A.J. SCUDIERE

NIGHTSHADE

FORENSIC FBI FILES ✦ BOOK 11

BENEATH
MEMORY

"There are really just 2 types of readers—those who are fans of AJ Scudiere, and those who will be."
  -Bill Salina, Reviewer, Amazon

For *The Shadow Constant*:
"The Shadow Constant by A.J. Scudiere was one of those novels I got wrapped up in quickly and had a hard time putting down."
  -Thomas Duff, Reviewer, Amazon

For *Phoenix*:
"It's not a book you read and forget; this is a book you read and think about, again and again . . . everything that has happened in this book could be true. That's why it sticks in your mind and keeps coming back for rethought."
  -Jo Ann Hakola, The Book Faerie

For *God's Eye*:
"I highly recommend it to anyone who enjoys reading - it's well-written and brilliantly characterized. I've read all of A.J.'s books and they just keep getting better."
  -Katy Sozaeva, Reviewer, Amazon

For *Vengeance*:
"Vengeance is an attention-grabbing story that lovers of action-driven novels will fall hard for. I highly recommend it."
  -Melissa Levine, Professional Reviewer

For *Resonance*:
"Resonance is an action-packed thriller, highly recommended. 5 stars."
  -Midwest Book Review

1

_____

"Carly, look at that!" Mila pointed across the parking lot at the cherry red antique car.

"Is that it?"

"You know it is." Mila abandoned their conversation upon spotting the car and now she was abandoning her friend as she strode across the lot.

As she touched the paint, a shiver of warning ran up her spine, but she ignored it. It was just a car.

A Cherry red Ford Falcon. She checked the back—it didn't say "f u t u r a." Thus, this one had a stick shift—just like the one she'd almost bought.

Moving closer, Mila peeked inside, glad when a second chill didn't seep in.

Given the fantastic weather, the owner had left the top down. The old tops didn't have push buttons, they had to be cranked up and down—not an easy task. The seats were pristine white leather with red stitching holding each piece in place. The steering wheel was obviously original, but now shiny with decades of use. However, the dash looked like it had some work.

This could be the same car that she had almost bought when she was eighteen. Her grandmother had given her $1,000 toward her car for her high school graduation. Her father had given her their old

Chevy for a trade in, making it possible to go to college with a car of her own.

Her search for used cars had taken her to a '63 Ford Falcon. Was this a '63? It looked like it.

The one she'd considered had lived just down the street from her and, somehow, she'd never seen it all the times she'd passed by. The owner said it was very drivable, but her father had talked her out of getting it, noting that the repairs would be more than a college student could afford. Her mother had commented that it didn't have seatbelts.

All of that was true.

And, to date, she'd never owned her dream car.

"You like it?" A voice called out to her.

"I do!" she called back, finally turning away from the shiny, pretty car to look. A man strode through the lot toward her, looking a little more casual than she would have guessed given his car. "Is it a '63?"

Her friend Carly stood back, arms crossed, watching the conversation. She'd seen Mila go nuts over red Falcons before. She'd learned to just wait.

"Very good. It's a stick though," he told her as she leaned forward, being careful not to touch another person's clearly babied car.

"I know. The Futuras were early automatics. But not this one. And I can drive a stick," she added the last bit as if to clarify that she could, in fact, drive the beautiful piece of machinery.

"You know your cars." Leaning against the side, he crossed his arms and looked at her, his head tilted.

Mila moved a few feet away, not sure if she was moving away from him—he had her cornered between the car parked next to it and the curb—or if she was just checking it out all the way around. "No. I know a few things about *this* car. I almost bought one years ago, and I've wanted one ever since."

"No one can drive a stick these days," he countered.

"My dad thought I needed to know."

The man nodded. He was probably about her age, darker skinned, dark-haired, dark eyes shining. *Did she know him?*

He seemed happy that someone was taking an interest in his baby, maybe that she was a fellow enthusiast. Up close, the casual clothing gave away the expensive watch on his wrist and the shoes that looked like they cost more than her whole outfit. He probably had four more cars like this at home.

He was opening his mouth to ask her something else, waving one hand almost as if he would offer her a chance to drive it, but she didn't hear anything he might have said.

Mila had taken a step, her foot hitting a pothole in the parking lot. No big deal. She just dropped a few inches further than she expected. As her hand shot out for balance, she laid her palm against the hood of the car.

White light flashed through her senses.

Mila jolted again.

She was inside the car, in the passenger seat, laughing. The man driving was her husband. They wound their way along an open road, clinging to the side of a mountain. Tall trees lined both sides of the narrow pavement. California.

How she knew that or why she even saw that made no sense.

Looking down, she saw the ring on her finger—shiny and new. It matched his. They hadn't yet told their parents they'd eloped.

With a sucked in breath, Mila yanked her hand back.

"Are you okay?" Both Carly and the man asked it together.

"I'm fine. I just stepped in a pothole." It was true, even if it wasn't the truth.

That had been far too bizarre. A faint buzz filled her senses like background noise. She was opening her mouth to say thank you and walk away, but the man didn't see her move. He simply started explaining what he'd done.

"I had the seats replaced. I installed seatbelts. If you look—" he pointed over on the side. The belts hadn't looked out of place to her modern sensibilities, but they weren't native to this car. "Do you know how much work it is to find someone who will install seatbelts on these things?"

She actually did. She'd looked into it at eighteen, hoping to convince her parents she could afford the car. But she hadn't been able to find anyone. At least he had. As she moved around the hood, thinking she'd exit between the other cars, she told him the same argument she'd gotten from specialists who didn't want to alter the original design. "You generally don't need them as much because the car is so heavy."

He nodded along with a grin, once again pleased with her knowledge. "Exactly. I get it. It's an antique and no one wants to damage it. But I'd like to drive it around and I would also like to live through the experience."

Something about the phrase grabbed her, clenched at her heart, and her hand went out again, balancing against the passenger side door for stability.

Her knees buckled. This time every muscle in her body went haywire just before her hand made contact with paint and metal. It didn't stop the memory from forcing through though.

This time, she was the one driving and her husband wasn't laughing. The trees were different. Somehow, she knew they were all the way across the country. Michigan? Ohio? More importantly, they were running—running hard from something that had them very, very scared.

The lake loomed in front of them, cold and dense. She'd heard about what went into the lake. They wouldn't survive if they went off the road. She cranked the wheel hard, taking a rough turn in the large boat of a car.

She could feel how it handled, the clutch resisting, all limbs operating the machine, every cell of her body tense with fear. Whoever was chasing them, wanted them dead.

2

—————

Brian tossed and turned, unable to sleep. Though he was usually a good sleeper, tonight, vivid dreams plagued him.

At one point he'd set down the book he was reading, letting it fall on the covers beside him. If he even rolled over to set it on the bedside table, he might wake himself up again. So he let his brain float away.

He relived the moment the woman—her name was Mila, he'd learned—had come up to the car. He'd been ready to dispense his usual *Do not touch my car*. But for some reason, when she turned and looked at him, he hadn't said it. She hadn't been touching it anyway. Not then.

His friend Paul had been watching, not bothering to run and catch up. After the two women had left—Brian hadn't even noticed at first there had been a second woman there—Paul had asked him, "What was *that?*"

"Weird. But she really liked the car though," Brian had answered, watching Mila walk away with her friend Carly. Mila had looked out of sorts but turned back to look at the car as if Cherry might have been responsible for it.

"Lots of them do," Paul had pointed out, as if to say, *and you don't act like that for them.*

As his brain faded into sleep, Brian relived the whole scene. *Had he told her he named the car Cherry?* Why would that even matter?

This was good though. This wasn't the kind of odd thought that would jolt him awake. Not like the feeling of falling into cold water and dying. Not like the feeling of being shot at. Or running uphill through the mountains, ankles twisting on the roots of the tall trees on either side of him, his breath huffing. Behind him, his hand had been clenched in a slightly smaller one, just as slick with fear as his own. The two of them dodged through the woods … chased.

No. When he'd woken from that one, he'd realized they were being *hunted*.

He'd died in his dreams that night, how many ways? Five? Ten? Fifteen different times? He'd lost track.

The clock had said 4:13 a.m. the last time he looked.

This reliving of his conversation with Paul was a last ditch effort to actually find some rest. When the two women were gone, he and Paul climbed into the car, pulling the heavy doors shut.

With the old school key in the ignition and the engine rumbling—one of the last that had been built to stay on the road forever—Brian backed out. He pulled onto the freeway, heading for their next destination: A reptile convention at one of the big warehouses at the edge of the city.

In his hazy, half-asleep mind, Brian didn't know much about it other than what Paul had told him. His friend already had more than one lizard and, apparently, he needed one more. This was the place to go to find the best breeders. Brian had agreed not only to go along and spend his day but to drive.

It only then occurred through his foggy memory that he would need to fit an aquarium and a lizard into the backseat of his precious Cherry. He glanced back, trying to figure out where he could put it. Should it be buckled in? Could he convince Paul to put it in the footwell?

There was plenty of space in the old behemoth, but suddenly Brian didn't see the seats as they were. The leather was dingy and gray, as it had been when he bought it. On the back seat sat a black duffel bag of shiny nylon. It was zipped shut and he didn't know why, but he knew it was full of money.

Shocked, Brian turned to ask Paul if he'd brought the bag—only it wasn't his friend beside him. It was a woman with red curly hair and wide green eyes that sparkled with some kind of devious secret. Her wide smile told him they'd made it! Whatever *it* was.

The car was both newer and older at the same time and Brian couldn't quite put his finger on what those things were. He stared at the woman, and she'd said exactly what he'd somehow always known she would.

"We did it! We are *set!*"

He didn't agree with her. Somehow Paul's voice broke through the vivid scene he was seeing.

"Man, why are you looking at me that way? What is going on?"

Brian whipped his head to check the back seat again only to find it empty. There was just the pristine white leather with red top stitching exactly as he knew it should be. "Dude, I don't know."

"Well keep your eyes on the road. That was creepy."

Brian had kept his eyes strictly on the road. No more looking into the backseat after that. It hadn't happened again.

Now, as he tried to fall asleep one more time, he went through the whole cycle again: Mila at the parking lot, her leaving with the odd look on her face, her friend with an arm around her, asking her if she was okay. Then getting in and backing out of the lot, merging onto the freeway,

But then he remembered it there again: the bag of money, though he'd never actually seen any money. He only saw the bag. That it was stuffed with cash was just something he knew.

As he lay in his bed, comfortable in the high thread count sheets that he loved, with his soft, fluffy pillows stacked around him, he heard the gunshots again.

His body twisted, toes clenching into his sneakers, pushing into the dirt as he tried to run away. Why had he been wearing jeans? Why would anyone run through the woods in jeans?

This time, as the shots fired again from behind him, he felt the fire in his side as his body convulsed and he bolted upright in bed.

He'd fallen asleep again, hadn't he?

His breath sucked in and he put his hand to his side expecting to pull it away wet and bloody. But he hadn't been shot, he'd only met a woman in the parking lot.

What the hell was going on?

3

E leri stood on the bluff, a light wind picking at her hair as she watched from her high vantage point. Though the air was warm enough, she had to consciously uncross her arms, pull out her camera from the bag slung across her body, and take pictures like she was supposed to.

As she looked down into the clear, glassy water, she saw the bubbles from the divers. Up and down they went. Sometimes they came up empty handed, sometimes they held evidence aloft, the piece rising out of the water first like a sword to be handed to Arthur.

Only Eleri didn't feel victorious at all.

She'd been here three days, waiting. The divers had started with a grid search, and now that they'd actually found something, they were going down and pulling things up piece by piece.

Though she and Christina had watched as each item came up, they stayed out of handling it. The closest they got was wandering through the evidence laid out on tarps. Though the FBI team was cataloging everything thoroughly, the two NightShade agents had both taken their own pictures. They'd asked before they touched anything, even though it was their case and the team was technically working for them.

Not that Eleri had ordered any of this. It had all happened on Westerfield's orders, of course. But still, both Eleri and Christina knew better than to mess with evidence.

Christina had found them this vantage point. Up on a small bluff, it stood away from the rocky shores the divers and the team struggled to navigate. It afforded them a place to watch and talk undisturbed.

"I'm not sure why Westerfield thinks it's a NightShade case," Christina said.

Eleri could only shrug as she rotely snapped a picture of a diver surfacing with another object in her hand.

Eleri hadn't spoken much these last few weeks. The one time she had truly talked it hadn't turned out well. So she was counting on Christina to suffer through her bullishness and her high walls. She could only hope Christina understood, because if her partner shut her out, she would lose the one person she had left.

"Do you think we'll see the bodies today?" Christina asked.

Eleri noticed her partner had moved to asking more questions, as though that might force Eleri to make replies where she otherwise wouldn't. She answered, "It's been three days. If they don't come up soon, then I don't know what we're going to do tomorrow."

The crane had already been scheduled to come hook on to the back of the car and pull it from the water. Though whether or not that was something that could be pulled off remained to be seen.

"They have to find the car first." Christina still looked out over the water, as if knowing this was easier for Eleri if they weren't face to face.

"They found pieces," Eleri pointed out, realizing that she'd spoken almost voluntarily. *Interesting.* On the one hand, she was proud—this was progress. Maybe she was coming out of her funk and on the other hand, it was a funk she didn't want to come out of.

She was scared, sad, and angry. So angry that she'd been assigned to this case when she had other things to do. Unfortunately, she needed NightShade for the other things she had to do.

She had to go along to get along. She was just grateful that Christina had put herself back into active duty, saying that she wanted to be on this case, and that she would only be active duty if she were Eleri's partner. Eleri had not yet thanked her for the sacrifice.

It wasn't a slap in the face to work with Agent Pines, only a slap to have to work a case without Donovan at all.

Looking down again at the tarp, Eleri counted items. So far the divers had brought up two hubcaps, a few odds and ends, and a suit-case full of clothing. Eleri wouldn't have thought that luggage would change so much over time. It was definitely older, but she didn't know enough to peg the year or even the decade it came from.

The suitcase had been full of women's clothing. Men's clothing had been found, too, but just a few pieces stuck to the rocks along the way down. But a second suitcase hadn't been found and this one had come up still closed.

Two "recreational" divers had gone down earlier in the week, supposedly for shits and giggles. Eleri figured that was a fat lie, with the lake being as cold as it was. The weather was in its warmest season, so this was when the divers went "recreational" diving. But they were most likely treasure divers.

There were rumors of so many amazing finds at the bottom of Superior and confirmation of so many more. It seemed these two hadn't found their treasure. Five days ago, they'd come up terrified.

Eleri figured they deserved their nightmares. If they were looking for treasure here, then they should have known enough to expect they might have found something like this.

According to their statements, they'd seen an old car with two bodies still inside, relatively preserved. Though a report from two terrified "recreational" divers wasn't something Eleri put a lot of stock in, Westerfield had deemed this a NightShade case. On top of that, he decided he needed Eleri on it, ASAP, instead of looking for her missing partner.

Her chest felt tight, but it had felt that way for weeks. Her hands clenched the camera as if the camera were at fault for all her prob-lems, when, in fact, her problems were likely her own doing. She had sent Donovan away with only a prayer that he would live.

Now it had been weeks and she didn't know if he was dead, alive, somewhere in between, or what.

She was looking through the viewfinder, her jaw already clenched, when she saw a diver come up. Usually, their hands came up with an object in them—always a gray paint can full of seawater and evidence. The divers hammered it shut beneath the surface to preserve what was inside, so all the onlookers knew was that they'd found *something*. They could gauge a rough size from the volume of the can but that was it.

The team lead for the crime scene workers had a comm to the

divers, so she got a verbal report on each object as the divers found it. But Eleri wasn't part of the communications. She couldn't even hear one side of it when she and Christina were up here.

From her vantage point, she watched as the team abandoned the tarp and ran toward the edge. The diver awkwardly cleared the water, his hands empty this time. But even from this distance she heard his exclamation.

"We found it!"

4

"It's getting close," Christina said.

Though Eleri would have expected more excitement in her voice for a situation like this, Eleri couldn't drum her own up either. As she stood beside Christina, she only responded by nodding in agreement. The day was beautiful. The air was crisp but not cold, the sky a wild shade of jeweled blue, the water beneath her begging it to solve its mysteries.

But she wasn't capable of feeling any of it.

The divers had gone down again, this time following careful diagrams to strap the tow line around the axle and the car frame. It was imperative to balance the car's weight correctly and only hook onto the frame. If they missed, the car could tip and fall into the depths of the lake. They could lose everything, which was why they'd already brought the bodies up.

Eleri watched for the bubbles again. Christina had requested as few divers as possible to minimize the number of people with exposure to the evidence. Eleri had no brain power to think of these things and had left it all to her partner.

The four divers had showed up each day, and rotated in shifts of two, carefully timing each dive. The lake was cold enough that they needed to minimize their time under water.

They were lucky to have found the bodies in the middle of summer.

Then again, maybe it wasn't luck. Lake Superior was never warm enough for the kind of wetsuits Eleri associated with diving. She was scuba certified, though she'd never done it much. Certainly, with Donovan as her partner, going into the water was more of a recreational thing on her own time and not part of her work.

Just the thought of him clenched at her heart. *Donovan should be here.*

Forcing her attention to the pair of divers waiting on the shoreline for their counterparts to return, she thought it through again. The two "recreational" divers who'd first found the car were likely only out here now because this was as warm as it would get. They would have had to have had dry suits, too. Nothing casual about it.

There was a pause in the turning of the winch that was slowly dragging the car up. The divers below were guiding the car where they could, calling up when it caught on something or needed a moment so they could turn it one way or another.

From what Eleri had seen from the grainy underwater pictures, the car had been positioned on a ledge. It had likely plunged into the water decades ago just a little over from where she now stood. This meant the dive team had needed to approach from an angle.

The ledge was about fifty-ish feet down, stopping the car from falling into the depths and being lost forever. It appeared it hadn't moved since it first rested there. Now, the team would haul it up.

The divers were trained in underwater forensics, so while they'd needed extensive instructions on the towing, Eleri trusted them to push and pull appropriately, making sure evidence didn't get damaged as it came up from the cold depths.

"It stopped," Christina told her, and Eleri knew that was a signal that the divers had been down long enough.

They would slowly time themselves rising and then switch out with the others.

Nothing would happen for a while during the time that the change occurred. However, Eleri didn't budge.

"Eat," Christina commanded easily as she pulled energy bars from her pocket and handed one to Eleri.

Peeling the wrapper, Eleri took a bite but didn't taste it. She only pushed forward, knowing that she needed to do *something*—maybe she simply needed to solve this case so she could put a checkmark on

Westerfield's forms. Then she could tell him that if he didn't send her after her partner with the full support of the FBI that she would be gone.

Their boss had insinuated that he knew something, but he wasn't sharing any intel about Donovan with them. It was the only reason Eleri hadn't left the job already.

She chewed the bite and swallowed what was basically a knot of food before taking another.

Christina tugged at her sleeve. "Come on. Let's go check the evidence again."

There were a few new things on the tarp, things that the divers had carried with them each time they came to the surface. Eleri and Christina needed to check each piece and make their decision of what was to be done with it.

It was a five minute trek down from their vantage point. Eleri reminded herself again that she'd agreed to take this case because it was Westerfield's undercover agent that she had handed a wounded and near-death Donovan to.

Her boss should be her best source of information about her partner. She couldn't afford to lose that channel, even if it had produced nothing by now. Donovan had been gone for over a month and SAC Westerfield hadn't been able to tell her if Donovan was even alive.

She was alternately despondent and livid. She'd known almost no other emotion since this assignment had been handed to her. Now, she picked her way across the rocks, leading until Christina reached out and tapped her on the shoulder.

"Drink," she said.

Eleri didn't argue. Christina had also quietly changed their liquids from water to sports drinks, plausibly trying to get as many vitamins, nutrients, and minerals into her partner as she could.

Appreciative of the help, Eleri tried to say so. But she found she simply couldn't make the words come. So she unscrewed the cap, took a long swig and resumed picking her way down the rocks. She was also grateful for the heavy treads on the work boots Christina had suggested. She probably wouldn't be alive, or at least not upright without Christina right now.

It didn't help that upon receiving news of this assignment, Eleri had basically extorted her boss for an extra twelve hours before she was due here. In that time, she'd flown across the country, met up with her boyfriend, and told him for the first time the things she was capable of. She'd talked him through the biggest secret she'd ever kept —telling him she was from several long lines of witches and spell-casters and showing him what proof seemed reasonable. She lit a fire in her own hand, and then in his. She altered his vision so he would see her as someone else. She'd given him one of her Grandmére's gris-gris for protection.

Those had been the only spells she'd cast in her despondent state. And doing it had been a shitty decision. Avery had not taken the news well at all. He'd yelled at her to get out of his sight and called her vile names—the worst of which were surprising despite her imagination of all the ways her big reveal could go wrong. He'd not spoken to her since.

Eleri wasn't even sure of his reasons. Was he mad because she had skills that he seemed to think made her inhuman? Was he mad that she had lied to him for so long? That she'd had these skills and let him believe that she was an ordinary, everyday FBI agent? The only upside to Donovan being missing was that her numbness allowed her not to care so much about Avery.

She paused for a moment, taking another long gulp from the bottle of sports drink, then screwing the cap back on before she picked her way further down. She ate with goals in mind. She'd finished the energy bar, and she would finish this bottle, too. *Check.*

She moved methodically—a twisted ankle at this stage of the game would do her no service. In a few more meters, she'd emptied the bottle and she and Christina were standing at the edge of the tarp.

One of the techs welcomed them back, her blonde ponytail whip-ping in the wind and attempting to sting her in the eyes though she seemed not to notice. "We definitely need you to make a decision on this one." The tech grinned and motioned to a still-sealed can. "When the car shifted from the winch pulling it, this jostled loose. So they grabbed it."

The divers had been smarter than she'd given them credit for. They'd been saving everything they could given the possibility of things going awry and losing the car into the trench forever—or at least until better tech was invented.

"Are you ready?" The tech asked. Leaning over, she used to small hand tool to pop the lid.

With their heads close together, Eleri and Christina peered into the clear lake water that had been collected with the item but as they pulled back, Eleri looked at Christina.

The divers had pulled a gun from the car.

5

"I'm not a forensic pathologist." Eleri held one hand up, refusing the offer from the local M.E. to perform the autopsy. "We're just here to observe." Eleri motioned between herself and Christina.

Agent Pines didn't have a medical background and putting the two of them on the same footing was a little odd. They hadn't discussed whether Eleri would expose or hide her physiological knowledge and Eleri herself wasn't sure if she should speak up even now. The ME didn't seem to notice anything odd.

"Then if we're ready?" Dr. Rasmussen asked them, the older man's white hair shining behind the clear face shield as he turned to begin.

Paying attention with only half an ear, Eleri looked away from the body on the table, despite the fact that she knew she should be paying closer attention. For a moment, she could imagine it was Donovan doing the work. She would have been hovering beside him making her own observations. Instead, she stood back, her gear on, her phone in her gloved hands because she hadn't yet touched anything.

It all felt bizarre and wrong.

This autopsy was unusual in many ways, but one was that Eleri had asked that the body not be removed from the bag until the autopsy started. The M.E. should do all the prep and record everything himself. The body had waited almost two days, untouched, while the other work was completed—until she and Christina were available.

He began by unzipping the bag.

Eleri's mind again wandered, this time back to her wish that the body could be brought up in a large container filled with lake water, almost like the paint cans used for smaller pieces of evidence. But it had been impossible. That type of collection didn't exist in the normal world. Bodies were usually so decomposed that there was little to no evidence to worry about preserving. But, here in Superior, things were different.

She'd heard rumors of ships that sank in the early 1900s. Cruising full of passengers, they had hit something or malfunctioned and the whole thing sat now at the bottom. The boat, bodies, and everything on board was hundreds of feet down—cold, dark, and with such a unique bacterial composition, that if they were ever to be found, they would be pulled up completely intact. She'd heard of shipments of food, people and even early model cars—all now sitting at the bottom of the lake.

Hence, the two reckless divers had been treasure hunting when they'd run into these two bodies. These two victims of the lake had not been skeletal but still remarkably intact. No wonder the divers had flipped out and called the police.

So as Eleri watched, and the zipper on the black bag pulled back, the face appeared. It looked to have only been in the water for a day or so.

An eerie shiver ran down Eleri's spine. She ignored it.

The car had been a classic and they suspected the bodies had been down for close to sixty years, maybe fifty if the car had been on the road for a while. But the suitcase had been newer, and the blond tech said the clothing inside hadn't looked like it was from the sixties or seventies.

For the first time, something sparked in her, though it wasn't deep, and it wasn't her usual curiosity—maybe just mild interest. She leaned forward, studying the wet red hair that hung in loose waves around a wide face. The woman's eyes were open, a mossy shade of green. Her mouth wide. Her t-shirt ...

The doctor moved and blocked Eleri's view for a moment. He continued recording his observations of the body and the clothing. So Eleri remained quiet, not touching like she would have if Donovan had been on the job. She watched as he rolled the body back and forth deftly removing the bag from underneath.

Usually corpses came to him naked, clothing already removed and collected for evidence. But Eleri hadn't wanted to miss seeing those steps. Her eyes glanced to the other table, to the still-zipped bag where the man waited. The woman's t-shirt with the band name splashed across the front bothered her, but she didn't have the bandwidth to sort it out.

Raising a hand, she waited until she got the doctor's attention. When he looked up, he stopped recording, and she motioned toward the body and asked, "May I?"

He seemed confused, which made sense. Technically, she was in charge here. But she waited for him to nod before she reached for the girl's hand. Chipped, pink-painted fingernails moved ever so slightly. The body had been down there for decades but moved like she was freshly dead.

However, Eleri still hadn't figured out why this was a NightShade case. There was a perfectly good *scientific* explanation for what had happened here. People had known for quite some time about the ability of Lake Superior to preserve everything. So why was *she* here?

Carefully, she flipped the hand over and saw what she wanted. Looking at Christina, she commented, "We'll be able to get fingerprints soon."

The skin just needed to dry out a little. Setting the hand back down, she stepped away from the table and motioned for Dr. Rasmussen to resume his work.

Christina pulled Eleri aside. "The car was a sixties model, but it looked a little worn. So maybe it went down in the seventies?"

Eleri nodded.

"Then the bodies have likely been down for close to fifty years," Christina said. "Do you think we'll be able to match fingerprints to a missing persons case?"

Eleri shrugged, the clothing didn't quite match the sixties, she thought. But what did she know? "I can only hope so. We have her and we also have him."

The other body bag remained zipped, though Eleri had peeked yesterday, seeing his face. His dark skin and short, tightly curled hair made her wonder if the timeframe hadn't played into the two of them going missing. They appeared to be a couple, though none of that was certain now. Matching wedding bands shouldn't give the assumption that they were married or even to each other.

Piece by piece, the doctor removed the clothing from the body and placed each piece into an evidence bag. Obviously a pro at this, he lifted one arm, tucked it in one direction, then rocked the body and peeled the shirt without assistance. Even though the woman wasn't large, handling literal dead weight wasn't easy without knowing all the tricks.

He folded the t-shirt and placed it last onto the top of the items in the bag. This time, it was Christina who raised her hand, waiting while he stopped the recording and asked her, "Yes?"

"Can I see the shirt?"

He nodded oddly as if to say, "of course, it's your case" but he spoke to the recorder instead as he went back to his work.

Eleri followed Christina, but stood back as she watched her partner reach in and pull out the shirt. Christina held it up, showing off the band name on the front. Then she turned it around to look at the back before saying, "Holy shit! Look at this, Eleri."

6

Mila woke in a cold sweat, sitting upright and breathing heavily. She picked her phone up from the bedside table, checking the time. 2:34.

Sunlight streamed in the window and answered her question—it was 2:34 p.m., not a.m.

She had already learned she could no longer sleep at night. Apparently, she couldn't sleep during the day either. Waiting a few moments, she let her heart slow as she shook off the memory of the dream.

Her pajamas and exhaustion had been her constant companion for the last several days. She'd simply stopped sleeping restful sleep. She was haunted by dreams of all kinds of things that didn't make sense. Though she knew when it started, *Why had it?*

She developed some kind of sudden-onset, severe insomnia.

When she did sleep, some of her dreams were wonderful. Some were nightmares. Some simply confusing.

But through all of them wove the thread of a life cut short.

Was it hers?

In one, she'd been eating breakfast with friends in a 24-hour restaurant in the middle of the night. They'd gone to a concert and gotten rip roaring drunk. Christy was high as a kite, though Mila wasn't.

In the dream she was confident this was something Christy did all the time. But it didn't matter, because real Mila didn't know this Christy to actually worry about her so much once she woke up. *But why did this Christy keep appearing in her dreams?*

In the last one, four of them sat around a very large table. The restaurant was packed despite the hour, probably because they weren't the only ones who'd gotten hammered at the stadium and walked the five blocks to the only place open after the VIP party had let out.

The hostess—far too regal of a term for a restaurant such as this—was at the front of the place, disappointing a group of young men. She told them the wait would be long.

Then Christy waved them over. At the time, Mila remembered thinking one of them was cute. But *now?* She frowned at her hands, twisted into the bedcovers. She didn't think he was cute. He was ... His hair had looked *permed.* What the hell?

The young man had waved back and before anyone else had a say in it, they were all sitting at the large table.

Mila looked around her room now, trying to figure out what her brain was subconsciously trying to tell her. The guys had been wearing shorts and high socks with colored bands around the tops. They'd had classic style sneakers. And ...

Mila put her hand to her forehead, thinking it would be best if she simply forgot this.

Some of the dreams had been scary. Some had been sweet. Though she'd found herself attracted to one of the members of the group, mostly the dreams struck her as insanely bizarre.

Realizing she was fully awake and too scared to go back to sleep, she threw off the covers and padded into the kitchen. After pouring herself a bowl of cereal, she sat down in front of the TV by herself.

Before this, she'd been proud of owning the small home. She'd bought it herself and covered all the bills on her own. She even had savings for things like when the toilet got clogged or a windstorm took a few shingles off the roof. Most of her friends complained about paying bills but, to her, it was a point of pride. Every time something got done, every time she repaired damage or improved something in her little fixer-upper home, she was proud.

But right now, in the middle of the afternoon, on a Sunday, it simply felt lonely.

She ate quietly at the small table in front of the couch, queuing up the television just so someone would talk to her. The true crime shows she usually watched popped up, but now, she passed right by it for a romance series.

Grateful there was something else to watch—even if it was cheesy drivel—she was halfway through the bowl of cereal when the spoon paused on the way to her mouth.

The young man in the restaurant, she hadn't recognized him. In this dream, she'd been meeting him for the first time! But he was the same one she'd seen in that odd flash of images several days ago. The one who had been running beside her through the woods.

7

"Anything yet?" Christina asked from behind her.

"Nope." Eleri shook her head.

"Energy bar gone?" Christina asked next.

"Nope." Eleri picked it up from beside her and held it up, irritated as she showed that she'd only managed to get through a third of it. Dutifully, she took another bite. Christina would keep reminding her until she finished it. But she shouldn't be angry that her friend was caring for her.

She clicked her way around the fingerprint on the screen. She'd rolled the prints herself from both the young woman and the young man the following day after Rasmussen had done the autopsies.

Now she was doing the matching. Eleri could do it herself faster and better than if she sent it in for testing. She had access to every print from all the different FBI cases around the country, and she could request relevant local databases as evidence came in. But as she tapped away, she found herself still wondering why this was a Night-Shade case.

So many times, it became obvious that something was very bizarre from the get go. She also knew, however, that sometimes Westerfield sent them out onto cases that had absolutely no obviously paranormal pieces. Those cases were simply very difficult to solve. Thus, it required agents with special abilities to root out the clues, figure out who should be investigated and proceed from there.

Eleri had been well known for her hunches during her days in the FBI's Behavioral Analysis Unit. So well known, in fact, that she'd been accused on more than one occasion of knowing too much about the serial predators they hunted. Between the accusations, the subsequent investigation, and her own onset of anxiety and paranoia, she'd wound up in a mental hospital. Westerfield had plucked her from there and brought her into his specialized unit.

That had been a number of years ago. She'd been partnered with Agent Donovan Heath ever since. She'd worked with Christina on more than one occasion before, as NightShade was mostly a small, close-knit division. Or so Eleri had thought until their last case had revealed an undercover agent that none of them had previously known about.

Though she hadn't at first, she was now questioning her boss's decisions. Her SAC had given each of them cause for concern over the last few years and only recently had the agents figured out they were all thinking the same thing.

Had Westerfield simply put her on this case to keep her from investigating what had happened to Donovan?

She had to consider the possibility.

She felt trapped on this case. She'd been physically trapped in previous situations—not surprising for the kind of work that she did. But she'd never before suffered this kind of low-grade panic that she was *stuck*. She needed SAC Westerfield and the power of the FBI in order to find her partner, but it felt as if it might be Westerfield and the power of the FBI that were keeping her from finding him in the first place.

With a shake of her head, and another bite of the energy bar, she looked back to the screen and resumed clicking at the image of the fingerprint. The young woman's first finger was rolled with ink, printed, then uploaded onto the large screen in front of her. She wasn't a fan of digital uploads. Eleri searched for splits, conjunctions, and terminals. Clicking on each one, she added arrows where necessary and labeled each point of interest with the proper color.

There was no known minimum number of match points nationally for fingerprints. Some states required as high as twenty points that matched before a legal identification could be declared. Some thought investigators should just determine if the fingerprint matched for themselves. Eleri was a stickler for hard matches, having once seen an officer declare he already knew who the fingerprint belonged to and just glance at it on the screen and declare it a match. Hence she was unwilling to hand this one over to the usual techs.

Eleri believed the likelihood of a match was unlikely given the time between when the victim disappeared and now. Even though it wasn't what they'd originally thought.

Clicking as many points as she could find in the fingerprint, she scanned the black lines, with their pink, yellow, and blue dots and arrows aiming everywhere. She was out of points to mark. So she clicked the button, letting the automated search do whatever it could. Unlike in movies and television, it didn't flash fingerprints and mugshots on the screen, discarding them visually as it went. That wasn't how the system worked at all. It simply chugged while she waited.

Eleri took another bite of the energy bar, then swiveled the stool around and faced Christina. They occupied a room in the Duluth offices of the Minnesota Bureau of Criminal Apprehension. This agency was the state version of the FBI. Most states had one, and she was glad the locals were willing to let the two FBI agents use the space and equipment.

She spoke up, her voice often feeling unused these days. "That was a good find on the shirt yesterday."

Christina has simply tipped her head and nodded. The victim's shirt had bothered Eleri but Christina had been functioning at a high enough level to put the pieces together. The t-shirt said "Bon Jovi" on the front in the band's logo. No big deal, except when the car was pulled up, it had been identified as an early 60s model. That band hadn't been around until the mid 80s.

Christina had been right about another thing: It wasn't the kind of shirt that had been sold at a store, but the kind one got at a concert. She'd turned it around, where the white print—still so very well preserved—listed tour dates from 1985.

Thus, the car had already been relatively old at the time these two had gone down and the missing persons search window had changed from the 60s to the mid-to-late 80s. The shirt might not have been new when the car went down. But these two had still been alive in 1985.

Everything had been so well preserved that there were none of the usual decomposition measures to help gauge time since death. But the shirt had given them a window they'd not expected.

Behind her, the computer pinged, and Eleri swiveled around to check the top twenty best matches the system had spit out.

Unlike on TV, AFIS didn't say "this is your match." While pieces of the system were computerized and automated, much of the work depended on human input. It only matched the information Eleri input on her side to the information some other investigator had uploaded on the print they had. Then it churned out best matches.

The first print wasn't her young woman, nor was the second. The work was tedious. Oftentimes Eleri could look and easily see that it wasn't the same fingerprint, that the lines and swirls simply didn't match. But she documented carefully, not knowing what later might need to go to court. Fingerprints were the kind of evidence that NightShade could hold up when prosecutions were on the line. They couldn't say "I'm a witch and I cast a spell" or "I had a hunch." "It obviously wasn't the right fingerprint!" certainly wouldn't work for hard evidence either.

The energy bar had disappeared, and the sports drink was empty by the time she was on the seventh fingerprint. She turned around and grinned at Christina. "Bingo!"

8

"She's Jennifer Barnes," Eleri told Christina. "This one is a match."

Christina dropped her papers where she was sorting pictures of evidence and trying to decide if there were more tests that needed to be run. In a moment, she was hovering over Eleri's shoulder, looking at the screen.

Though matching fingerprints certainly required training, Christina was more than adept at looking at the two side by side prints on the screen and agreeing that they needed to pull this file.

With the touch of a few buttons, Eleri discovered that while the prints had been uploaded, the file wasn't. That wasn't uncommon with old evidence and cases—things were getting scanned as local personnel had the time or as the municipality had the budget. Eleri didn't think it was really anyone's priority and she was just glad that anything had matched.

It took another thirty minutes to contact the local office in Northern California—where the print was from—and find a real person who could rummage through their storage and pull the original paperwork. Eleri eventually hung up and swiveled the stool around. "We probably have some time to kill while we wait. What do you have?"

"Far too much clothing. Most of it, upon inspection—" Christina waved one hand over a series of photographs of sodden clothing that had been pulled up. "Appears to fit the two occupants of the car."

Though the suitcase had been closed tightly it wasn't by any means waterproof and had been soaked through long before the divers had discovered the car.

"Now assuming that's Jennifer Barnes, our John Doe's fingerprints should be next?" Christina asked.

Eleri nodded. Maybe she should have done his first. The autopsy revealed a very recent wound on his right side. It appeared to have been from a bullet grazing him. Or maybe more than just a graze. He still had the stitches. Eleri had noted during the autopsy that they'd been placed by a pro. Hopefully the missing persons report would help pinpoint a timeframe to look for a hospital visit for a gunshot wound. But it would still be an awful lot to even attempt to go through hospital records from a several year range in the eighties.

Not the path she wanted to have to pursue. Eleri looked up at Christina. "The gun?"

It had been labeled a priority, as guns often were.

"That came back this morning." Christina tapped her finger on her tablet almost as if to motion *over here*. In reality, she was pulling up a document that had been sent. "It's been fired. And they are currently looking to match the rifling to any known crimes."

"In the eighties," Eleri clarified.

Christina offered only a sigh. "Exactly. A case as old as this is going to be a mess."

"I'm not a bad researcher," Eleri said, "but I really wish I'd paid more attention in the archiving classes."

Christina only nodded in agreement. "Me, too."

"The car?" Eleri asked next. It was a 1963 Ford Falcon, which she had only recently learned was less than a decade after VIN numbers started to come into use. Luckily, this car was a model that used them.

"Still hunting down the registration," Christina said, her tone conveying the resignation at the kind of work that would be, too.

Eleri already knew the vast majority of what they would be looking for—just like the missing persons report—would only exist on paper. Eleri had already run into more than one case where paper records had been destroyed due to natural disaster, crime, and all sorts of other issues. Some places had digitized their old records, and she could only hope that was the case more often than not with this case. But given the number of agencies she was already looking into, she couldn't hope for much.

Behind her, the computer dinged, and she turned to see what had come in. Though she didn't recognize the email address per se, parts of it let her know that it was coming from the Sutter Creek Police Department. "It looks like I've got my report."

Once again, Christina hopped up out of her chair and came to stand over Eleri's shoulder as she pulled up images of paper reports on the large screen where she'd been working on the fingerprints.

"Her mother filed the report," Eleri said, trying to scan through it as fast as she could without blocking Christina's view or flipping the screens too quickly.

Christina motioned to her, and Eleri moved to the next page. "Mother and father both interviewed. They reported her missing in July of 1987."

It matched the concert shirt, Eleri thought. The couple had simply been driving a vintage car. With the way Superior preserved things, it was no wonder the team had been twenty years off on their estimate of when the car had gone down and how old the bodies themselves were.

Christina spoke again over Eleri's shoulder, having looked further down the screen than Eleri herself did. "Both the mother and the father report they hadn't heard from their daughter in over a month despite multiple attempts to contact her ... they'd left messages on her answering machine ... contacted her friends. Her friends said they hadn't seen her."

"Why didn't they go over and check for themselves?"

"It looks like they were in California and the daughter was living in Georgia." Christina moved her finger down the page as she motioned for Eleri to scroll further.

But there was no next image.

Crap. Eleri clicked back to the email where—of course—everything was written out. Had she read the whole thing the first time, she would have known the file was incomplete. However, the officer assured Eleri her team would be looking for the rest of it. "So we have no dental records, but we at least have the fingerprint."

Christina added, "And no photos. So we're assuming who we have here is Jennifer Barnes."

"Hopefully our John Doe's prints match and that helps us." Eleri tried to push forward, but she felt the fog crowding her brain. It was the same barrier she always ran up against now. *Something was wrong. Donovan should be here.*

Christina, though she also missed Donovan and worried about Eleri, hadn't been his partner. She hadn't worked with him practically day in and day out for the past several years.

Her brain still worked. Christina said, "I know where to look."

9

"Yes, Mom." Eleri grumbled as she stared at her turkey and cheese on wheat sandwich.

She'd tried to order a salad. Christina had told her no. Christina had countered with a burger and they'd arrived on the turkey sandwich as a compromise.

Ultimately, it didn't matter. She wasn't eating it anyway.

Christina motioned with her finger, a small scooting gesture as though that might make the sandwich fly into Eleri's face and have her chew it and enjoy it.

Dutifully, Eleri picked up the sandwich and took a bite. She didn't taste it, though. When Christina again motioned for her to eat, Eleri fought the urge to yell, "You're not the boss of me!" But she was enough of an adult now to know she clearly needed someone to be the boss of her. Luckily, Christina changed the subject.

"We need help."

Eleri raised one eyebrow, as if to ask if Christina thought this because Eleri wasn't pulling her own weight. She almost laughed. Her weight was much easier to pull these days.

"No really. We need someone who can help us with this case. And to help us find Donovan."

Eleri swallowed suddenly, the knot of food a little too big, but she managed to get it down the right pipe. "Who can help find Donovan?"

The problem was that she had handed him over to an undercover agent who'd whisked him off to ... *no one knew.* They all suspected he'd been taken away to a doctor who knew how to work on his kind. But it was likely a doctor working for the mafia—at least that was how Eleri thought of Miranda Industries.

Was Donovan alive? Was he dead? Was he healed or did he need more surgeries? Had they run out of money to care for an agent who was trying to shut them all down? Were they going to indenture him into the mob?

Clearly, they couldn't just release him into the wild. He'd been thrust into the inner workings of a shady international corporation. At the time, it had been the only option to save his life. Eleri was now grateful that she hadn't thought of any better solutions since then or she might have been beating herself up more than she already was.

"I don't know how to do more." That was why she hadn't been doing it already. When she had the spare time—mostly in the evenings since she wasn't sleeping much—she checked records in Florida, tried to figure out the strongholds where Miranda might have placed him.

She'd tried to log into Donovan's email repeatedly to see if he'd sent anything to anyone. Not that she knew his password. She hadn't gotten in. If she had found he'd been in it and he hadn't contacted her, she would be overjoyed for about three seconds, and then it would turn to deep, dark anger. But she hadn't gotten in, so that was all moot. She'd found absolutely no evidence of her partner's existence after the day she'd handed him over.

Christina pulled her back to the present. "We need someone who knows how to research. We need help on this case, and we can justify the cost: we've got missing paper files from decades ago. We do need the hands."

Eleri didn't comment, just digested both the thoughts and the food. Extra hands would make it go faster. Extra hands would get Donovan back sooner. And doing it that way might not trigger SAC Westerfield that they were more looking for Donovan than working the case.

"So far," Christina added, "There's nothing about this case that smacks of anything we can't share with an inside investigator."

"Are you suggesting we get another agent?" Eleri was not looking forward to discussing this with her SAC.

He didn't take kindly to requests for extra agents. It wasn't as if this case had run away from them—more like Eleri was trying to run away from it. "If we do get another agent, how would we have them looking for Donovan? We're already doing what we can on our own time."

"I've been thinking …" Christina put the last bite of her own burger into her mouth but didn't say more.

It was taking everything Eleri had just to show up and do the bare minimum on this case. Cases deserved attention—the kind she didn't have right now.

"One—we see if we can get Wade on this." Christina gestured with her last french fry.

"Wade would be perfect." She simply hadn't considered that he might be available. He knew Donovan. He might be able to find Donovan by scent alone … if the trail wasn't cold. "But we'd be asking him to infiltrate Miranda."

"Not really. We're asking him if he *wants* to. Donovan is his friend, too."

For a moment, Eleri had a flash of memory from when the two men had first met, each of them recognizing instantly what the other was, even though Eleri had been almost completely clueless. Wade had been her friend for well over a decade and she'd never known what he was until Donovan had curled his lip and bared his teeth.

"I didn't tell you, because there wasn't much to report, but Wade and Noah have both checked in with me. Wade just hasn't found anything we can use yet."

Pressure pushed at the back of Eleri's eyes as small epiphanies rocked her. She'd thought she was looking for Donovan and Christina was helping her. But that was all wrong. They were *all* searching for Donovan. As closed off as he was, he'd still made very deep ties in the group of agents.

And so had she.

"I should quit and go look for him." The words just came out, though she knew she'd chosen to stay so she could get information from Westerfield. It was just that none of it was working.

"If it were that easy, you would have already done it." Christina motioned toward the door. "But you would have to leave the job to do it." She lowered her voice. "And we don't know if you can come back. Westerfield is playing a game we haven't cracked yet."

When Eleri didn't say anything, Christina added. "Wade should be finishing his current case here in the next few days. He's just wrapping up paperwork. I'll ask if he's willing."

Why would anyone be willing if she wasn't?

Eleri couldn't help but blame herself for all of it. Still, Christina seemed to read her mind.

"We're all willing to help. This isn't just on you." She paused. "You'd come looking if it was me."

Eleri felt another flood of emotion she wasn't prepared to handle. *She would.* She would have dropped everything or stayed with the job, whichever was better, if Christina were missing. She'd thought she was alone this whole time. But she wasn't.

"As soon as we close this one, if Westerfield hasn't found him yet, I'm going solo. I'll find him," Christina assured her.

Eleri hoped it didn't take that long. But here she was, weeks out from his disappearance, having made no progress at all.

"Plus, like us, Wade's in NightShade and he's been in longer than us. He might be able to access records of the undercover agent you handed Donovan over to. Maybe with each of us doing pieces of the work, we can sneak under Westerfield's radar and find the agent."

"That's why Westerfield wants us close!" Eleri knew she was late to this party. Christina had been babysitting her in her grief and fear, but it was well past time to wake up and fucking function. "He's sacrificing Donovan to protect his undercover op."

"That's what I think." Christina nodded. "But we won't let him."

They sat in silence for a moment, both absorbing what they'd finally said out loud.

Then Christina pulled them back to the present. "So, we see if we can get Wade, but we have the authority to add our own researcher."

"As long as they've been vetted," Eleri pointed out. Half her turkey sandwich sat untouched, but she felt more focused than she had since she'd loaded Donovan into the back of the SUV and watched her dying friend driven away.

"Right," Christina grinned. "I think we can get away with hiring Jesse Nash."

10

Mila sat in her car in the parking lot as she took a bite of her pop tart and looked in the rearview mirror. The concealer hadn't quite hidden the dark circles under her eyes.

This was the third day she'd been sitting here. Each time she told herself to drive away and abandon this stupid project. She wasn't a stalker, she told herself now, though she had to admit that her actions didn't support that. But the nightmares were taking everything from her. She had to find him ... whoever he was.

What if he didn't come back? What if he already came back and he wouldn't be back again for another month or so?

But Mila didn't know what else to do. So she sat in the car, scanning the lot constantly looking for the antique red car. *Cherry,* he'd called it. She didn't like that the name ringed true to her memory.

She couldn't see all the parking spots, but she could see the entrance and exit to the lot. Each time before she left, she went around the whole loop. Each time when she came back, she ran it again. Just in case he'd come in while she was away.

She had to pee so bad. With a muttered curse, she set the half-eaten Pop Tart down on the passenger seat beside her. Cranking the engine, she put the car in gear. Hers wasn't a '63 Ford Falcon. And now she wasn't sure she wanted one anymore. Her little Civic would do just fine.

She headed several shopping centers over, pulling in at a fast food place. Using the restroom as quickly as she could, she next hopped up to the counter for a coke and fries. Not that it was any better than the Pop Tart she'd abandoned but she didn't like using the restroom without paying for it in some way.

Back in the car, she settled the drink in the cup holder and the fries in the empty one made for whoever her non-existent passenger was. She'd barely talked to anybody for three days. Her designs had been shit and everyone had noticed. If she hadn't called in sick, she would have been sent home.

Mila didn't think she'd slept more than four hours in a row for the last several weeks. All of it traced back to the moment she touched that stupid car.

She needed to find it again, to find *him* again.

Then again, she was beginning to think maybe what she actually needed was to find a good therapist. Maybe a psychiatrist who could prescribe medication.

She'd been living another life in her dreams. The pieces were starting to come together ... the man, the car, the chase ...

Why it had happened when she touched that car, she didn't know. But she needed to. Some big chunk was still missing and the drive to find it was compelling her to do these things.

With her coke in one hand, Mila pulled back into the restaurant's parking lot. She made a loop around, checking out all the cars and not seeing the classic Falcon. Her same spot was open, and she settled into it.

An hour later, as the afternoon waned on, his car drove by.

It had to be him, right? There couldn't be that many of that exact car in the world, let alone in this city.

He didn't pull into the lot but pulled past. He must be going into the shopping center.

Cranking the engine, she slammed the little Civic into drive and practically peeled out of her spot. Mila told herself that she had to be cautious, she couldn't look like she was following him. But having had no training in it, she probably looked exactly like she was following him.

11

"Please don't touch my car!" Brian called out to the woman who was standing near it.

She was turned facing away from him, standing next to the driver's side door. Her hand tentatively reached out, as if she wanted to touch but didn't feel she should.

He kept Cherry pristine, and he didn't like people touching his baby. Brian was about to call out again when she turned and looked at him.

"You!" he said, startled.

She looked almost as if she'd been crying this time. Last time she'd looked vibrant. His brows pulled together. "Are you okay?"

She seemed almost startled that he might ask. But if she looked in the mirror she should have seen she didn't quite look okay. It had been three weeks since he'd seen her the first time. It bothered him that he knew that.

Had that been the first time he'd had the visions? He couldn't call them anything else now. He wasn't certain what they were, but he was confident that he didn't like them, and he didn't like her association with them.

She shook her head. At least she knew she wasn't all right.

He stopped walking toward her, staying near the trunk. Maybe it wouldn't be wise to get directly into her personal space. Was she mentally ill? She'd seemed fine before.

She looked at him as though she needed something from him, and he already didn't like it before she spoke.

"I've been having the weirdest dreams ever since I touched your car."

It wasn't an accusation, but he felt it like an arrow piercing his heart—or maybe a shot through his right side, like a bullet grazing flesh.

Everything in him shut down.

No, she could not be saying that. In that moment, he denied every odd dream and every weird thought he'd had. Had it really started for him when she touched his car? It was enough that he was having these dreams. If she was having them too ...

He didn't ask her name or where she was from. Brian simply pushed forward, practically forcing her to take a few steps back, allowing him to get to the driver's side door. "Lady, I don't know who you are or what you want. Please get away from my car."

"Sir," she said. "I'm sorry. I was just curious. It started when I—"

He slammed the door and revved the engine, drowning out her words, not quite knowing why he was being such an ass.

The old car was not the same kind of quiet that new ones were, for once, he was grateful. Hitting the clutch, he jammed the car into reverse and pulled away from her. It was all he could do to be just cautious enough to not hit her. He didn't want any ties to this woman, whoever she was.

He did not have the ability to process that she might be having the strange dreams, too.

Behind him, she called out, her hand waving. Running a few steps, she seemed to think she might catch him. As if he would suddenly change his mind and stop. Then, as he got a little further away, he saw that she took out her phone and snapped a picture of his license plate.

12

———

"Wade will be in Florida in two days," Christina announced the next morning. Eleri felt her heart lift.

But then … "Is that the smartest thing?"

She wasn't convinced Donovan was still in Florida. He probably hadn't been for some time.

"Let's find out." Christina tapped at her phone before Eleri had a chance to say anything.

Within moments, Wade's voice came over the line, "Christina!"

"And Eleri," Christina added.

"It's good to hear from you both," Eleri could hear it. "Any news?"

"Sadly, no," she chimed in.

Eleri had known Wade longer than she'd known Christina. She'd met him during her early days in the Behavioral Analysis Unit. His team had tapped her for a couple of cases and at the time she'd had no clue that the NightShade division existed, nor that Wade was a part of it. She'd never suspected what he could do.

Christina said, "We wanted to talk about you heading to Florida in a few days."

"I thought that was the plan. Honestly, I'm just double-checking the paperwork on this last case. Crossing the I's and dotting the T's, that kind of thing."

Eleri grinned. She didn't think he could say the phrase correctly anymore.

"Why?" he asked. "Do you have other ideas?"

Eleri's heart settled a little deeper into her chest. These were her friends. They weren't making decisions behind her back. Florida was simply where the conversation had likely gone. Christina and Wade had been doing the work that she herself couldn't do.

Clearly, following Westerfield's orders and waiting for the FBI to find him wasn't getting the job done. So she told Wade. "We don't have actual other ideas. We just wanted to get the brain trust together and talk it through." She paused and sighed. "I suspect he wasn't in Florida for more than a week or two. However long it would take to heal."

There was a moment's pause then Wade's voice came back on. "I think you're the senior-most medical person here."

That position should go to Donovan. Well, she had plenty of physiology though the majority of her training was about what happens to bodies *after* they died, not while they were living. But Wade was a physicist and Christina had a degree in law.

She made her best guess. "I would think a week or maybe two before they could move him. It would depend on how much surgery he needed and what kind."

He'd been shot, bleeding and near death. He hadn't even been in human form at the time, so she couldn't call 9-1-1. She'd considered tapping a local veterinarian. But again, the vet would have noticed something was off about Donovan's physiology, and none of them wanted that. Donovan might not have survived it. He'd needed a surgeon who knew what he was and how to handle that.

She didn't have time to get him to the de Gottardi/Little compound in the Ozarks. So Eleri had done the best she could at the time. She'd reached out to the wolf who'd been tailing them.

"I would have imagined Miranda would want to save him. If only for information." As Christina said it, Eleri cringed.

The thought had crossed her mind that they might torture her partner for information. Though she welcomed one of them coming after her, she couldn't make the chain of information get to that endpoint. She couldn't even think about them torturing Donovan, especially not after he'd almost died. So each time she thought it, Eleri had immediately pushed it aside.

"Well," Wade said, clearly thinking. "What if I start there? I go back. I trace Donovan's steps—at least what we know of them. Then I look for Miranda Industries shell companies in the area."

That had been the whole problem. She and Donovan, and eventually Christina, had been on an investigation that wasn't related to Miranda, but an employee of a Miranda shell corporation had been killed in the process. Miranda had sent Victor Leonidas—their own investigator. The issue was that when he'd crossed paths with Donovan, Donovan had smelled him and known there was another wolf in the area. And that the other wolf was following them.

"I think we look for Leonidas, too," Christina said. "Eleri and I are stuck here in Minnesota for a little while at least."

Even so, Eleri had been digging where she could. Each night she tried to follow the tracks of the NightShade operative who had been embedded with Miranda Industries for almost five years. He needed to stay hidden for his own safety. And probably for Donovan's now as well. So Eleri hadn't pushed too hard when she hit roadblocks.

"How do we find him?" Eleri asked.

Christina jumped in again. "We tried going forward and we can't find him that way. So we go backward."

Eleri looked up and frowned at the same time as Wade's confused voice came across the line. "What?"

Christina filled them in. "We find out everything we know about him from *before* he went undercover and we use it to pressure Westerfield into giving us his information."

Interesting idea.

Maybe Christina was right. Westerfield had proven he wouldn't give them what they wanted without pressure—not about Donovan or his undercover agent. If they could find special agent Victor Leonidas, they could probably find Donovan, or at least get information where Donovan's last known location was. It was better than what they had right now. And looking for Donovan hadn't been working.

Eleri now hoped that maybe Wade going to Florida was the best idea. They talked a little more, finalizing Wade's plans.

But before they finished, Eleri's phone dinged.

She looked at Christina, holding her own phone up so her new partner could see what was on the screen.

"We've got stuff coming on this case, Wade," Christina said.

"No worries. I've got work to do here. I'll let you know once I'm boots on the ground," Wade told them before hanging up.

Christina turned to Eleri. "What's that?"

Eleri grinned. "They traced the VIN number on the vehicle!"

13

Eleri leaned back as Christina announced, "The car is registered —*was* *registered*—to Benjamin Hartman of Stanislau County, California."

The two of them had come in to the BCA offices early this morning. They'd stopped early last night, wanting to spend the evening putting their efforts toward finding Donovan.

They'd pulled out maps, pinpointed the Miranda Industries shell companies they'd found on the last case, and searched until they found a few more. Eleri had called Jesse Nash and left a message but, unfortunately, had yet to get a return call.

She was beginning to wonder if maybe she was too late. Though Jesse had done some work for Eleri and Donovan on their last case, Eleri had no idea if that meant the investigative reporter would be willing to do it again. Surely, she hadn't sat around with no work in the meantime.

Jesse was now the mother of an elementary school-aged child—a stepchild she'd inherited when her husband was murdered. There was every possibility Jesse Nash would not call them back at all.

Eleri fought back the pressure that pushed at her because if they couldn't get Jesse, who would they get? Who would be good at the work? Who could pass the Bureau's inspection and also understand that things were a little off? And who could possibly do that in the kind of timeframe that Jesse could? Mostly because Jesse was already cleared.

Eleri told herself it would work out. She told herself she would not ask Christina to push Jesse into accepting the assignment. That wasn't fair to her partner or the reporter. So she swiveled her chair around to her screen and typed in what new information they had.

They'd come back to the BCA because their temporary pass codes here gave them access to all the databases in the state. Logging into FBI systems using their own passwords and codes gave them secure access to most all Bureau databases as well. In moments, they had information about Benjamin Hartman.

The owner of the car in the lake was possibly the man who'd been found in the car. Maybe even *probably*. Eleri figured that was likely given his birth date and the possible timeframe in which the car went down.

But as of yet, the two agents couldn't be sure. Jennifer Barnes' info said she—and therefore *they*—had been alive in 1987. The clothing in the suitcases indicated the car had gone down sometime before the mid 90s—a very different date range than they'd initially expected.

After a few minutes of both agents tapping on their keyboards for more information, Eleri turned to Christina. "Any photographs of Benjamin Hartman?"

"None." Christina didn't even look away from her screen.

"Then we start with his family." Eleri tried not to look at the time, and ignore that Jesse Nash still hadn't called them back.

Though they struggled to find pictures or fingerprints or anything else useful in IDing the body, they did manage to hunt down one of Benjamin Hartman's survivors. A few minutes later, Eleri found a phone number for the woman who hopefully was his mother.

Eleri punched the numbers into her cell phone, holding it out between her and Christina. The line rang a good number of times before a curious, deep voice answered.

"Hello?" It was the kind of voice that spoke of decades of cigarettes, and yet still remained melodious and beautiful.

Given the timing and the age of the voice, Eleri had to wonder if perhaps the phone wasn't an old model still attached to the wall. The curiosity in the tone indicated the woman had no idea who was calling, not even that it might be an unknown number.

Eleri started in gently. "Hello, my name is Eleri Eames. I'm with the Federal Bureau of Investigation."

She'd used the full name of the Bureau, having learned that a lot of older people had watched enough TV and movies to have a reaction to the letters "FBI." And that reaction was almost always negative.

Eleri continued, "Am I speaking with Mrs. Ella Hartman?"

"Yes Ma'am. I am she."

Eleri almost grinned at being "ma'am"ed by a woman probably fifty years her senior.

"What did Tyrone do this time?" the old voice asked, melodic weariness tingeing every word.

The tone let Eleri know that she should have done more research before calling this woman. *Was she just being stupid? Was it because Donovan was missing and she really was operating at half mast?*

"Apologies ma'am. I have no information on Tyrone. I'm calling about Benjamin." She paused letting that absorb. "Benjamin Allen Hartman."

The silence on the other end of the line let her know she'd found the correct person.

"Did you find him?" The voice asked softly. Before Eleri could answer, the woman added, "I'm assuming you found his body."

She wasn't sure yet. That was the problem. Given the complete lack of information on Benjamin Hartman in any database from after the mid-eighties, it was hard to tell. Unlike with internet access today, the timeframe created a difficulty pinpointing an exact date when all activity stopped.

There was no social media to check for the last post. No up-to-the-minute banking records. In the eighties, people frequently used checks and credit cards were often just accepted and filed days later, then the banks processed the funds days after that. The person might have disappeared or died in the intervening time. The record didn't stop when the person did, not back then.

However, the issue that this woman suspected her son was already dead made it more likely that his was the body they pulled out of Lake Superior this week. But Eleri didn't have enough to say "yes."

So she said what she could. "Ma'am, we do have a body and we're not certain if it's your son."

Though if this woman was as sharp as she already sounded, then she would have put together the facts. If the FBI was calling her, it was about her son, or it was something very very close.

Eleri pushed forward. "I'd like to ask you a few questions about Benjamin."

"Ben," the woman corrected, but then there was another pause and Eleri wasn't sure the woman would continue. But then she sighed. "I've known he was dead for years. So now ... go ahead, ask me your questions. Though I'm not sure how this will help me."

Eleri was afraid she'd get hung up on, so she was opening her mouth to try to fudge some kind of explanation. It felt too much like a lie, though.

Luckily, Mrs. Hartman spoke again. "Was he with that woman?"

14

"**B**enjamin got out," Mrs. Hartman told Eleri once she decided to trust her.

"And Tyrone? You mentioned him first," Eleri pushed back as Christina nodded toward her. She'd sat by as a silent player on the call, but her expression said maybe the brother was important.

"He never did. In and out of prison, that one. Benjamin though? He got that one arrest and ..."

He had an arrest? They should have found that!

Unless their guy wasn't Benjamin Hartman. The doubts were creeping at the edges now. The car was registered to Benjamin Hartman, but they couldn't jump to the conclusion that his was one of the bodies inside.

Christina was already taking notes, pushing the paper across to Eleri to cue questions. There was only one word on the page. *When?*

"When was he arrested, ma'am?" Eleri asked.

"I don't remember exactly. He was seventeen—" Christina wrote that down quickly. "—and he got charged with possession."

"Possession?" Eleri pushed.

"Cocaine!" The woman said it with an emphasis at the end of the word, letting the agents know that she was irritated by something about this arrest.

"I hate to have to ask this ..." Eleri needed the information. "You sound upset. Are you mad at him for having cocaine? Or are you upset about something else?"

"He didn't have cocaine!" Mrs. Hartman said forcefully, and Eleri felt herself pull back at the force of the accusation. Though whether it was just a mother's words or the truth, she didn't know.

Mrs. Hartman set her straight quickly. "If you told me it was Tyrone, I would believe you. I would believe you seven ways to Sunday and back, because Tyrone actually did the things he's gone down for. But Benjamin, he didn't."

There was a heavy pause, then the woman continued, her tone having changed to explanation. "Ma'am, my son is Black."

Those few words were thick with unsaid meaning. Eleri nodded, then spoke because the woman couldn't hear that. "I understand, ma'am." She wasn't quite ready to add, "I too, am partly African American" because was she? Her Grandmére had been something else. Eleri's mother passed for white a lot of the time, so much so that even Eleri had been surprised to learn how much of her heritage was Black, Haitian, and more.

"He was out with some of his white friends," Mrs. Hartman went on. "I had warned him he'd be the one who got in trouble."

Eleri felt her heart sink. "The others weren't also arrested?"

"No, ma'am." This time the tone held only resignation.

Once again Eleri only said, "I understand."

To an extent, she did. Her own mixed parentage had left her open to incidences that she was certain were racist in origin, and many others that she thought were but couldn't quite prove. But, in much of her life, she'd had the privilege of the very wealthy. She simply hadn't run in the kind of circles where the things that happened to Benjamin Hartman would happen to her. So she said she understood, but she also knew that she could only understand in an intellectual sense.

Pausing for another moment, she waited for notes from Christina that didn't come. She hoped Mrs. Hartman would fill in the spaces. It seemed, once she was going, the older woman was happy to do so.

"That charge kept him from finding work! He did eventually convince somebody that the charge was fraudulent, even though it was on his record. That man was wonderful and hired him. But when the boss's boss found out about it, Benjamin was immediately let go."

Oh no. Eleri couldn't imagine thinking she was okay and then later being fired for a charge that she hadn't actually committed. The FBI trained part of her brain reminded her that this was his mother's version of events and it might be a bit too rosy.

So Eleri moved the conversation in a slightly different direction. "When did you know he was missing?"

"In the late summer of 1987." The answer had been sharp and ready. *The same as Jennifer Barnes.* "He was good right up until before then. He was doing better, he said. He stayed in touch, loved to tell his mama that he was making a better life. Then he just quit communicating."

Eleri asked another question, but these kinds of things had to be broached with tact and delicacy. Unfortunately, she was the only one to ask though she likely didn't have any finesse these days. "I've looked through our records, and I didn't find a missing persons report on him. Did you file one?"

Eleri expected answers like Yes or No. And then she would have to figure out where the report had gone or why there were no records of it. Or she could ask why the mother hadn't filed one. Those would all be valid and expected paths.

She was not prepared for the answer she got.

"I *tried*." Again, the emphasis at the end of the last word told Eleri the woman was angry about this, too. *But what did that mean?* "Can you explain?"

Christina was looking at Eleri again, the pinched skin between her brows suggesting that she was having the same reaction as Eleri.

"What does it mean that you *tried* to file a missing persons report?"

"I went down to the police station, and I told them my son was missing and they needed to investigate it. The woman behind the desk said I didn't qualify."

Eleri and Christina looked at each other with eyes wide. *He didn't qualify?*

"How would you not qualify for a missing persons report?" Had he not been gone long enough? Then she would just go back later. If her son was the man in the morgue, then he hadn't re-appeared.

Eleri was as confused as she'd ever been.

But Mrs. Hartman had a tale to tell. "The woman pulled his record and found the charge for cocaine and decided he was a druggie who'd just gone away and decided not to talk to his mother anymore."

"They still should have filed the report," Eleri told her. They were obligated to do so.

"Yes, ma'am." Mrs. Hartman understood what she'd been denied, and Eleri felt the rage simmering in her own chest.

"They *should* have filed it!" The melodic voice had accepted the insult but still held the bitterness. "But they told me not to worry about it and she said again that Benjamin didn't qualify to have a report filed."

"They didn't tell you to come back later, after he'd been missing longer?"

"He'd been gone almost a month by the time I tried to file an official report. And no, they told me not to come back."

Holy shit, Eleri thought, but tried to keep her tone neutral. "And where was it that you filed—tried to file—that report?"

"It was here, ma'am. I have lived here my whole life. In Crows Landing."

Fingers flying, Christina searched a map, finding the area even as Mrs. Hartman added, "Just outside of Modesto."

Another pause filled the space between them, while Eleri desperately tried to formulate another question. Once again, it was Mrs. Hartman who aimed them where they needed to go.

"The thing is, just before he disappeared, my Benjamin called me. He said he met a woman and that he was in love. He said I would like her, and he told me that they were suddenly wealthy and that he was going to buy me a proper house."

That was very interesting.

"Did you believe him?" Eleri asked.

"Of course. Ben didn't lie. He told me he had over three hundred thousand dollars."

"And he didn't say where he'd gotten it?" *This had taken an unexpected turn.*

"No ma'am. He didn't."

Just then, Eleri's phone interrupted them with a buzz and a pop up letting her know that Jesse Nash was calling her back.

15

"No, I don't mind at all," Jesse Nash said. "The timing is actually perfect. Ciara wanted to go to summer camp and I couldn't tell her no. So this will help me pay it off a little faster."

Eleri's heart soared as soon as the reporter agreed to take the assignment. "When can you start?"

"I'm driving Ciara to camp this afternoon. It's about three hours each way. I'll get home tonight. Is tomorrow morning okay?"

"Of course." Though, Eleri thought with what she already knew of Jesse, there was every possibility that woman would start once she got home from dropping her step-daughter off and might even stay up all night. Eleri suspected it would be a combination of missing her child and having the drive to crack a case.

"Is it in Florida?" Jesse asked. It was the next smart question and it made sense.

Eleri and Donovan had only found Jesse in the first place because they were where she was—in Florida. She'd impressed them by cracking pieces of their case for them.

"No. In fact, it looks like it's going to be research all over the US."

"Travel?"

Christina hopped in. "That depends on what we come up against and what our SAC will fund."

They spent a small while working out the logistics, then Eleri laid a list on Jesse, including research items regarding Jennifer Barnes, the

VIN for the car, and anything she could find on Benjamin Hartman. She updated Jesse on what they had. "As of right now the Benjamin Hartman who owned the car appears to have left little digital footprint."

"Interesting," Jesse said.

"It's causing trouble," Christina added. "We have a body on the table that we believe is this man. But with no digital footprint, we're struggling to match anything."

"No fingerprints?" Jesse asked. "No history of arrest? No one filed a missing persons report?"

Jesse was on top of all of it, Eleri thought. "Those things are exactly the problem. It's not a current case. It's from the late eighties or maybe nineties."

Eleri laid out what they'd already found leaving out a few key pieces.

"So he's about sixty now?" Eleri could almost hear Jesse doing the quick math in her head.

"He disappeared sometime around eighty-five though."

"Ah, so the body is skeletonized remains?"

"Not exactly," Eleri hedged, thinking of the perfectly preserved body in the morgue. Despite the preservation that the morgue employed the body was decaying more rapidly now than it ever had before.

Jesse's confusion came through in her tone. Though Jesse had FBI clearance, Eleri hadn't yet cleared the entire case through Westerfield. She was once again hoping to get forgiven rather than getting permission.

"We know Jennifer Barnes was alive as of June of eighty-seven. After that, it's a crapshoot," Eleri struggled with what she could and couldn't say.

The three continued on with Jesse urging them to narrow down the disappearance window, and Eleri suggesting that they truly couldn't. At this point, all they had was the visual age of the bodies. She would readily guess that neither of them had made it to their sixties. It was problematic though, since they didn't know that they actually had Benjamin Hartman on the table. The young man they had could be much younger than Hartman. Jennifer Barnes didn't appear to have had any plastic surgery. But people looked younger longer these days. Though the clothing and the coincidental times they'd gone missing made it unlikely, it was entirely possible they'd only been underwater maybe six or seven years.

Eventually, after a call that had taken much longer than Eleri planned, but made her feel much better than she expected, they hung up.

"What are we up to next?" Christina asked.

"Just digging." Eleri didn't like the word. "At least we have Jesse to help us with it now, but we still have our own digging to do."

Jesse couldn't access fingerprint databases. Eleri or Christina had to do all of that.

Christina sighed. She didn't appreciate the research any more than Eleri did, though they both liked what it yielded. "Do we have more coming in?"

"We've got more coming in off of the car now." Eleri watched as Christina's brows climbed closer to her hairline in surprise. Eleri grinned. "The techs pulled all kinds of prints off the paint and chrome."

"I mean, I know you can get prints off a car after it goes in the water. Depending on the water and the timeframe," Christina added.

In fact, if a person hadn't washed their hands recently—or had rubbed some particularly oily portion of their body, such as the back of their neck and then touched a clean car—the fingerprint could stay for quite some time.

"Here," Eleri tapped a few keys and brought another image up on the large screen. Spending another day at the BCA in Duluth hadn't been her idea of a good time, but at least it was yielding information. "Look at these pictures."

The tech had dusted the car doors and the dash with the luminescent print powder and then put a UV light source on it.

"Wow. How are they even going to pull an individual print out of that?"

It was a mess. Fingerprints overlapped everywhere. The door handles were covered with them to the point where it would be impossible, as Christina suggested, to pull one from the multiple overlaid marks. Some were smeared, but many were clean.

Eleri felt pretty confident she could follow the lines and whorls and put one back together. She might actually do it, but it would be for their own use. It definitely wouldn't hold up in court.

"Here's the dash." Eleri pointed then flipped to another picture.

"The inside door handle." She flipped the screen again. "And the trunk."

"Alright." Christina looked carefully, bringing her face in close to the screen. "There are a few places where we can get some individual prints."

"Exactly," Eleri agreed. "And the techs did already send over the clean ones that they could find."

Nodding and stepping away, her partner added, "I don't want to work on finding images of Benjamin Hartman anymore. Not now that we have Jesse on it. I might just be duplicating her work."

Eleri agreed. "But what should you work on?"

It felt wrong to have a pile of work if her partner didn't also have it, but Eleri was their certified fingerprint analyst. She either did this herself or spent time reading through matches some other analyst had found.

"I'm pouring through the other evidence. There is some stuff coming in about the clothing, and the car. I'll just sort it all." She sounded resigned, but Eleri turned back to her screen and the meticulous work of pulling and labeling the prints. There were several steps required before she could even load them into the system to find a match.

Sure enough, a few minutes later, Christina grabbed her attention again. "I've got some evidence that narrows our window for the car going into the lake."

Eleri looked over her shoulder, having been clicking on arrows and circles, and trying to lay out one of the fingerprints before feeding it into the system. It didn't visually match, either Jennifer Barnes or Benjamin Hartman.

"This might be a real clue."

Turning the stool around she devoted her attention to Christina. "How so?"

"Remember the tech at the scene commented that the clothing looked wrong?"

Eleri nodded.

"It didn't match the car. We thought then that the car went down in the late sixties or early seventies. They found now the clothing was actually from the late eighties. The Bureau put an analyst on it, who determined the original make. Nothing in the suitcase was produced after 1987."

"So chances are they died before 1990," Eleri said. They had to be careful. Even though both parents had reported the two missing at the same time, assuming that was when they died could be a colossal mistake ...

"Yes." Christina's answer surprised her. Eleri waited while her new partner looked back at her screen clearly reading from what they had. "Given the purchase dates and the range of clothing that was in there, the analyst didn't think this woman would have gone more than three or four years without a new piece of clothing—especially given things like the concert T-shirts and such. She concluded this woman would likely have had new shirts or such had she been able to do so in her last few years. She checked manufacture dates and found one piece that didn't exist until late 1986."

Eleri was absorbing that. The window for the car to have gone into the lake was getting smaller and smaller. Even as she was trying to put all the pieces together in a way that made sense, she heard a ding from Christina's computer. "What was that?"

"Well, that's good," Christina replied with a grin as she looked at her screen. "The ballistics report is back on the gun."

16

"You look *off* again," Christina said. "I thought the last few days were getting better."

Eleri sighed and felt her shoulders fall. "What is *better*? Accepting that Donovan's not here anymore. I can't believe that he's …"

She couldn't bring herself to say the word *dead*.

"I'm confident that he's not." Christina reached across the table and covered Eleri's hand with her own in a gesture that Eleri hadn't expected from her fellow agent.

"Why don't you think that?" The question was sharp, driven with a dagger-like force, though Eleri hadn't intended it to be. *Did Christina know something she didn't?*

"I don't believe it because you don't. I have a feeling that you would feel it if any of us was gone."

That feeling had been the only thing keeping Eleri going. Surely, if Donovan had left the earth, she would know. But she didn't know much of anything. She was opening her mouth to ask Christina what she should do, when her friend seemed to get ahead of her.

"Have you cast a spell to find him?"

"Of course, but they don't work. They all fall flat." Just like her taste buds and her usual excitement about a new case. She wouldn't take any of it for granted in the future.

"Interesting."

"No. It's disturbing. Frustrating." The last thing Eleri would have called it was *interesting*.

"No." Christina shook her head, her gaze turning toward the ceiling as she thought it through. "It's *interesting*."

"Why?"

"Eleri, you're a very powerful witch—"

"Who has to focus her emotion to get anything! And I'm too scrambled to focus! I haven't even had any decent dreams."

"Wow." Christina tipped her head. "That's telling, too. I think our first order of business is to fix your focus."

Why hadn't she thought of that? Eleri wondered. It wasn't that she hadn't thought of casting a spell and looking for Donovan. She'd *done* it. She'd cast fire and watched it sputter. She'd poured clear water, boiled with herbs and strained, for scrying, but seen nothing. As a last resort, she'd pulled out her pendulum and a map and let it cast over Florida.

The pendulum not only hadn't pointed her to a place, it simply hadn't moved at all.

In fact, all of her questions about Donovan—even when she'd brought herself to ask the most disturbing, *is he dead?*—hadn't moved the pendulum at all.

So she'd been casting spells and watching them fail. *But she hadn't tried to fix the root of the problem.* She had simply gotten frustrated and angry and walked away. Now she shifted her attention.

"I'm not quite sure how to fix it," Eleri told Christina.

"Well, obviously we need to find you some emotional focus. I don't know if that's yoga, or—"

Christina stopped as Eleri's face scrunched up.

"Meditation?"

Her face scrunched harder. For all that she had to do to focus when she needed to cast a spell, meditation was one of her least favorite things. Right after yoga.

"Long walks in the woods?" Christina was reaching.

Eleri laughed. "Pina Coladas and getting caught in the rain?"

"Maybe." At least Christina was grinning.

Eleri felt a real smile, and that—her first genuine feeling in some time—might be the first step.

Then she leaned forward. "Can you push me?"

Christina could make anyone see, hear, or feel whatever Christina determined. She'd had a bad history with using it for her own personal gain and now limited herself to using these skills only on the people they were chasing as part of a case or to force answers to questions the team needed in order to save lives.

Before Christina could refuse, Eleri leaned further forward. "I'm asking you to do it. You don't just have my permission. You have my *request*."

"Maybe," Christina replied. At least she was considering it. "We need to think about what exactly to do first, so that it works."

Yes, Eleri thought as she leaned back. They needed this to work. It had to work so they could find Donovan. She'd been failing at it by herself. So maybe the trick was to not do it by herself. But then her brain snagged on something Christina had said earlier. "Why did you say it was interesting that I couldn't find Donovan?"

"Because you should have found something. You didn't get any answers?"

"Nothing," Eleri confirmed.

"Which is exactly why I think he's still alive." This time it was Christina who leaned forward. "We know what Miranda can do, at least part of what they're capable of. You should have gotten an answer when you looked for Donovan, even if it was the one you didn't want. The fact that you didn't get anything ..." Christina paused. "I think it means he's still alive. Because the only reason I can think of that you would get *no answer*, is if someone blocked you from seeing it."

17

Mila had charged the hiking boots to her credit card. She was spending out every last vacation day she'd banked at work and still wasn't sure if they'd figured out yet that she almost definitely wouldn't make it back by the time she ran out of leave.

She'd packed a small bag and hit the road, having made it to southern California before she stopped. This was Jennifer's old grounds. And maybe the key to putting all these strange memories to rest.

Hiking up through the woods near Los Angeles, she found the new boots gripped the ground well, but they also gripped her memory a little too tightly.

On a normal day, she would have cared. But the dreams hadn't stopped, and she'd felt compelled by a force stronger than herself to pursue them. Hope spun out like a gossamer thread that, if she could find out what they were, they would stop.

So she was just north of Los Angeles, hiking in the Hollywood Hills. Everything around her felt right, but also wrong. The whole town had felt right, but also wrong. There were places she'd driven past and suffered a fleeting thought of "There used to be ..." But there was no way she could know that.

She'd only been to Los Angeles once before, as a child. Surely, she didn't remember things from back then. At the time, she'd come with her parents. Her father was speaking at a conference and her mother had taken Mila and her brother around to see the sights.

She remembered the Tar Pits and the Hollywood sign. She remembered seeing the beach and thinking it wasn't quite as pretty as the ones in North Carolina. So she couldn't have remembered driving down Ventura Boulevard and thinking about a grocery store beyond the big parking lot. Or a nail salon that had sat on the previous corner. Or the restaurant she'd gone to out in Porter Ranch.

Now, standing in the woods, the trees and the dirt and the scenery felt almost like home. But again, something was off. Something she couldn't quite place.

Mila stopped her hike and peered through the trees to the city beyond. The vantage point here was not quite panoramic, but it was still beautiful. Even the fact that she could see Griffith Park Observatory felt normal.

Why did she feel like she remembered *it? And would any of this ever go away?*

Shaking her head, she turned and picked her way down the other side of the hill. It wasn't quite a mountain. Was she going to get lost? She found she had a mild amount of confidence that she wouldn't. She also had a heaping dose of not giving a fuck.

She'd snapped that picture of the license on the Ford Falcon and found a site to enter it. She'd done it all from her phone as she'd stood there in the parking lot. Relatively quickly, the site had popped up the name Brian Abadi. A few more quick searches and she'd found his face and basic information. He was an investment banker, lived in a high rise apartment. He'd graduated from Wharton.

Brian Abadi was the right guy. He wasn't driving his friend's car or anything like that. She now had access to his social media and knew where he worked. Though she hadn't found a unit number, she did now know where to find him.

Mila had debated reaching out to him again but, in the end, she had decided to travel on her own. Brian Abadi certainly didn't seem to want anything to do with her. Maybe by the time she got back home—*if* she still had a job or *if* she still had any functioning brain cells left—she would be able to tell him something that would make him listen.

18

E leri had settled herself back at the desk, once again scrolling through images of fingerprints from the car. Several had matched Jennifer Barnes the others had matched their John Doe.

Whether he was actually Benjamin Hartman or not seemed to be taking a while to confirm. Hopefully Jesse would be able to get the arrest record sent from Stanislaus County Sheriff's Department for Benjamin Hartman's cocaine bust all those years ago. Most likely it was a paper file somewhere. Precincts varied quite widely in their ability and desire to get old records scanned. Eleri understood why it still hadn't happened in so many places.

Hence, why Mrs. Ella Hartman could tell them that her son had an arrest record that Eleri and Christina still hadn't been able to pull up. That record should contain prints they could use to match or rule out the man in the morgue.

There were other prints to deal with though. These prints from the car belonged to more than just two people. Some fingerprints were individual and clean. A few came in sets, where a person had touched with their whole hand. She even had a partial palm print on the trunk. She'd gotten palm prints from both the victims once the skin had dried enough to make a decent copy. But she didn't expect Stanislaus County to have been taking palm prints in the early eighties unless they were way ahead of their time.

Evidence was piling up that someone who was neither of the two bodies they'd found had been around the car. Her clearest finger-prints looked as though someone had reached up and pulled the trunk closed.

When that had happened, Eleri didn't know. She had one set of three fingers with clean, clear marks. That the prints were on a background uninterrupted by dirt or other prints or smears, indicated this person had touched the car at some point after it had last been cleaned. The clarity of the prints told her it had happened close in time before the car went into the water.

Once again, Lake Superior with its lack of degrading bacteria, had preserved the evidence beautifully.

Eleri had high hopes to get a hit on those, but first, she had to put in the time to mark the fingerprints up so the system could read it.

"Check this out, Eleri." Christina's voice carried from behind her.

Christina had spread out at a table, with printed paper copies of what she needed. She preferred being able to scan all of it at once, instead of having to remember where the docs were and tap through them on a tablet or a screen.

"What have you got?"

"I just went through the ballistics on the gun. It's a trip."

"Oh?" Eleri swiveled the chair around. She needed a break from the lines and arrows. She'd done the prints herself to speed up the process but she was about to go cross-eyed. She knew fingerprint techs for whom this was their whole job and she now wondered how they didn't all need glasses.

Blinking a few times, she tried to focus on her friend but found it hard. Christina was already talking excitedly.

"So they fired a bullet from the gun brought up from the car and checked the rifling from the barrel."

Eleri nodded. That was standard procedure to see if the gun had been at known crime scenes. "So it matched?"

It must have or Christina wouldn't be bubbling over like this.

"It was used in a supermarket robbery."

"What?" Eleri's brain scrambled trying to move five different directions at once. Ella Hartman had said … "His mother told us he said he had just over three hundred thousand dollars. Would a grocery store have that much?" She paused and tried to calculate. "In the summer of 1987?"

"Well," Christina added more information, proving that nothing was ever easy. "It's associated with a *string* of grocery store robberies in Los Angeles in that year. The total take was over two million."

Would that add up? "How many places did they hit and how much money does a standard grocery store have on hand in 1987?"

"I don't know," Christina answered. But she didn't look up from her screen, just tapped quickly until she said, "It's easily a hundred thousand in cash in a big store these days."

Eleri thought for a moment then added, "And in 1987 a lot of transactions would be cash, much more so than today. Was it a big store?"

"It was in the valley in Los Angeles. So most likely, yes." Christina tapped at her keyboard again. "Looks like it was very profitable."

"Murder?" Eleri asked.

Christina still seemed to be reading from the screen. "The MO was for two masked assailants to open fire with handguns and automatic weapons. In this one that it matched to, the armored truck drivers who were standing chatting with grocery store employees were murdered immediately upon the assailants opening fire. No negotiations are apparent from any witness statements. The armored truck employees had already successfully accessed the vaults and stood with bags of cash in their hands."

"Holy shit," Eleri said. The murder hadn't been a mistake. It had been part of the plan.

Then again, it was difficult to get money away from security like that without committing murder.

Christina still hadn't looked up, but she confirmed Eleri's theory. "It wasn't just a robbery. They seemed to know that was the only way they could get the money. And they had the timing down."

Eleri was trying to sort the pieces floating through her brain. "Between the clothing and the missing persons report ... same year."

"Exactly." Christina finally looked up, a gleam in her eyes. "And Benjamin Hartman told his mother that he had three hundred thousand dollars."

"I'm still trying to figure if that's the amount they would get from robbing a grocery store, though," Eleri pointed out.

"Hold on a sec." Christina put one finger up for a moment, then resumed her work on her keyboard. "This gun traces to this hit and one more in the string. They happened around Los Angeles that entire summer."

"Not just the two associated with this gun?"

"Nope. There were ten robberies total before the killers quit."

"But if this one only matches rifling to two robberies then they didn't always use the same guns. Were the police sure it was the same people?"

"Same group at least. They had to be associated given the MO and timing and witness reports."

Eleri absorbed that, too. "And no one knows where the gunmen went?"

"Nope. In fact, this rifling on this gun only pinged now. This is the first hit … over thirty-five years later," Christina added.

They both paused for a moment, their brains working as puzzle pieces seemed to snap into place.

"Two gunmen at a time?" Eleri asked not liking where this was going. "Male or female?"

"That's just it." Christina looked up and shrugged. "They wore black, and they were bundled up, a little bit bulky. People commented that they knew something was wrong the moment the two walked in. They kept their faces down and away from cameras until they pulled the ski masks on. It was apparently difficult to tell if they were male or female."

The two bodies laid out at the morgue were starting to tell a different tale …

19

"Let Jesse handle it," Christina said for probably the fiftieth time. Eleri agreed, though. Jesse could handle looking into Benjamin Hartman. Jesse could look into the string of grocery store robberies in the late eighties in Los Angeles. Jesse could do standard background checks on Jennifer Barnes, especially now that it was a distinct possibility that she was one of the grocery store robbers.

It was the fourth straight day in their assigned research room at the Duluth BCA. Eleri was tired of these white walls and black desks. At least the internet was solid.

"There were ten robberies," Eleri reiterated, as if the pieces would fit better if she said them out loud. "And there appear to be at least four different killers."

Christina nodded along.

Eleri continued listing what they knew. "The rifling evidence on bullets collected from the scenes reveals at least nine different guns were used in the killings."

Eleri and Christina had done some of the work themselves, despite the "Jesse can handle it" mantra. They wanted to have some pieces in hand so they could match it to what Jesse found later. The intent wasn't to grade her work, just to double check in case Jesse came up with different information than they did. The mismatch would let them know quickly that conflicting information was out there.

Still, she and Christina had stopped early because as Christina kept saying, "Let Jesse handle it." That didn't stop Eleri's brain from churning through what they had though. "So why keep this one gun? Why not keep more of them?"

Christina only shrugged in response. "That's a question to be answered later. Though ..."

But Eleri could see the gears start turning. Her questions were triggering Christina to work through it too. "It's possible they kept more than just this one, but that was the only one to survive the accident."

Eleri hadn't considered that possibility. So much of the car had seemed intact that it was easy to believe they had everything. That wasn't a given.

One of the suitcases had come open from the back seat, and men's clothing had been found all along the rock wall behind the car. It had clung to pointed rocks, stuck in crevasses, and simply laid on small ledges for decades, leaving a trail pointing to where the car rested on the larger ledge below.

There were cuts and the scratches and dents on the car that looked relatively new. Given Superior's fantastic preservation, that told the investigators the damage occurred either right before or *as* the car slid down into the water.

It had been a bumpy ride. They knew this. Had the ledge not existed exactly where it was or had it been any narrower or any host of other factors, it was entirely likely all the evidence would have been lost to the depths and never found.

"These are questions to be answered later. Right now, we need to be looking into our Miranda wolf." Christina pulled them both off the track they had wandered down. She was right. *Jesse could handle it.*

Eleri jumped in. "Victor Leonidas."

They had found his name from their searches just after Donovan had disappeared.

To date, Eleri had no idea why she had trusted him at the time— only that he'd been the one option she had. All they had known was that he worked for Miranda and he was a wolf. Still, he'd seemed unwilling to interfere in their work as long as their investigation didn't interfere with *his work* at Miranda industries.

When Eleri had been panicked, it was because Donovan hadn't even been conscious to help make the decision. But Eleri had handed her wounded and dying partner to this man—if not readily then at least reluctantly.

Now, looking back, she wondered if it was some kind of gut instinct that had told her it would be okay. She wondered if maybe agent had recognized agent—that, no matter how well he covered it, his like kind could spot him. Much the way Donovan had recognized early on that he was a wolf.

"We've spent enough time on this case." Christina declared. "We can't bring back anyone from the robberies. The string stopped at the end of the summer of 1987. There's nothing we can do today that will change by tomorrow."

Eleri couldn't argue. No one was in danger of not only these robbers, and murderers, but even from copycat killers. If there was closure to be had, it was likely most of the families had found it long before now.

Waving her hand at the equipment in the room, Eleri asked, "But where do we look?" She meant physically where should they pull the information.

"Here?" Christina offered.

Eleri shook her head. When they logged into FBI databases, everything was recorded. What searches they entered, what keywords and terms they fed the databases, and which cases they eventually looked into, would all be noted.

Being tracked was never a concern that Eleri had in the past, because who cared? She'd never needed to justify the things she searched or pulled. But this? "If Westerfield sees what we're doing …"

"Let him!" Christina argued, her own hands flying up in the air. "Let him know that we've had enough of waiting and getting nothing! He can help us, or he can get the fuck out of our way. And if he fires us, well then we didn't really have access to the FBI information he promised, did we?"

If their searches made Westerfield fire them, then there was no reason to stay. Finding Donovan was her top priority, even when it didn't look like it. Her whole reason for running this case was to maintain access to FBI information. If they couldn't actually dial it up and use it, then they didn't actually have it. Christina was right.

Putting their effort into this case afforded them nothing in the search for Donovan except lost time.

She looked to her temporary partner. Eleri adored Christina. But she wasn't Donovan. "So we're just going to use the BCA system?"

"And FBI records when we have to," Christina said, her tone firm. She'd already made up her mind and Eleri couldn't argue the logic.

With a deep breath, she put her fingers on the keyboard, and ignored the case she was assigned to, as she typed in the name "Victor Leonidas."

20

"I need to see the doctor." Wade stepped forcefully inside the door.

The young woman in the bright blue scrubs had only reluctantly opened it for him after he'd flashed his badge. Though that had changed her response, he still didn't trust her.

He'd tried to get in as a polite, if early, visitor first. She'd refused, saying the office was not yet open and pointing to the sign indicating he should come back at 8a.m. He absolutely did not want to come back at 8a.m.

For starters, there were enough animals in here—already scenting him and starting to make small noises from the back—that if he came in while pet owners had their animals loose and near him, it could become problematic. He and Donovan, and others like them, tried to only encounter other animals in small numbers. A lone person walking their dog at night worked fine in most cases. Some dogs barked, some came up and fell in love with him immediately, others were just a little standoffish. But a place like this, where the animals were already uncomfortable, didn't play well.

He could tell that many of the animals in here were in pain just from the smells of the place. Many others simply didn't like that they were being treated for a medical condition they didn't fully understand. Others didn't like being boarded and away from home or exposed to so many other animals and unusual smells. So no, Wade did not want to come back at 8a.m.

Also, he already knew the doctor would most likely not want to have this discussion with him when other clients and creatures were here. Wade didn't pull the badge out again—he wasn't here on official FBI business, so what he had done was just a little bit illegal.

The receptionist or tech or whatever she was started to reach for the phone, but then seemed to change her mind. "I'll go get her."

Yes, he thought, she wasn't just going to say *hey, someone's here to see you.* She was giving him the side-eye and she was going to let her boss know that the FBI was at their doorstep.

It took a few moments, as though she were making him wait simply out of spite. He didn't care. When she came back, she only looked at him with a haughty expression and said, "She'll see you now. Through that door."

Pointing to one of four exam room doors, she explained. "Go through the exam room, out the back side and turn left. It's down the hall."

She wasn't going to escort him, but Wade preferred it that way. He could leave her surliness behind at the front desk.

Slipping through the series of doors he noted the odd scent as he got closer. *Wolves had been here. Recently.*

Maybe that shouldn't be a surprise given that he believed this was the doctor Donovan had been taken to. That meant this doctor treated wolves and it might also very well mean that she was a Miranda Industries operative. Wade may have just set foot in the snake pit.

He figured his worst case scenario was that he got captured. Then he might be able to work on the inside to find out what had happened to Donovan. After talking with Christina, he was as convinced as she was that Donovan was alive. If Eleri couldn't sense anything, then someone was actively blocking the signals.

If Donovan had passed away, there would be no need to hide him. In fact—though Wade hated to think it—why wouldn't they have just dumped their friend's body somewhere and left it for them to find? So Donovan must be alive.

The scent grew stronger as he made his way down the hall. By the time Wade had his hand on the doorknob, he understood better what he was walking into. He opened the door and saw her.

Behind the desk, the doctor was already on her feet, one lip curled, long fang revealed.

"Dr. Booker," Wade said, trying to keep his tone convivial.

"Agent," came her reply, reminding Wade that he'd flashed his badge and that maybe the nurse was surly because she realized she hadn't been sharp enough to get his name. In that brief moment, Wade decided not to give it until pressed.

There was a brief pause as both wolves stared, acknowledging that each knew exactly what the other was. It was a surprise Wade had not quite been ready for. Trying to re-start a conversation, he asked, "Veterinary school?"

"It suited," she said, the syllables clipped and curt.

"Makes sense." They always needed someone who could treat their kind. He would have asked if she was familiar with his family name, but since she didn't know it already, he didn't. "I'm following up on a patient of yours."

She nodded and seemed to know where he was going but forced him to say it.

"An FBI agent that was brought to you after hours." He rattled off the date and all the information that he could about Donovan— enough to give her what she needed to answer his questions, but hopefully not enough to ask questions of her own if she hadn't been the doctor who'd treated his friend.

She sighed, her shoulders dropping as she motioned him to sit. Sinking into her own office chair she took a deep breath before saying, "Obviously, I remember him."

There were so many things Wade needed to ask, so many more things he wanted to know. But in the end, he asked the most important question. "Did he survive?"

21

E leri took a bite of her pizza, finally hungry. It felt good to *want* to eat again. It felt good to know that Wade had made it to Florida.

But that was only part of what they needed. They'd had the pizza delivered to their suite, allowing them to talk freely. Barring anyone having slipped in any listening devices, they should be safe here. They'd rented the rooms both above and below theirs and on either side, assuring they had no neighbors who might casually hear something. Then they'd reinforced the hall door as best they could.

It was time to hash this out.

Eleri started in. "Leonidas went straight into the FBI, no other career or degree for something else first."

Christina nodded. "I couldn't find anything about why he was so focused, but I'd be interested in asking his parents and siblings what they remember. Because yes, it looked like he had this goal from relatively early on. I even pulled his high school transcripts."

Eleri raised one eyebrow at that but found herself taking another bite. "Excuse me. You got *high school* transcripts?"

"Yes. It was in his FBI application. His high school had a retired police officer teaching classes. So Victor took political science and even an investigation course."

"Wow. That does put his desire to be in the Bureau way back. It explains though, how he wound up on such a big undercover assignment at such a young age." Eleri felt another puzzle piece click in.

The man had gotten an undergraduate degree with dual majors in political science and law enforcement then applied to the FBI Academy before he even graduated. "He got in on his first try." Eleri added

Eleri could feel the pieces of her brain starting to function and the fog that she had been working under was lifting. Unfortunately, that made the fog she had been in only more obvious.

On a normal day, she would have remembered all of the numbers, but now she looked at her notes. "Leonidas was a four-point-oh student in high school and managed a three-point-eight in college. So not quite the complete overachiever, but close."

Christina followed from there. "He graduated third in his class at Quantico. He got assigned to a tiny branch in Bend Oregon then soon, was promoted to Portland. He made three arrests in three different small cases there. And then *boom*, Westerfield snatches him up for NightShade."

"How long after was that?"

"Three years in the Bureau at that point." *Not long.* He'd been pushing his mid-to-late twenties by that point. Being that young wasn't uncommon for agents who had come straight to the FBI and gone directly into the field—much like Eleri herself.

She was still considered young in many of the Bureau circles. Though, having seen the other agent's birthdate, she found she had just over two years on Leonidas. Eleri had been tracking his time before he joined the Bureau, and Christina had been following after he joined up.

Christina had volunteered to do the research that had her tapping FBI traceable databases so that it would all track back to her agent number, leaving Eleri free of blame. It meant—if Westerfield took issue—Eleri would be free to stay on the case and have access to information.

Picking up the thread more now that Eleri had run out her portion of the timeline, Christina added, "He closed a handful of cases through NightShade, but like most of the rest of us, eventually he ran into Miranda Industries."

Miranda was simply too big, with their fingers in too many pies for a NightShade agent *not* to run into them eventually.

"In fact, check this—" Christina said. "I went at it from a different angle pulling information on Miranda. You would think, given the way Miranda operates that the NightShade division would be the primary investigator."

"We aren't?" Eleri found that odd.

Miranda had wolves running drugs and even some selkie, merwoman who'd been operating for them. When people were strange, they hid in plain sight, or they seemed to go to work for Westerfield or Miranda. At least, that's how it looked right now to Eleri.

"I think we wind up with a lot of the cases in the end," Christina said. "Westerfield keeps finding and handing them off to his own agents."

Eleri winced even as she took another bite. "I'm sure the other SACs love having Westerfield snag their cases from them with no real explanation."

"Given the notes I'm finding, that's exactly how it goes," Christina told her.

Ouch. Eleri didn't think her SAC handled that correctly, but he walked a fine line of getting the right cases into the hands of his agents and their odd and special collection of "talents."

Christina chewed then added, "Leonidas ran a handful of Night-Shade cases. I got the name of his partner: Harrison James."

"Is he still NightShade, or is he undercover too?"

"Better. He's retired," Christina said, and Eleri felt her eyebrows rise at that information.

Retired might be good. Retired meant he didn't have a current SAC that he was beholden to. Westerfield shouldn't be able to tell him what he could and couldn't tell them. Harrison James might just be a font of information.

"So check this, though. Harrison James leaves the FBI entirely after this Miranda case. And, it looks like Leonidas didn't go undercover on purpose."

22

"What do you mean Victor Leonidas didn't go undercover *on purpose?*" Eleri was leaning forward, her elbows on the small coffee table.

"It looks like he and Harrison James ran into Miranda Industries on one of their cases."

"Miranda captured Leonidas?"

"Not quite," Christina told her. "James and Leonidas let their Miranda operative get away that time. But on the next case ..." Christina continued, and Eleri sat listening with rapt attention. "They ran into another operative, only this time it went the other way and the Miranda operatives captured Victor."

"Oh, damn. That's a hostage situation." It was the only thing Eleri could consider off the top of her head.

"It's hard to tell." Christina shrugged. "Eventually, they let him go. But his official report simply read that they didn't want to be responsible for an FBI agent. Also they believed he didn't have anything that would stand up in court. So they felt it wasn't in their interest to hang on to him."

Though Eleri was trying to line up all the pieces, Christina kept going. "When he returned, Leonidas reported that he allowed Miranda to think he had turned."

"Wow," Eleri said. "So the FBI thinks it's got a mole in Miranda and Miranda Industries thinks it's got a mole in the FBI."

Christina nodded along. "The question is, which one of them is right?"

Eleri didn't know.

From the moment two agents had showed up at her family farm to investigate her younger sister's disappearance, Eleri had known she was meant to be in the Bureau. Even when she'd resigned her position with the Behavioral Analysis Unit and checked herself into a mental health clinic, she had spent much of her time wondering what she might do next. Because she still considered herself to be the same woman who'd always carried that badge. Being an FBI agent wasn't something she *did*, it was what she *was*.

But she didn't know Victor Leonidas. While she didn't understand quite how it happened, or what drove them to do it, agents had gone rotten before. They'd taken money and payoffs; they'd been blackmailed and hidden evidence and basically worked for whatever crime syndicate was giving them what they wanted. She had to ask, "Is Leonidas getting payoffs or anything like that?"

"Initially, it appeared his reward was just getting out with his life intact."

Eleri tipped her head, *it was a fair bargain.*

"But later, we start seeing income into his accounts."

"Where did you get all of this?" Eleri asked

"Oh, you're not going to like it." Christina offered a wry grin and Eleri had to laugh.

She was imagining all kinds of things, but not Christina's next words.

"I called Westerfield, and I pushed him to give me the information."

"Holy shit, Christina!" Had she not been sitting on the floor, almost stuck under the edge of the coffee table, Eleri would have hopped up. "He's going to kill you when he remembers."

"I don't think he will." Christina looked to the side in a thoughtful manner.

"This is Westerfield we are talking about. So you pushed him? And then what? You pushed him to forget that you pushed him? And then you pushed him to forget that you made him forget that you pushed him?" Eleri was getting more confused as she spoke.

If there was one thing about SAC Westerfield it was that he seemed to understand everything.

"I pushed him slightly before," Christina said. "Remember? We've run tests on him."

"You're right that he doesn't seem to remember that one," Eleri paused for a moment. But did he not remember it or was he playing them? "Do you trust that?"

"Not entirely." Christina answered quickly, letting Eleri know she had the same concerns.

But what Eleri thought and what Eleri would have chosen didn't really matter. Christina had already done the deed. Now she could only hope that Westerfield didn't notice he'd been manipulated.

For a few moments, the two women were quiet as they ate the last few bites of pizza. Christina didn't even ask, just stood up and motioned for Eleri's permission. Closing the box, she headed toward the small kitchenette aiming for the refrigerator. But, once she opened the door and looked inside and at the large pizza box in her hand, she changed her mind and dumped it in the trash.

Though she was simply waiting for her partner to return to the conversation, she still wasn't quite ready when Christina sat down on the other side of the table. "I think you're right that Westerfield may catch on to me. And that's why I'd like your help."

"My help?" Eleri couldn't push anyone. But even as the thought wormed its way through her head, she realized maybe she could. She'd learned a lot in the past few years. Though she'd used none of it in the last month, it was past time to start trying. She needed to not simply give up and get angry at an unmoving pendulum or the map.

So she asked, "What is it you think I can do?"

Christina grinned. "I have a few ideas."

23

Mila woke in a cold sweat, her breath soughing, her head pounding. Cold shivers ran her spine and she regretted leaving home.

She'd thought she could figure this out. That coming here would let her grasp at the memories that hovered just beneath the surface. That she could click some pieces into place and have a full picture. *Instead, the nightmares had gotten more intense.*

Another dream had robbed her not only of rest but of the ability to sleep.

Her eyes had flown open wide and the terror had translated to reality for a moment—the room unfamiliar, the bed hard, the space confining. But this was the hotel she'd rented by the day while she was here.

All this traveling around, all the searching that she had done, and she'd only managed to get the feeling that she was in a *known* place, if not the *right* one.

In her dreams, she ran through the woods—woods she now knew by heart, woods she would recognize if she could ever find them. *But did she want to?*

She wasn't sure anymore.

Each time, she was chased, the same man at her side, his hand gripped tightly in her own. She knew his face now, though she didn't believe she'd ever seen him in her life. If only she could get her dream self to look in a mirror, because she was pretty certain the woman in the dream wasn't Mila Panas.

She remembered her own whole life—and none of these things had happened to *her*. She'd also cataloged a handful of discrepancies in the dreams, not just the cherry red Ford Falcon, but the clothing, the stores, the signs in the windows ... they were all *off*.

The Falcon she had initially brushed away. It had been her dream car for so long. But, like Brian Abadi, she'd wanted seatbelts and a few modernizations she couldn't afford. Because Mila Panas wanted one, it made sense that her own desires would manifest in her dreams. That was precisely what she'd always been taught dreams were made of.

But in the rest of her now-rich dream world, there was nothing she could find that linked this information to her own desires or fears. She'd borrowed dream journals and interpretation guides from the library and looked everything up.

She now knew that if she dreamed of oceans, she likely had a decision to make. If she dreamed of a house, she was dreaming of her own inner self and thought process. An orderly house meant orderly life, and so on. She'd also learned that if she dreamed her teeth fell out, she likely had money troubles.

Great, she could look forward to dreaming that her teeth fell out because she was living on savings that she'd intended for other things. The money was supposed to be for home improvements, or just as a backup plan. At no point had she ever envisioned spending it to chase down someone she remembered but had never met.

Where was Ben?

Surely if she could find him she could put all of this away and return to her normal life.

Though it was only three in the morning, and the hotel room was paid through until eleven, she realized she wasn't going to get back to sleep.

Each morning, she went to the front desk where they made her check out and check back in. It was a system she wasn't overly fond of given that she wasn't sleeping well in the first place. But she was now petrified of going back to sleep.

This dream had taken her and the young, tall, thin black man—the one that she now knew she loved—running through a different set of woods. Once again, they'd been chased and he carried a heavy black, ripstop nylon bag in his other hand.

Mila had to find that bag.

Standing up on shaky legs, she let her muscles adjust. She couldn't blame her body, it hadn't been well fed or rested for several weeks now. She flipped on the light and looked around.

Maybe she was really an adult now. Her home was better than the hotel rooms. She had all the channels she wanted. She had an insanely comfortable mattress on her bed. But the room itself wasn't why she couldn't stay.

The only thing she'd brought with her was a packed suitcase and her car, which she adored even if it wasn't a '63 Falcon. She plucked her bag of chips that she'd left on the dresser and pulled it open. Grabbing a way-too-expensive bottle of water from the mini fridge, she ate an inappropriate breakfast.

Between bites of chips and swigs from the water, she grabbed a towel in the bathroom and wiped the sweat of her dream away. Then she got dressed, piece by piece, putting clothing on or tucking it back into the suitcase.

Faster than she'd expected—3:28 according to the red lights on the hotel clock—she was ready to go. She didn't even need to bother checking out this time, just left the plastic key on the dresser and she carried her suitcase down the back staircase.

Outside the door, the darkness of the night didn't hit her with the chill she was used to. Instead, it was balmy and warm. She hadn't expected to hear crickets just outside of Los Angeles, but they sang a background song that again sounded of deja vu. Even the birds didn't quite sleep.

Looking up into the trees, Mila saw what she was hoping for: a flash of blue. She smiled. A pair of blue macaws must have escaped from someone's home—they now seemed to be nesting nearby. Each day of her stay, she'd caught sight of them several times, swooping by in a bright flash of color. They were unique and odd and nothing like her dream.

Right now, she needed the bizarre sight of a blue Macaw outside of a cheap hotel in Southern California to help keep her anchored.

Throwing the suitcase in the trunk, she remembered her mother long ago having told her not to ever let someone look in the back window and see she was traveling. She slammed it shut and climbed in, not quite knowing what she was doing. But she put the car in gear and tapped an address into her GPS.

It was going to be a long drive to Minnesota.

24

Eleri ran through the woods. Her white night gown billowed behind her, her bare feet pressed into the earth, making soft crunching noises on the cover of colored leaves that littered the path.

The leaves were wrong, but they were right.

It wasn't fall. She shouldn't be seeing reds and oranges and yellows, but they were here. But she knew she only had to go a little further to make it to the tiny house with the corner porch.

She ran farther and faster. Though she made progress, the trees all looked the same. It would have frightened her had she not come here many times before. She knew these paths, and she knew—or she hoped she knew—what lay ahead.

This was Grandmére's house. This was not the shotgun home her great-grandmother had owned in real life in the Lower Ninth Ward of New Orleans. This was where Eleri saw Emmaline, her younger sister, for years after she had disappeared. This was where Eleri visited Grandmére after she'd died. This was where Grandmére told her what she needed to do.

But the last time Eleri had come bursting through the door, she had passed Alesse Dauphine in the kitchen.

The thought now chilled her heart and slowed her feet on the path. It had not been Grandmére in the rocking chair last time. Instead, it had been an unknown older woman. The more Eleri thought about it, the more she was convinced that she had come face to face with the goddess Aida Weddo.

Who would be waiting for Eleri this time?

Would Grandmére be back in her house where she belonged?

Eleri was no longer running. Instead, she cautiously picked her way along the path. Branches reached out in front of her, and Eleri grabbed at one to pull it aside so she could pass without getting scratched.

She didn't remember the branches—or anything that hindered her path to the house—from before. The ground itself should have sticks and small rocks, roots that would trip her as she ran, but it never did. It always seemed as though the woods *wanted* her to get to the house. So the branches seemed a bit unusual, if not foreboding.

Eleri ducked low under one yet still felt it tug at her hair. Had it moved?

Only a little further.

Noticing as she always did that though she was once again in the white nightgown and barefoot in the woods, she wasn't cold. Still, so many little things seemed *off*.

She caught a glimpse of white railing through the trees and picked up her pace. Reaching out, she pulled back supple branches and twisted past or ducked under them. She moved faster than she planned.

Quickly, she emerged into the tiny clearing. Eleri always came to this side of the house. The door sat at a 45-degree angle, the two sides of the porch making a perfect triangle—just enough space for a person to stand and be greeted.

The white railing called to her, pristine and bright, somehow always shiny and new though she'd been visiting for decades. Moving cautiously, she stepped across the small lawn, the green grass new. It was all at a uniform height, as if someone continually mowed it, or more likely it simply knew not to get any taller.

As she stepped forward, her hand wrapped around the wooden railing, her foot moved up the one step, bare foot resting on boards. No matter how old Eleri got, the house never aged. The porch was tiny, and she cleared it in a single step, reaching for the doorknob. She twisted it but it resisted. *Locked.*

In a burst of frustrated panic, she twisted it again, harder, only to have the knob give way beneath her terror that she'd been shut out. It had been a stupid move. If the door was locked, it was locked. But the second time it opened easily, almost as though the house were playing with her.

She didn't like it. The house wasn't supposed to play. It was supposed to tell her what she needed to know. Show her what she needed to see.

Stepping into an empty living room, she remembered that the last time she'd been here had been too long ago. Then, the place had been full of small children. This time, the house had an eerie feel, making her think this wasn't the only empty room.

Eleri leaned forward, tipping her head and looking down the short hallway to her left before continuing straight ahead. The living room sat still and calm, something about it said that it had been unused for quite some time. She stepped through the archway into the dining area and turned to her left, heading through the opening leading into the square kitchen.

She sucked in a breath, not having realized she was holding it. This time, none of the Dauphine sisters stood in the space. Finally, calming herself down, Eleri stopped and tried to feel the house, to actually *listen*.

She didn't sense them here. Hopefully, that was a good sign. Though she had no doubt they would be back.

It bothered her to no end that they had found this place. She could only hope that they hadn't truly found it, but that the house had manifested the image to warn her.

Still, she padded softly through the kitchen and around through the back room. For the first time, she heard noises and signs of life. The repetitive squeak sent a rush of relief that exactly what she hoped was happening: the rocking chair was occupied.

Sometimes, she came down the hallway so that when she opened the door, she faced whoever was in the chair. This time she was coming up behind the chair.

The tall person occupying it wasn't Grandmére. Something about the weight of the creak and the speed at which it slowly rocked told that this wasn't the old woman either.

It was a man in the chair. He had dark hair longer than she expected. His shoulders were thinner. He rested in the space, not acknowledging her.

With a burst of adrenaline and a rapid flutter of her heart, Eleri ran around to the front of the chair.

"Donovan!" she yelled.

But he didn't open his eyes and as she looked frantically around the room, a dark shadow hovered beyond the window and drenched the small house in darkness.

25

"Donovan is alive!" Eleri breathed the words as she opened her bedroom door and found Christina already awake.

Her new partner was already dressed and standing at the kitchenette counter in the main room of the suite. Christina had been stirring a mug of coffee, but at Eleri's words, the spoon stopped clinking and stood still.

Christina slowly turned her head. "What makes you say that?"

"I saw him!" It was difficult to get the words out. Her heart was still racing. She felt as though she'd clawed her way out of sleep, but she was excited nonetheless.

"The spells worked?" Christina asked, beginning to move again, her hand reaching for the coffee and lifting the mug.

Eleri had known her friend was a coffee drinker but right now the room smelled wonderful. The scent was the first thing that let her know she was actually here, back on Earth. She breathed deeply, but Christina was waiting for an answer. "I don't know."

A frown replaced the questioning expression.

The night before, Christina had said she'd thought of several things that might help Eleri get her spells working again. So Eleri had listened intently and let her friend talk her through a few attempts. All of which had failed—remarkably so. Maybe, in part, because Christina was watching over her shoulder the whole time. Still, Eleri had been willing to try anything at this point.

Christina had been smart enough though to think beyond Eleri's original spells. They'd gone back and started with the basics, making sure that the problems were *these spells* and not the work in general.

Though Eleri had struggled with lighting a flame and basic scrying, they'd managed to make them work. Eleri had breathed a deep sigh of relief at seeing and feeling her skills start to come back.

But with the pendulum at the ready, they'd not asked to find Donovan. Instead, Christina suggested they look for their SAC.

"Where is Westerfield?" Eleri had spoken out loud and not just a little self-consciously. It was much easier to speak to inanimate objects alone. But her embarrassment evaporated as the pendulum began to swing. It had gone right to his office in Atlanta.

"Interesting." Christina had leaned over the map they'd spread onto the table and tried giving the command herself. "Find Wade."

Again, the pendulum sprung to life, slowly moving back and forth, until it pinpointed a spot in Central Florida.

"I mean, it could be because you know where Westerfield and Wade are already," said Christina.

"That's valid." So Eleri had looked her friend in the eyes, her fingers still laced through the thin, elegant chain that held the pointed rock. "So ask me something I don't know."

Christina watched Eleri's face. "Where's my brother?"

Eleri hadn't known Christina had a brother, but the pendulum had once again begun to move back and forth. It traversed Missouri, then headed to Nebraska, where it came to a rest in the upper corner.

"Is that where he is?" Eleri asked when it stopped.

Christina nodded.

"Are you sure?" People did move around, and the snark in her voice had only somewhat been intentional. "What if he's traveling?"

"What if he's dead and buried?" Christina replied too quickly. "And right where it's pointed."

Eleri felt her heart stop. *What a shitty thing she'd said.* She hadn't been thinking and she hadn't been open to sensing anything either.

"Well, your pendulum proved it works. So the fact that you get no answer for Donovan probably means something is in the way." Christina didn't seem to hold a grudge, and Eleri had learned something new.

"How do we get around it?" Eleri headed back to the subject she was more comfortable with.

Christina laughed, not bitter or cold but true mirthful laughter. "I don't know! You're the witch."

It was a term Eleri still had yet to get used to, but she hadn't thought of anything. So before she'd gone to sleep, she'd thumbed her way through her Book of Shadows hoping to find a spell to break a spell. Though she'd found several, two of the three required multiple witches to be on hand. She did not think Christina qualified as two or more practiced witches. And the last she didn't have the materials for. She would have to get them.

Now Christina stared at her, coffee mug in hand, demanding that Eleri's wandering attention come back to the present. "What happened? What did you do?"

"I dreamed last night, dreamed of Donovan."

"And that's enough for you to know he's alive?"

It was a good question, and it made Eleri pause a moment—not because she doubted the question, but because she wasn't sure how to tell Christina that she knew.

She'd dreamed of this house since she was a child—always something awaited her there. Something that was always proven to be true, even if that something had taken twenty years.

Aiming for the middle ground, Eleri said, "It's a dream I've had many times and a dream that often tells me things, true things. This time, Donovan was waiting for me."

"That's good to hear." Christina's shoulders visibly relaxed, for the first time truly letting Eleri know that Christina didn't miss Donovan less, she just held herself together better. Now, with obvious relief, Christina took a sip of coffee and pulled back quickly because apparently it was still just a little too hot.

"It is good news," Eleri told her. "Because Donovan is alive, but I don't think he's safe."

26

Eleri got dressed, ate breakfast, and then sat down in the main room of the suite, looking at Christina and feeling at loose ends.

She didn't know what to do. Donovan was alive! She was finally confident of that. But she was just as confident that he wasn't okay. But where and how should she even start looking?

Should they go to the BCA and work on the case? Just thinking about that twisted her into knots. It was the right direction for work, but the wrong direction for everything else.

They had information on Victor Leonidas now. Were they ready to press Westerfield to give them what they needed on Donovan? She was opening her mouth to ask Christina exactly that when her phone rang.

Motioning to her new partner, she grinned and held up the phone. "Hey, Jesse!"

Not very professional of her, but she didn't feel she had a professional relationship with the investigative journalist ... or about anyone right now.

Jesse didn't know that Donovan was missing or that Eleri felt like her world had been unraveled. So she dove in. "Have I got information for you!"

"Wonderful," Eleri said. Though it was, in fact, great, it wasn't what she truly needed. Still, she liked Jesse, and she had to do this.

Jesse wasted no time diving in. "The 1987 string of grocery store robberies. Let's start there."

Eleri could practically hear that Jesse was sitting in front of organized information. Her next words confirmed it. "I'm sending you what I have. But let me break it down. The investigators never closed the case, but ultimately believed there were four separate perpetrators—*murderers actually*—who mixed and matched which pair went to which store at which time."

Interesting, Eleri thought. *Smart, too.* It meant they had planned the whole string, or at least to have a string of robberies, up front.

"They successfully robbed nine stores, but did not successfully rob the tenth, because the stores were catching on and were too prepared. But they did flee."

"No one has ever identified them, right?" Christina had been listening intently.

"There were suspects, but no, no actual IDs. What we have is random footage from the stores that gives us enough to know there were four of them. They knew what they were doing and kept their faces away from video cameras. They managed to stay relatively unknown. Except for one thing." They could hear the smile in Jesse's voice. "I'm sending you the video on this."

Eleri was excited and it was difficult to wait. She was glad she was interested in the case. She still needed to work it. If they were going to press Westerfield, they would have to prove they were making forward progress on the thing he'd tasked them with. Westerfield would absolutely be tit for tat on this.

It took a few moments in which Christina tapped away on her tablet and pulled up the video. "Ready."

As they watched the short clip, they saw a handful of people coming from the parking lot toward the store front. Two red circles delineated who to follow. Eleri needed that. She understood they approached as regular shoppers, not letting anyone get a good look at them until they were inside and just away from cameras, then they pulled their hats down—showing for the first time that they were actually ski masks—and pulled out guns. As the two got closer, one of them looked up at the camera, but about half the other people in the video got their faces captured, too. Without the red circles, Eleri would have known nothing.

"The store installed this just three days before they were hit. This seems to be the perpetrators only mistake. Still, the investigators weren't able to identify the face. Even running it through more modern facial rec systems."

That made sense, it was a grainy shot. But Eleri looked at Christina and saw her new partner shake her head ever so slightly. Eleri agreed. *This was not the face of either of the two bodies that lay on the table.*

It didn't mean they weren't involved. But it did mean that Eleri and Christina couldn't confirm that they were.

"Also," Jesse added excitedly, "we have fingerprints from one of the locations. I've sent those over to you in the first batch of information as well."

"Wonderful," Eleri said. She could match them to the bodies. Though these faces didn't match, maybe the fingerprints would. "Is this evidence from the same store hit?"

"No. The camera was from the eighth store that they hit. The fingerprints are from the third store hit. As of yet, we don't know if they know that they left the prints behind."

Eleri loved that Jesse kept saying "as of yet," as though she was going to crack a case of grocery store robberies that was over thirty years old. If anyone could, it was Jesse.

"Anything else on the robberies?" Christina asked.

"A few little threads here and there that don't yet mean anything," Jesse told them. "So I'm not sending that stuff yet. There's plenty that I've managed to confirm to keep you busy, and I'll keep digging as long as you want me to."

Christina leaned forward talking directly to the phone. "Yes, we want you to keep digging."

"On it!" Jesse replied. "Now onto Benjamin Allen Hartman. I'm sending a file on him, too."

Jesse was smart, sending the information in separate emails, batch labeled, making it easy for them to find what belonged to one portion of the case and what belonged to the other. Christina once again tapped away loading what Jesse had sent, while Eleri held on to the phone.

She didn't need to, but it seemed to be her job. She leaned over watching as Christina pulled up reports then a photo.

Her eyes flew wide, and her mouth opened as the picture popped up. "That's him."

"Who?" Jesse asked from the other end of the line.

Eleri had just given away information that maybe she shouldn't have. Too late now. "That's our John Doe."

"So the man in the car was the owner of the car?"

"That's what we suspected but this is our first confirmation." Even if it wasn't a legal ID via dental work, fingerprints, or DNA, the picture was pretty solid.

"Well," Jesse said, as if she could hear Eleri's thoughts, "in the batch of information that I sent you on him are the fingerprints that they took when they arrested him on cocaine possession."

Even better. That *would* provide a legal identification. Pictures were good, but dead bodies didn't photograph like live ones. And it had been thirty-plus years. It was entirely possible, maybe even probable, that the John Doe looked like Benjamin Hartman's picture, because he looked like Benjamin Hartman. People borrowed their siblings' cars all the time. Though, as Mrs. Ella Hartman had told them, Tyrone was alive and well, and much older.

"Perfect, we'll finally be able to make a legal ID." Christina filled in where Eleri hadn't.

Jesse's tone changed then. "That cocaine charge? It was bullshit."

Eleri and Christina's eyes met. They'd only told Jesse that he'd been arrested on charges and not passed on Mrs. Hartman's information. Eleri had to ask, "What makes you say that?"

"Even in the report ..." There was a pause from Jesse and maybe a throat clearing, "I get that it's been a long time since he was arrested. But I just didn't think we were still that openly racist in 1984."

She huffed out a breath and Eleri and Christina both held back, letting the reporter continue. "The report clearly states that they found four people in possession of the cocaine. It also says they only arrested Benjamin Hartman. The report actually states that the three they let go with verbal warnings were white."

"Wow." Once again, Eleri wasn't able to think before speaking and she let it all roll out. "It *says, We arrested the black man and let the white ones go?*"

"No, but there's a description of each of the men they arrested, as they checked driver's licenses and such. Then, in the report, they make it clear that they decided—*through no evidence in any of what's written!*—that Benjamin Hartman was the sole possessor of the drugs."

Well, Eleri thought, *Score one for Ella Hartman.* She'd been right.

Jesse was still going. "It appears after that his employment record is spotty, which is fully understandable! A cocaine possession isn't quite a light thing."

"Did he serve time?" Christina asked. They'd not looked any further into this, letting Jesse handle the work.

"Doesn't look like it. The judge seemed to recognize what it was and let him off with probation."

But it didn't erase the charge, Eleri thought. *And it could never erase all the damage.*

"And there's one more thing. Well, there's a ton of more little things, but there's one more big thing," Jesse said.

"What is that?"

"I found a marriage license. In June of 1987, Benjamin Hartman married one Jennifer Barnes."

Christina and Eleri looked at each other again.

Suspicions confirmed, Eleri thought again. The two had been wearing what looked to be a matching set of wedding bands. "That's really great information. All of that's in the file?"

But even as the words left her lips, she knew it was all there and more.

They thanked Jesse for her work and clarified what to do next before hanging up.

"I think we have to go in and do fingerprints," Christina said.

Eleri still wanted to leave, to rush to Donovan's side. But she couldn't say those words out loud and she couldn't do it. She had no idea where to go or what to do to find him.

"I know," Christina replied to what she hadn't said. "But I think going into the office is the best thing. We need to figure out how to use the information we found on Leonidas yesterday. What's our best move to pressure Westerfield? I'm concerned if we go at it too quickly, we might play our hand wrong."

Eleri nodded. It was a good point. Westerfield might very well have seen that Christina was checking his agent's files already.

So, they gathered their things and as they were getting ready to leave the suite, Eleri's phone rang again.

She looked down at the screen.

"Wade!"

27

"Wade!" Eleri called his name out as she fumbled answering her phone.

Christina had her hand on the doorknob but stopped at Eleri's exclamation. Quickly, they both turned and headed back toward the center of the room.

"Hey, Eleri, is Christina there?" he asked.

"Yes, hold on!" It took a moment to get her bag off her shoulder, sit down and actually hold the phone where she could put it on speaker. Once she had it and Christina had said hello, her need for information about Donovan took over. "What did you learn? Anything good?"

There was a pause, letting Eleri know it wasn't nothing.

"There's good news and bad news." Another pause. "And weird news."

"Give it to us in any order." She was hungry for information. The shadow outside the window at Grandmére's had her more than concerned. But she had no idea what it might mean.

Was Donovan dying? Was someone stalking them? With everything blocking her from getting more information, all she had were these small, unclear clues.

"I found the veterinarian that Miranda wolf took him to."

Eleri realized then that they hadn't yet told Wade what they learned about Victor Leonidas. But first, she wanted to hear about Donovan. "The vet fixed him up?"

"Yes." *Best news ever.* Even if it didn't really mean Donovan was still alive all this time later. Still, Eleri felt a layer of stress peel away and Wade's next words came through clear. "Donovan stayed with her for a week, then he was moved by people from Miranda Industries."

"That makes sense," Eleri said, her hope blooming. "It means he survived the first week."

"Yes," Wade agreed, "And the vet said she thought he was on the way to recovery, though it was a very concerning wound."

Eleri knew that. His pulse had been weak and thready by the time she'd given up handling anything herself and handed her best friend to a stranger, hoping only to save his life. She had to remember that even if she never saw him again, if Donovan was alive, that was what she had chosen. And what she would choose again, if the alternative was to have him die in her arms.

"I would have been more surprised had it not been very serious." It was the only part of her thoughts she could say out loud. Though she knew she should take a breath, she couldn't. "What else did she say?"

"Over the course of the week, she did three separate surgeries. First, simply stopping the bleeding and keeping him alive. Then repairing internal organs."

"Obviously, she's worked on Donovan's kind." Eleri heard the words before she could stop herself. Christina and Eleri both almost flinched. Donovan's *kind* was Wade's *kind*.

Luckily, Wade didn't seem to take any offense. "Yes, that's the weird part. She and her partner are both wolves themselves."

"Running a veterinary clinic in Central Florida?" Eleri asked, a little stunned. The wolves she'd met were in the FBI, or at the de Gottardi/Little compound in the middle of nowhere in the Ozarks. Working for Miranda industries, or—she had to admit—stalking her in Florida.

Wolves liked places with open, undeveloped land where they could run. Eleri would not have thought that that would be Florida. Not until her last case, at least. But she and Donovan and Christina had found more than one cabin far enough back in the woods to hide a wolf or a family of wolves. Enough room to give them space to run miles and miles when no one was looking. She had to concede that it was a better option than she would have guessed.

"That was the good news?" Christina pushed.

"Part of it. The bad news is the vet, Dr. Andrea Booker, has no idea where they went after the Miranda Industries people took Donovan away."

"She didn't ask?" Eleri hated the panic in her tone but neither Christina nor Wade seemed to fault her for it.

"She says she can't ask, and it sounds like she doesn't want to know."

"So this is the bad news? What's the weird news?" Christina asked.

"That the vet was herself a wolf. I was not expecting that." Wade huffed out a breath on the other end of the line.

Eleri had been shocked by it too, but now that she thought about it, it made sense. Miranda Industries was in the drug trade, among other things. Surely there were people getting shot and injured all the time. A wolf, who was also a veterinarian, was the perfect physician for all the creatures Miranda seemed to interact with and employ.

"So, is there other good news? Bad news?" Eleri pushed.

"I guess the mixed news is that Dr. Booker, and her partner, Dr. Spivy don't want to work for Miranda Industries. They didn't go into veterinary care to join the mob. They simply wanted to be able to provide medical care for the wolves that lived in Central Florida. So they built their practice with a whole back room and the capacity to care for someone like Donovan."

It was the perfect setup for a veterinary office. All of the extra material could be passed off as part of an office caring for large, wild animals. Hell, the bank had probably given them loans to cover the extra machinery and supplies. But Wade was still going.

"The bad news is they're both too petrified of Miranda to help me try to find Donovan."

"You offered that the FBI would help get them out, right?" Christina asked.

Eleri had wondered the same thing. *Would* Westerfield offer to get the vets out, though? Or would he use them as pawns? As undercover informants of his own, adding to what Leonidas might bring back? She didn't know.

At one point in her career, she had trusted Westerfield, following blindly where he sent her, believing she was doing the right work. But lately, his instructions had become more and more concerning.

Now he'd left Donovan behind with no word to her that anything was being done to find him ...

"They don't want to touch the arrangement they have." Wade sounded resigned. "They don't like Miranda, but their offices are *very* well funded now."

That would make it harder, she thought. But Eleri switched topics. "Do you think it's possible that Westerfield is embedding Donovan as a second undercover agent?"

No sound came from the end of the line. Christina turned and looked at Eleri, her expression clear that she'd not considered that before. Now all three of them were worried about it.

28

"The fingerprints match," Eleri announced for the umpteenth time as she swiveled on her stool to face Christina.

It had been a long morning. Between the phone calls and interruptions, they'd been late getting here. She didn't care one bit. Then they'd worked on what they needed to for the case, each agreeing that they were just keeping busy until they figured out how to pressure Westerfield into giving them information on Donovan.

Eleri had been slow this morning and even now she still wasn't quite ready to present anything solid to Christina about how to approach their boss. She wondered if Christina had had any brilliant ideas of her own. Their intent had been to think about it separately so that they didn't sway each other in hopes that they could come up with the best possible answer.

Now she sat here with no ideas. Eleri was ready to call Westerfield and make demands now. She wanted to leave and get in the car, get on a plane, fly to wherever Donovan was, and bring him home. But she had no idea where that was. She had no idea if he was in any shape to travel.

The shadow outside of Grandmére's window still concerned her. She didn't know how to explain it to Christina, but it had left her with a sinking feeling she couldn't shake.

"Which fingerprints?" Christina asked, bringing Eleri's thoughts whiplashing harshly back to reality.

"Benjamin Hartman. The body on the table is Benjamin Allen Hartman."

"That's good to finally know for sure." Christina seemed thoughtful about the idea but didn't add anything.

Eleri nodded along as if she could do anything more than sit here and be near to useless. "I'll look at the prints from the robbery next."

It was faster to match the fingerprints herself than to put it into queue and wait for a tech to be available.

Turning back to the computer, she pulled up the prints. But something from the back of her thoughts nudged at her until she turned around and looked at Christina. In the past she would have called it a hunch. "When did Miranda Industries begin?"

"I don't understand." Christina looked at her oddly and Eleri tried again to explain.

"It's a huge global conglomerate. But even places like Exxon and Nabisco started somewhere, on some date."

Christina seemed to catch on but added, "Sometimes they began as railroad companies that then got into oil or whatever, so we might not know when this version started."

"But they all have a starting point. What is Miranda Industries' starting point?" Eleri pushed.

"That's a great question."

Eleri had no idea if anything would pan out from it, and she had no reason to believe this case was related to Miranda in any way, but it sure stank of the kind of work she'd seen from them lately, just smaller potatoes. Honestly, it could have been some Minnesota mob family that was all long since dead, or now legally into dry cleaning.

But Eleri needed more about Miranda to help find Donovan. If she could find holding places around the country, maybe she could find where she should start looking.

Christina had been going through data for the case. But even as Eleri felt the new idea take hold, her partner simply shoved her work aside and began searching.

Turning back to her own work, Eleri began the diligent tedium of marking up the lines on her screen. She expected nothing from this. The fact was this was a cold case. AFIS first began coming into use in the eighties. But it wasn't a database, like people thought. It was just the program that matched fingerprints put into other databases *by* humans. There were local and state databases and though all should have been uploaded to a national system by now, the reality was that prints were still scattered and hiding in all kinds of local troves that no one had checked yet.

Every old print was still dependent on people having the time to upload archived records into national databases. If the person whose fingerprints were on file for the grocery store robbery had done something else, then when they had been entered into any kind of national database, they should have pinged. That would have matched the grocery store robbery offender to something else, or someone else.

Eleri knew all of this to be true. But it depended on people on both ends uploading the information and having correct information to link back to. Still, she had to assume for a case as high profile as this, it would have had some priority and been uploaded. But nothing had pinged before the case fell into her hands. So, she worked methodically, but didn't expect anything to pan out.

Her brain wandered away from the work, still worrying about where Donovan might be and what the shadow outside of Grand-mére's window might represent. She was growing confident that it was less metaphorical and more literal.

Her difficulties at staying focused were compounded by thoughts of what Wade had said about Donovan surviving his surgeries. And that Miranda Industries had come and taken him away. Interestingly enough, Eleri had thought she handed him *to Miranda Industries* the first day, but apparently the wolf had taken her partner to a veterinarian he knew, and Donovan had only truly been in Miranda's hands a week later.

At least he'd still been alive.

Wade had explained the veterinarians felt stuck. They were definitely afraid of Miranda and the Miranda workers. But they also enjoyed the perks of having a clinic that was able to do all kinds of charitable work as long as they handled the Miranda operatives that came in needing their care. Eleri wondered how often that was.

"You're not going to believe this," Christina interrupted her morbid thoughts, and Eleri spun around again, glad to be distracted from the monotony of the fingerprints before she went cross-eyed.

"Miranda Industries began in the fall of 1986."

Eleri couldn't help it. "You have got to be shitting me. Is it coincidence?"

"*Could it be?*" Christina replied, but her expression made it absolutely clear she didn't believe in coincidences. At least not this kind.

"Did it start as a shell corporation?"

"Maybe?" The question in Christina's voice led to the next explanation. "It was founded as a vending machine service company. They shipped and stocked buildings and campuses with vending machines that they provided all the maintenance and supplies for. The business got a small cut of the income."

Eleri frowned. She remembered a long time ago in coursework at Quantico that certain businesses made good drug running fronts. Vending Machine companies were on that list. Also, Eleri knew, sorting that out was made more difficult by the fact that legitimate vending machine companies could also make money hand over fist. "So, they just got bigger and bigger, then branched out into drugs?"

"Looks like they were doing something really wrong. Almost no income for the first year." Christina was scanning something on her screen that Eleri couldn't see. Then she looked up at Eleri. "What made you think of this?"

"Wondering why this was a NightShade case. Just a hunch."

Christina offered a knowing grin before going back to reading from her screen. "So they struggled the whole first year then, all of a sudden, no more struggles. Guess what they got?"

Christina was looking up at her again, this time with a sparkle in her eye.

"A sudden infusion of cash?" Eleri guessed. It couldn't be coincidence. But the pieces were lining right up.

In her head, it worked. Jennifer and Benjamin had to have been two of the robbers on the grocery store heist. Miranda had taken the money and the two of them had gone into the lake—cleaning up all of the evidence, at least until the gun had been found with the car.

Christina was nodding along. The sudden infusion of cash was correct.

"Wealthy parents who just 'helped them out'?"

Christina shook her head no this time.

"Bank loan? Venture capital?"

Two more nos. "Then I have to go with random acquisition of just over two million in cash?"

Christina smiled and nodded. "Yes, exactly that."

29

Brian followed the woman through the woods, her blond ponytail bobbing like a beacon.

Her name was Mila, she'd said, but he knew nothing else about her.

At least that's what he told himself. He knew much more than he was willing to admit.

She knew something about his car. From the first time he'd seen a cherry red Ford Falcon, the car had become an obsession, and when she'd talked to him the first day, Mila had sounded the same. Though that was before she'd acted completely batshit crazy.

Her story had sounded so familiar to his. He'd seen one as a kid and instantly known it *needed* to be his car. He didn't have a pension for antiques, just for Ford Falcons. For whatever reason, it seemed this stranger, Mila, felt and lived all of that with him.

That's the story he went with.

But the day he'd met her, the dreams had started. Not the kind with random images or things that morphed, but realistic stories that he *lived*. More than once he'd gotten up and done a search. Yes, Pepsi did have that logo and it looked almost identical to Coke's current cursive. He'd googled until he found out about parachute pants and paper jackets ... and then he stopped.

He didn't want to know more. But the dreams kept coming, and though Mila wasn't in them, she was the cause. So he followed her now. She was driven by some inner need that he told himself he didn't have.

Despite the fact that he needed sleep, he was out here in the woods, in his nice shoes and the suit that he'd worked so hard to get. He'd put so much effort into being the right kind of moneyed. His coworkers who went for sushi with him during the day wouldn't understand his ease in the trees. But they also wouldn't understand that, in the evenings, he still ate Spaghettios from a can. He peeled the wrappers from the slices of his cheese and made white bread sandwiches with Miracle Whip.

Though he'd worked very, very hard to take the boy out of Canton, Ohio, he hadn't been able to take the little rundown neighborhood and the money that never seemed to quite go far enough out of himself.

Taking a few more steps Brian felt his sneakers gripping the leaves and rocks and roots on the path as he picked his way through the woods, trying to keep his distance behind Mila. She didn't need to know that he was here.

Sneakers? He'd been wearing his nice shoes and his suit, but *no.* Looking down again, he now saw a tracksuit. *It was fleece?* None of this made sense.

He wanted these dreams to stop.

The last thing he needed was more interaction with Mila. Because, when she spoke, she spoke to something deep inside him. Something that reached even further back than the memories of nights the heat had gotten turned off and his mother had huddled the boys together in a pillow fort in the living room. His mother had sold them on the idea that it was fun.

The feelings about Mila had the same kind of sensation: That somewhere in his past, she'd been fun, but looking at it now, he could see the rough edges of poverty.

In the case of Mila, she'd been fun and wrong and more than she was. She'd been an idea and an ideal that he clung to. Brian wasn't quite sure what was gnashing at the edges of his thoughts now.

Ahead of him on the trail, Mila looked around as if sensing that she was being followed. He stopped abruptly, hanging back and ducking behind a tree like a rank amateur. He hadn't tried to trail anyone since he was a kid. As he took a deep breath, he stepped back and immediately cracked a twig, but she didn't even seem to notice.

After her cursory check of the surrounding areas, and obviously coming to the false assumption that she was alone, she pushed on forward and Brian scrambled to catch up.

Mila was fast. She had a bag over her shoulder—not the black ripstop nylon bag that for whatever reason had become so comfortable in his memory—but a different one. She wore it slung crossbody almost like a backpack. All the while Brian hung back and watched.

Until, at last, she stopped. This time she didn't check behind her but looked upward. She turned and faced different trees as she stood in the middle of four large trunks. Raising one hand to her forehead, she shaded her eyes from the sun that didn't filter through despite the daylight and looked off into the distance.

He couldn't help it, he turned and looked. There was a faint line of mountain tops through the trees that surrounded them. *What was she even looking for?*

But it seemed she wasn't going to go any further. Standing at the base of one tree, she counted as she paced, placing her feet heel to toe, heel to toe. Then, almost in the middle of the small opening that was slightly off the path, she set down her bag, and unzipped it and pulled out a small shovel.

Then Mila began to dig.

Brian sat bolt upright in his bed, sweat pouring off of him. He looked down. No nice pajamas for him, not like the brands his new friends recommended. Not like the guys who'd grown up rich or adapted to it far better than he did. For him it was old cotton boxers with an even older tank top.

His twelve-hundred thread count sheets were soaked.

His shoes? He'd thought they'd changed partway during the hike, but that was just an effect of the dream. The taste of American cheese lingered on his tongue for some reason. But, taking deep breaths, he tried to calm himself.

He'd slept plenty but rested none. He considered calling in sick to work, though he'd never done it before. In the dream he'd left home and was following her, but he was grateful that wasn't his reality. *Would it be?*

Whatever Mila was on to, she was like a dog with a bone. She'd left her job and was hunting, though he had no idea what for, but she was traveling all over the country.

Brian didn't know why he knew this to be real. Mila—whoever

she was to him and whatever the hell she was doing—was actually in the woods in Minnesota.

Probably not right now, he thought, as he looked at the dark edges of his blinds. Tapping at his phone on the bedside table, he watched as the time popped up. It was the dead middle of the night. Minnesota was even in the same time zone as him and it had been daylight when he followed her.

No wonder she looked around and believed she was alone. *She was.*

He wasn't even sneaky at following her. He simply hadn't been there.

Now he did what he'd done each time he had one of these awful dreams. He messaged his therapist for an appointment. But though he knew he should talk about all of it, he would not tell her about Mila and the strange dreams. Instead, he would tell her about Spaghettios and beans and American cheese. He talked to her about the times that he felt inadequate. And he listened when she tried to change his internal monologue that he was as good, if not better, than the others given the effort it had taken to earn his spot among the elite.

He didn't answer when she pressed about other things bothering him, and she would press. Even though this dream had triggered the appointment, and she would ask why he'd left a message at four a.m., he would not tell her he was dreaming of the blonde woman who shared whatever link he had to the cherry red Ford Falcon.

30

"Oh, you're going to love this." The sarcasm dripped from Christina's voice.

They were once again at the BCA in Duluth—still without a good enough plan to get to Westerfield—and Eleri didn't think there was much of anything she could love about any of it right now. "What?"

"The techs pulled two sets of fingerprints from the gun."

"Oh, lord." She slumped further down, the stool not allowing it. "I'm tempted to farm them out."

"It'll be two to four weeks for results," Christina reminded her.

"I hate you," Eleri replied drolly. "Don't make me think of that."

"Apologies." Christina grinned up at Eleri from where she sat at her arranged desk. Her laptop sat open in front of her, printed documents were strewn across the black surface in a pattern that only made sense to Christina. It was a sight Eleri was becoming familiar with. "I was merely pointing out that if you farm them out, it will be two to four weeks before you get them back."

Eleri waited, that part was already very clear.

"So if you wait three or four days to do it, you're still much faster." Christina waved her hand up and down at the large monitor and console Eleri had been using. "And if you wait, maybe you don't go cross-eyed."

She made a good point.

Christina kept making it. "It's not like this case is going anywhere, is it?"

"No," Eleri sighed. Her friend was right, she wasn't going to kill herself over a case she didn't want and shouldn't have. "The one thing I could imagine happening—the thing that might be time sensitive— is that our investigation has signaled people who are involved. Such that they are now going to be able to disappear or cover up evidence because we're being slow."

"That's not good," Christina conceded, but her face didn't quite match the words. She folded her arms and leaned forward on the table, her head tilted as if she had a secret. "But do we really care?"

It hit Eleri like a ton of bricks. *Christina was right.*

The goal in solving this case was only in pleasing Westerfield. They'd already given Mrs. Ella Hartman some level of closure about her son. That had not been a fun phone call, but Eleri had been through much, much worse. The worst part was that the woman had basically already come to terms with it and Eleri and Christina had opened old wounds.

They'd been able to tell the woman the name of her son's new wife. Then they'd had to break the unfortunate news that the young woman was pregnant and—barring surprise genetic tests—it had been Ella Hartman's grandchild.

They'd not yet been able to answer whether the deaths were accidental or murder. Eleri suspected this case would walk the gray line somewhere between. People didn't just drive their cars over a bluff into Lake Superior for no reason. Suicide didn't make sense despite the fact that they hadn't found the money that Benjamin Hartman had told his mother he had.

The odd infusion of cash into a very early Miranda Industries would indicate exactly where that money had gone.

In the end, Christina was right. Aside from the fact that this all now seemed to link back to Miranda Industries, which Eleri thought just had to be her luck, she had no real attachment to this case. No attachment to Jennifer Barnes and Benjamin Hartman. No attachment to the cherry red Ford Falcon the evidence team was still combing over. And no real concern about the two sets of fingerprints on the gun.

"So, what do we do?"

"We have to get to Westerfield?" Christina countered deftly. "What ideas do you have? We have to pick one."

Assuming Westerfield wasn't already completely up to date with their searches into Victor Leonidas, and that Westerfield hadn't already fully predicted what they were going to do next, Eleri still had no clue.

Christina was looking at her and Eleri felt the need to confess. "I've come up with exactly nothing except blackmail."

"I can go for blackmail." Christina smiled. "What exactly are you thinking?"

"That we threaten to out Leonidas if Westerfield doesn't hand over Donovan." Eleri still only had the partially formed thought. It sounded even less solid as she said it.

"Do we think that he's not looking for Donovan? That he already knows where he is?" Was Christina playing Devil's advocate? Or was it a legitimate question?

Eleri didn't know. But as she started talking, the ideas gelled. "I think that Westerfield sees Donovan as someone he's now got inside Miranda Industries and he's letting it play out. I think he's waiting to see what they do with Donovan."

Christina didn't counter that, only added, "I have an idea of what they do with the people they recruit."

That was terrifying. Donovan wasn't at full health. But she'd held those thoughts at bay because there was nothing she could do about them right now.

Shrugging, Christina admitted, "That's the same idea I had. We go to Westerfield and we tell him that we will publicly let Miranda know that Leonidas is an FBI agent unless he pulls Donovan immediately."

"Can we do that? I have no doubt that I can stomach ruining a five-year investigation, but I don't know that I can let the brass at Miranda turn on another agent. He'll probably end up in a ditch."

"If we can't save him. And all this assumes Westerfield knows where Donovan is and can extract him."

Eleri pointed out, "I don't know if it matters. What if he doesn't know where Donovan is? Then Donovan is just as missing as he is now. And can we make Westerfield give us the information we need from here?"

"Here?" Christina asked. "I think we need to head to Atlanta to do this."

"You want to see him face to face?" Eleri hadn't considered that.

"I think we need to. Anything less and we won't know what's going on."

Eleri nodded. Christina's skills worked best up close and personal. Eleri's spells could work from a distance, but she could sense things better in the room with someone.

The question was how did they get from Minnesota to Atlanta without Westerfield noticing? They could drive or book a commercial flight. They'd have to work that out.

But Christina was still going. "First, we gather up whatever you need and then we cast whatever spells we need to before we leave the state."

"What spells?" It wasn't like Christina to have a menu ready.

"Well, we need to knock Miranda Industries' protections off of Donovan. We also need to make Westerfield receptive, and we need to do anything we can to find Donovan." Christina waited until she nodded. "You said you had spells for those. I'm aware that I'm just your lowly assistant, but I'll do everything I can. There's got to be somewhere around here to find the supplies that you need."

Eleri felt the knot loosening and reforming in her chest. These were good solid ideas, things that she probably should have thought of a while ago. Each day her brain felt clearer. Each day that she no longer took her orders from Westerfield and was told to sit by and wait idly while he found her partner, she felt a little stronger.

The spells she cast the other night hadn't seemed to have worked at the time, but clearly they'd opened something. Christina's plan could be a winner if each of the little pieces worked the way they were supposed to ...

31

Eleri's head whipped around as the young woman started up the trail toward where she and Christina stood. The blonde ponytail bobbed along as though the woman didn't even see them.

Quickly Eleri's eyes darted to Christina. *What should they do about the intruder?*

That Christina only looked at Eleri and shook her head but didn't speak was odd. Her expression asked without words, *What are you looking at?*

When Eleri checked back down the trail, the woman was gone, though the image was seared into her brain—Wide smile, blue eyes, straight blonde hair pulled back, hiking boots that looked new, jeans that maybe didn't. She'd had a bag slung cross body as though she were carrying a rifle or such.

But she wasn't there now. *What had Eleri seen?*

Chances were she'd conjured it.

"I caught something, but it's not really there," she told Christina as she turned back to the work at hand.

Picking a spot out in the nearest National Park, they'd followed the trail and then Eleri's instincts. When they stepped slightly off the path they came to a small clearing with four tall trees. In the middle of the space was a freshly dug divot in the soil.

"Somebody already dug us a fire pit," Eleri had declared as she and Christina had both set down the heavy bags they carried.

Inside were the copper bowl, the Book of Shadows, the herbs they needed and even snacks for them in case they got lost. Heaviest were the jugs of water. Well, maybe them and the book. They brought a gallon of tap water for cleaning. Also a gallon of purified and blessed water that Eleri had set up before they had each tried for a long nap to get ready for tonight. They carried an empty jug that they'd filled along the way with local stream water—another good option for spells.

She pushed the bowl down into the loose earth and added the stream water to start. Next, she sprinkled the herbs into the swirling clear liquid repeating words and phrases her Grandmére had taught her.

They'd spent much of the afternoon finding their supplies. Christina had looked up local witchcraft shops and they'd wound their way around and out of Duluth. More and more, Eleri was not surprised to find quality supplies a bit off the beaten path. Luckily, they'd found a good one less than an hour away. She hadn't been forced to make do or decide whether she needed to dry any of her own herbs. For all that she was her Grandmére's direct lineage, she did not seem to have inherited that skill.

Now she stood facing the bowl as it swirled with little flecks of dried plants. Her white t shirt hung over her jeans—all cotton and natural fibers. She'd issued similar instructions to Christina, and she had to trust her roommate had managed it. Both had to kick off their shoes before starting this and Eleri had already fudged some of it.

She should be wearing only white, or nothing at all, but standing here in her t shirt and underwear on a just-south-of-cool Minnesota night in the national park was absolutely not what she wanted anyone to find. The image of the blonde woman had made her think, *what if someone saw them?*

They were clearly casting spells. She looked across the space at Christina, who hesitantly raised her own two hands to match Eleri's. Would she pull out her FBI badge and say this was official business? Technically, it was. Instead, she just hoped no one came by.

Closing her eyes, she tilted her head up and felt the air shift as Christina did the same, mirroring Eleri's movements as she'd been instructed to.

Already, Eleri felt more present, more focused. She'd tried several times since Donovan disappeared to cast spells and everything had been blocked. Now she felt the energy of the forest moving. It came in at her fingertips and swirled out of the soles of her feet through her socks that were slightly damp from the loamy soil. With just the blink of a thought, she could reverse the flow. She wondered if Christina felt it too.

The crackle and pop as the flames started in the bowl let her know it was working. Or, at least, it was starting to.

Though she wanted to simply look for Donovan, there were other tasks to do first. She asked Christina. "Are you ready?"

"Not quite." There was a pause, a break in the flow of energy, and Eleri watched as her friend pulled a folded piece of paper from her back pocket and scanned it over, quickly re-memorizing her portion of the spell.

Eleri smiled.

She might not have Donovan, but she wasn't alone. Together, she and Christina and Wade would find her partner. For a moment she paused and let herself feel that. How many years had it been? When she'd been in the hospital, she'd felt Wade was the only one she could call. Now, despite the pain and the grief that she tamped down and refused to feel, her life was much, much richer, and she would use that.

"Ready," Christina told her, and Eleri nodded.

Her hands had fallen so she lifted them again and began to chant. Once. Twice. Three times through.

She paused and, with a small nod, motioned to Christina. They moved in tandem, opposite sides forming a circle around the flames in the bowl. They stopped at each other's original positions. This time, when Eleri repeated the words, Christina joined her.

The rush of their combined voices hit her in a way that Eleri had not been expecting. The rich, deep tones of Christina's alto rang and matched into hers. Though she was only supposed to go once through, she couldn't stop.

The chant kept going, feeding on itself. She watched as Christina continued as well, despite that it countered her instructions. The flames rose higher, reaching almost to her chest.

Impressive. The slim column of orange and yellow, with flicks of white and blue, was tall. It started a foot or two below the level of the ground, given that they'd put it into the freshly dug hole.

Eleri had not cast a spell with anyone other than Grandmére before and had not expected Christina to be such a powerful ally.

Twice more around, the chanting continued, their voices intertwined in a way that Eleri could almost see lifting into the treetops, reaching up just as the flames did. At last, she had to cut the power and send it with emotion. First, she needed Christina to add her own push. The spell should harness Christina's powers, too.

But, because this spell had not gone quite the way she thought it would, she stopped abruptly, not giving warning. Christina's voice cutting off at exactly the same time, their wonderful synchronicity only making the spell stronger.

Eleri leaned forward, her palms aimed toward the bowl, and said, "Special Agent in Charge, Federal Bureau of Investigations, Night-Shade division, Derek Westerfield." Then she nodded to Christina and with one last whoosh of her breath, the flames reached higher up into the trees before completely disappearing.

The air felt ionized but empty.

The spell had gone, hopefully doing its job.

"Did you push?" she asked Christina.

"I pushed for your spell to work and for him not to have any idea that it happened."

It was the best they could hope for. Behind her a twig snapped, and Eleri spun around once again to see the blonde woman coming up the trail. This time, she moved through the exact same piece of forest that she had before. Clearly, she was only an echo of something that had been here.

"What are you looking at?" Christina asked.

"I don't know," Eleri replied knowing her confusion could be heard in her voice. Turning back to her new partner, she added, "But her name is Mila."

32

Wade pulled his lip back to bare one long fang. Though hopefully no one saw it, it was just an innate reaction as he stayed hidden in the parking lot.

He he stayed just out of sight, watching the proceedings from between two minivans. Jesus, why did these people have minivans? Just further proof that the best place to hide was in plain sight.

He'd wound up here after starting at the physical address of a shell corporation he'd found that linked to Eleri and Donovan's last case. JP Talley had been one of the first known victims of that killer, but his death had triggered an investigation by Miranda Industries—just to be certain his death wasn't tangential to their business. Talley had been murdered for an entirely separate reason, but it had given NightShade further information about the conglomerate and what they were up to.

Wade had come looking now, to find who they'd replaced Talley with and what they might learn about Donovan's whereabouts. Instead, he was surprised to find there were only four employees despite the size of the office. He'd trailed three of the four, and the third had led him here.

He'd also tried to strong-arm doctors Booker and Spivy at the Veterinary Clinic hoping to force them to hand over information to the FBI about the Miranda cases that they saw.

They'd refused. Spivy had been adamant. "We do not give the

government data about wolves."

"Even wolves that are doing what these wolves are doing?" Wade had pushed. He'd first fed them information about what was known about Miranda's tactics in hopes of swaying them. It hadn't worked.

"I don't know what these wolves are doing. Just like I didn't know what your friend was doing." Spivy had held her hands up, palms out, as though surrendering. Her point about Donovan was a beacon to her willful ignorance. She'd then added, "And I *do* know that they're providing us the ability to care for families who don't have the means and cannot get care at hospitals."

Wade understood that, but what she was balancing it with was beyond concerning. He'd left with a sour taste and none of the help he wanted. Was it possible the vets were just scared? He'd not expected them to defend the practice.

Without their help, he was left with only his own research and his own nose. It had been too long since Donovan had been there to follow any kind of scent trail. In fact, with Booker and Spivy both being wolves—and all the other wolves that they'd brought through the clinic—Wade couldn't find Donovan at all. He'd need to find a very recent scent and follow it.

He'd wasted most of a day following the faint scent that he thought might be Donovan. It had yielded nothing. But, interestingly enough, when he'd followed the car from the shell corporation, he'd wound up here. Where he'd picked up the scent of the wolf from the clinic. He still wasn't sure it was Donovan, only that someone had been both places.

So now he lurked between the cars watching the goings on. He wanted to search the name on the building and reverse check the owner but didn't want to ping anything nearby, so he snapped a picture and decided to look later.

Here, the parking lot was full. People were coming and going with a purpose. Wade needed to step away from his spot. If they were wolves, they would come to their car and scent that he'd been lingering here. It wasn't normally a problem in most of his FBI cases, but with wolves around, he had to be careful.

He still had no idea where Donovan was or had gone. But he had figured out that the veterinarians, while not bought into Miranda—and even quite ignorant of Miranda's information—were definitely feeding people back and forth.

He watched, understanding that something important was going on in the building, even if he couldn't see what.

Leaving the parking lot, Wade stepped carefully to the side. He had an option to go left or right but chose right because it would get him closer to where he'd stashed his own car in case he needed to get away. He stepped slowly and carefully, his two main needs at odds.

The slower he moved, the more his scent lingered, and the more easily one of these wolves would be able to follow it. But the faster he moved, the more likely he was to crack a twig or make a noise that their sensitive ears would pick up and they would know now that he was here.

He aimed for the middle, working his way around and hoping that the building—though situated on a state road—was backed enough by woods and national park land that they wouldn't think anything of the occasional noise.

Twenty minutes later, he'd worked his way in close enough to hear a conversation in the back parking lot. He'd once again been surprised. Though he thought the empty cars out front were too numerous for the few employees he'd seen at the other building, this lot was full. This was where the action was.

They didn't give any indication that they'd heard him coming. They were making so much noise of their own it was difficult to make out the words, but clearly some sort of deal was going down. Behind him, a car zipped past, the trees had muffled the sound until it got close and hopefully also hid him from view.

Turning, he caught sight of the vehicle. It didn't surprise him that it was a state trooper car, but it did shock him that it pulled into the front lot, bypassed all the parked cars, and came directly to the back.

Wade felt his mouth fall open. The state trooper had either walked into something she wasn't prepared for or ...

As he watched, she climbed out of the car, in full uniform, gun on one hip, taser on the other. Had she walked into the biggest ambush of her life?

No. She smiled and talked jovially to the men. They were wolves, he could tell, and she joked with them as though they were old friends. In moments, she was back in her car, packages in hand.

Wade's heart dropped. This was going to be even harder than he thought.

33

Eleri's nerves flared as she and Christina calmly waved their badges to enter the Bureau building in Atlanta.

Had Westerfield been pinged that they had arrived?

Chances were, yes. She knew she'd be safer if she made that assumption. She was confident he had his fingers on his agents, wherever they were. Whether it was by following their badges, having them check in regularly, or some otherworldly means that she hadn't quite managed to duplicate herself, she didn't know.

Smiling, Eleri and Christina kept up small talk as they entered the long hallway after passing through security. Though Westerfield might be alerted, there was no reason to let anyone else know that anything was afoot.

They had no guns, no weapons other than their intellect and their information, but if Eleri had her way, this would definitely be an ambush.

The building was large, the hallways long, and it took a few minutes to get to the correct floor. Then they headed down the long hallway to the office where Westerfield worked. There were a few other rooms that he presided over—temporary offices for agents who were in the area, research rooms almost like the one they used in Duluth at the BCA, and places for NightShade agents to work and access databases locally without having to worry about their Wi-Fi being hacked or information refused due to poor security options.

An elbow bump from Christina let Eleri know she was holding her breath—and that it was obvious. She tried to calm down. If their spells had worked, then Westerfield didn't see them coming. If their spells had worked, Westerfield would talk, and he wouldn't filter the information he gave them. If their spells had worked ...

She took a long slow breath as they approached the office door with his name on it. As she reached for the knob, once again Christina offered a very slight elbow. Hopefully, the move was small enough that the others in the hall didn't notice.

Christina lifted her hand to knock. *Were they using proper protocol before they set off a bomb inside his office?* Eleri wondered.

"Come in."

Interesting. The tone in his voice let them know he wasn't surprised to be interrupted and also that he didn't seem to know who was on the other side of the door.

Sure enough, as Christina swung the wide plank door inward, he jerked just a little, revealing that he'd not expected the two of them. His expression changed from surprised to weary as Eleri passed through and Christina followed, turning and closing the door behind her.

His tone was droll. "You should be in Minnesota."

"We were." Eleri tried to let all of her anxiety go. There was no way to truly be ready for a conversation like this, but she'd prepped as best she could. "I'm *assigned* to a case in Minnesota, but where I *should* be is looking for my missing partner."

"I told you—"

"No, you've told me nothing!" she cut him off sharply, surprised at the rage that fueled her unusually sharp answer. Maybe it wasn't the best way to negotiate, but it also might be a good idea to let him know that she was not the docile puppet she had been in the past. "One of your own agents is missing and you've done nothing to find him. So yes, there is a case in Minnesota, and you've assigned me to that case. But where I'm *supposed* to be is radically different. So, we're going to start from there."

"Look, Eleri ..." He should have said "Agent Eames."

Her eyes narrowed. Luckily, Christina, who was a little more logical, managed to step in. And Christina did it right.

"*Agent Eames'* partner has been missing for over a month. You've not reported to us what you've done to find agent Donovan Heath."

"I've told you I have other agents on this matter."

"Wonderful." Christina didn't miss a beat and even offered a saccharine smile. "What are the names of those other agents?"

Christina stood still, letting him know that she was waiting and that this was information he should be able to give.

"It's an undercover op," Westerfield replied calmly.

"It's not that far undercover." Now Christina was on the offensive and Eleri was glad. "Is Agent Victor Leonidas in contact with Agent Heath?"

Eleri tried not to look sideways at Christina but to stand beside her to add her stare and weight to Christina's threat. But Christina's arms slowly crossed. They were all tired of Westerfield's bullshit.

"So you figured that out? Good for you."

"A long time ago. It was the only reason that Eleri handed Donovan over to him in the first place."

Not quite true, Eleri thought, but she let Christina spin the tale as she saw fit.

There was a pause. Westerfield leaned back and absent-mindedly picked up a quarter from his desk. Seemingly without his input, it began to walk back and forth across his fingers.

Eleri appreciated that they were making him at least a little nervous. He didn't have a ready answer. But she needed one.

"Agent Leonidas is operating in a different section of Miranda Industries. He's no longer with Agent Heath." The words were calmly delivered though not comforting at all.

So Donovan was still in there and it sounded like he was alive, but who had he been left with?

"And you're doing what to send him to extract agent Heath and get him back into the hands of the FBI? Or even to get him proper health care?" Christina shifted her weight, looking more like a mob boss than an agent as her expression slowly headed deeper and deeper into a scowl.

"Look. According to my contacts inside Miranda Industries, Donovan is still healing." That was it. Her SAC paused and waited as if to say the next move was theirs.

Eleri jumped back in. "Are you suggesting that after more than a month, he's not healthy enough to leave?"

"I don't know."

"You *do* know," Eleri retorted. Then she leveled an accusation that she'd intended to hold back. "Have you planted Agent Heath inside Miranda Industries to use him as an undercover operative?"

A slight twitch on her boss's face told her it wasn't an unheard of proposition to him. But whether or not he'd actually done it, she couldn't quite read.

Her anger flared and she wished she could pause, take deep breaths, and close her eyes for a moment. She would turn her palms toward her boss and at least attempt to read him like a damned book. But he was far too well aware of what she could and maybe what she couldn't do. And there wasn't the time for her efforts anyway.

"We won't back off of this," Christina announced, softly but firmly. "And, if you make any movement to interfere with us, we will go public with the fact that not only does Miranda Industries have an FBI agent against his will, but you left him there and refused to let other agents free him."

Christina took a small step back and Eleri wondered why her new partner was starting the motion of extracting them from Westfield's office. She certainly hadn't gotten all the answers she wanted.

"We'll work the Minnesota case as we see fit." Was all Christina said. No one had yet mentioned that they'd found a tie between the new case and Miranda Industries.

Eleri wondered if Westerfield had gone through their files.

Maybe he had. Anger flared across his features. "You'll work the Duluth case as *I* see fit."

In a sudden flash of movement, Christina leaned forward, slapped her hands down on Westerfield's desk, and practically growled, "*No. And we will go about finding and extracting agent Donovan Heath.*"

Westerfield started to rise, but something flared in Christina's face. Eleri wondered if he sat back down of his own accord or if she had pushed him to do so.

Christina hadn't yet moved. Her voice was furious but soft, still Eleri heard every word. "If you make any movement to interfere with us, we *will* go public with the fact that not only does Miranda Industries have an FBI agent against his will. But that you, *personally*, left him there."

"That's not—"

"I don't care," Christina interrupted. "I don't care if it's true or not. When I put it into the public domain, it will become the truth!"

Eleri could see Westerfield's teeth grinding. His eyes darted back and forth between the two of them. Whatever his unique skills were, none of the agents had ever been quite sure what those skills might be or what the limits of his abilities were.

But he knew that between Eleri's witchcraft and Christina's ability to push people, they could bury him.

"We're done here," Christina announced.

Taking her cue, Eleri turned and followed her new partner out the door, slamming it behind them.

As they walked away down the hallway Christina muttered, "Good!" though Eleri still didn't know quite what that meant.

34

They were back in the car, with Eleri clicking into her seatbelt, as Christina started the engine.

She was obviously still angry, though she managed to hold onto it.

As they were alone in the car, Eleri finally pushed. "I don't understand what was good."

"He did it. He gave us a lot of information."

"I don't think he knows where Donovan is," Eleri countered, not liking that. She'd hoped she would just squeeze an address out of him, but it couldn't be that easy, could it?

"Me either." Christina turned and looked over her shoulder having learned to drive before the use of backup cameras. The tires caught the slightest hint of the squeal as she raced her way out of the parking lot.

The rental car would need to be returned or extended soon. They'd flown down here as driving would have taken too long off the case. Too long not searching for Donovan. Too much time to warn Westerfield that they were up to something.

"I don't think he'd expected us," Eleri finally added.

"No and that was good." Christina watched the road, but Eleri could tell the question was directed at her. "Did you hear what he said?"

How should she respond to that? She was pretty confident she'd heard every word, but clearly she'd missed something that Christina had picked up.

There was silence in the car until the next stoplight, at which point Christina finally turned and looked at her. "He said he had *contacts* inside of Miranda."

Holy shit. Eleri had not caught the plural until Christina repeated it. "And if it's not Donovan ..." she worked the information as pieces started to line themselves up.

"There's Victor Leonidas ... but he's the only one we know of. Donovan isn't a contact that could give information about Donovan. So that means another agent ... Maybe a confidential informant?" The light changed and Christina pulled forward. "Maybe someone inside Miranda that flipped?"

After a brief pause, Christina announced "I'm hungry. You?"

Now that Christina mentioned it? Yes. With a nod, Eleri held on as Christina took a sudden sharp turn right without signaling.

"Is this good enough?"

Eleri nodded as they pulled into the drive thru. Obviously, things were rolling in Christina's head if she wasn't even trying to get Eleri to eat healthier or eat more. They didn't talk while they ordered. They didn't even open the bag of hot food until Christina tapped on her phone a little bit, found a nearby park and pulled into the parking lot.

With a quick look around, they declared it acceptable. It was the middle of a weekday and relatively empty.

"Christina," Eleri motioned to her partner as she grabbed the bag. "Let's go sit at one of the picnic tables."

Still needing to calm down after the meeting with Westerfield, she took a few slow deep breaths through her nose and out her mouth as she walked. She could hear the well-manicured grass crinkle under her feet. She heard water in the distance, a small pond too uniform in shape to have been anything other than man made. The flap of wings of a couple of white swans behind her. The ice clinked in the paper cups Christina carried behind her.

Better. Not great, but better.

Eleri brushed acorns and pine needles off the table before declaring it good enough and beginning to lift the individual food items out of the bag. It was only after she'd sat down and taken the first bite that she began to speak. "If Westerfield has a confidential informant, that would mean that he's trying to get to someone higher up in the chain, right? Is he trying to take down all of Miranda industries?"

Christina, now a few bites into her own fries, frowned and shook her head. "I don't know. It would have to be someone high enough up to do damage. Someone who could implicate the big guns. The peons wouldn't have access to any of that kind of information. So flipping them wouldn't do Westerfield any good."

"The same would apply if he has another agent in there. Someone besides Leonidas."

"True," Christina conceded. "And if it's a confidential informant, they'll have to get some level of immunity in exchange for their work."

"Unless it's just some grunt who's got a grudge against Miranda and is doing it out of the goodness of their heart." Eleri offered up.

"A possibility. But even a grunt who's far enough up the chain to cause problems is going to need immunity."

True, Eleri thought, going for her own fries and then trying to find a place to put her ketchup.

Silence lingered between them for a few moments as they both thought. But then Christina set her burger down and looked at Eleri.

"Leonidas has been inside Miranda for *five years.* If Westerfield is going after the whole operation, why hasn't he at least taken some people down by now?"

"But has he?" Eleri asked. "I mean, it's possible we just don't know about the arrests. It's also possible Leonidas is turning these people over to the local authorities."

"Or, as Wade told us yesterday, the local police might be in on it. It sounds like Miranda has their fingers in all kinds of pies." Christina sighed. "It sounds like the kind of operation where you cut off one head and another grows back. So, I'm not sure what Westerfield thinks he's going to accomplish."

"We should definitely see what we can find on that." They each took a few more bites, again thinking in silence, chewing, swallowing. Eleri satisfied the hunger in her belly but not her brain. "There's something else bothering me."

Christina looked up and Eleri continued. "I didn't catch it when he said that he had contacts. But you did. Since you said it, I've been replaying it in my head. And he didn't say *agents,* he said *contacts.*"

This time it was Christina who nodded thoughtfully. "He didn't say *informants* either."

Eleri shook her head. "If the spell worked, and Westerfield spoke to us without filters, then he does have contacts inside Miranda."

Eleri couldn't believe what she was about to say. When she'd first joined NightShade, she'd trusted this man implicitly, if only because he was her SAC, and she had no reason not to. But in the intervening years, his instructions and information had become more and more sketchy. More and more clues had been dropped.

"Do you think …" Eleri asked, finally putting her growing fear into words. "That one of the pies Miranda has its fingers in is Westerfield?"

35

"Holy shit!" Eleri blurted out as she scrambled to answer her phone. She fumbled the device, glad that she was in the passenger seat this time.

She had to wonder what had prompted this call and at the same time why it had taken so long.

"Walter!" She was thrilled to hear from her friend and fellow agent, and it showed in the tone of her voice. Christina, who'd already been glancing at her oddly as she failed to answer the phone three times now lit up.

"Are you having any luck?" Walter asked, seeming to know that she was already on speaker.

Despite the fact that they hadn't communicated in weeks, the first thing out of her mouth if they'd located Donovan would have been, "We found him." So, they all instantly knew that no one had.

"Nothing really. Just little bits and pieces of progress." Eleri hated admitting it.

"The same here." Walter sounded almost defeated, but Eleri wasn't going to let them give up.

"Like what?" she asked.

"I don't think he's in Florida anymore."

"We think the same thing. We'd found the veterinarians who treated him."

"What?" Walter sounded surprised by that, and Eleri was just as surprised that their tracks hadn't overlapped. How many different options were there to move an injured wolf out of central Florida?

"Just a few days ago, Wade located them. They said he was moved after about a week, though he wasn't fully healed."

"Hold on," Walter said.

"What are you doing?" As Eleri asked the question, she realized she hadn't phrased it well at all. Still Walter caught on that she meant "What are you doing to find him?"

"I tried to get his last known location while finishing a case. GJ and I tried to work both but ..."

Eleri almost heard the next words before Walter said them and she filled in, "It was nearly impossible."

"Yeah. Westerfield talked me into—"

Eleri suddenly caught on and finished this one, too. "—believing that you'd find him faster if you stayed with NightShade, with the FBI."

"Shit!" Walter's surprise was genuine. "You too?"

"Us, too." She told Walter about what they'd been trying to do.

"You just went and saw him in his office?" Her surprise was evident. Then again, neither Walter nor GJ had Eleri or Christina's skills. They wouldn't be able to push Westerfield to spill information he didn't want to. They were also both new to the job. Eleri—and even more so Christina—had some seniority to throw around.

After a moment's pause, Walter added. "You two do have some mad skills."

Next to Eleri, Christina kept her eyes on the road but grinned softly.

Sometimes it was difficult to forget that Walter's unique talent was simply being a badass. The other NightShade agents had something that couldn't quite be defined. Walter just lined things up and knocked them down everywhere she went. GJ's special skill was her ability to connect things and crack codes. But again, Eleri didn't think there was any element to it that was beyond the definable.

She asked about Walter's partner. "And GJ?"

"She's doing more work on the case and feeding me information so I can roam and see if I can find where the fuck they hid Donovan."

Interesting, Eleri thought. Walter and GJ had split up where Eleri and Christina had more split their time. Wade had simply gone off on his own, taking leave and using the agents with FBI access to help guide him. At least they seemed to have their bases covered even if the progress was agonizingly slow.

Eleri would not let herself think that anything bad could happen to her missing partner while she was looking. If he died just before she got there, she'd never forgive herself.

But she was going to connect everything she could. Now that Walter and GJ were reporting in, she told them about Wade's findings. Finally adding, "I mean, I think he's got fantastic Miranda information, but it's not helping us with Donovan."

"Oh, but it is!" Walter added suddenly. In the background Eleri heard a shuffling almost as though the other agent was shuffling through large paper maps or such. "The drug trade that runs out of Central Florida goes up to the North Carolina coast."

Eleri felt her brows pinch and her head tip. Next to her, Christina also looked at her with a question in her eyes.

"Trace it for me?" Eleri asked Walter and a few moments later the other agent had walked them through drug testing that took the origins of the seized drugs to ports in Miami.

"They've tested the products from what they seized at the port and tested product elsewhere and matched it back to Miami."

Several cases ago she'd seen that firsthand.

But Walter was still going. "And they funnel it up through Central Florida because it's less populated."

Despite the density in Orlando, there were wide open swaths of land.

"Given the chosen trafficking routes, avoiding populated areas seems to be their major goal." Walter said. She rattled off several Southern freeways and state roads that she'd found to be carrying Miranda's illegal merchandise.

"But where does it go after that?"

"It's interesting." Walter hadn't been idle even if she hadn't been communicating with them until now. Eleri understood. Walter and Donovan had been as "together" as either of them could be. Losing him had been a blow to all of them, and it took a while to crawl out of the grief and blame.

But Eleri could use some *interesting* right about now.

She and Christina had left Westerfield's office in Atlanta, climbing into the car and heading north for no reason other than that they had nowhere else to go. They'd flown down but not booked a return flight because they didn't know how long it would take. So they'd just aimed the rental car back in the general direction of Minnesota and the hotel room they still held.

They didn't know enough to do anything more than Wade was already doing. And even that had hit a snag, because Wade had found a drug track but not their missing partner.

Perhaps Walter could be of help there.

"The route goes to North Carolina and then back toward Nashville. A second route goes straight—or straight*er*—to that same spot and swings a sharp left heading for Los Angeles."

Eleri pulled up the map they were following on their way back to Minnesota, trying to remember if they would pass through Nashville. They'd set up the route, but she hadn't really paid attention.

But as she looked, she saw they could simply swing left. But they were not prepared for a trip out to Los Angeles. Eleri had packed a small bag with all of her most important things. She and Christina could make this happen but even as she was working through the logistics, trying to alter their map, Walter added more.

"So it's not Nashville, but a small area just east of Nashville. Miranda has a hub there—"

"That's White Nationalist territory," Christina interrupted.

"What?" Both Eleri and Walter blurted that at the same time.

"There are several large camps or compounds around there. The Southern Poverty Law Center does a 'Hate Report.' That area always has issues."

Of course, Christina read the report. Eleri should have, too.

"Dana and I worked a handful of cases there." For once, there was no dark tone to Christina's comment. She'd come a long way since losing her partner in a case Eleri and Donovan had worked.

Walter knew about Dana, but maybe not the gravity of the loss, and she kept talking. "There's a hub there and the route splits. The majority goes west toward Los Angeles. From there it goes up the California coast for distribution. But at the Nashville/Cookeville area split—"

Eleri took her best guess. "It goes north to Minnesota?"

36

Eleri slid the plastic key into the door lock at the hotel. The place was equipped with phone app entry, but the majority of agents never used it. Even the key cards were hackable, the phones only made that easier.

Stepping into the room brought an odd sense of deja vu. It had been a long drive, but they'd come straight back to the hotel. None of the NightShade agents they knew closely could claim any real familiarity with the area, but it had made more sense for Eleri and Christina to come here—where they were already assigned. Walter had aimed for Los Angeles, where she'd lived for several years.

Walter probably even still had connections. Given that she'd lived in a street encampment in the downtown area for a while, chances were some of the people she knew had been involved with Miranda Industries one way or another at the time. Or maybe they now were. MI offered a way out for struggling people.

Walter was growing more convinced Miranda had smuggled Donovan out of Florida along one of their trade routes. If he wasn't up and walking, then they had to transport a fully grown man—probably in a hospital bed—and that would require passing through checkpoints that were known to be friendly or at least amenable to looking the other way.

Eleri knew that, if he was conscious, Donovan would have made his case to any official checking the cargo. So it was necessary that the route where Donovan had traveled was policed with people they knew they could bribe.

The whole thing was a gamble. She was almost irritated that it was leading them right back to this case as if the case itself *wanted* or *needed* to be solved.

Exhausted after yet another far too long drive, she was grateful to be back in a room where she knew the bed, where her clothing already waited in the suitcase in the corner. All she needed to do was unpack her essentials.

Her overnight bag held few essentials other than her toothbrush and deodorant. She had however, packed and traveled with her copper bowl, heavy book, candles, herbs and more. Her necessary craft items were now moved back into the large suitcase and tucked away at least from the eyes of anybody who wasn't specifically looking for it before she brushed her teeth.

Her head swam as her body fought for sleep and she tried to figure out if she was missing a step in her routine. It nagged at her, but she was too tired to care. She could fix it in the morning. Managing to just make it into her pajamas, she tumbled into the bed. Sleep was desperately necessary even as she felt guilty that she wasn't actively looking for Donovan right now. Resting was a lesson hard learned.

She awoke from a deep fog hours later with a sharp gasp. The sunlight seemed to almost illuminate a small quick knock from the door. Then it opened a crack and Christina peeked in. "You okay?"

"Yeah," Eleri almost added, "just a dream." But she wondered how many she would have to have before she came to the realization that she should never just brush off her dreams.

"Anything good?" Even Christina knew to ask if Eleri had seen anything useful.

"I saw Donovan. He was standing, healthy. He looked good. But he was on the bluff where the car went over."

"Hmm," Christina mused, but didn't add anything.

Eleri knew that her partner was having the same kinds of thoughts she was. The dream likely wasn't predictive. It wouldn't make any sense for Donovan to be here. Then again, if Miranda Industries had smuggled him somewhere safer, somewhere less populated ...? Maybe he would be here. Maybe it *could* be a predictive dream.

Putting the pieces together in different ways didn't yield anything helpful. Eleri turned toward the window, squinting at the bright light pouring through the sheers. It came at her in a steep slant. It was still early.

She practically glared at Christina as she lingered in the doorway. "How are you awake?" She waved one hand up and down her partner's body and added, "And you're *dressed.*"

"Well, that's a little something we need to talk about."

Uh oh. Eleri threw the covers back, her feet swinging down and touching the almost-too-perfect carpet.

"We were too tired to notice last night," Christina announced as she turned away.

Shit, Eleri thought, a mistake they never should have made. The time in the car had been spent worrying. She'd gotten high on the excitement that Walter had finally reached out and that they'd had information to share. It had all worked together to pull the plug on the tension that had held Eleri taut and her body had simply fallen into sleep.

Now, stepping into the main room of the suite, she saw Christina standing with crossed arms on the other side of the space. Eleri took the hint in her partner's glare to go no further.

"See anything?" Christina asked.

At first, she didn't. The coffee table remained where they'd left it, still with the small pile of napkins Christina put there for them. The staff hadn't scrubbed the room. Eleri and Christina had straightened it before they left and hung out the *do not disturb* tag. It was still on the doorknob when they came in last night. Eleri had at least checked that much.

They'd even told the desk when they checked in that they didn't want room service for the duration of their stay unless they specifically requested it. So, Eleri figured everything was in the place they'd left it.

Then she saw something odd. "There's a housekeeping note beside the coffee pot." It had grabbed her attention for some reason.

"Exactly," Christina said before Eleri fully processed it.

Christina said the words out loud. "Housekeeping wasn't in here. It's obvious they didn't change the sheets or do the work. So why do we have two fresh packs of coffee and a note?"

"Because it's not a housekeeping note." Eleri nodded along.

The question was *who had been in here and why?* She'd packed everything important because of this exact possibility, and it wasn't the first time her room had been rifled through. Even though Christina had carried an overnight bag with only a change of clothing, a pair of pajamas, toiletries, gun and badge, Eleri's bag had been twice as big. Right now, she didn't regret a single pound she'd carried.

It was clear from Christina's expression that she'd already read the thing and put it back. But Eleri was stalking across the room, scanning the handwritten "thank you" scrawled across the front of the notecard. She recognized the less than perfect writing, though it took a moment to place it.

Her gaze flew to Christina's. "Leonidas."

"Again," Christina said. The man had a knack for getting into their hotel rooms.

Picking up the card, Eleri held it gingerly by one corner as if she might be able to lift fingerprints off of it, or as if any prints she found would matter. Inside, it had only the words, "We hope we cleaned your room to your specifications" and it wasn't signed. But it was clear from the handwriting who it was from.

But what did it mean?

"What was he here for? NightShade or Miranda?" Eleri asked. It was hard to tell with an agent working both sides.

"This is why I couldn't get back to sleep." Christina tapped the corner of the card, motioning for Eleri to turn it over.

As she did, she gasped at the words.

37

Brian heard the knock at his door. Though it was still very early, he was dressed in a three-piece suit. In shoes that cost more than his mother had spent on groceries for three months for the entire family. He had a haircare routine that also put him out a pretty penny. Had his mother known, she would have tsked her tongue at him and told him the cheaper stuff was just as good.

One thing he'd learned once he started making money: the cheap stuff was *not* just as good.

He'd skimmed as much as he could from his salary, sending what he could back to his family. The money he'd sent had grown smaller over time though he still spent a sizeable chunk on his mother each month. But most of his ties with everyone else from the old neighborhood had been severed.

Moving up meant moving away. It meant he didn't run in the same circles anymore and they couldn't understand him, or maybe just that they *wouldn't*.

His older sister had quit speaking to him, angry that he'd tried to help them out. She'd angrily yelled that anything he gave them was charity and therefore unacceptable. Then she'd gotten equally angry when he didn't help them. Brian got the feeling it was her husband mostly who protested, but he also seemed to have a love/hate relationship with the expensive gifts Brian had started sending in lieu of cash.

If not for his mother, he wouldn't have seen any of his family for going on ten years. As it was, he hadn't seen his sister, or his niece and nephew in three. Though he continued to send the kids nice gifts for their birthdays, he'd taken the money Angela and Scott refused and invested in a savings account. And he bought himself high-end hair products and a fancy car.

His mother still lived the kind of life that brought knocks at the door at all hours. He didn't. So the sound was a surprise and it had him on edge.

Telling himself the sound likely signaled a delivery at an odd hour and the wrong door, he pushed the knot of his tie into place. He grabbed for the knob, swinging the door wide without thought.

There, in the otherwise empty hallway, stood Mila.

She looked less professional than she had the day they'd met at the brunch restaurant. But she now looked far more determined. That first meeting, she'd been excited about his car, then confused.

Now she stared at him and didn't say anything.

Was she waiting for an invite? Was she accusing him of something? He couldn't tell.

He wanted to say, *I saw you digging. What the hell were you doing?* But to say that, he would have to admit that he had seen her in his dreams.

He did not want to tell her she'd robbed him of blissful nights. She'd stolen his rest and his time—making him think of her and the car and being chased through the woods. When he'd started sleeping again, he'd gratefully believed it was over.

He was tired of his co-workers asking him if everything was okay. He claimed he'd simply gotten sick, though he'd never been sick a day in his life.

"Let me in, Brian," she finally demanded when he didn't speak. The tone of her words matched the harsh expression on her face.

"I don't think that's wi—" He didn't even get the words out.

She was already brushing past him. Apparently, it hadn't been a request. Mila moved quickly down the short hallway, stopping in the living room and maybe for just a moment admiring the view of the sunrise.

That view had sold him on the apartment. Because it wasn't like he got to be here very often with the hours he worked. The last several days he'd taken leave and he'd managed to see the city in every phase of daylight. But today he was done with all of it. He'd gotten up on time, put on his suit, and was ready to go back to work and resume being Brian.

He'd pushed so hard to become the Brian Abadi he'd always intended to become. So, it somehow figured in a dirty game of universal *fuck you* that she would show up today.

"Are you still having the dreams?" she asked.

"No." It wasn't quite a lie. The disturbing images hadn't been gone long enough for him to say that with confidence, but he wasn't above faking it.

Turning away from the city view and back to the center of the room, she once again pinned him with a hard stare. Her head then tipped, a smirk growing on her lips, as if she knew. She uttered only the word, "Liar."

They stared at each other for a few moments in silence. Finally, he broke first and asked, "What were you digging for?"

Brian had thrown it out as a test, but the surprise on her face told him either she'd passed the test or he'd failed.

This was confirmation that he didn't want—that the dreams hadn't been the inner workings of his brain trying to puzzle together the pieces of his life. She'd actually been there in the woods that he recognized, surrounded by the tall trees. She'd stood in the center of the circle of pines, digging—just as he had seen her.

Now, Mila stepped closer to him, her expression changing from surprise to focus. Instead of telling him what she was digging for, she narrowed her gaze and said, "It wasn't there. It wasn't where we left it."

Such an odd choice of words. As if she and he had been digging out near the Great Lakes at some prior time. But Brian could account for every moment of his life except that one time he'd had surgery to take his wisdom teeth out. It hadn't happened that day when he was twenty-one. And it wasn't happening now.

He had to get to work. He didn't have time to deal with any of this. Grabbing her roughly by her upper arm, he dragged her toward the front door. He would simply toss her out, follow her into the hall and click the lock behind them. He would make sure she left.

But what could he do about the fact that she clearly knew where he lived? Also, she had no problem showing up at his door unannounced. He didn't know the answer, he just had to get her out of here now.

She didn't fight, just let him tug her along. But as he reached for the doorknob, Mila twisted her arm, yanking it back and grabbing his attention. "Brian, stop!"

She repeated the words until at last he stood still and quit trying to reach for her.

"I didn't remember, but after I dug it up and there was nothing, I remembered. It wasn't there because we moved it." Staring at him with a look that crossed determination and trepidation, she said, "I know where the money is."

38

"Ugggghhhh." Eleri growled at her own thoughts. Not the best thing to do in public, but she hadn't stopped herself before she did it and now Christina was looking at her oddly.

"What now?" Christina asked. They were sitting at a small diner they'd found after a very disorganized drive around while they discussed the morning's finding.

The inside of the note card had said *We hope we cleaned your room to your specifications.* Which now sounded a bit odd to her. But on the backside, it had simply said *he's alive.*

"I want to go into the lab and solve this case," Eleri announced.

"What?" Christina sounded almost incredulous. The case had always been secondary to finding Donovan.

"I know! I'm not sure why, but we do know that one of Miranda's routes tracks up this way. If Donovan is in Los Angeles, Walter will find him." Eleri did have complete faith in that.

For a moment, she thought back to the woman she'd first met sitting in a homeless encampment, squatting in a chain-link-fenced square block of downtown Los Angeles. Walter had been brilliant even then.

"Agreed." Christina nodded. "So is Walter leaving GJ to the case while she hunts down Donovan?"

Eleri nodded and shrugged at the same time. That was the impression that she had gotten as well.

But Christina was still going. "Is GJ forging Walter's name on the documents? Or do they just think that Westerfield isn't going to notice that one of them isn't working?"

"I don't even know," Eleri said, tapping the fork she hadn't used rhythmically against the tabletop. Then she turned back to her best explanation for her own odd feelings. "Aside from LA, the other major tracking path for Miranda Industries leads right to here."

"Coincidence?" Christina asked.

"I don't see how it can be." Eleri was looking up into the far corners of the restaurant, her gaze not even seeing what was there. Her mind tumbled and turned, less as if she were driving her thoughts and more as if she were rolling down a hill.

"So not only does the Miranda traffic path lead here, Leonidas is actually here as well. Or at least he was." Christina looked like she was working to put all the pieces into one picture. She didn't tap a fork, but her first finger made a small rhythm on the tabletop itself.

Both of their brains were working, letting out the excess steam in the tic.

"I do want to work on this case now." Eleri announced again.

Christina's finger stopped moving, and her eyes caught Eleri's. "Do you think it will lead us to Donovan?"

"I don't *think* anything. And that's the problem. I just *want* to get back to the case." Christina looked at her for a moment, and Eleri struggled to explain. It was difficult because she didn't really know it herself.

"I have no idea why I want this. Is it maybe just that I'm afraid I'll find out that Leonidas is wrong? And if I figure out that Donovan is gone ... I'll have to live with that. But I don't know what the feeling is. Maybe just a hunch." Eleri's shoulders lifted, her hands came up, palms pointing toward the acoustic tile ceiling in the old restaurant. "It could be anything. It's just what I *feel* like I should do."

"You're right, it *could* be anything," Christina conceded. "But with you, it's almost never just *anything.*"

Eleri felt her gaze drift right back to her partner's. It was an odd truth, one she'd had to learn to live with over the years. She'd spent her life chasing hunches and thinking that they were only that. It wasn't even until she was in her early twenties that her Grandmére had looked her in the eyes and said, "Why do you keep chasing your hunches?"

Eleri hadn't known. She was about to say, "It's just what I've always done," but Grandmére had answered first.

"It's because they're always right. Humans are not complicated creatures. We do what we get rewarded for. And you, my dear, are constantly rewarded for following your heart and your hunches."

It had stunned her at the time to realize the rightness of that one statement. She had never really been wrong. She'd been a little off, or not interpreted something correctly. She'd sometimes believed she needed one step when she'd actually needed two or three. But she'd *never* been led astray.

Why had Grandmére not told her then of her family's history? Had she been waiting for Eleri to discover at least some of it on her own? Eleri might never know. She still hadn't even seen Grandmére in the little house in far too long.

"Here's the thing," Christina said. "I don't have any fucking better ideas! I mean, we'll look and we'll see if we can trace any Miranda trafficking in the area. We'll check all those leads, but I don't think it's going to fill up our days. We might as well solve the damn case, if only to keep from staring at the walls. We can always abandon it as soon as we get a better lead on Donovan."

It wasn't a bad thought. Finding missing people was long, dull work with a lot of wall-staring. They'd all learned it the hard way.

"Is it worth driving around town and looking for Donovan?" Eleri asked.

"I don't see why not." Christina held her hand out and Eleri knew instinctively her partner was reaching for the keys. Eleri readily handed them over, having driven here and pocketed them upon arriving.

The server showed up just then, and with a few quick motions they sent her back for the check, even though their food wasn't quite finished.

"Let's do that first." Christina said as soon as the server was out of earshot. "I'll drive, you can cast whatever you can, and tell me wherever we need to go. If we run into anyone to question, I can make them tell us what we need to know."

It was a wonderful solution for them, Eleri thought, and shitty for anyone they ran into. But at this point, she didn't think she really cared. She nodded to her partner. Any appetite she'd had had fled in the excitement of a new idea.

"But after that," Christina said, "We head back into the BCA and we try to figure out what other fingers Westerfield has in Miranda ... besides Victor Leonidas. Then we work on whatever the case hands us."

Eleri was nodding slowly along. Christina was an excellent partner. She took Eleri's feelings and urges and turned them into plans and actions.

Eleri didn't think they would find Donovan today, as much as she wanted to. But maybe they could find one thing that would lead them to the next thing.

They were heading out to the car when her phone rang. She looked up at Christina with a smile on her face. "It's Jesse."

39

"Jesse, what have you got?" Eleri looked around but quickly decided that climbing into the car gave them the most privacy.

Jesse caught on, waiting a few moments until she heard car doors close. "Are you good?"

"Yes," Christina replied for the both of them. "What did you find?"

"Check this: there's a bit of a connection about the missing money."

"The missing money?" Eleri asked, had she not put all the moving pieces together correctly?

She assumed Jesse was referring to something from one of the robberies. Or maybe the difference between the total of the robberies and the funding that Miranda Industries had started with.

"Yes, it was exactly $342,517.72"

"What?" Eleri asked.

Jesse sounded excited, though Eleri hadn't quite put all the pieces together. "Remember I said Miranda started with a certain amount of funding, and there was a certain amount that had been stolen across the grocery stores?"

Eleri had been right? "Yes."

Beside her Christina nodded along.

"So, at the ninth and last successful robbery, the grocery store reported the missing amount was—"

"$342,517.72!" Eleri filled in.

"Right! And it is also the exact amount of difference from what Miranda Industries claimed in the start-up paperwork."

"That's stupid!" Christina sputtered as Eleri whipped her head around to her partner. But Christina was still going. "They started a business with an exact amount that was known missing?"

"Apparently they did," Jesse added. "And no one questioned it until much later."

"Who questioned it?" This time it was Eleri who was being confused.

"Give me a second, I'll get there," Jesse told them, and Eleri trusted her.

"So, the Albertsons debacle—"

"Albertsons?" Eleri asked.

"Yes, over the course of the nine robbery/murders, a variety of grocery chains were hit. All were in the Los Angeles area and there were nine different stores, but six different chains. Sav-on, Lucky, and Albertsons were all hit twice. The tenth was a different chain."

"Do you think they were planning to hit all of them more than once?" Eleri interrupted.

"No telling. Because the last one—the tenth—went south and everything ended," Jesse told them. "Or at least that's what everyone thinks. Despite a few similar robberies in the years since, there's no evidence of this continuing on later."

"I still don't understand," Eleri said. "What does that mean *it went south*? Weren't guards killed at each of the stores?"

As she had read, some of the companies were sending three and four guards on each run. And they'd still been hit despite lookouts. The robbers managed to get *into* the stores unnoticed, which was their best trick.

Some of the guards had survived the attacks. From what Eleri had seen, and what Jesse had said earlier, some of the guards had decided it was over or that it wasn't going to happen to them and had gone out in their usual pairs and about their usual business.

That had seemed to be the case with the guards at the last store.

"So all—or I guess—most of the money winds up in the hands of Miranda Industries." Eleri tried to sort everything out.

"Except for the take from the ninth store—an Albertsons—and that money went missing." Jesse's tone lowered. "It's never been found. Kind of a DB Cooper thing."

Eleri looked to Christina. They hadn't yet told Jesse that Benjamin Hartman had told his mother he had made just over $300,000. They also had a gun that had fingerprints that matched fingerprints associated with the other robberies. Even if they didn't match his or Jennifer Barnes's fingerprints.

Her head was starting to hurt.

Christina popped in. "So do we think Miranda was behind the grocery store robberies?"

"Hard to say?" Jesse said before Eleri could even open her mouth.

Eleri would have said *yes,* but Jesse's next words stopped that line of thinking.

"Miranda Industries was a new business that was failing until several months after the grocery store robberies stopped, when it got a sudden infusion of that exact amount of money. So, it's a fair guess that it's a lot of the same people involved."

Criminal roots for a criminal organization. It made sense. Now MI had her partner and she had two dead bodies that she didn't quite know what to do with. But Jesse was still going.

"There's an underground group, a kind of 'Citizen Sleuths' trying to solve old cases. Some of the online channels are big for that kind of thing. That's who eventually dug into the money and they're full of information."

Jesse seemed to be waiting for an opinion, but Eleri didn't have one.

She'd heard of this kind of thing before. It had been citizen sleuths who had identified that the Original Night Stalker and the East Area Rapist had similar patterns. They'd pushed to get the DNA matched and renamed him the Golden State Killer. It was citizen sleuths who'd done the work and pointed police departments in the right direction years later to catch him.

So, while they were sometimes a pain in the ass they were just as helpful as harmful.

"I've joined the group looking into this and they are digging way back. They've used online research, the occasional investigative reporter who travels, and more. This particular group has solved or played a hand in solving a lot of cases. One thing they're trying to bring attention to is missing Indigenous women in the western United States. So that's where a lot of their effort is going these days." Another pause, but then when they didn't have questions, Jesse kept plowing ahead. "But there is a treasure trove of information on Miranda cases and a lot of people with a lot of knowledge about this chain of store robberies in Los Angeles in the late 80s."

Another pause.

Then, just as Eleri figured it out, Jesse said it. "I need your permission to start asking questions."

It would bring the case back into the light. People would start wondering why, and how Jesse had what little tidbits she might need to trade to get information or get a legitimate foothold in the group.

"Do it."

"Excellent. I'm on it."

But Christina added more. "We need you to follow up on the suspects in the grocery store robberies. Give us fingerprints for any and all of them that you can."

"Interesting ..." Jesse let the word draw out and proved herself as sharp as she always was. "You have a set you can compare against, right?"

Eleri grinned, of course Jesse put it together. "We do."

40

N*o, no no!* Wade thought as he watched the large semi in front of him take the exit.

It couldn't be, he thought. But it could and he knew it.

He was maybe even more familiar with this road than the trucker in front of him was. Had the driver yet figured out that he was being followed?

Though Wade had considered ditching his own car at a gas station and hijacking another one, so far it hadn't been necessary. He would have done it if he knew for certain Donovan was in the truck in front of him. But as it was, he was simply following a shipment. If he had to lose it to stay undiscovered, he did.

Originally, Wade had gone back to the building where he'd seen the officer and the drug deal. For several days he'd watched as several smaller bundles were handed out—half seemed to go to officers from various organizations. The other half to people like random soccer moms, men in business suits, and the occasional teenager in a hoodie. After following a few of the smaller handoffs, he'd found the trails led to meth houses or were getting handed out in apartment buildings in rundown sections of town. A few had gone to very nice high rises in nearby Orlando.

None of it had impressed him. And none of it had made him think that maybe Donovan was on the other end of things here.

So Wade had gone back and watched until he had seen a truck.

They'd loaded it with pink plastic-wrapped pallets, none of which seemed to be holding a human being. If they were, whoever was in there was dead or would soon be. Nothing about it suggested to Wade that this was Donovan, but it was a way out—a way they might have moved him.

Though he could stay here and monitor the activity for longer, Wade's goal wasn't to follow the drug trade, it was to find his missing friend. And he was growing more and more convinced that Donovan was not in this building. It was just a way-station and he could only hope the path he was following was the one they had taken Donovan on.

When the semi had pulled out of the lot, so had Wade.

He'd hung back, his silver sedan trailing several cars behind. He'd picked it off the rental lot for the sheer purpose of blending in. It wasn't even shiny, a little more of a gray matte. But at this point, he had been following the truck for long enough that—if the trucker had any idea what he was actually hauling—he was going to be good and paranoid about the car that was constantly just a little bit back from him.

After the first hour, Wade had managed to get up close to the cab of the vehicle at a truck stop and place a tracker on it. Then he allowed himself to hang back. Hopefully it was enough. Hopefully the trucker had no idea that the little silver sedan had been just out of sight for miles and miles.

Also, Wade had driven these roads plenty himself. He knew it was more than possible to find another car pacing him on the road for the entire trip. It didn't mean a person was being followed, it simply meant someone was going the same direction.

Hopefully, if the trucker recognized the car, that's what he would think.

According to the tracker, the semi pulled off at the next exit. Wade followed, taking the exit but driving past the truck stop. He saw that the large vehicle was parked there and continued to the next restaurant on the small road.

Finally, he was able to run inside and relieve himself. He did not like being on someone else's schedule. But he ordered food and watched the tracker sit in the other lot. He ate in his car, to be ready when the dot moved. And, in the middle of his meal, the tracker started down the road again.

Whatever the trucker had done on his stop, he was faster at it than Wade.

Starting the engine, Wade watched as the dot drove past where he was before shoving the last of his sandwich into his face and pulling out. That had been fifty miles ago and the last hour had been blazingly uneventful.

But now, at this interchange, the trucker had made an odd choice. He was no longer heading north. The route went up to Minnesota— to where Eleri and Christina were already working. They'd sent Wade information, some of which they gathered on their own, some of which they'd had Jesse Nash researching for them again.

Wade had agreed with all of them: There were likely two possible routes, one to Los Angeles and one up to Minnesota. It couldn't be coincidence that Eleri and Christina's current case was there.

The question was, was it the case that had brought them to that point? Or had Westerfield found them a case at the place he needed them?

Wade hadn't teased that one out yet.

Hand over hand, he took the turn for the exit, getting a little close behind the truck as his heart picked up rhythm. He didn't like this. His feelings had settled into his foot and onto the gas pedal. He'd been going just a little fast.

Now, he lifted his foot a bit, letting the car slow and the truck pull further out in front.

Good, he thought. The truck couldn't see him anymore. It shouldn't be suspicious.

But what wasn't good was the direction the truck was headed. He knew this road because it would take him home.

41

Eleri had just sat down when a knock came at the door. She and Christina turned, frowning at each other, but Christina quickly added, "Come in!"

The BCA official didn't even set foot in the lab, just stuck her head in. Was she an agent, or maybe an analyst, or from the mailroom? Eleri couldn't tell. It was something about the Duluth office, they all looked the same.

"We've been hacked," she announced.

Eleri quickly pulled her fingers back from the keyboard, as if touching it might infect her with whatever computer virus was going around. When she'd sat on the stool and faced the large monitor it had felt a little too familiar. This at least cured that.

She swiveled around to face the woman. "How so?"

"Unknown yet." She shook her head at them, obviously just running around and warning agents in the office … or maybe just them?

"Is my screen going to pop up with a laughing face and a ransom note?" Christina asked, her own fingers held at a distance from her keys now.

"No. Worse."

Eleri and Christina waited, as the tech stayed leaning through the doorway, her head in, her feet out. "It's subtle and we're trying to figure out when it arrived."

Oh, Eleri thought, *not ransomware*. This was not the kind of hack that was going to ask them for money or threaten to lockdown their files. It was ...

"They're pulling data." The BCA officer looked around the room as though that might tell her something, but added, "capturing keystrokes."

Ouch.

"We have no idea why," she said as if she had no clue why anyone would want to tap a state criminal database.

Eleri and Christina looked at each other. Only then did she seem to catch the interaction between them, and step fully into the room. Her hands stayed loose at her sides though the rest of her was clearly tense. She was not just a messenger, because in that moment Eleri knew that she knew they weren't fellow BCA agents.

In fact, maybe she knew that simply because they were in this room. *Was this space reserved for visiting officers from other agencies?*

The tech's tone reflected Eleri's revelation. "You guys show up. You're tapping FBI databases from here, right?" This time she pointed at the floor as if to drive the point home.

Eleri and Christina nodded. "Does our presence match the date that the hack started?"

"We're not sure. We can trace it back to a week ago. But whether it goes further back, we don't know yet."

Eleri didn't like the way her organs twisted. "We were already here then."

The woman nodded. "I remember. I authorized your clearance. I mean, it's possible it goes back to before you were here and we're not confident about when. But right now, the timing looks suspicious."

"It does," Eleri admitted before realizing she might sound as if they'd knowingly brought it. Quickly Eleri stepped off her stool, moved back a few paces, and lifted her hands. "Please feel free to check."

"This is my personal computer," Christina said, also offering it up for inspection.

The woman only nodded along and said, "I'll get my tech guys in to check it."

"We'll be calling an FBI tech as well," Christina told her. But that wasn't a threat, just standard procedure.

They all knew Christina and Eleri had been granted access to all the databases by the grace of the BCA. Minnesota's Bureau of Criminal Apprehension had not in turn been granted access to all FBI databases, or even to Christina's personal computer. It could be a touchy moment. But Eleri was hoping it would be a quick one.

God forbid they had managed to bring the virus in with them. They had brought Christina's computer, but it should be very locked down, as should everything in here. Safety from hackers and criminals gathering protected information was the whole point of them coming and using this office.

While it was possible the hack was entirely unrelated to them, Eleri didn't like the coincidence. It was more likely that either they had brought it with them unknowingly, or their presence here had attracted the hacker. Neither option sat well.

The woman looked back and forth between them, her short bobbed haircut turning gray, but still clearly red. She seemed as if she couldn't decide if she should trust them or not. Still, she held out a hand toward Christina. "Gwen Parrish, Tech security."

"Special Agent Christina Pines." Eleri watched as her partner held out her hand, shaking Parrish's hand with enough enthusiasm to be clear that she believed she wasn't the breach.

Eleri watched as Parrish then stepped toward her, her hand held out again. She had no social choice but to comply. "Special Agent Eleri Eames."

She didn't add the case they'd pulled out of Lake Superior was connected to thirty-year-old cases in Los Angeles and possibly something much larger. What she did say was, "How familiar are you with Miranda Industries?"

Gwen Parrish's eyes flew wide and Eleri and Christina turned to each other is surprise. It was clear that she already knew who they were talking about.

42

Three hours later, Eleri's stomach growled. She was more than ready to leave the BCA, but she was stuck here for the unforeseeable future.

Though the office they'd been using was compromised—the techs had found the virus on the computer she'd been matching prints on—Christina's computer had nothing. Eleri and Christina both had breathed an audible sigh of relief when the two techs working the room had declared it so. It meant both that Christina's personal computer was not the source of the hack and also that they could still use it as long as they could hook into the secure FBI system, a feat that was much more difficult without a local agency providing the kind of security they wanted.

However, given that they'd thought they'd found safety, and the BCA had already been hacked, maybe it would be just as safe to login from their hotel room. Not something Eleri was looking forward to.

It was Gwen Parrish who motioned them to sit at the long black tables as the techs checked out the system for malware. "Can you please tell me why you brought up the name of the company that we believe is the most likely source of the hack?"

It had taken a moment to figure out how to respond. *How much could they tell?* Though Eleri and Christina had been working it on their own, the BCA techs that had helped out on scene already knew plenty. And what they didn't know they seemed smart enough to put together.

While the two of them debated something Parrish seemed to have expected, she pulled the phone from her pocket and tapped away on it. Eleri wondered if she'd already cleared it, making sure that someone wasn't capturing her keystrokes. It turned out that Parrish was head of security here, so Eleri figured the woman was confident.

But instead of answering, Christina asked, "Do you know what Miranda does?"

She leaned forward, waiting for her answer, elbows on the clear surface in front of her. The stance looked odd to Eleri without her papers spread all around.

Parrish raised an eyebrow. "It seems to me that Miranda Industries does whatever the hell it wants. We know they run drugs. We suspect they're trafficking humans—" Eleri flinched at that. "They're International."

Parrish said the last part as though she were informing them of this fact. "And that makes it hard to pin things on them. The best we can do is shove them out of our territories, but we don't seem to be able to *stop* them. Before we know it, they're back in. They use seemingly legitimate businesses as cover. The businesses themselves— when we line it all up—are clearly not legitimate. Pretty much every legal venture that Miranda supports fails. Most likely on purpose, declaring bankruptcy within a year or two, but it provides cover for moving money in the meantime."

Interesting, Eleri thought. The FBI had followed up on similar ideas that that was how MI was operating. But having Parrish confirm it only solidified her concern that Donovan was in the hands of people who wouldn't hesitate to use him in whatever way best served them.

Parrish didn't seem to catch Eleri's flinch or the interaction between her and Christina because the woman just kept plowing forward. "They ran cocaine and crack in the nineties. They've added oxy and are running fentanyl now. They've got patches that are solid enough counterfeits of actual pharmaceutical supply grade medication that we found them in pharmacies, getting passed out with prescriptions."

"What?" It made more sense for the drugs to go the other way—

pharmacies illegally selling off stock or more likely being robbed for it. Then pharmaceutical grade stock would wind up on the street.

"What's the benefit of running street drugs into pharmacies?" Christina asked, clearly as confused as Eleri was.

Parrish placed her hands flat on the desk in front of her and looked at them almost as though she were conferring a secret. "The counterfeits are higher grade—higher dosing—than the legal batches. Thus they are dispensing much higher amounts of fentanyl than the patient is supposed to be getting. We've spot tested and found them in at least five different pharmacies clustered in some wealthy suburban areas of our largest cities."

Interesting, Eleri thought again.

"Don't drug sales tend to cluster in the less wealthy areas?" Christina asked. The two of them already knew that drug use was rampant across socio economic levels. Wealthier communities simply had slightly more legitimate ways of procuring their drug of choice.

"That's just it," Parrish told them. "It took us a while to figure it out. Wealthier people are less likely to be procuring street drugs and more likely to be getting prescriptions that are then filled legitimately at pharmacies, even if the prescription itself isn't legitimate."

This, Eleri was already familiar with: Doctors overprescribing for kickbacks. There were plenty of documentaries about it already. But Christina put two and two together before she did.

"So, patients are going in for one level of prescription. Then they're getting a higher dose—"

"With poorer time release!" Parrish pointed out, "So it hits them faster."

"Then when they go back for their next prescription, it's not high enough and they turn to other sources."

"Exactly. Or even better: they blaze through one prescription and can't get the next one refilled, leaving them seeking out other sources or other drugs."

That, Eleri decided, was insidious and also disturbingly well planned out. "So, you likely have connections between both the doctors making the prescriptions and the pharmacies handing out the substituted medications."

Parrish nodded. "But I thought you were working on the case of the couple pulled out of the car from Lake Superior." Her eyes bored into them, and she demanded, "What aren't you telling me?"

43

"I needed this!" Eleri declared as she bit into the burger. Her stomach had been begun growling long before Parrish was satisfied that she had enough information from them.

She and Christina were at least satisfied that they'd held enough back. They'd shared details but made no mention of Victor Leonidas or of the fact that they suspected there were other agents undercover in Miranda Industries.

They had asked Parrish if the BCA had their own people tucked into Miranda. She hadn't been able to say for sure, but had replied, "I know we had them at one point. As far as I know, we still have some, but I'm not privy to the details."

Miranda Industries was huge. It wasn't a surprise there were multiple agencies investigating them. What was surprising was that the Bureau hadn't told the BCA to step down. Where the two agencies interlaced? But for the Bureau, the Miranda Industries case was handed to NightShade—with good cause. *Did the BCA know what kind of people worked for Miranda Industries?*

"At least it's good to see your appetite back." Christina grinned and shrugged.

For whatever reason the food now was oddly satisfying. She didn't think it was a coincidence that she'd had the dream that Donovan was alive and then Leonidas confirmed it just before her appetite returned.

Donovan was out there, and they would find him.

On the other side of the table, Christina, looking concerned, set her burger down. "What are we even doing now?"

Eleri shook her head. *What kind of question was that?*

"What's our main purpose?" Christina clarified.

Easy. "Find Donovan."

"Exactly. So, what's our main purpose with this case?"

Not so easy. "Initially, we were simply looking into the bodies that they pulled out of the car."

"Right," Christina sighed, gesturing now with a French fry that she had dunked in ketchup. "The FBI was called in to identify two bodies. That was really the whole job."

Eleri was catching on. "Why would we be called just to ID bodies? But now it's much bigger—the two bodies weren't just any two bodies, not someone joyriding who'd gone over the bluff and into the water. They're actually connected to a decades-old crime."

"Exactly," Christina said, "and that's connected to the founding of Miranda Industries. Miranda Industries is connected ..."

In her head, Eleri could hear the song *ankle bone connected to the leg bone* and so on.

Christina was still ranting. "Everything we found has spun this further and further out. Each time we pull a thread, we don't unravel the sweater in our hands. We discover we're holding a thread to a whole new sweater."

"It did loop back around though," Eleri said. "Our goal is to find Donovan. Miranda Industries has Donovan. Our case loops back to Miranda Industries."

"True, however, Westerfield sent us here for *this case*." Christina had shoved the fry angrily into her mouth and was now tapping on the table as if that would help her make her point. "Westerfield sent us here to identify two bodies from a car pulled out of a lake for a case that ultimately turned out to be connected to Miranda."

"So how did he know?" Eleri asked.

Christina clearly didn't have the answer. "Did Leonidas tell him this was a NightShade case? Or maybe someone else tucked into Miranda alerted him?"

"Or maybe Westerfield just knows these things ..." Eleri let the comment hang. A moment later she spoke just to cover her own unease at what she'd said. "So, if we have all these connecting pieces, why don't they connect back to Donovan?"

"That's just it," Christina replied. "I think they do. I think they have to. Westerfield knows we want to find Donovan and he sent us here. Leonidas is here—he left a note in our room, and he knows what we needed to hear."

Eleri nodded along.

"There's a hack now, capturing information from the BCA offices that *we went to* with this case, and the BCA already suspects the hacker's from Miranda. They don't want money. They want information, which sounds very much like Miranda."

Eleri agreed with all of it.

Christina added, "Assuming it's MI, they now have the fingerprint data you pulled."

"Is that news to them, though?" Eleri finally had something to add. "If the two people in the car were involved with Miranda, *we're* only just now discovering it, but Miranda Industries would have known it for thirty-plus years."

"True. But then why hack the BCA?"

"Well, Jessie did send us several more fingerprints of suspects."

"Which you then matched to several people," Christina gestured with another fry, though her plate was almost empty.

Eleri still had a couple of prints that she hadn't matched yet. That was what she was going to do today. "So, Miranda knows what we know. They should know who their own people were in the grocery store robberies. If two were Benjamin Hartman and Jennifer Barnes, then they only have two more, or whatever support team was there with them."

"Why hack the BCA to find out what they already know?" Christina pressed.

That question set Eleri's wheels turning. "They wouldn't. It's too big of a risk. Clearly, the hack is already traced somewhat back to them. Parrish seemed to think it was them even before we said anything."

Christina nodded along. "So, the answer is: they didn't hack in to find what they already knew. *They didn't know.*"

It took Eleri a moment to put the pieces together. "That means that Benjamin Hartman and Jennifer Barnes weren't the robbers. But then how did they get the money?"

"And is Miranda really after $300,000? From 1987?" Christina asked.

As Eleri blinked, she once again saw the shadow passing outside the window at Grandmére's house. Was the hack the shadow she'd been warned about?

And if it wasn't the warning the shadow was meant to be, *what was still out there stalking them?*

44

"Hold my hand," Mila demanded.

Brian sat in the passenger side of his own car, finally having let her drive the cherry red Ford Falcon. He'd insisted they take this car, despite what was considered horrifyingly shitty gas mileage in today's numbers.

She was certain this wasn't the car she had died in—it was simply very, very much like it. She was grateful for the seatbelts and anti-lock brakes he had added though the car handled like a boat. It was responsive enough on the turns, but heavy and lumbering enough to make her concerned that if she got too close to a Miata or a Mini Cooper, she might drive right over it and never notice. Yet it was all disturbingly familiar to her.

The sense of déjà vu was overwhelming enough that she thought she might just slide right into Jennifer Barnes' life as she cranked the key and started the engine. Though she'd only test driven the one Falcon for sale around the block, this car felt like she knew it.

"I'm not holding your hand," Brian protested.

"You need to!" She held her hand out, waiting for his fingers to lace through hers, though he still shook his head at her about this one last thing. The few times he'd touched her, he'd jumped back as if stung. Although why he hadn't anticipated the feeling when she had known it would happen, Mila didn't know.

He'd been having the dreams, and she knew that, too.

While, on the one hand, his being here beside her and driving cross country felt perfectly normal, on the other hand, she was still stunned he agreed to it.

She'd stood there in his apartment in the early morning light. He'd straightened his tie three separate times, before angrily calling into his office and telling them he needed more vacation days.

He'd practically yelled at her. "I was just getting ready to go back. I just finally slept a good night!"

She'd managed not to reply that she hadn't slept any. And that it wasn't fair that he'd found a good night's rest. It wasn't fair that he had a job to come back to. It wasn't fair that she seemed to know more than he did.

But she'd stood her ground and convinced him to come with her. She'd sounded like she knew how to do this, even though she had no clue. Mila was running on guesses and prayers. But she'd been bold enough to make him believe tracing the old route was the only way to stop the dreams.

She'd told him it would work.

She hoped like hell it could.

So, when she asked him to hold her hand, all she was trying to do was level the playing field.

"I'm driving so that you can do this." So that they didn't have to stop and lose any time for Brian to catch up. They could have flown, but certain things she'd said or offered had given Brian weird reactions.

"Hold my hand, Ben," she'd told him, not realizing until he looked at her oddly that she'd called him *Ben* again.

She tried again, her hand still out, palm up, waiting for his. "You need to know these things before we get to my mother's house."

"She's not your mother." He doubled down and Mila knew that both of them were right.

But Mila would recognize her mother.

"You can't walk in there blind," she argued.

"Why not?"

"Because it's not safe!" She was getting frustrated, not sure how much Brian would believe until he saw it himself. He'd agreed to come out here, he'd agreed to let her drive, *so why wasn't he taking this one last step?*

Driving with one hand, luckily not needing to shift on the freeway, she shook her hand at him, gesturing once again for him to take it. "My name was Jennifer Barnes, and you were Benjamin Hartman. We were married."

That part always made Brian shake his head at her. But it didn't matter, she knew all of it to be true. Though she'd had trouble finding Benjamin Hartman online, she'd easily dug up old yearbook photos of Jennifer Barnes and recognized the face she sometimes saw in the mirror lately.

She watched as, reluctantly, Brian reached out and placed his fingers through hers. But once he committed, he doubled down. He grabbed on tightly and she watched as he tensed, understanding what he was seeing as the two of them connected.

She saw the little wedding in Vegas.

The black ripstop nylon bag tossed casually into the back of the car.

She felt Brian's fingers flinch as Benjamin told her how he'd found the money.

They'd put up a map and thrown a dart, deciding to head to Minnesota.

She felt another twitch in Brian's fingers as she tried to keep her eyes on the road. But Brian's eyes turned to her as he realized that part of the reason he had taken the money was to support their new family.

Mila nodded. Jennifer had been about eight weeks pregnant.

It was only later as he picked his fingers out of hers and tugged his hand back to his side of the car that he asked, "Do we have to go see Mrs. Barnes? Can we just get the money?"

Mila shook her head.

"I don't know how to get to it without letting her know who we are."

And that was the $300,000 question, wasn't it? Because Mila was beginning to wonder herself: *Just who was she?*

45

"I'm sorry, I thought you'd be asleep."

At the sound of the click of the bedroom door, then Christina's voice, Eleri opened one eye.

She'd been sitting on the floor in front of the coffee table in a classic lotus position, simply because it was comfortable and kept her still. She found if she merely sat on the couch, she fidgeted. If she tried to stand, she would pace.

In front of her, the blue flame that glowed in the copper bowl sputtered but didn't quite die.

"It was a reasonable assumption," Eleri admitted. Maybe she also should have been practicing her search in the bedroom. But the small couch in the center of the suite was more comfortable against her back than the pillows had been. And the coffee table held her supplies better that balancing them on the comforter. She'd yet to figure out how she would have explained to a hotel that she'd somehow spilled water, herbs, *and fire* on the bed.

Eleri heard a few soft steps as Christina tried to backtrack, but she stretched her legs out and shook her head. "Don't go, it's fine."

Taking a deep breath, she let go of the spell and watching as the fire softly absorbed itself into the water in the bowl. Slowly, the swirling of the herbs also came to a halt and Eleri shuffled a bit, moving to stand.

Christina stepped back into the room, "I'm sorry I interrupted. Anything good?"

"No," Eleri said. "Worse."

"Worse? How?" Christina leaned against the counter in the small kitchen area, her brows knitting together.

"Somehow things have gotten worse. I just don't know how."

"Were they great before now? And I just missed it?" Christina at least made Eleri laugh.

She had to concede that nothing had been good. Only the *nothing* had a holding pattern. Solving the case, threatening Westerfield, trying to find Donovan, and more.

"I'm up and I'm out here because I had dreams that Donovan was being chased," she told Christina with a heavy sigh.

"That's not good." Her partner turned around and began to run the faucet at the small sink. She moved things along the counter until Eleri realized that—despite the fact that it was 3am—Christina had simply gone about the business of making coffee. She ripped open one of the packs of pre-measured grounds to dump it into the top of the small coffee pot.

Eleri reminded her, "I believe Victor Leonidas left those for us. Do we trust them?"

Christina shrugged and dumped it into the pot anyway. "It's the same brand as what the hotel sets out. And the note card was the same one the hotel staff actually leaves. So I'm guessing he pulled these off of a housekeeping cart as he went by. Also, it's all we have left, and I need coffee. I'm willing to risk it."

Fair enough. Eleri offered a small nod.

"But tell me about Donovan." Christina continued her setup for the perfect tiny pot of coffee.

"That's just it, I don't know what to tell. I never know how to interpret it. So I don't know what's real."

Christina hit the button, turned around, and placed her palms downward on the counter behind her as though she were going to press up. But she just sighed at Eleri. "I get that you don't know exactly how they work, but you need to start trusting your instincts better. You're all we've got right now, the rest of our clues haven't panned out. If you think it's a warning, it is. It *always* is."

It was true. Eleri thought about the years she'd dismissed her dreams as hunches or coincidentally predictive. They never had been.

Only now, she wasn't dismissing it because she didn't think that she had the ability, she was dismissing it because she didn't want it to be true.

"I don't know that Donovan has been safe this whole time, but I think—as of last night—his situation changed."

"You think he became unsafe?"

Eleri nodded and altered Christina's words a little bit, though she wasn't quite sure what she meant by it. "I think he became actively unsafe."

Christina looked at the window as though she were looking out it, though the curtains were drawn. "So, we step up our efforts to find him."

Eleri could only nod along. She wasn't quite sure what that meant. What efforts had they made? They'd been tracking Miranda Industries shipments, solving the case at hand, and she'd been updating Walter. Walter now knew not only what they'd found about Miranda, but about Eleri's vision of the blond-haired woman digging in the forest from when she and Christina had gone out for her spell. She wasn't sure why, but it had all felt connected.

Several minutes of silence passed between them. The coffee pot began to chug and whirr, but Eleri couldn't say her brain did the same. She felt empty, with no direction, and far too much concern.

"Maybe," Christina said after a moment, "We stop chasing and we start baiting."

"I don't understand."

"Well," Christina—still waiting on the slow little coffee pot—sat down on the couch and laid back, her eyes darting to the ceiling as if there might be answers in the paint. "We've been going along and following evidence. We've been following whatever happened thirty years ago, and we've been following whatever's going on with Miranda right now. Wade is *literally* following a truck."

True, Eleri thought. They'd been trying to catch up to Donovan.

Wade, unfortunately, had let them know that one of the trucks had headed off toward the de Gottardi/Little compound, but hadn't updated them since. Eleri preferred to believe that his lack of contact meant that the news wasn't as bad as it had originally seemed. It did make sense that where there were wolves, there were wolves.

Miranda had definitely been looking to take over the de Gottardi/Little land. They'd tried before to hack into the family unit and recruit some of the members. So, while the move was concerning, it wasn't surprising.

"What do you mean *bait* though?" Eleri asked.

"We've been doing all this quietly," Christina pointed out. "Maybe it's time to get loud. To rattle some cages."

46

By 8a.m., the two agents had been up for hours. Taking advantage of the otherwise unusable time, they'd cleared their important things out of the room. They'd packed the valuables and files into the car so that housekeeping could finally come in. Eleri was looking forward to clean sheets and new cups by the sink when they got back. But in the meantime, they were dressed and waiting at the office door of Gwen Parrish, tech security.

"Hello. Trouble?" she asked, sliding the keycard at her door. Whether or not she intended them to follow her into the office, they didn't know but Christina moved immediately after and Eleri followed.

Parrish at least managed to be gracious about it. "What can I help you with, agents?"

Eleri had liked Christina's plan, and now she laid it out for Parrish. Each time she added another point, she nodded to Christina making sure that the two of them were in agreement. They needed Parrish on board. The woman didn't appear ready to jump in.

"You want me to hack Miranda?" She sounded more than just a little incredulous.

"Well …" Eleri leaned back in the chair as best as she could, faking that she was relaxed. The office was small, and she was fine, but had no room to move forward or backward, given the desk in front of her and the wall behind her. She now acted as though this idea were perfectly obvious. "They hacked the BCA. You shut them down. You may manage to keep them out now, but what have they suffered for what they did? Nothing."

"Actually, they'll be prosecuted to the full extent of the law."

"Will they?" Eleri asked knowingly.

Christina didn't even bother with a response. She merely tipped her head and raised one eyebrow.

"We *are* that law." Eleri added. "We're the FBI. You're the BCA. You are the agency that got hacked. Please tell me exactly what's going to happen to them for this? Who are you even going after?"

"It's a fair point," she conceded. "However, I'm not sure what I can do. I'm not the one to prosecute anyone anyway."

That was a problem Eleri had always had with the system. She could catch the bad guys, but unless she killed them herself the whole thing got handed over to someone else. Someone who hadn't been there. Someone who was supposed to be impartial. Someone who could be bribed and bought in a system that had enough loopholes for an entire circus to jump through.

Parrish at least asked, "How would I even do this? I'm not part of any kind of prosecuting or punitive committee."

Christina leaned forward now, her elbows awkwardly across her knees in the small space. Eleri tried to stay leaned back and casual looking, to not fidget. The plan depended on getting Parrish on board. Neither she nor Christina had the tech skills needed to do what they wanted. Perhaps GJ did, but Gwen Parrish had traced the Miranda hack. All she had to do was send something up the line.

Christina laid out their idea. "You follow the hack backwards to the origin point. You plant some kind of virus so that Miranda will see that the BCA used their code, used their hack to hack them. And then you see what kind of information you can get from it."

Parrish looked between the two of them. "That's not in my job description. I'm in security, not investigation."

"So, who does investigation?" Christina asked. "Can you get them on board? And why isn't getting your fingers into Miranda and what they're doing to the BCA also under the umbrella of security? The more you know now, the faster you can shut it down next time or block it from starting in the first place."

She looked nervous. Her eyes darted back and forth between them, her fingers touched things on her desk, the bow at her neck, and her glasses with no seeming pattern. But her expression was thoughtful.

Eleri could see the decision was not yet made. She and Christina sat quite close in the space, only the distance of the desk separated them from Parrish, but she couldn't see their feet.

Using only a slight movement of her foot, Eleri nudged Christina. In reply, Christina tapped her finger on the arm of the chair twice. Hopefully Parrish didn't pick up on either bit of communication. It wasn't anything they had pre-planned, or any signal they already knew, but Eleri understood. *Christina wasn't ready to push her yet.*

She'd pushed people to do her bidding in the past—maybe a little earlier in the process—as it was easier than talking them around to her way of thinking. Pushing someone to do what she wanted was always simpler than letting them decide for themselves. It was faster, and always gave her the outcome she wanted … at least immediately.

But Christina had lived with the consequences of having a gift she hadn't been mature enough to use wisely … And she regretted it to this day.

So now, Eleri played her last card to Parrish. "Agent Pines and I aren't usually partners. My regular partner is Agent Donovan Heath."

Parrish clearly didn't know what to do with the information. She needed to hear what had happened, but Eleri hadn't realized how difficult it would be to say it out loud. "Miranda Industries has him. They've had him for almost two months."

"And you're here working this case with the bodies in the lake?" Parrish sounded confused, and it was a reasonable question.

"We didn't have any leads on Agent Heath, but the case is now connected to Miranda. And it seems that something going on with this thirty-year-old case has made Miranda think it's time to dig into the BCA and see what we're finding out."

She realized she just laid the reason for the hack at the FBI's feet whether it was their fault or not.

"I haven't been able to locate my partner for months, despite the fact that the FBI has at least one undercover agent inside MI."

Parrish's eyebrows popped up. That was clearly news to her, and Eleri wondered if it would be news to everyone at the BCA. For the briefest of moments, she also wondered if she'd betrayed a trust that Westerfield had placed on them. But she found she gave exactly zero shits if she had. Now it was her turn to lean forward.

"It's been too long that he's been gone, but we've recently received word ..." She didn't say *how* she'd received the word, "... that my partner is in trouble. We need to make some random move in hopes that MI will reveal something in the process. We need to act, and not just follow along."

This time it was Parrish who sat back. She steepled her fingers like she was in an old detective show.

Eleri could see that the tech manager was considering it and she wanted to nudge Christina's foot again, but knew it was unnecessary. Sitting and waiting for Parrish to make this decision was knotting her up inside.

In the end, all she said was, "What you're requesting is highly unusual."

47

"She's so old," Mila's whisper carried to him, almost as though she had spoken it directly into his soul.

Brian didn't know what to do with the information. He knew Mila had not met the woman, Olena Barnes, before now. Yet, when Mila had insisted he hold her hand, he'd seen so much of what she knew. She knew this woman ... from a long time ago.

He now had so many memories that weren't his own. Of getting arrested on trumped up cocaine charges. He remembered watching young men he thought were his friends turn away. He remembered the sharp, hot feeling of betrayal. Now, though, looking at it almost like a bystander, he could see they were ashamed of their actions, just not ashamed enough to fix them.

He and Mila pulled up to the house in the cherry red Ford Falcon. Brian had distinct memories of Jennifer Barnes pulling a small photo album from her suitcase and showing him photos of her mother and father ... and pictures of this house on the hillside in California. She'd grown up here, just north of Los Angeles, closer to where he'd grown up than where they wound up.

Brian had so many bits and pieces of memories that he was trying to sort out and string together. He now remembered riding his car over the edge of the bluff. He remembered being petrified as he went —scared of what was in front of him, and even more terrified of what was behind him.

His side had hurt like fire and fury, and he knew that he'd been shot at the time—though Brian himself had never been shot. He remembered the feeling of the straps of the bag in his hand, the weight of it. He even told Mila about when he'd found it—that Ben had twisted his way around to an explanation. He knew better, but he'd taken it anyway in a bit of a fuck-the-system moment. But no one left bags with that kind of money lying around.

It wasn't randomly there behind his neighbor's garage for him to find. But that's what he'd told himself. He'd known William forever. William and Ben's older brother Tyrone had been friends and Ben was pretty certain William would have killed anybody who took that kind of cash from him. He was also pretty certain that William wouldn't kill him or that Tyrone wouldn't let William do it.

Except that Ben had to grab the money and get out fast. Tyrone wasn't there to protect him. He'd been picked up on something petty and was in jail.

Benjamin told himself that the money was just sitting there. It wasn't even in the shed. It was around behind, mostly covered by the grass that William's old man had let grow out of control, rather than buy a mower.

At the time Ben thought it was stubbornness, but Brian could see it through Ben's eyes and his own. To Brian, who'd grown up in a similar neighborhood, it looked less like stubbornness and more like a cover, so the old man didn't have to be embarrassed by his lack of funds for a mower or a service.

Still, Brian could almost feel the moment that Ben had seen the bag. He could feel the twists and turns in Ben's mind as he told himself it was simply lost and anyone could take it, and no one would miss it.

That was a whopper of a lie.

One that Ben and Brian both knew. Because Ben had gone directly to his mother and said he had to leave. He'd told her he had a girl to pick up. Brian could still feel the adrenaline in Ben's system as he'd done that.

He'd snuck around the back of William's house, empty of all people during the day, or maybe the old man was sleeping off a bender in the back room. No one drove by. No one commented or yelled at him as he grabbed the bag. But as he lifted it, he saw the gun underneath.

He'd not expected that, and he consciously didn't know why, but he wanted the gun, too. Brian guessed that Ben understood he might need it to defend himself from whoever he'd just stolen the cash from.

Reaching down, he pulled at the edge of his oversized t-shirt and used the fabric to hold it by the barrel. It might be leverage in the future. Popping it into the trunk of his car, he'd left the neighborhood for what Brian knew now was the last time.

Ben had headed out to pick up Jennifer.

But Brian couldn't find the memories of where the bag had gone. *Mila said she knew.*

So instead of taking him directly to this house, she'd taken him into Los Angeles, given him directions up and over one of the canyon roads. That drive had churned deep memories inside him despite the fact that he'd never been to the city before.

She'd sent him driving on one of the state roads winding out through the hills and into the trees. He didn't even recognize the name of the township where her mother paid her taxes, but he knew the road ... or Ben did.

They'd arrived and seen the house. Though clearly well maintained, it hadn't been updated since Jennifer was alive. Now, Brian turned to Mila and said, "Do you think she kept it because her daughter was missing? Because she was waiting to see if Jennifer came home?"

Mila nodded. "I'm sure she did."

Olena Barnes was out in the front yard, digging in her garden. Now, she seemed to have caught on to the fact that a car had stopped at the bottom of the drive. Given the looks of the road, and the expression on the woman's face, Brian figured that wasn't something that happened often.

"We have to go and talk to her." He wondered if maybe she, too, recognized the car.

Mila climbed reluctantly out of the passenger side as if she would rather sit and watch rather than act.

He didn't know why, but he reached out to hold her hand and together they climbed the driveway.

Olena Barnes was on her feet, her gardening gloves off, though she still held the tool loosely in her hand. Something about her spoke of a quiet devastation. As they approached, she offered a *hello?* under-scored with suspicion.

Brian let Mila take the reins as she announced, "I'm here about Jennifer Barnes."

He wasn't prepared for the single tear that rolled down the woman's face. She shook her head looking at the pair as though they were old friends of Jennifer's who'd maybe come to see if Jennifer was home.

"Are you here about the funeral?" she asked.

Mila seemed startled by the question. "No."

The two of them had known that Jennifer and Ben were no longer alive. It couldn't have been a coincidence that Mila and Brian shared the same birthday, a mere four hours apart. But ...

"Funeral?" Brian asked. "Why now?"

Olena Barnes now looked as confused as they did. But she spoke. "Jennifer has been gone for thirty years, and I only just found out a week ago that they found her body."

That was news to him, and to Mila.

The woman sniffled back the emotions that rolled off her in waves. Brian wished he didn't have to feel them, he'd felt far too much these past few weeks.

Something changed in Mila beside him, he felt it in her touch, or maybe in the connection they shared that he still didn't want.

As her fingers slipped from his, she stepped forward to hug the woman. She took a gulp of air as she tried to quell her own tears and said, "Oh, Mom. I'm home."

48

"I'm going to fall right into bed ... facedown, probably," Eleri announced as she and Christina exited the car at the hotel.

As usual, they looked around, but saw nothing. Duluth had been relatively calm as cases went. They'd put themselves in a far more precarious situation driving to Atlanta than anything they seemed to have done here.

Christina shrugged. "Parrish just texted me that the trace is set. So, we just have to wait. I'm exhausted, too."

The sun had barely set, and there was still so much to do on the case. Fingerprints were still waiting to be matched. It was the kind of thing Eleri never would have let sit on a case before, but she just couldn't muster the concern to care right now, nor could she muster the energy to do it. They'd both been up since well before the sun and they'd both run out of fuel.

There were still threads to be pulled, but Jesse Nash was out there unraveling the yarn even as they sat in Minnesota and worked other angles. Eleri figured the case could wait. Her work could wait. The only thing more important than sleep right now was finding Donovan, and she had no leads to follow on that right now.

Using Christina's key card, they headed in through the side door of the hotel and down the hallway. The elevators were located only in the center of the building. *A weakness,* Eleri thought, but not enough to make her switch hotels.

The elevator doors finally pinged and as Eleri breathed a sigh that she was one step closer to a bed, her phone rang.

Looking at Christina, Eleri backed away from the opening elevator. Maybe because somebody might be coming out of the elevator, but mostly because she didn't want to climb in if she was on the phone. With a nod that told her to take the call, Christina stepped to the side with her.

"Hello, Mrs. Barnes?" Eleri answered the phone and saw the surprise on Christina's face at that. But then she blurted out, "You *what?*"

"There's a young woman here who claims to be Jennifer."

It took Eleri a moment to process that. Even then it didn't work. "I don't understand."

Thirty years after filing a missing persons report for her daughter, Olena Barnes had finally been told that her daughter had been dead all along—likely even before the report was filed.

She could be having some kind of psychogenic break, Eleri thought now. But in this business and with the cases Eleri had seen recently, she wasn't going to write it off that easily.

Something bothered her though. Olena Barnes said a *young woman* claimed to be Jennifer. If Jennifer were actually alive, she wouldn't be young. She'd be twenty-plus years older than Eleri herself.

"Let me get this straight ..." Eleri didn't want to put the phone on speaker. They were standing just around the corner from the lobby of the hotel. Though it appeared empty, it wasn't late enough at night to count on it staying that way. So, she held the phone up and let Christina put her ear in close. Eleri asked, "Jennifer showed up at your house?"

"Well, not quite."

A silence hung between them until Eleri asked, "Can you please explain?"

"I don't know if I can." There was exasperation in Mrs. Barnes' voice, but also a hint of tears and relief. "But I'll try. This evening I was outside gardening and a car pulled up at the end of the driveway. It was an old car ... like the one Jennifer told me about."

Eleri's eyes darted to her partner and Christina mouthed the words *red Ford Falcon?*

Eleri was shrugging as Mrs. Barnes said, "It was one of the classic

Falcons, like the one Jennifer told me her boyfriend—husband, I guess—had. Anyway, this couple walked up the driveway and said they were here to talk about Jennifer."

Eleri felt her brows pull together. *Who would even do this? Was it someone from Miranda?* She wasn't ready to ask that yet. But that was where her thoughts went immediately. Christina's clearly did, too. Was this related to them putting the tracer into the Miranda system? Had MI already reacted? Even for them it seemed too quick.

Olena Barnes likely had no idea what Miranda Industries was or how much trouble she could be in ... Eleri didn't ask. She prompted, "So this young woman ... she looks like Jennifer?"

"No." The woman answered, though again there was a hint of happiness in the woman's voice that Eleri couldn't quite place into the right position for the conversation. "She's much younger. She was born three months after I stopped hearing from Jennifer. About two and a half months after I filed the report."

Eleri mentally did the math on that, trying to make note of the date. Given the date she couldn't be an unknown child of Jennifer's, but Olena Barnes was talking again.

"She knew things, Agent Eames. She talked about her friend Christy and things she couldn't otherwise know." There was a pause, then the woman added, "And she knew that Jennifer was about eight weeks pregnant when she died."

Side by side, Eleri and Christina froze. *Who could have known that?* They'd found out during the autopsy. So, someone in the medical examiner's office here in Duluth could have shared the information. Eleri had called Olena Barnes and told her the news herself only a handful of days before.

"Did you tell anyone about that?" she asked now.

"No." There was another sad sigh. "My husband is gone. I've been dealing with the fact that Jennifer is dead and has been all along. I live in a big house up on a hill. I don't really have neighbors—"

That was concerning to Eleri, something she hadn't put together before. Then again, she hadn't expected Olena Barnes to get visitors. From the look on Christina's face, she was developing the same concerns.

"I didn't share that information with anyone. It didn't seem wise."

It sounded almost as though Mrs. Barnes might have done some math of her own and understood that the eight-week-pregnancy had superseded the three-week marriage.

Perhaps someone in Duluth had leaked the information, Eleri wondered. But even as she tried to make it all line up, Mrs. Barnes added, "She knows things. She knows things that only Jennifer would know."

49

"Like what?" Eleri asked quickly before pulling herself together and trying to frame the question in a more professional way. "I'm sorry, what things did she tell you that only Jennifer could have known?"

"She knew that I keep my parents' wedding rings in a small carved box that sits on the mantel. She knew that my father made the box himself as a young boy and carried it with him when they came here from Belarus."

But if the rings had been there for over thirty years, then someone other than Jennifer must have known about it. As she looked to Christina, she saw her partner's eyes narrow as she shook her head. Christina wasn't taking this as proof either.

"She remembered the car we used to drive when she was small. It was a large, white, country cruiser with wood side paneling."

There was a smile in the woman's voice, but Eleri didn't share it. *Also, not proof.* It was the kind of thing anyone halfway decent at pulling a con could find out.

"I know what you're thinking," Mrs. Barnes confided. "You think I'm foolish for letting her in my home."

Yes, Eleri thought but didn't say. It was incredibly foolish. So, she asked the next question she had to. "Is she there now?"

"Yes. She's sitting on the couch across from me with her husband."

"I'm not her husband!" a voice chimed from the back. "I'm not even her boyfriend."

"But you're Ben," Olena Barnes sounded confused, she wasn't even talking to Eleri, and Eleri was getting more confused.

Someone claimed they were Jennifer ... and there was also a Ben? Benjamin Hartman? But how? It was all too bizarre.

But Eleri reminded herself that her entire division of the FBI dealt in *bizarre*.

"I have Ben's memories," the voice said. "But I'm not Ben."

Eleri felt her eyes snap toward Christina, but Olena Barnes continued.

"She knew things that only Jennifer could know. Stories from trips we had taken. A fight we had when she was small. She walked into Jennifer's room, which I have to admit I've left almost untouched for thirty years. I mean, I changed the sheets on the queen size bed, but she walked in and pulled Jennifer's diary from under the night-stand. I had no idea it was there! But she knew!"

"What's her name?" Eleri asked. Had the woman given any name other than that of a dead woman?

"Her birth name is Mila Panas. And the young man with her is Brian Abadi."

Immediately Christina turned away, her fingers flying over her phone. She would only have access to standard search engines and wouldn't be checking any FBI databases, but it was a start.

Still, Eleri remembered the vision of the blond woman digging in the woods. Her name had been Mila, though Eleri didn't know how she knew that.

Within moments, Christina was holding up a picture of a young man on a "Thirty under thirty" list.

Staring at the picture Eleri asked Olena Barnes, "Can you describe the young man?"

"Of course! He has dark short hair, dark skin, a neatly trimmed beard, round eyes. A kind face."

Lord, Eleri thought, the woman was sitting on her couch with two people she didn't know who had come into her home pretending to be her missing daughter and recent husband.

Eleri couldn't dismiss the possibility that something more was going on here. She would be completely remiss in her job if she simply let this slide on Olena Barnes's word that these people were exactly who they claimed they were.

Christina's fingers had begun moving again, but this time she shook her head, indicating that the search for Mila Panas wasn't turning up pictures. She showed Eleri the list of links it had generated, but no images.

Eleri had a sudden idea. "Mrs. Barnes, can you tell me, is Mila a young woman with long straight blond hair? Blue eyes and a wide smile?"

"Yes! Yes, she is!" Olena exclaimed. "Do you know her?"

Even Christina was looking at Eleri. *Oh God.*

"I don't," Eleri said. "But I may have an idea."

Tucking the phone under her ear and holding it with her shoulder, she motioned toward the north, hoping Christina caught on. Then, using both hands, she motioned digging.

"Mrs. Barnes," she said out loud. "My partner, Agent Pines and I are still in Minnesota. We will be coming out to see you, as well as to meet Mila and Brian very soon. However, we have another partner who happens to be in Los Angeles right now."

No, Eleri thought. *She didn't* happen *to be there—this was no coincidence. It was all tied together. They just had to find out how.*

"Her name is Special Agent Lucy Fisher. I'm going to send her directly to you. And I'm hoping that she can be there very soon. I'll call back periodically to check in and update you. Please answer your phone when I call."

"Absolutely. Of course! I'm going to get Jennifer and Ben ..." There was a pause as she seemed to realize she'd used names that weren't legal. And maybe the people in front of her didn't want to be called those names. "I'm going to get them some dinner."

"All right," Eleri conceded. There was nothing she could do while she was currently on the other side of the country. "I'll talk to you soon."

She hung up with a heavy sigh. Christina was already in the middle of another call now, and she hung up, too, having set up the local police to drive by every fifteen minutes.

"I don't want to send them up to the house," she told Eleri. "We don't know who these people are. We don't even know if they're human."

Ouch. But Christina wasn't wrong.

"I've got Walter on the way," Eleri was at least able to announce that after a few quick texts. "I told her to drive like a bat out of hell."

"I noticed you lied to Mrs. Barnes that she would be there soon. She has to be at least an hour or more away."

"I didn't want the two to know how much time they had to hide Mrs. Barnes' body." Eleri stared at the textured wallpaper that lined all the public spaces in the hotel. Her brain was fried. Her heart twisted. Her worry through the roof.

Trying to quell her own anxiety with a deep breath, she asked, "Do we try to find a flight tonight?"

She looked at her phone. They'd been up for hours, and she was beyond exhausted.

"To what point?" Christina asked. "Walter will be there hopefully in less than two hours. And we need sleep. There's nothing we can do now."

This time, when they hit the button for the elevator, the doors popped immediately open. The box had likely been waiting for them the whole time they'd been standing there.

They rode in silence up to the third floor where Christina once again swiped her card into the door lock. Eleri let her eyes fall shut, her body letting her know that it had had enough for one day. But as Christina pushed the door open, it caught on something.

Eleri stepped forward now, her brain not working fully, just curious. *Had housekeeping left something behind?*

It was difficult to see around her partner, but Christina held a hand back, motioning Eleri to stop. So, she only craned her neck a little. The room was dark, but the hallway light illuminated a limp hand and a pool of blood seeping into the carpet.

50

At last Wade turned the engine on and pulled away.

He'd been sitting back just off the gravel drive, unable to fully hide the car and hoping what he'd done was sufficient. He'd trailed the truck when it turned onto a freeway that made him nervous. Then he'd gotten even more nervous as the Miranda Industries cargo got closer and closer to the farm where he'd grown up. A place that had come under attack from MI operatives far too recently.

But the truck had not gone to the de Gottardi/Little farm as he had feared. Still, it had come precariously close.

Another farm, some twenty miles from his home, afforded this gravel drive the truck had taken. It had pulled up to a small cluster of buildings and finally parked. Wade had hopped out to see what was happening and he'd had a clear view as the truck driver had been greeted with open arms.

A handful of people had swarmed from seemingly empty buildings, clearly expecting the driver. Within moments, several pallets had been removed from the back, put into storage, and then everything had been closed up. They'd all gone on about their day.

Wade had photographed all of it.

But the truck driver didn't seem inclined to linger. Seeing his delivery was done, he swung back up into the cab of the truck and began the arduous process of turning it around.

Wade had run.

The small sedan he drove was the same one he had driven all the way from Florida. If he was seen, he might be recognized—especially out here. He desperately needed to *not* be seen. With his foot on the gas, he was grateful he'd rented something small and didn't have the problems the truck did. A quick, three-point turn and he was heading out again.

At least the truck had to go slowly out here on the gravel. Wade hoped no one would hear the noise he made—at least not over the noise they had made.

He didn't know who owned this farm. He didn't quite know where he was or on whose property. Given that they were unloading things from a truck that had originated from a Miranda shell corporation, Wade was rightfully concerned about the people he was watching.

Had he tripped some kind of sensor when he'd pulled onto the property? It was safest to assume that he had. He wasn't even sure where the property lines were. Though he was confident he'd walked onto the property, had he also parked on it? How good was the security?

He might have been watched.

Now, he simply needed to get away. Speeding up, he decided he no longer cared if the gravel flew or if he looked odd. He looked odd just for being here. Flying down the road as best as a rental sedan could, he listened as the gravel pinged off the undercarriage. The damage to the car didn't matter. Damage to him would.

Five minutes later, he pulled off the gravel onto a two-lane paved State Road. This, at least, could not be their property. But it didn't mean that he was safe yet.

His immediate thought was to turn toward home. He would find protection in numbers there. But alerting those he had been following—who might now be following him—that he was one of the de Gottardi/Littles might bring unwanted heat onto his own family.

Instead of turning right, he turned left. Once again, he hit the gas, though this time at least it had a much greater effect. So far, no one had appeared in his rearview mirror, but he still wasn't quite ready to breathe a sigh of relief.

Fifteen minutes later, when he'd seen nothing suspicious, and heard nothing that made him concerned, he pulled into the nearest large gas station and truck stop. Hopefully, there would be safety in numbers here, even if the people here weren't like him. The truck driver or anyone from the farm wouldn't just come execute him here.

He hoped.

Pulling in between two other cars, he tried to hide the car and himself as he pulled out his phone. First, he checked the tracker on the truck, only to find that it was still at the farm.

Damn. They'd found it and left it. Because he'd seen the actual vehicle pull out. The tracer was now useless.

But there was nothing he could do about it, so he dialed home. After a few introductory remarks, and a *we haven't heard from you in a while*, he asked, "Who owns the farm twenty miles to the north?"

"Hold on." He waited a moment then heard, "The McLarens do."

Wade frowned. "We know them, right?"

"Somewhat. Not friend, not foe. Just there. Growing beets and government subsidies from what I understand."

But Wade told his cousin, "I just followed a Miranda Industries truck to that farm. They unloaded several pallets of what I'm pretty confident is either pure or cut cocaine."

"Holy shit!"

"I just wanted to see if you knew anything."

"I guess we know something now," his cousin replied.

Wade quickly hung up, getting to his next call. It was to Eleri, but it rang through. He left a voice message, initially thinking he would just tell her to call him back.

He almost pulled out and headed back to the freeway to wait for the truck to pass him again, hopefully on the way to Minnesota. But he dialed Eleri one more time. This time when he got voicemail, he put everything he'd seen into the message.

In case he wasn't as safe as he thought he was.

51

"You shouldn't be in here. This is a crime scene!" The rough voice made Eleri slowly look up.

She barely moved but couldn't help it, she knew the scorn showed in her eyes.

As she reached toward her back pocket, she saw the officer reach for his gun. Again, her expression clamped down, her eyes narrowed. She was irritated with him and hoping he didn't try to draw down on her.

She'd been kneeling over the body, not stepping in the blood pool. If he'd looked at the scene at all, he would know she wasn't messing with the evidence.

"Officer." She wasn't able to keep the rude undertone from her voice. He didn't have the gun drawn yet but he certainly had his hand on it.

"You need to step out of there, ma'am," he commanded.

"No," she replied, the full force of her voice pushing the anger off her. This time she didn't doubt that she could blow him backward before he pulled the gun. "*You* need to step out of here. *We* are the FBI and this isn't your case."

She paused as his expression changed from surprise to suspicion.

Was he misogynistic because there were two women in the room? Or was he just naturally suspicious? She found she didn't have the energy to care. "I'm going to reach into my back pocket and pull my badge."

His eyes flew wide at that, though, honestly, she *could* be reaching into her back pocket for some kind of weapon. He should have had the sense to realize there was no way she had a gun stashed back there. Women's pants didn't come with pockets big enough for that kind of storage. With one hand up, she slowly stood, reached back, and felt through the several items she carried. Luckily, the leather wallet was large, old, and well-handled. There was something about that that felt familiar and comforting to her.

Pulling it out, she flipped it open in a practice move. He stepped forward to read it. But she cranked her head quickly as if to tell him *Don't you dare.*

He would be stepping into the pool of blood that she herself had carefully navigated around. The words she said were, "I wouldn't want you to mess with any of my evidence."

Instead, she closed the badge and tossed it to him, too angry to deal with any of this.

Who had even called the police?

Christina must have been thinking the same thing. Eleri finally looked over her shoulder to see Christina had also stood and had her badge out.

The officer examined Eleri's badge carefully. She could see the moment he conceded that she outranked him. He motioned then as if to toss it back to her. "Do not toss that into a pool of open evidence!"

His fingers and his face clamped down a little tighter. She was too tired to be nice. She was too concerned to even force herself into decent behavior.

There was a woman dead in her hotel room right behind the door and all their things had been tossed.

So, she looked up at the man in uniform and said, "If you're going to be staying, can you just hold on to it?"

She shouldn't snap.

The dead woman on the floor wore the uniform of hotel staff. Eleri could only assume that whoever had broken into their room had done so either coincidentally while the hotel staff was in here or *because* they were in here using the staff and their master card key as an easy entry. So far, she'd seen no signs of anyone forcing their way in, but she was smart enough to know this body might not actually be staff. The uniform alone didn't make it so.

Looking up to the officer, this time she was at least not irritated at his very presence. "Who called you?"

Because she had called the medical examiner's office and the Duluth BCA crime scene team, but not the local police.

"Dispatch received a frantic call from the hotel operator."

Why? Eleri thought. She and Christina had mostly closed the door once they'd seen the body. There hadn't been anyone in the hall when they'd come in.

But the officer was still talking. "They said someone was walking down the hallway and saw the door slightly open. Thought they saw blood, heard someone say *a body.*"

Well shit. That could have happened. They hadn't closed the door all the way. They were waiting for the BCA to lift prints, do a more thorough inspection of the doorknobs and the lock mechanism to see if they had been picked in any way. So they hadn't fully shut the door, only nudged it nearly closed with the toe of Christina's shoe.

So yes, the door had been ajar. And, yes, there was blood all over the carpet.

The woman's throat had been slit, a move that concerned Eleri.

This was a murder that wasn't performed in anger, and it likely wasn't performed in surprise. It may even have been completely premeditated: Follow the housekeeping worker into the room, over-whelm her, slit her throat, take what they could. It was a murder to remove a witness.

She and Christina had already discovered that every single piece of their luggage and every object in every room had been tossed. None of Eleri's things appeared to have been stolen and Christina couldn't find anything missing either. But it had clearly been thor-oughly searched.

Luckily, they didn't have any boxes of evidence lying around. Most of it was digital. The few folders Christina normally tucked under the mattress had been carried with her since they'd asked for the room to be cleaned.

Which meant the housekeeper had been murdered in cold blood and nothing had been gained for it.

Eleri looked to Christina. "We need to check the car."

They'd been too tired to carry the things back up. They hadn't seen anything at the hotel during their whole stay. They'd mistakenly believed the car to be safe and that not touching or looking at the trunk meant anyone watching wouldn't even be alerted to the fact that anything was in there. The car had the best security system they could get, and nothing had pinged.

Eleri was now ready to beat herself up. She'd seen the shadow outside the window at Grandmére's. The idea that the hotel had been safe was foolish. She'd seen the threat and somehow managed to forget or dismiss it.

In the dream, she'd been at Grandmére's little house. The shadow had passed just beyond the window of *her home.* This room, this hotel —it was her home right now. The shadow was just outside.

And now it had been inside.

She hated how many times the visions only made sense after everything had gone wrong. But Christina was nodding, already picking her way across the carpet. She stepped carefully on the papers they had thrown down to make a footpath. As Eleri worked her way past the body, up on her toes, managing not to step in any of the blood nor touch the edges of the door, she tried not to blame herself again.

Finally, she made it into the hallway, where she held her hand out for the officer to hand her FBI credentials back to her. "Can you do us a favor and watch the room? We need to go check our car."

He nodded, though whether he was pleased to get an assignment from an FBI agent or maybe even mad that there was a murder and it wasn't his, she couldn't tell. But she and Christina walked by leaving him in charge as they headed to the staircase at the end of the hall.

If things were going south, the staircase was more open than the box of the elevator.

Shit!

This was Duluth.

This was one of the endpoints for Miranda Industries in the US. From here they would head further north into Canada. It occurred to Eleri for the first time that perhaps the officer had not been called by the hotel but was somehow in Miranda's pocket. Could he have been a cleanup crew intended to remove the body before Eleri and Christina returned?

But they were out of the room and there was nothing she could do about that now.

She and Christina did need to check the car. Evidence folders were in the trunk. In the back seat was her duffel bag with all of Eleri's supplies.

Two minutes later, they were outside in the parking lot. Christina looked up to the third floor as if she could see through the walls and know what was going on in the room.

"Do you think the officer is MI?" she asked.

But Eleri was already shrugging. "The thought occurred to me, too."

They needed to get back quickly, but they also needed to check everything. They had their hands on the car handles, popping the trunk, opening the doors, checking everything as fast as they could. Even as she did it, Eleri thought of the fingerprints they'd found on the Falcon—the ones that hadn't belonged to Jennifer Barnes or Benjamin Hartman.

"Everything seems to be here," Christina announced full of relief. "I don't see any evidence that anyone got in."

"We keep it on us at all times now," Eleri said, hefting the bag, glad she had her things in her own hands again. Now she wondered what the room would look like when she returned.

But as she slammed the car door shut and turned around to head back inside, a chill shivered down her spine.

52

Eleri woke with a sharp gulp. She sat upright in the bed though, for once, she couldn't quite remember the dream that had taunted her.

That was something she wasn't used to.

Had last night been a dream?

She looked around the room, remembering the harsh feeling of knowing the hotel door had bumped against a body. She could feel the tang of copper in her nose—Donovan could have told her if the woman was diabetic or had metabolic problems, but Eleri just knew *blood*. She remembered the face, fallen to the side in death, the sightless eyes staring straight ahead.

Now she looked around the room. The bed was wrong. The light was wrong. Even the feeling of muddiness in her head was off.

No, she remembered, *last night was not a dream*. She and Christina had moved to a different hotel at 4a.m. after the body had finally been removed. After the BCA crime scene techs had done everything they could that Eleri and Christina had needed to oversee. After she'd sent word to the FBI and told Westerfield that he needed to get in touch with Victor Leonidas ASAP.

Leonidas needed to let them know what the hell was going on.

Eleri let a slow breath out as she remembered. Looking to her side, she reassured herself that her duffel bag sat on the bed next to her. It wasn't ripstop nylon and didn't have $300,000 in it. But it did contain her copper bowl, the small hand-sewn sachets of herbs she'd collected, and the stitched bags that held the crystals Grandmére had left her.

Those things were all here. But her toothbrush and her clothing were still a part of an active crime scene.

Luckily, she'd learned as a newbie agent to carry a complete extra outfit in the car at all times. Now she was down to zero extras but hopefully that would remedy itself soon.

Standing up, she covered the short distance to the window and pulled back the curtains. No blackout shades here. Who even thought that was okay in a business hotel? No wonder she was awake.

She'd gotten enough hours of sleep, or at least she thought she had. Hopefully, she wouldn't wake Christina this time. Sitting cross legged on the bed, she tapped away at her phone. She already had notifications that some of the evidence from last night was in. Westerfield must have put a rush on it.

Though she was grateful for the knowledge, she had no idea whose side her SAC was on. She wouldn't have been surprised if he'd held it up and made them wait. But here it was, waiting for her when she woke.

Reaching out, she pulled her laptop from where she'd set it on the other twin bed. As she opened it and listened to the faint chug of it coming quickly alive, she looked out the window and wondered if she could drive thru somewhere this morning and buy a large, high-calorie, frothy coffee drink. It seemed like the kind of day for it.

It wasn't really even morning anymore, but she yawned.

Eleri pulled the laptop across her bare legs and began tapping into the system. The dead woman had been quickly legally identified. And there was no obvious link to Miranda Industries ... if the information was complete.

The hotel staff had been questioned quickly and reported a female staff member missing. They hadn't seen her for a while, and she had been assigned to clean the rooms on this floor. So, Eleri and Christina had been relatively confident who she was even before they'd left last night.

But an analyst must have been up all night working, because the report also checked for spare accounts, unexplained income, and extravagant purchases or family members with the same. She lived a quiet life and hadn't ever been more than five hours away from her home. Eleri's heart hurt for her. She'd been caught in a crossfire and Eleri didn't even quite know who the enemy was.

Reams of information had been sent. Fingerprints in the room matched almost entirely to Eleri and Christina, though a few random others had been found. The analysts had even sent her scans despite the fact that they were doing their own AFIS matches. The case had depended on Eleri to do the matching—until now. But Eleri and Christina no longer had a stable base to operate from, nor a known safe BCA office where they could tap FBI databases.

Eleri clicked over to several other scans she had saved and felt the corner of her mouth pull up. From a quick visual glance, one of the partials sure looked like it could belong to Victor Leonidas. *Not a surprise.* They knew he'd been in the room.

Was he responsible for this? Just how deep undercover was he? He had been embedded with Miranda for years. What kind of loyalty would MI expect him to show? Had he come to toss their room and the housekeeper had had the sheer bad luck of being present and Leonidas had been forced to dispose of her?

Eleri didn't have answers to any of these questions, but she noticed she was still giving him the benefit of the doubt. She did that for all her fellow NightShade agents. She'd done it for SAC Westerfield, but she was starting to doubt the wisdom of that benefit.

On the other side of the door she heard the soft padding of Christina's feet and the whispered words "You up?"

"Come in," Eleri called back and watched as Christina shuffled her way in, sinking onto the empty twin bed as Eleri scooted around to face her partner. "I dreamed something weird last night."

"How could you not?" Christina waved her hand back and forth, as if to indicate everything that had gone wrong. "What did it tell you?"

"That's just it. I don't remember it."

Luckily, Christina took that in stride the same as everything else. "Are we going to Los Angeles?"

Eleri shrugged. "Walter seems to have that well enough in hand."

Though, when Walter had reported in just an hour after they'd found the body, she'd let them know that Mila Panas and Brian Abadi had managed to slip away from Olena Barnes. Neither the agents nor Mrs. Barnes had any idea where the two had gone or what they might have wanted at the Barnes home. But it seemed more and more like they had arrived with an agenda that wasn't just about speaking to the woman Mila had called *mom*.

"What are we doing then?" Christina asked, and Eleri felt that deep in her soul.

There was both too much to do and nothing to actually start on. But something pushed her to say, "Wade should be getting close today. I'm curious if the truck he's following will lead him here. So we watch out for that."

Christina seemed to amiably agree, and at least Eleri didn't feel she'd missed anything obvious. But something about the dream she couldn't quite remember scratched at the back of her brain. "I think we go out to the cliffs where the car went over, and we start retracing paths. It all connects somehow."

53

"It looks like it would have happened here." Eleri pointed to the ground. "The trees here are young. It was possible then, though no car would be able to drive through here now."

She watched as Christina turned around, looking all directions from the center of what Eleri believed was the path the red Falcon must have taken on its final dive into the water.

"It makes sense." Christina took several steps forward, watching the ground as she moved.

The rest of the land was open—easy enough to drive through— but not quite open enough to put a car exactly where the Falcon had been found.

"The tree line makes it look like the forest moved in the last several decades. If they didn't drive through here, I don't know how the car could have gone down where it did." This time, Christina moved to the edge of the bluff, where she looked over into the dark, cold water.

There were still marks from where the truck had been planted to winch the Falcon out of the lake. Also where the backup crane arm had been anchored. The car had needed to come out straight up.

Eleri could almost see it replay in her mind. They'd done a good job, but it hadn't been easy. Figuring out exactly how the car had wound up there in the first place—thirty plus years after all the evidence out here had eroded away and been trampled over—was harder. Eleri back traced those movements the best she could.

The car had been stuck on a ledge, the back axle catching on a protrusion from the side. It wasn't quite a sheer drop downward, and likely the Falcon wasn't the only thing that had gone over, just the biggest and the one that got caught the shallowest.

She was still thinking it through as she stepped back. "But why would they have run off the cliff in the first place?"

Christina paced what they now believed must have been the path the car followed.

"What would make you drive off of a cliff?" Eleri spoke out loud the thing that continued to most bother her about the scene. "Why would they be driving up here anyway?"

"Same as we did," Christina suggested. "Or sightseeing."

Jennifer and Ben weren't sightseeing. He had a fresh bullet wound in his side. There was missing money. Their deaths hadn't been casual or even purely accidental. She was still trying to work it into something usable. "The money they took was from Los Angeles. So why come here?"

"Maybe *because* it's far from Los Angeles." Christina shrugged then waved her open hand at the edge. "And I'm thinking you don't go over this cliff unless you're drunk or high or being chased."

Eleri crossed her arms as the wind picked up. Wade had called. He was now less than thirty minutes away and she was looking forward to seeing one of her oldest friends. But she tried to get work done before he arrived. He would bring new information with him, and it would all scramble again, she knew.

"So, the logical conclusion," Eleri added, "is that they were being chased because they stole a sizable sum from Miranda Industries—"

Christina added, "And in those days, it was a much more sizable sum."

It felt to Eleri as if some of the pieces were being put together, but she didn't have the whole picture yet. Just glimpses. "So maybe they didn't necessarily come here. Maybe they were driven here—I mean pushed this way *because* Miranda was chasing them."

"Whatever it was that got them to Minnesota, I think Miranda was literally chasing them when they went over the cliff." Christina was looking at her now, as if asking if Eleri agreed. She did. Christina kept going. "Maybe it *was* an accident. Maybe they thought they could ditch the car in the water and swim away unseen."

But even in the summer, Eleri knew, the water was far too cold to be survivable for more than just a little while. Certainly not if they were trapped in the car or knocked out cold from the impact.

"If Miranda knew that they were in the car and Miranda knew that they had the money … Why didn't they try to get the money back?" Christina asked.

She was no longer standing at the edge of the cliff but had paced another handful of feet back. At least that made Eleri worry a little less that something might happen and her friend might go over and into the water herself.

A cloud passed in front of the sun casting a shadow across them. It was swift moving but Eleri felt it more as a metaphor than a meteorological happening. She turned and looked down the long slope that led to the bluff and saw only a single car in the distance. The small gray sedan made her smile.

In her pocket, her phone buzzed. Pulling it out, Eleri was prepared to see Wade's name. But it was Avery's instead.

She froze.

Could she answer this?

Christina looked out over the bluff again as if putting pieces together.

The phone buzzed again, but Eleri decided she couldn't deal with Avery right now.

She looked down the road until the phone stopped buzzing. Wade was almost here, but he was still several turns away. Her brain hopped to another point and she said to Christina, "But they had the money in the car, and MI was chasing them, MI would want the money. All they would have to do was send divers down." Eleri pointed out. "So maybe MI did dive for it, and they got the cash back."

"But they didn't," Christina countered. As Christina turned around, Eleri saw her face change as she also saw the car in the distance and waved to Wade.

It would be a few minutes before he arrived though, and she kept talking. "They didn't get the money. MI started up with exactly the missing amount less. So, whether or not they sent divers for it, they didn't find it. The money wasn't in the Falcon and—whether or not they knew that upfront—they had to have eventually figured that out."

The small gray sedan was pulling up closer, but Christina used her last few minutes to point out a whole new set of possibilities. "It would seem the very fact that the divers found the car a few weeks ago is what triggered this whole chain of events. The divers found the car and the bodies, then we got called in, and that in turn notified Miranda that the money was in play again all these years later."

Eleri nodded along as she casually pulled her phone out and looked. No message. She put it away again. She looked up at Christina. "That sounds about right. But who are Mila Panas and Brian Abadi?"

They knew at least some of it. Though Christina's quick Google search hadn't turned up much on Mila Panas, the following morning the analysts had had plenty to say. The two were young hip up and comers—Abadi more than Panas—from the Chicago area. Aside from the fact that they were obviously traveling together now, there was no known prior connection between the two.

Panas' credit cards had pinged all over the US in the last few weeks, and Eleri had not been surprised to learn that one of the places the young woman had visited was Duluth, Minnesota. She had no doubt now that the hole where she and Christina had set the copper bowl to cast their spell looking for Donovan had been dug by Mila Panas just prior to their visit.

"Did they bury the money near here?" Eleri turned to Christina, even as she could hear Wade's car slowly getting closer. "I saw Mila digging. And, if she actually thinks she's Jennifer Barnes, then maybe she knows where the money is."

With a slow dawning realization, Christina began to nod. "That may mean our job right now is less about the two bodies in the car and more about finding Mila Panas and Brian Abadi and protecting them. Because no matter how they know that information, simply knowing it puts them in Miranda's sights."

"Exactly." Eleri said, at last turning around at the sound of an engine stopping behind her.

The small gray sedan had finally arrived. With a smile on her face, she stepped forward to greet her old friend.

But it wasn't Wade who climbed out of the car.

54

"This is petrifying."

Mila heard the terror in Brian's voice, but she disagreed. "It's *exhilarating.*"

"You're just like her." He said the words as an accusation.

He meant she was just like Jennifer. Mila didn't know if the comparison was good or bad. She only knew that it pleased her an inordinate amount that he was admitting that he had all of Ben's memories—that he remembered Jennifer Barnes and what she was like. In no way was Mila in love with Brian Abadi, but she remembered being in love with Benjamin Hartman. He and their coming child had been her everything then.

When they'd been forced over the cliff and they knew they were going into the water—in those last few moments when she still had hope that they would survive—she'd reached out and grabbed his hand.

Mila remembered the shock of cold water. She remembered coming to, slumped against the dash of the large car. Hitting the water had thrown them into the dash far harder than she'd ever expected. Mila had not been prepared for an accident in a car without seatbelts, but now the ripstop nylon bag once again sat in the back seat of a cherry red '63 Ford Falcon, and somehow seemed to set the bad memories to rights.

Brian made almost as much money in a year as was still in the bag.

At least that's what Mila had put together from where he lived and what he wore and the title on his business card. She hadn't made any "30 under 30" lists, and she certainly wasn't going to make them now that she'd left thirty behind several years ago. But she was doing just fine for herself. She didn't need a bag full of stolen money. Because that's what she knew it was.

"What are we even going to do with it?" Brian asked. "We can't run away and start over."

"Why not?" Though the prospect of living with Brian Abadi wasn't high on her list, she really wanted to know what his protest was.

"It's a digital age, Mila. There's facial recognition. The second you use your card at a gas station, they know where you are. Everything tracks and, no, I'm not going to a cash only system and putting black war paint on my face so the cameras can't recognize me." He paused and huffed out a breath. "We have to do something with this. I think we should go back to the FBI agent."

"Really?" Mila frowned at him. Turning from her position in the passenger seat, she studied his profile. Despite the fact that they were on the freeway and moving fluidly with traffic, his knuckles were white on the steering wheel. It was just one of their problems but they were not keeping a low profile in his very recognizable car.

People smiled and waved just for seeing them out in an antique with the top down. Mila smiled and waved back. Brian mostly looked like his lunch didn't agree with him.

Though dread settled around her heart at the idea of going back to Minnesota—back to a place where she had clear memories of dying—she knew they needed to go there first. Still, that certainty quelled her fears that she might meet the same untimely death twice.

All she said was, "Something is there, and we need to go. Whatever it was, we didn't finish it the last time."

55

W ade felt a knot twisting deep in the pit of his stomach. He was supposed to reunite with Eleri and Christina, but someone else had beaten him here.

Whoever the man was, Eleri was stepping back from him. The mystery man had arrived in a gray, four-door sedan, and it looked like he'd only just arrived himself.

Wade had expected a happy reunion and, instead, he was facing an intruder. Worse, he was looking at the intruder's back and had no idea who he was, or what the threat was, only what he could read from Eleri and Christina's faces.

Opening the door, Wade climbed out and slammed it shut behind him. Letting them all know he was there. As the tall man turned around, Wade took note of the dark hair, blue eyes, and intense expression. He had broad shoulders and a look that was almost too prescriptively casual—as though he were trying to appear so but wasn't.

The wind shifted and the scent made Wade growl.

Wolf.

Behind the man, Eleri took a step forward. Now that he wasn't facing her, her expression changed, and her mood clearly shifted.

"Wade!" she called to him with an exclamation point at the end of his name. "Welcome. This is Victor Leonidas."

The man whipped back around and looked at her, clearly startled that she knew his name. To which Eleri replied, "We aren't as dumb as you think we are."

Wade was walking into something he wasn't prepared for, so he had to be prepared for anything.

"Who was the woman in our hotel room?" Christina demanded.

Wade was grateful that they had brought him up to speed and he already knew about the unfortunate housekeeper. And that Eleri and Christina's room had been tossed. *Was this the man who had done it?*

Tipping her head so Eleri could see around the large blockade that was Victor Leonidas, she said to Wade, "He's Westerfield's man, an undercover NightShade agent embedded in Miranda Industries for almost five years."

So, this was the agent. Wade had known there was someone—or several someones. With a few quick steps, Wade moved around to the other side of the man, lining himself up with Christina and Eleri. All three of them faced the newcomer, or maybe the old comer. Though Wade had been an agent in the NightShade division for a long time, he clearly hadn't worked with everyone.

He waited for Leonidas to answer Christina's question.

"I don't know her, and I don't know what that was about." It wasn't much of an answer.

"So, what you're suggesting ..." Eleri tag-teamed her way in, "is that you came into our room, left us a note, and then later someone came into our room and left us another message—only this one involved a slit throat and blood on the floor."

"I don't think they were supposed to leave you anything other than the knowledge that they'd been through the place. It's my understanding it was more of a threat."

Some threat, Wade thought.

But Leonidas stood with his hands on his hips. He seemed irritated more than anything else, even though that didn't make sense to Wade. But Eleri had already switched topics, letting this one go.

"Where's Donovan?" she demanded.

"That's just it ..." This time Leonidas' eyes looked upward, the blue sky dotted with cotton ball clouds belying the tense conversation that was taking place here on the cliff. And instead, he answered, "You don't know who you're working for."

"Westerfield?" Christina asked. "No, we don't know everything, but we know that we don't."

The other agent nodded slowly, taking that in, and Wade recalled conversations he and Donovan and Christina and Eleri had had in Florida—in which all of the concerns the various agents felt had started to congeal. When he learned he wasn't the only one who thought it was a possibility that Westerfield wasn't on the up and up.

"So, where's Donovan?" Eleri pressed again. "Is Westerfield leaving him in Miranda, attempting to create yet another embedded agent?"

Something in her phrasing made Wade realize that she and Christina also suspected that Leonidas wasn't the only finger their boss might have in Miranda's pie.

When Leonidas didn't answer, Christina got more aggressive. "You said he was alive, so where is he?"

This time, the undercover agent looked them square in the eyes. "When I left you that note, I'd seen him the day before. He'd been removed from his medications, and he was up and around."

Wade could see Eleri's reaction to that. The intense relief that streamed through her was difficult to separate from his own. They'd all felt the loss of Donovan Heath keenly.

Then Leonidas added, "But the next day he was gone."

"What do you mean? *Gone?*" Eleri's tone was tense, her arms crossing and uncrossing, her body unable to find a comfortable position in this conversation.

"No one in Miranda can find him. At least not that I know of. I was hoping he'd be here with you."

But Donovan wasn't here. Eleri and Christina had gotten that note a number of days ago. That meant Donovan was absolutely missing for that long. But there wasn't time to press Leonidas for more answers, because an ominous convoy of large, dark SUVs was coming up the trail along the bluff.

56

Behind Leonidas' shoulder, Eleri could see three black SUVs racing up the trail.

"Do you know them?" she asked calmly.

His expression fell. "Shit. I didn't think they'd follow me here."

"What did you tell them? That you were going to come *take care of us?*" Eleri almost lifted her fingers to make air quotes but realized at the last moment that she couldn't afford to let anyone in the distance see her do it. Leonidas' cover might depend on her playing along. Then again, her life and her friends' lives might depend on something else. She didn't know yet.

"Do they suspect you?" Christina asked.

"They might now!"

It hadn't occurred to Eleri, until the moment Christina asked, that this could do more than just blow his cover. It could get him killed. But she wasn't ready to die for it herself. "Were you prepared for this?"

"Always." He reached behind his back, pulling a gun from where he must have had it stashed in the waistband of his overly contrived jeans.

Eleri raised an eyebrow. Surely the people in the SUVs couldn't see that from the convoy.

"You either need to beat me within an inch of my life and leave or let me capture you." He waited a heartbeat as he waved the gun at them and mouthed a soft, "Get out!"

Eleri wanted to ask if the gun was even loaded, but the convoy was very close. They would be opening doors and pouring out in just a moment, and she had no idea if each car held two people or ten.

"Where would we go?" Wade asked as the tires screeched behind Leonidas, effectively blocking in the car Eleri and Christina had arrived in.

Wade's sedan was at least a little further back. Maybe they could run for it. But as she watched, the last SUV in line swerved slightly, squealing its tires and placing itself directly across his back bumper. *Too late.*

Leonidas offered a whispered, "I'm sorry," as he rushed at the three of them.

Eleri would have pulled her own gun, but hers was loaded. And she knew to never point a loaded gun unless she intended to kill her target. She wasn't there yet, but her brain had jumped into hyperdrive even as she stepped back to avoid the man rushing at her.

Leonidas was an FBI agent by training, he wouldn't carry an unloaded gun. And, as a Miranda operative, he wouldn't hesitate. If anyone at Miranda had discovered him carrying an empty chamber, he would have been laughed out of town. His cover would have been blown either as an agent or an idiot.

So, Eleri was confident now that there was a bullet in that chamber staring her down. And, unlike an agent, he didn't rest his finger alongside the trigger. He had it in place where a twitch could kill her or one of her partners … one of her friends.

Eleri, Wade, and Christina continued slowly stepping backward, getting closer to the edge of the bluff as doors slammed and military-black-ops looking soldiers began to unfold themselves from the SUVs. She saw all of that in the periphery. Her focus followed the barrel of the gun. He would hit Christina. Maybe he was aiming right beside her.

Eleri was reaching for her own gun when she stumbled. Leonidas swung quickly, once again aiming at her. This wasn't the first time she'd seen down the barrel of a gun, but it was maybe the first time she wasn't confident the person aiming at her was willing to shoot.

Her brows pulled together, her expression narrowing at him as she tried to read his intentions. Probably not a good look. But she got nothing but the roaring of a sea or the tv static of her childhood. *Why couldn't she hear him?*

Behind him, she now saw a contingent of bodies lining up. Some had handguns, but most held longer range rifles. For a moment she was struck by the sheer militaristic scenario of the operation.

Beside her, Christina and Wade's eyes flew wide, and she realized they'd seen this before at the de Gottardi/Little compound.

These soldiers had helmets and protective eyewear. What appeared to be kevlar vests, and deep toned camouflage. They were much better protected than any of the agents. If she wanted to kill one, she'd have to hit the groin area and open a femoral artery or take out the neck or lower jaw. Those nearly impossible shots were her only options.

She could slow them down with a bullet to a limb, maybe explode the bone and stop them from coming even if it didn't kill them. But the idea of shooting someone in the kneecap as they moved was utterly ridiculous. Only the very best marksman even stood a chance of it. At Quantico, they were trained for kill shots, center mass only. But with the protective vests all it would do was leave a bruise.

She needed to make a decision and fast. And she needed that decision to happen in conjunction with two other people she couldn't quite communicate with.

Or could she?

With her hands down at her side, Eleri splayed her fingers wide and hoped no one noticed. She took a deep breath and closed her eyes, wondering if she would feel bullets ripping through her body as soon as she stopped looking. But she didn't.

The center of her mind opened, and she reached out to Christina and Wade. Even as she asked them to speak with her, she felt another fourth presence entering her circle.

Leonidas?

No. Someone else. But she didn't have time to process it.

Though she was confident she could now hear them, she'd acted too late. Her eyes flew wide, as she heard Wade growl.

She snapped her head to the side to see Leonidas tackle him. The undercover agent managed a few quick steps back as Wade stumbled backward from the heavy hit and tumbled over the side of the bluff.

57

Eleri stood frozen as she watched Wade disappear over the edge. There was nothing she could do except pray that he didn't hit anything on the way down.

Or was there?

Once again, she regretted that she had not grown up with her Grandmére's training. Her grandmother had disappeared and left Eleri's mother to be raised by her own grandmother—Grandmére. Her mother had left as much of that culture and knowledge behind as she could. The chain of passage had been broken and what should have come naturally to Eleri didn't.

Turning, she pushed her hands out toward where she'd last seen Wade, as if the motion alone could keep him away from the rocky sides of the bluff. The fall was far but shouldn't be fatally so. Hitting the water could be the worst of it, but it should cushion him from anything he encountered underneath it.

She didn't hear if he'd splashed into the cold depths or not, because Christina grabbed her, yanking her hands out of position and pulling her into the thin cover of the young trees.

In that moment, Eleri heard the sharp, heavy pop of a bullet leaving a chamber. A second pop was accompanied by a young tree next to her shattering into splinters and shards.

"Come on!" Christina hollered, dragging her away from Wade, whom she could now only hope was safe.

Reaching out behind her, Eleri snapped her fingers, putting him in a bubble of safety as best she could without the level of focus she was used to.

She knew now that her anger could generate big effects, but could her fear?

"Hide us!" Christina hissed.

Eleri no longer heard the pop and retort of individual guns, only the dull thuds as they hit the trees near her. Was Leonidas shooting at them, too? Was he going to let them die to maintain his cover? And even if he wasn't, was there anything that he could do to save them?

With a quick raise of her free hand, Eleri clenched it into a fist near her heart. Her eyes closed out of habit, and she stumbled as she attempted to cast the spell mid stride. Christina yanked her upright, keeping her moving forward.

Eleri tried once again. This time, she whooshed out a breath and felt the spell take hold. The next tree that popped and exploded was far behind them.

"Stop," Christina commanded softly, the two of them having reached the older tree growth where the thicker, wider trunks offered them better cover.

Looking out beyond the trees onto the open space of the bluff, Eleri could see that the MI gang in their military garb had stopped shooting. The muzzles of their long guns swung back and forth, as if unable to find a target.

Both Eleri and Christina breathed heavily as they stood together, silent, until Eleri attempted to take a step to one side. Christina yanked her back and they listened together as the leaves crunched under Eleri's feet.

Leaning in close, Christina whispered, "Did you stop them from seeing us? Or did you also stop them from hearing us?"

"I don't know." But so far, none of the guns had swung to aim towards them again.

Christina turned slowly, picking her way, stepping her foot down softly and Eleri wondered would anyone see the leaves move on the forest floor? Would they sense a distortion in the air and shoot at it?

The pair made it three steps and she was breathing out a heavy sigh of relief as she heard the voice in the distance behind her announce, "We've got a witch."

Son of a bitch. If they hadn't known before what she was, they all did now.

But of course they did. These were Miranda Industries operatives. They were wolves. Christina had been at the de Gottardi/Little compound when Miranda had worked in concert with the Dauphine sisters.

Hell, if these guys had worked with the Dauphines, then they likely expected Eleri's powers to be far greater than they were. Could she use that to her advantage?

"Then shoot everything!" One voice commanded, and again the bullets began flying.

The tree right next to Eleri exploded before she could even react. But Christina was faster, grabbing her hand and tugging her toward the ground. Quickly, they scooted behind two separate tree trunks, the pair of agents no longer touching.

Eleri felt the tree she squatted behind shimmy as it took a hit meant for her. Another voice entered the fray "Stop, stop!"

"If we kill them, we kill them!" another countered with the tone of a shrug.

At least the number of bullets seemed to have lowered.

"We can't cast against them," another said.

The words were softly carrying on the air and Eleri reached up and snapped her fingers, amplifying the sound. With the change, she heard a soft tread come from a distance on her left and she turned her head slightly but didn't see anything.

The trees were denser here. Despite the afternoon light, the shadows were long and dark. The next voice came clearly: Victor Leonidas.

"They might have hidden themselves, but we can find them. It's probably better to take them alive."

Jesus, Eleri thought. Was this Leonidas' version of being on their side?

Christina popped up motioning to Eleri, and they began running, but behind her she heard the noises of velcro ripping. With a quick look back, she saw two wolves were already down on all fours.

She'd never seen Donovan change. She hadn't been at the de Gottardi/Little farm when the wolves had come out in force. But right now, she was watching Miranda operatives throw off their protective gear and lean forward, shoulders rolling, hips twitching.

Collarbones moved in closer as the hair that ran naturally heavy on their arms appeared to get just a little longer and thicker.

The wolves came in shades from pale brown to pitch black. And they were coming.

"Run!" Christina yelled.

58

Christina pitched forward once again, waving her hand back until it connected with the hand Eleri swung forward to catch her. It was better for many reasons if they were linked.

Holding on tightly, they pushed forward. Eleri again pulled her free hand into a fist, moving it close to her chest and once again attempting to cast her invisibility spell.

Did it even matter though? The wolves had good eyesight but far superior smell. Could she cover their scent? She had no idea, but she needed to try.

Her foot caught tree roots as she wasn't looking, and she flailed downward harshly. Christina caught her again. This time though, the fall had been grand enough that Eleri felt the sharp pain as her arm yanked and extended to full force.

She was on one knee, but quickly managed to get her other foot under her, still holding her hand clenched in front of her chest. She looked up at Christina, "I have to cover our scent."

Because Christina had turned around to face her and haul her back to her feet, the conflict in Christina's eyes was clear.

Keep going? Or maybe stop and make the spell work better?

Christina tugged her upwards. "Do it."

"Push them!" Eleri countered as she dropped her hand.

Christina turned until she spotted the two wolves closest to them.

With the earlier spell still connecting them, Eleri felt and saw all that her partner did.

Christina sighted the first one, but Eleri fought to not pay attention. She needed her focus for her own work and Christina could make him believe he didn't see them. She could make him believe he shouldn't walk their direction at all.

As Eleri began whispering the first words to herself, she could hear the soft padding of his feet as he turned away. She opened her eyes briefly, wondering if any of it had worked. She felt the change as Christina set her eyes on the second wolf, but a third and a fourth had appeared.

They were no longer fighting with guns and bullets, but with claws and fangs.

Eyes clamping down tightly, holding her focus just on her words, Eleri recited them faster. She could still sense wolves approaching and she had to spend a portion of her attention on them.

If she couldn't see them, they could attack her or Christina with no warning whatsoever, because if Eleri's spell failed, they would be down for the count.

She peeked again, seeing Christina turning to yet another wolf and working on altering his plans. Eleri began the third round of her recitation. The whole chant, cycled three times through, needed to be complete for the spell to take root, though hopefully it was already beginning to work.

Several of the wolves were sniffing the air as though they suddenly didn't know which way to go. The ones further back seemed confused by the ones up front not knowing where their prey had disappeared to. One had even walked past Christina and Eleri and she wanted to take a moment to be glad that it was working but she couldn't spare it.

If more wolves were coming, her spell had to hold against them all. Christina was pushing them one at a time, and that was the best way to weave her particular brand of magic, but maybe it was time to think bigger. She had done it before, making an entire room of FBI agents believe the space was on fire.

The collective hallucination had been beyond realistic. Eleri had felt the heat coming off the walls, even as she had wondered how the walls could burn so hot so fast. She thought of it as she finished the third round of her spell and all she could do now was pray that it held. She didn't have a good enough sense of smell of her own to know if it had worked or not.

She turned to Christina. "Can you set the woods on fire?"

From the look in her partner's eyes, it was a novel idea. She'd been pushing the wolves to not come near them or not sense them or simply *want* to look the other way. But a fire could create enough distraction that the wolves should fear for their safety. Eleri and Christina—knowing it wasn't real—could run through it and maybe get away. Then they would have to find Wade, but one thing at a time.

Though the wolves knew that Eleri was a witch—and they might even believe she could start the fire—would they believe they could pass safely through it? Would they have any idea that it was an illusion? Even Leonidas likely didn't know what Christina's power was. Eleri was hopeful.

Christina nodded and took a step forward, planting her feet. It would take a moment for her to shift what she was doing, to aim it toward the entire lot of them.

Eleri stood watch as the wolves at the back of the pack aimed directly toward them. Whether the two agents were visible or not, whether the wolves could scent them, she didn't know.

Automatically reaching to her hip and her gun holster, she flipped the strap aside—her chosen holster was not quick release. She wanted everyone to know that if she'd shot someone, she'd had the time to think it through. Her thumb moved to the safety even as she lifted the gun and aimed.

She would hit these wolves between the eyes while Christina lit the forest on fire.

But which wolf might be Leonidas? Was he still out there beyond the trees looking human or had he joined his Miranda brethren here in the forest?

She didn't recognize his wolf form, not having seen it more than a few times and only in glimpses. She wouldn't know if she was hitting him, only that MI's sheer numbers made the odds that it was him lower. Still, it made her hesitate to pull the trigger.

Too bad, she decided, she couldn't be forced to make that decision. She sighted on the closest wolf, tilting her head slightly to aim her eyes down the barrel of her FBI issued gun. She was taking a slow breath and readying herself to pull the trigger when, beside her, Christina jolted forward.

Her partner was on the ground, on her hands and knees, a wolf on her back before Eleri could react.

She reached for her partner out of instinct, hoping to help her up but time spun out through her own terror. They'd thought all the wolves were in front of them, but at least several must have looped around behind.

Eleri had barely realized she needed to look behind herself when she felt the paws on her own back. As the force of the hit made her stumble and lose hold of Christina, she pitched face forward toward the forest floor.

Her adrenaline—already spiked—sent her thought process into the stratosphere. She twisted as she was hit and tried to maintain her grip on the gun. Hopefully she could shoot him as she hit the ground.

But she wasn't quite fast enough. The roots of the forest floor seemed to rise up and smack hard into her shoulder blade. Her head almost grazed the bark of a nearby tree, though she managed not to smack into the trunk and maybe knock herself out, her already too-slow responses weren't enough.

She tried to pull her arm up to shoot at the creature she still hadn't quite brought into focus, but her arm wouldn't move. It took a split second to realize the creature was on her and holding her limbs down. It was leaning in too close for her to execute any of her plans. Her arm was caught, pushed across her body. Though she held onto the gun, it was at an absolutely useless angle.

The wolf stood over her, on her, his paws pinning her shoulders, his mouth open, his breath fetid in her face.

She was thinking so fast that the world ran in slow motion. How could she save herself as he lunged in close, his jaw snapped down, fangs clicking together. Eleri jerked back, smacking her own head into the tree trunk this time. She managed to evade him though he missed by mere centimeters.

With a livid snarl, he opened his mouth and pulled his head back to gain speed for a second strike. Eleri used the chance to lift her gun, hoping to get it up under his chin even though his powerful paws still pinned one shoulder. But she only managed to strike him in the flank, putting his aim just a bit off. He still snapped at her, but the force of her unplanned strike sent him slightly to the side.

He would not give up. He would keep coming, and he did.

His rage rolled over her in a low vibrating growl as she wondered if Christina and Wade were even still alive.

Pulling back away from him as far as she could, Eleri found no way to escape a third time. The open jaws struck out at her face and she knew this would be it. If she survived, it wouldn't be pretty.

Only at the last moment, the pressure of his claws digging into her shoulders shifted. The teeth didn't make it to her skin. She didn't hear the snap of his fangs. Her eyes squeezed shut, as if not seeing him could stop it from happening.

But with the odd feeling, her arms came loose from where she'd been held. Her eyes finally opened to see the wolf lifted bodily off her. In her surprise, she raised the gun to shoot at him.

But then, beyond the wolf, she saw a familiar face.

59

The water was freezing cold as it swirled around him and sucked him downward.

Had he hit his head? Wade didn't know, but his skull pounded and he could feel himself drifting away. He likely only had moments before his body stopped responding all together to the signals his brain sent.

But as his lungs tried to open and his mouth fought to stay shut, the need for oxygen propelled him upward. With his eyes open, the water stung, but he could see light. He could see threads of his own red blood swirling past him, too. *Not good.*

Swimming was not his strongest suit, but he was passable in both forms. Aiming upwards, he cupped his hands and only as he got near the surface did he have the concern about gunfire coming in.

He could hear the pop of bullets beyond the surface of the water, probably somewhere on top of the bluff, but it seemed at least no one was shooting down toward him.

Breaking the surface with a massive inhale, Wade gulped for air. He spent a moment—far too long for his safety—simply balancing his need for oxygen. He was treading water, feeling the last of his heat seep from his body even as he did it. He didn't have time to stay here and make decisions.

Luckily, he was close to the bluff. Unluckily, it didn't appear it would be easy to climb. Looking side to side, Wade checked for better options. But the shoreline where he could just walk out was far enough away that he would likely become too hypothermic before he could get there.

Up. He had to go up.

It would put him into the line of fire. He could hear the guns overhead. And even the words, "They've got a witch!" came to him. In case he hadn't been scared enough when he went into the water, that managed to ratchet his fear up even higher.

He'd seen the Miranda operatives and their gear. They came ready to kill. He'd seen them like this before, at his own home. At least the rage warmed him.

With a few short, angry strokes, he was at the edge of the bluff, reaching up and trying to haul himself out. But his fingers didn't hold well, and his wet clothing tried to suck him back down under the water. He tried again, kicking hard, thinking that if he could propel himself up far enough, he could haul himself higher and out of the cold, dense lake.

But even as he made it halfway out, the khakis he'd been wearing —with wonderful cargo pockets full of the things that he'd always needed—were now lead weights. They were attached to his legs and belted around his waist and pulling him under. Wade could think of only one solution.

With one hand, he reached out to wrap his fingers into the nearest small gap in the rocks. But the rocks were worn mostly smooth, with just a few gaps here and there, just enough to make himself believe that he could—with enough adrenaline—perhaps free himself. Sticking his hand into the closest one he found, there was nothing to hold onto. So, he splayed his hand wide, turning it sideways and using it like an anchor, while he used the other to begin working at his clothing.

His wet shirt had to go first. It was one of his favorite plaid button-downs, and much harder to peel off now that it was wet and stuck to him. The white t shirt underneath had to go next. He had to keep letting go of the wall and switching which hand he used to anchor. It was taking far too long, and Wade could feel his core body temperature dropping as he did it. By the time he fumbled with his belt, he was also kicking his shoes off simultaneously with his feet because he was running out of time. His fingers weren't working well, his fine motor control already gone.

At last, he'd managed through sheer force of will and fumbling movements to peel it all away. Reaching up with one hand, he grabbed for the nearest hold and felt his finger slip against the rock. He realized what he needed to do.

Holding on for all he was worth, still half in and half out of the freezing water, he started. Grateful that at least the air was somewhat warmer, if not quite warm enough, he rolled one shoulder, altering where the socket sat. He felt it sink into a slightly different location. He watched as the hair on his forearms stood on end, looking thicker. Flexing his fingers, he felt every bone in his hand shift and move and curl. Then he watched as what most people mistook for normal fingernails extended.

Flinging his arm upward by force, because he lacked the fine motor control to do more, Wade sunk his newly exposed claws into the tiny gaps of the rock. He hauled himself higher with sheer brute strength and force of will, then rolled his other shoulder.

Slowly he climbed as he shifted one limb at a time. Shoulder blades pulling back, ribcage rounding as his muscles pulled him into his new shape. He was out of the water and dripping but no longer held back by sodden clothing. But he wasn't warm, he wasn't safe, and he wasn't anywhere near done. He was clinging to the side of the bluff, and if he stopped, he would fall back into the water.

Wade was certain he wouldn't survive it a second time.

He had no body heat anymore, and no idea if he would be of any use by the time he reached the top of the bluff. He honestly didn't know if he even had enough left in him to reach the top. With a growl from the depths of his core, Wade flung his other hand upward, claws sinking into the tiny cracks and crevices where a finger wouldn't fit, and he hauled himself up.

60

"Donovan!" Eleri exclaimed, her happiness at seeing him upright, and apparently hale and healthy, overshadowing the fact that they were likely both about to die. Worse yet, they would likely die at the hands of Miranda Industries.

With his grip on the wolf's scruff, he held it up and threw the creature back into the distance.

But there was no time for reunions. Eleri yelled, "Behind you!"

She'd managed to maintain her grip on her gun despite getting tossed around like rags, but now it was handy. No longer pinned, she pushed herself upright and aimed for the wolf coming up behind her partner.

But just as she was about to pull the trigger, she stopped. There was just enough distance for hesitation. *What if it was Leonidas?*

This wolf was a dark brown, almost black. Leonidas' coloring—though he wasn't the only one, not by far. A lighter color wolf she would have shot with no concerns. She counted down, letting the undercover agent alert her if it was truly him.

Three.

Two.

It snarled and growled, leaping toward Donovan. *Not enough time to get to one!*

Eleri pulled the trigger several times in rapid succession. Though the wolf continued its arc, it went limp midair. The two agents let it flop to the ground unceremoniously, dead.

With his hand out, Donovan reached down and pulled Eleri to her feet. In tandem, they turned around to find Christina standing, shaking, blood ran freely from cuts on her arms and across her shoulder. Another oozed blood down the side of her face.

Eleri almost asked "Are you okay?" But the question was ridiculous. Clearly, Christina was still alive but, no, she was not okay. Only then did Eleri notice the gun hanging loosely in Christina's hand.

"I set myself on fire," Christina said softly as if to no one.

The words would have made no sense coming from anyone else, but Eleri understood. At some point in the middle of being attacked, Christina had figured out that she needed to startle her attacker. Making herself seem to be suddenly ablaze must have worked. The wolf had likely drawn back for a moment—

"I shot him," she said into the air.

"*Good.*" Eleri reached out to take Christina's hand, then turned to Donovan. "We have to get out of here."

"Wade." Christina said, and Eleri shrugged.

"I don't know where he—"

"No. *Wade.*" This time, Christina pointed over Donovan's shoulder where a caramel-colored wolf was desperately hauling himself up over the side of the bluff.

It appeared that no one had noticed him except Christina. If he was lucky, maybe he could blend in with the Miranda Industries operatives. His head turning as if he knew exactly where to look, he met her eyes.

Eleri saw her old friend in there. Thirteen plus years ago, when she'd met Wade, she'd never envisioned this.

"He's probably cold," Donovan said, already moving toward the bluff. "Maybe hypothermic."

They couldn't just let him try to blend in. He might not make it and one of the soldiers would likely sniff him out sooner rather than later.

"I don't want to draw attention to him, they could attack." Eleri didn't like where they were. Wolves were behind them, Christina was hurt. Wade was at best far less than one hundred percent, and Donovan looked good, but she didn't know that for a fact.

"How do we get out there?" Donovan asked, searching through the trees as if there might be a path or better option.

"Can you walk?" Eleri asked Christina not sure if she was surprised when Christina nodded.

Though she took her first step, her partner faltered a little, and only then did Eleri realize there was a gash down her thigh as well.

Though Donovan could have thrown Christina's arm over his shoulder, he was taller than she was, and it might have hurt more than it helped. Eleri stepped in, buffering Christina and holding her upright.

"You lead," she told Donovan, "I'll try to cover us."

"I'll push," Christina offered though her voice held no force. Maybe now that she was battered and bloody the last of her ethics had slipped away.

Though Eleri understood Christina's desire to only use her skills when she was certain her reasons were solid and the need extraordinary, this was a fight for their lives. Christina's willingness to use a skill she'd tried so hard to mitigate and minimize was greatly appreciated.

Behind them, wolves paced the forest, noses to the ground. Eleri held tight to her gun in her free hand, her other wrapped around Christina's waist to support her. She wanted to just shoot them as she saw them. Let them drop dead from bullets from an unseen source, their bodies left in the woods. Miranda could deal with the clean-up later.

But she couldn't swivel easily. She couldn't take aim. So periodically she tried to look back over her own shoulder and Christina's. Still the wolves milled about trying to follow the duo who had become a trio. With grunts and whines, they communicated with seeming ease. If only Donovan and Wade could understand what they were saying.

Looking back to the bluff, she saw Wade was hauling himself up the last few inches. He fell onto the rock and grass, in worse shape than she'd expected. Had he been shot?

Wet and bedraggled, his every effort was put into saving himself. A lone black wolf further down the bluff checked both left and right before trotting toward Wade.

Was it Leonidas? Eleri wondered. Was there any way to ask? Was he even known by the name Victor Leonidas to the people at Miranda? She didn't know, so she couldn't even just call out to him.

But why the hell was she so concerned about protecting his cover? He had stood by as they'd nearly been slaughtered and Christina had been injured.

Just as the wolf reached Wade—obviously out of energy and easy pickings—the wolf turned and looked once. Though he didn't seem to see anything, he offered several short, sharp barks.

Whatever it meant, no one answered, and no one came to help.

Donovan, still moving forward, his long legs eating up the distance, turned back and said, "It's Leonidas."

Had he scented the man? Recognized him? It didn't matter; she trusted his assessment and kept pushing forward, feeling better. Leonidas might be undercover, but he most likely wouldn't kill Wade in cold blood.

As she got closer, she could see that Wade was breathing heavily, clearly exhausted. Blood matted his fur, still flowing from a gash on the back of his head. He wasn't even shivering, which concerned her more. So, she wasn't surprised when Donovan didn't seem to even assess his friend, but just leaned down and picked him up.

Could he do that? He'd been shot and on death's doorstep not that long ago? Had Miranda put them all at risk again so soon?

Standing Christina upright and making sure her friend was balanced, Eleri pulled her fist in close to her chest, hoping she could cast one more spell. Sadly, she was willing to let go of her friend before she was willing to let go of her gun—it was by far the safer option, though nothing about this was safe.

Christina took a labored breath and looked around. As Eleri clenched her fist and cast her spell, she heard a whoosh and crackle that startled her into opening her eyes. She watched in surprise as the entire forest burst into flames.

61

"It's the car. They recognize the car. We're easy to follow." Mila said.

She huffed out her breath with anger that masked her fear. Reaching across the center console, she grabbed on to Brian's arm. But just as quickly he shook her off, too tense to deal with both his own thoughts and her.

Behind them, the black SUV came closer. It was out of a nightmare or a bad action movie. And it was making a point so they would know they were being stalked, coming threateningly close before backing off. Then it would do it again. The road they were on now was small enough that there wasn't any traffic—or any witnesses— besides the two of them. The chances that this was some random dickhead were low. Too low.

She'd been concerned earlier, when the small silvery blue hatchback had followed them for so long. Surely bad guys wouldn't drive an economy car. Would they? But the small car, though it had paced them for hours on end, had done nothing ... Until it had switched out seamlessly with the larger SUV. It was almost like a dance and that had made Mila even more nervous. The car she was certain was following her was not only on its game enough to track her and Brian easily but was well enough coordinated with a full team to be able to switch out.

It had been a long, long drive. Mila was the one who'd insisted they push through, though now she wasn't sure why she'd done it.

Brian must be having the same thoughts. "Why did we come here?"

She shook her head. "I don't know."

"You said you *knew!*" his anger countered her uncertainty, and he smacked the palm of his hand against the old, thin steering wheel.

She squeezed her eyes and flinched. He wouldn't hit her, or at least Ben would never have hit Jennifer. *Brian?* She would have said no, but now she wasn't certain. She also remembered they'd had a gun in the car. Ben had stolen it from his neighbor, found it under the bag.

But now? She didn't think they had a gun this time.

She was the one who'd fucked up. "I knew we needed to come here, but I still don't know why."

The weather had been balmy days ago when they left Los Angeles, now it had turned cooler, just a little bit crisper the further north they had gone. Each time they took a turn, she remembered the roads. There was only one stretch where she'd felt it was entirely unfamiliar. It had bothered her enough that she'd eventually looked it up and found that the highway had been reworked and shifted about ten miles east fifteen years ago.

But now, as they neared the bluffs, the roads were old and familiar. Though they were much more built up than she remembered, the view in the distance had stayed mostly the same.

"Why are we here?" Brian pressed.

Mila noticed he didn't ask "Where are we going?"

As they turned onto smaller and smaller roads, the dark SUV with tinted windows stayed close behind them, sometimes even hugging their bumper. Unlike the smaller economy car from earlier in the trip, this one gave Mila no doubt that the driver meant harm. Had it actually been local assholes messing with a tourist, they should have peeled off and turned back miles ago.

No, this was for them. It was about them. It was about the money.

Turning her head from side to side, Mila swallowed harshly as if that action alone could make the flashes of memory go away. She heard the rev of the engine as the black SUV pulled precariously close behind them and held her breath until it slowly eased back again.

She'd sat in the passenger seat and ridden these same roads a lifetime ago.

"There's nowhere left to go," Brian said, "Except up toward the bluff."

He didn't want to go toward the bluff, Mila knew. She too remembered what happened the last time the two of them had been up here. Just like before, there had been a car chasing them—not a sleek black SUV like this. She couldn't even remember what it had been. Her memory wouldn't focus or allow her to turn and look over Jennifer's shoulder to see it. She only retained the memory that it had been there.

Reaching out she once again held onto Ben's hand ... *Brian's* hand.

"I'm not going over the edge again," Brian declared harshly.

She agreed, or she wanted to agree. She had gone to Olena Barnes' house and even recognized the woman as *her mother*. She had so many memories of Mrs. Barnes, wiping her head with a cool cloth and taking her temperature with a mercury and glass thermometer when she'd been sick as a kid. She remembered eating cereal together on Saturday mornings from brown-flowered Corning-ware bowls. And she could feel the way her lip curled when her mother insisted that she pose for a picture in the matching tops her mother had handsewn.

It had been embarrassing. The clothing was clearly homemade, her mother only passable with the sewing machine. It was awful as a teenager to be forced to wear anything, let alone the same outfit as your mother. Looking back, though, Mila could see the love and the pride and the gesture, and she could feel Jennifer's irritation, too. All of it existed in her now, the whole story.

Still, it hadn't stopped her from leading Brian down the steep back yard, toward the dock on the little lake. She'd gone into the shed her mother hadn't used since her father died. Jennifer had hidden her weed in there for a long time, and her mother had never found it. So, she'd felt comfortable leaving the black nylon bag of cash in there, too.

Mila had pulled away the crap her father had piled on the dirt floor ages ago. She remembered all of this as she dug her way into the dirt at the back of the shed and found the bag that she shoved there so many years ago. Her mother apparently hadn't touched anything in the shed since Jennifer had left.

What a life Olena Barnes had lived. She had lost so much. Mila recognized her as 'mother' and she felt all of it. Still, Mila and Brian had come and had disappeared. She'd barely found her daughter and Mila had stolen her away again.

This time, though, she intended to return. To explain everything. To be a daughter to the woman even if she couldn't be Jennifer.

Then the black SUV had pulled up behind them. Now, it was herding them toward the bluff.

Mila regretted every single one of her decisions. It seemed that for all she remembered and all that she knew, she should have made better choices. She should have been able to make it turn out better this time.

Had she thought she could find closure for Jennifer out here?

What a fool she'd been. The thought was jarred from her brain as the black SUV tapped on their bumper. Her head snapped backward into space in a car that had no modern day headrests. And her choices hadn't made any of this better … Only worse.

All she'd done was lead them here so they could repeat history.

62

Eleri stopped at the edge of the bluff but could only stand still for a moment as she surveyed the wolves still in the trees.

She didn't get to stop and be grateful that the four of them were back together. Wade and Donovan having arrived almost simultaneously was a stunning and welcome surprise. The rest was not.

Wade, at least, she knew how he got here. Donovan? Eleri still almost believed she was hallucinating though, right in front of her, Donovan made strides toward the cars with Wade draped, heavy, wet, and still bleeding, in his arms.

Behind them, the wolves ran toward them, fleeing the perceived forest fire. Though some went the other direction, a handful were coming fast their direction. Eleri didn't run, she had to trust her spell held, but mostly what she held was her breath.

With a shift of her stance, Eleri tried to bolster Christina better as they picked their way through discarded clothes and weapons. Her partner's gait was off, noticeably weak on one side and it worried Eleri. But they had to keep going. God forbid the wolves got back to their abandoned belongings and changed quickly enough to pick up the guns.

"Wade's car," she told Donovan, pointing to the back. Though they were all partially blocked in, his had the best shot at escape.

"Keith," Wade muttered, offering only some mild movement in Donovan's arms with the faint word that appeared in her head.

She wasn't even sure what he'd said.

Keith?

As much as it made no sense, it was wonderful that he was following the conversation.

Then he added, "In the lake."

Keys! Eleri realized.

She was listening to him in her mind, the old spell must have held! She'd cast it between her and Donovan before she'd handed him into whatever care or hell he'd been in for the last weeks. It must have been a broader net than she thought.

Could she hear the Miranda wolves? Or did the wolf in question need to direct his thoughts toward her?

There was no time for such academic pursuits right now. "He shifted," she told Donovan, who raised an eyebrow as if to ask if she'd caught the stupid.

She wanted to laugh and cheer, but in getting Donovan back, she might have lost Wade or Christina ... or both.

"He peeled his clothing to get out of the lake!" Eleri clarified, "And his keys went with them."

Donovan nodded and shifted direction.

As of yet, no wolves seemed to have seen them—or scented the fresh blood from Wade—though their haggard crew was walking through open space. The lack of wolves didn't help them with the next piece, or the next. In the movies, people reached under the dash, pulled out a few wires, and started a car, but it didn't work like that in real life. Certainly not in a modern car or a rental.

She almost laughed, hysteria bubbling up in her at the thought of calling her roadside assistance to come out and let them in and give them a backup key. She couldn't cast a spell to start the car or manufacture a key. She could push and pull things, not do alchemy.

Behind them, wolves paced the edge of the forest. A quick glance over her should revealed odd behavior. They checked themselves over, a few took the daring risk to jump back in to save friends. But others stood back and looked at the burning trees with a suspicious eye.

She didn't know how long she had before they figured it out ... or before Christina's energy drained low and the vision disappeared.

She remained grateful none had seen them yet, but as she turned and looked the other way, her grasp around Christina's waist faltered. Her right hand still gripped the gun tightly as she watched several of them approach their discarded items and start to move.

Eleri's eyes widened as they began to shift and stand up on two feet. *It was fascinating.*

She almost stopped and watched in awe, but for the fact that two of her friends were possibly near dead.

Miranda's soldiers stood upright in their nakedness, no shame whatsoever. Several men and women walked bipedally back toward their clothing. They looked around, their human expressions easier to read. They were confused, and desperate to find their quarry.

One even cut just in front of Eleri and Christina. Eleri pulled back, jolting her injured friend, and grateful that Christina had the sense not to yelp or gasp. Though, from the sudden tension in her limbs, Eleri could tell the sudden move had hurt her.

"Our car," she whispered to Donovan.

As soon as the soldier reached down and picked up her things, Eleri began moving, and quickly ushered them out of range. Had the operative scented the air? Did she know she'd come so close to her prey? It didn't seem she had. It took several forced long breaths to slow down Eleri's heart rate.

Then she turned to Donovan. "Your car?"

"Don't have one."

Curiouser and curiouser. How had he gotten out here without a car?

Hers had three SUVs at various angles behind it, that would make her escape difficult, but not impossible. At least she hoped. The car was close, and it would have to prove to be rugged, but unlike Wade she did still have her keys.

Though she feared the loss of immediate access to her weapon should she need it, she re-holstered her gun to grab them.

Their little band couldn't run. They made their way slowly toward the rental car. Wolves passed through and around them. One walked right between her and Donovan as they both squeezed their eyes shut and held their breath and prayed that no one could sense them in any way.

Could she stop the wolves if they attacked? It was better not to find out.

As they got close, she clutched the keys and realized clicking the button to unlock the car would alert everyone. But then she remembered she hadn't locked it.

It seemed ages ago that she and Christina had been the only ones up here. They'd been retracing the scene from thirty years ago and brick by brick piece after piece had fallen away and left them with this horror.

She and Donovan went to opposite sides of the car and as they stood still, they looked at each other over the roof. Once they started opening doors, they'd bring the wrath of the wolves directly to them. The fire in the trees was already starting to wane and Eleri took it as a sign that Christina was declining. From the looks of it, she couldn't even tell if Wade was still alive. She'd gotten no messages from him again that would confirm he was still in there.

"We have to get in quick," she whispered to Donovan.

He nodded, still holding the weight of his friend in his arms. Wade's breathing had become slower and shallower; she'd only now realized it as Donovan stood motionless for a moment.

With a small nod, Donovan turned to her. They would time their moves and make it fast.

She stood across the car from him, on the passenger side, Donovan waited by the driver's side backseat. She was going to load Christina and he would load Wade.

Donovan looked around, not making his move, and it took Eleri a moment before it clicked. He was waiting for the wolves to be as far away as possible, which had to happen randomly because they didn't see the four FBI agents standing there.

Then he looked down at Wade and back up at Eleri. "It's the best we're going to get." Then he added, "Now!"

He set Wade down, his friend's feet barely touching the ground as Donovan threw the car door open wide. With one hand, he basically threw Wade inside and shoved the back door closed before scrambling around to the other side.

Eleri yanked her own door open and pushed Christina in, but Christina at least was upright enough to force her away. "Go!"

Trusting Christina to get herself settled, Eleri ran around the back of the car. The front was aimed toward where the wolves were, and she couldn't risk getting any closer. Because, as soon as the doors had swung open, heads had turned. The wolves began running directly to them, even if they couldn't see the agents, they knew something wasn't right here.

Some of the operatives came on two feet. Others, on all fours, were faster. Eleri slammed her door shut as one raked his claws down the hood of the car.

63

S tarting the car, her heart felt as if it were beating as fast as the RPM of the engine. Eleri slammed her foot on the gas, jolting the car forward and throwing the wolf on the hood to the ground.

She felt the sickening rock of the car as they rolled over some body part. She didn't care about his life. Everyone she cared about was already in the car.

She couldn't go backwards. One of the SUVs had parked bumper to bumper with her in an attempt to block her in.

But the road just trailed off as it reached the bluff, so they would simply drive over the grass and exposed rock surface. If she scraped the bottom of the car, she wouldn't care. She *couldn't* care—there wasn't room for it.

Eleri spun the wheel and realized the rock in front of her rose too far out of the ground. Fearing getting caught—high centering the car —she swore, then slammed the gears into reverse. If she ran over the wolf again, she would forget about it later, she promised herself.

Beside her, Christina winced at the movement and still tried to put her seatbelt on. At the same time she tensed in the seat, simply trying to stay in place as Eleri slammed them around.

Donovan was looking over the seat into the back, reaching his hand out and seeming to pick through what they'd left there. "Is there anything here I can use? Any clothing or blankets?"

He quickly gave up and began peeling his shirt.

There wasn't even a change of her own clothing in the trunk like usual—not after the hotel room had become a crime scene. She was wearing the last of what she had as they hadn't been back to retrieve anything yet.

Shit! Of all the times to have a bag with a copper bowl, a handful of herbs, a book, and nothing else!

She hit the shift, again slamming the car into reverse as she shimmied it forward and backward. The MI operatives had jammed them in better than she'd estimated.

The wolves threw themselves at the hood and the windshield. At least three wolves clawed at the back, but she didn't care. Eleri leaned over and put her arm on the back of Christina's seat as she twisted her head around and peered through the back window. She could see guns being raised in the background.

"Get down!" she yelled into the space of the car, no longer caring what the wolves saw or heard. Lowering her own head even as she backed up further than she needed to, Eleri managed to slam into another one of them. A sickening crunch of bones and the yelp of a human voice shuddered down her spine, but she told herself again that she didn't care.

She and Donovan ducked quickly, but Christina wasn't so fast. A gunshot ricocheted through the car taking out the back window. Then the front window answered with a pop and a hole and an instantaneous spiderweb. This car was not bulletproof.

Eleri could still see enough though, and she slammed the gear back as far as it would go sending them into drive. Smashing the gas pedal yet again, she lurched forward. The car lifted and tilted as one wheel hit rock and another soft grass. Then the ground traded beneath them and the car rolled them the other way.

She had made it onto the gravel at the end of the road and aimed her way down the hill. Gravel sucked, but it was better than grass and rock, and she followed it. Speeding down the path as best she could, they rocked and hit ditches. Christina's groans had to be ignored or they'd all wind up dead. Eleri swallowed the thought down.

What would she do if one of them died while they raced away?

Then she heard behind her the sound of doors being slammed and engines starting. Enough of them must have changed back to bipedal to operate the cars.

Sure enough, Donovan's face popped into her rearview mirror as he huffed out a scared, "They're coming."

Three large black tinted SUVs—the same ones she'd seen rolling their way up the bluff when she'd stood there talking to the undercover operative—were now hunting her down. Then and only then, did it occur to her that she might have hit Victor Leonidas. Still, she found she couldn't dig up any concern. It was entirely possible he'd led Miranda to them. Whether by accident or not, it didn't matter to her. Two of her closest friends were in bad enough shape that she could only hope they would survive this day.

Behind them, one of the SUVs spun its tires as they hit the gravel. Eleri was grateful that the crappy road slowed them down, too. Another wove its way in front of that one, taking over the lead position as the second one got its bearings. Operatives climbed into the third quickly, as intent on loading their weapons as themselves.

Her sideview mirror hadn't cracked at all and as she glanced back she started making contingency plans. MI soldiers could shoot and hit the back of the car and likely all the occupants would be fine. But if they took out a tire it would slow her down—maybe send them off the road and kill them. At least slow them enough to get caught. Eleri began to weave back and forth every once in a while, just enough to make aim difficult.

Her mouth opened with a scream that never erupted as she swerved back to avoid a car coming the other way. A large red boat of a car, it tried to keep to its own side. Her swerve was just enough to miss it, and no one else in her car seemed to have noticed.

Jesus, she was going to have to watch out for cars, animals, and even people. Her breathing had ratcheted up with the near miss and wasn't slowing back down. Just as she managed a few deep breaths and to pull her focus back to the road, the pop of gunfire behind them confirmed her fears and had her checking the mirror again.

She could now see one of the operatives was hanging out the side window of the car like a fucking idiot. He wasn't going to hit them. If he did, it would be sheer luck. Still, he was sending bullets their direction and she would have to watch out for them.

But, in the other car, it appeared one of them had shot out her own front windshield to be able to sit anchored in the passenger seat. She was going to be more of a threat.

"Maps!" Eleri yelled back at Donovan over the wind rushing through the now open car.

He replied quickly, "No phone."

Eleri began digging in her pocket but somehow Christina managed to be faster. So maybe her new partner wasn't quite as injured as she looked. Eleri could only pray that was the case.

With her phone handed back to Donovan, Christina once again, softly—at least as softly as she could—settled into a still position in her seat.

Eleri had been wrong. Christina had simply made a life-saving move. *She was not okay.*

As their tires finally hit the pavement, Eleri heard the squeal as they slipped then found their hold. Hopefully Donovan could find them a way out of this. The roads up here had been long and winding but if they could find a side road, they might be able to duck away and hide.

Behind them, though, were three different SUVs—any of whom could catch up or branch off, giving MI a huge advantage in this chase. They could waste a vehicle, or two, and still keep coming.

So, Eleri simply had to be the fastest. Keeping the gas pedal as far down as it could go, she took the turns at far too high a speed. Her passengers had to feel the tires lift on one side of the car. But rolling over was the least of her concerns as she heard another pop behind her and her sideview mirror exploded.

64

Their car had taken any number of hits from the bullets MI had thrown at them. But though they were still upright and driving, Eleri couldn't breathe safely yet.

Donovan had been worried about Wade and only able to throw a few volleying shots back. He'd managed to hit the lead car or blasted out a tire or just scared them. She couldn't tell, but the big SUV had spun out and crashed into the rock side of the road.

The other two chase cars seemed not to care about their dead or injured colleagues and the remaining two simply filled the missing space. The second car had taken the next turn at the same speed Eleri did. Though she had wished for an SUV, she changed her mind as she watched the big black beast tip and roll.

Good riddance.

Though she'd tried a spell to hide her entire vehicle from view, it hadn't worked. Hiding cars might be easier when she wasn't also driving. Or maybe she was just out of magic for the day. It didn't matter the reason, she couldn't let it kill them.

But maybe it *had* worked.

They'd pulled further and further ahead until she couldn't see the remaining car. *Had it given up?*

Her adrenaline was high, and her faith was low.

She turned to look at Donovan once again trying to calm her racing pulse. "How do we find a vet for Wade?"

She wanted to ask if he could shift back into his human form, but she hadn't seen him move at all in some number of miles. His head wound was still bleeding into the back seat. Even she could smell it now. Shifting was high energy—she knew that much—and she was petrified that Donovan would reply that there was no point.

It didn't escape her notice that she was asking for the very same thing for Wade that she'd asked for Donovan not so long ago.

She had no idea what kind of vet would be able to treat him here and what they would do once they x-rayed him. God forbid, they found a vet who knew exactly what her friend was. Apparently, the likelihood around here that a vet would know about the wolves was higher than in other places. But then the risk of the vet being in MI pockets went through the roof.

If Duluth, Minnesota was a Miranda Industries operating ground then they likely had vets already in place, just like in Florida. She could be handing Wade over exactly as she had done with Donovan. Only—this time—it wouldn't be unknowingly.

"No vet," Donovan said, "ER for Christina."

"But Wade—"

"I've got it." He sounded confident enough to push aside her fears. But then she realized that it might mean Wade wasn't salvageable.

Her eyes still turned and looked periodically using the remaining mirror on Christina's side of the car to try to determine if anyone was still behind them. Sometimes she simply had to swivel her head around and look. But they hadn't been shot at in long enough that both she and Donovan at least had resumed sitting upright.

For her, it was the only way to see through the shattered wind-shield. She tried to think of everything, and not miss a single option. She could handle the sickening crunch of running over a Miranda Wolf. She could handle it even if it had been Victor Leonidas. She had no issues with watching the black SUV crash and possibly kill the inhabitants or the other rolling as the body tried to collapse inward. But if she heard the silence of Wade passing because she'd made a bad decision, she would never be able to live with that.

Should they pull over somewhere and call an ambulance? But that would require knowing that there was an ambulance close by. Should she speed? She didn't have a red or a blue light to reach up and stick on the top of the car, like in one of those cool cop shows. Sure enough, as Donovan's directions took them into more populated territory, a police car pulled in behind them lights flashing.

Of course they did, Eleri thought with a sigh as the blue and whites almost gave her a seizure. The officer was obligated to check out a car speeding through town with shot-out windows.

Eleri tipped one hip up, still not properly belted in, but that was the least of her worries. She didn't care about herself, but she was grateful when her fingers swept through her pocket and closed on the leather wallet. It would be too windy and she might lose it if she tried to hold it open in the wind out the open window. But she had to try.

No, not the wallet. The badge. It came on a small holder, tight and compact.

She held it out the window, hoping the officer would recognize that she wasn't an average citizen blowing through his town.

From the backseat, she heard a voice on the phone and instantly recognized that Donovan had called 911. "What's your emergency?"

"My name is agent Donovan Heath, FBI. One of your officers is trailing my car with lights flashing. I need him to take lead and escort us with lights and sirens to the nearest hospital."

Smart move, Eleri thought. There was another question from the woman that Eleri couldn't make out. But Donovan answered, "I cannot pull over. I have two gravely injured FBI agents and we are on our way to seek treatment. You can turn your man into an escort or he can trail us all the way to the hospital. If he interferes with my agents getting proper care, I will be arresting him."

Wade and Christina might be injured, but Donovan was in full form. She almost smiled, but beside her a small huff of air came from Christina, letting her know just how damaged her friend truly was. But she had to wonder again, if Donovan was taking them to a hospital, had he written Wade off?

He wouldn't, she told herself. Even if she didn't understand the move he was making, that wasn't the kind of thing that he would do.

Within moments, the officer behind them had tweaked his sirens to give a couple of short blares, letting them know he was no longer in pursuit. The dispatch operator must have gotten to him. He sped up, somehow going faster than Eleri, who was at what she thought was the fastest possible speed that wouldn't get them killed.

As he pulled out into the empty oncoming lane, the officer stuck one hand out the window, his index finger up in the air, making a motion for them to follow.

Good.

It was past time.

She had held her breath for the whole drive. As they finally arrived at the hospital, she squealed to a stop under the portico reserved for the ambulances. Once again, she didn't care.

The officer who'd skidded to a stop in front of them was out of his car and at her door almost before she could climb out. She barely flashed her badge at him and pointed to Christina, the only human they had that was injured. Caring for Christina here had to be what Donovan intended.

Had he seen something in Christina's injuries that were worse than what Eleri thought? It was possible. He was an actual MD; she was not.

Christina looked bad, Eleri thought, but she turned back to the officer, realizing he was already running inside, and meeting up with the hospital staff already pouring out the sliding doors, gurney and saline bags and stethoscopes in hand.

Donovan may have worked mostly with dead bodies, but he'd told them everything they would need and set Christina up for the best possible outcome. He'd done a rotation in the Emergency Department.

Eleri saw a second team come out with slightly less force and gusto. She watched as the first team moved Christina onto the stretcher in a fluid, practiced motion and had an oxygen mask strapped onto her face almost before Eleri could see it happen.

Turning back, she watched as Donovan lifted Wade onto the other stretcher explaining, "He's an FBI canine and he saved that woman's life—" he pointed to the doors Christina had just disappeared through. Then he rattled off a list including packed cells, ringers, warming blankets, and more that he was demanding for what everyone thought was a dog in the ER. Anyone who balked was flashed his credentials and a warning glare.

He'd pull a fang if he needed to, she knew.

"We only operate on humans here," one of the nurses protested. But she helped push the gurney Wade was now rested on top of. He was partially covered under a blanket that looked to Eleri to be heated from a battery source.

They wouldn't operate on him, she knew, and it wouldn't be because they were a human hospital. She and Donovan wouldn't let them. The two agents stood shoulder to shoulder until the ER team reluctantly wheeled Wade inside. Maybe working on him in the bay would have been more acceptable, but he needed heat and access to supplies.

"I take full responsibility for him," Donovan said. When the nurse again tried to protest, he shut her down before she even got a word out, "I am a doctor."

She raised her eyebrow, skeptical of FBI agent and MD in one person, until Donovan rattled off his medical school and year of graduation before giving her another list of supplies. The woman ran off, hopefully to fetch the things and not to get her boss to come and explain to Donovan that it wouldn't be the case.

Christina had already been whisked away by a team hustling to get her safe. Eleri could only stay here with Wade and watch as Donovan steered him into the nearest empty bay and ran an IV into his friend. How he found a vein under all that fur was a mystery, but she was determined to act as if having a huge "dog" in the ER was an everyday occurrence for her.

Donovan slid a human oxygen mask awkwardly onto Wade's canine face. Then he demanded one of the nurses apply pressure to the head wound while he hung the saline bag from the pigtail at the end of the gurney. Luckily, a few nurses came back in to volunteer to help. If Christina had a chance, at least the people here would try to make it happen for her.

Turning back to Donovan, Eleri was about to speak as another scrubs-clad employee burst into the space.

Donovan brooked no argument from the woman who was apparently in charge of the ER.

"I need this bay for him." Donovan rattled off more commands. Whatever medical school jargon passed between them, it worked. Or maybe it was the badge that Eleri once again held up in her free hand.

Next to her, another nurse pushed her way through the curtains. "How did you survive that?"

She realized she'd left the car riddled with bullet holes and covered in both Wade's and Christina's blood right in the entry bay. She'd send the keys out with someone to move it or move it herself later once things had settled down. Nurses passed in and out as

Donovan worked. He didn't cut into Wade but hooked up machinery in complex patterns that Eleri understood but couldn't have done herself. One by one, the machines began to beep.

When Donovan finally stopped moving, she asked, "Is he going to make it?"

"I don't know."

65

Donovan stalked through the ER. The place felt strangely familiar though his position in it did not. Even the walking upright and free, clear-headed—or as clear-headed as he could be in this situation—was both familiar and new.

He was the obvious an interloper here, handing out orders despite not being in charge. He left Eleri watching over Wade, her hand resting on her friend's shoulder. Wade's breathing was shallow but beginning to become steadier once Donovan had fashioned a better face mask out of a cleaned out soda bottle.

Still, Wade wasn't out of the woods yet. His core temperature was shockingly low. Something Donovan wouldn't have known, if not for having interacted with those at the de Gottardi/Little compound and with the two veterinarians, who initially saved his life in Florida.

Not only was Wade's body temperature low for a human, it was concerningly low for a wolf. They tended to run hotter than normal humans.

Donovan strode to another care bay. There were only curtains—no doors—to knock on. He wasn't sure if it was better to whip the curtain back and announce his presence or slip in and possibly startle someone.

"Dr. Anderson?" he asked as he stepped in, noting that the woman's steady hands didn't flinch in the slightest.

No, it was he who flinched as he turned, surprised at the sound of Eleri's voice. "Donovan?"

Why was she behind him? But as he turned to look, she held up her phone. He simply shook his head. Whoever or whatever was on the phone was not as important as making sure that Christina had the proper treatment.

She was heavily sedated for pain and locally anesthetized for the work the ER doctor was currently doing. Donovan looked over Christina's left forearm where it lay propped on a small table with part of the necessary suturing finished—but only part. Now that the wound had been cleaned it was easy to see the damage was deep, deeper than he'd thought.

"What kind of subQ did you use?" he asked the doctor. She rattled it off as, on the table, a very woozy Christina asked, "Sub Cue?"

Turning again, Donovan grinned at her. "Subcutaneous sutures. You need your torn muscle repaired under the surface, then the skin sutured closed over that." He turned back to Dr. Anderson. "Will you be calling in the plastic surgeon?"

"She's already on her way." Dr. Anderson was laying subcutaneous sutures herself but was bringing the plastic surgeon in to do the surface ones with an eye toward minimal scarring.

Donovan felt the corner of his mouth quirk. Christina was not conscious enough to participate in this conversation. Perhaps she would have demanded Dr. Anderson, or even Donovan himself, lay the surface sutures in with a heavy hand and give her the best scar possible. But erring on the side of hiding it was the better thing to do.

Eleri looked at him one more time with her phone held up to him. Again, he refused her, watching as she stepped back beyond the curtains. He noticed now how crowded the small space around Christina had become. Still, it was good each time he saw her face.

He wanted her in here. He wanted his friends with him eating a good steak at a restaurant. Christina could have a beer, Eleri a soda, and he and Wade would eat their steaks almost bloody. This heart-pounding, worry-filled hospital visit was not the reunion he'd hoped to get.

Stepping around to the side of the gurney where Dr. Anderson worked, Donovan's eyes traveled up to look at Christina's face. Though she grinned goofily, she was far more battered than he'd originally thought. Small scratches marred her forehead, a rash had scabbed already at her left temple. Her right cheek had an open but clean gash that would also be waiting for the plastic surgeon.

Her eyelids fluttered only slightly. She was in there, but not completely, hopefully pain free. The drive down the mountain had to have been much harder on her than she'd let on.

Dr. Anderson finished suturing the ripped open muscle on Christina's left forearm and moved to work on her shoulder area.

"When is she going for a CT on the wrist?" he asked.

"Wrist?" a nurse asked as she stepped in through the curtains.

"I think it's broken," he added, still looking at Dr. Anderson who hadn't moved from her position, her hands steadily laying in sutures.

"I already sent another nurse with the request to get her in. She's priority."

He was grateful that Anderson had given Christina priority status, and hoped it was because she was an FBI agent. However, he was concerned that she was priority simply based on her damage.

"And her leg?" he asked, then kept going. "I'm assuming you are stitching the muscle and getting ahead for the plastic surgeon?"

"Dr. Gupta will do that. She'll likely follow them into the OR."

Multiple teams working on different portions of her body at the same time, Donovan thought. It might take hours for plastics to close the gashes she had. There was a window where infection could set in. After that timeframe—usually just six hours—it was no longer safe to close a wound.

Christina's leg was torn open in several places, and he wasn't surprised when Dr. Anderson, not even lifting her gaze from where she carefully stitched together the ripped pieces of Christina's shoulder, asked, "How did she get that wound on her leg?"

The others looked almost like knife cuts, but her leg sported three, long, parallel gashes and a fourth that cut across them. That would make it much harder to simply close the wounds.

He was trying to think of a good explanation when Dr. Anderson finally turned her attention to look up at him. Her blonde hair was pulled back in a ponytail, her bright blue eyes warped by the magnifying glasses she was using to look at Christina's wound. She demanded, "Tell me it wasn't that creature in my other ED bay."

"It was not him." Donovan said the words with all certainty.

But the doctor looked Donovan up and down, not missing the gash on his forearm. "You know you need to get that taken care of. I'll get our best PA and she can get you cleaned up and put butterflies on it."

He thought of protesting but the stern look in Dr. Anderson's gaze had him only nodding. Still, he was surprised by what she said next. "And we need to treat your friend, too."

Not sure who Anderson was talking about, as she was once again looking at the wound on Christina's arm, Donovan frowned.

Somehow, Anderson read the silence correctly. "The small one. Ginger curls, darker skin."

Eleri.

Anderson didn't even look up as she added, "She definitely needs to be treated for that bullet wound."

66

Donovan sat with Eleri next to Wade. His friend remained asleep, the makeshift soda bottle mask on his long nose doing the job. Donovan was grateful that he was more certain now that Wade was actually *asleep*. That he was resting after his ordeal, rather than barely hanging on, unable to open his eyes or function.

Eleri had finally been stitched up—the wound along the side of her calf had been a cut from a claw. She had another on her upper arm. This one had been from a bullet puncturing the muscle. She hadn't even noticed.

Donovan had felt and seen the wounds he had gotten during the fight. He'd simply ignored them. Eleri seemed to not feel her damage at all.

Dr. Anderson had demanded that if he was going to do such things as bring animals into her Emergency Department and demand that they receive a bay and a human bed, that he was going to get treated for his wounds. He'd agreed.

It was a fair trade.

Eleri still sat with one hand resting on Wade's shoulders, as if she needed to feel that he was still breathing.

Her eyes met Donovan's and he felt compelled to tell her, "At first, I was worried about Wade. Christina needed stitches but Wade was in critical danger. Now, I'm less worried about Wade ..."

But he didn't need to fill in the rest. Eleri did. "And Christina was more injured than you thought."

Donovan nodded. "She hides it well."

"She hides everything well," Eleri replied as the truth of that sank deep under his skin.

Christina had been recruited into the FBI in her early college days by Westerfield's predecessor. Apparently, they'd been watching her from high school on. Donovan had had an entirely different career for almost a decade before joining. Eleri had been a profiler, having gone into the FBI on her own before getting drawn into NightShade. He wondered what it was like for Christina having always been working like this. What little he knew of her, told him that her past powers had brought her both great rewards and devastating losses, and almost nothing in between.

Wade was likely the most emotionally stable of the four of them, having been brought up in an environment full of people like himself. He'd been encouraged to follow his dreams and his education. He'd been warned about the dangers he could face and trained to deal with them. But he'd faced the world knowing he had a place to come back to, a home should he ever need it. He had medical care from trained professionals who knew how to work on those like him.

He'd pursued his dream of a doctorate in Physics yet kept getting pulled back into the FBI—into NightShade. Whether that was because Wade loved the work or felt the driving need to keep his friends alive, Donovan still hadn't figured out.

For a moment, he flashed back to Eleri introducing him to her old friend. Donovan had smelled the wolf on him the moment they'd entered the room. Though he'd only known Eleri a very short while at the time, he knew enough to understand that she didn't know what Wade was.

The two men had almost gone into a full-scale, claws out, fangs gnashing, kind of fight right there, in de Gottardi's office at the Argonne National Labs. Now, he sat by the man's bedside, watching the light brown fur softly move with the slow rhythm of his breathing—still not fast enough or deep enough for Donovan to quite write it off. It was at least better than it had been.

Eleri's phone buzzed once again in her hand. She'd turned the ringer off at least. She answered "Yes" with no other greeting, letting Donovan know who it was. It felt bizarre not to have his own phone in his hand, buzzing simultaneously to let them know it was Westerfield.

She scooted around to Donovan's side of the bed, her eyebrow raised to ask if he was going to be involved in the conversation this time. With a silent but heavy sigh, he nodded.

"Sir," he said, speaking to his boss for the first time in well over a month.

"Glad you're back," Westerfield offered by way of greeting but, before Donovan could say anything else, Westerfield snapped, "Where have you been?"

Donovan rolled his eyes. What a stupid and shitty question. So, he said, "Everywhere."

"I need a full report," their boss demanded.

Good to know his boss was concerned about him. Then again, there was every possibility that Westerfield was angry that Donovan had escaped Miranda. It has crossed Donovan's mind more than once that he might be more useful as MI's prisoner than as anything else. He still wasn't going to stay, not voluntarily.

"Well, sir," he said, his capacity for bullshit having diminished by a great bit over the last handful of weeks, "I've just seen my partner for the first time in almost two months. I've got two injured partners here in the hospital whose status I'm still not fully confident about. And I haven't even had a damn moment to call my girlfriend and let her know that I'm alive."

He saw Eleri's face fly wide at that thought and she moved the phone as if to dial Walter, only to realize it was her phone they were talking on and she was already on the line. He almost grinned at her error. But said out loud, "You'll get your report when you get it."

He reached over to Eleri's phone and hit the red button, hanging up. Then watched as she tipped her head back and began to laugh at Donovan's brazen dismissal of their boss. But the sweet sound of her mirth didn't cover the odd gurgle that came from Wade.

Donovan's gaze snapped sharply to his friend even as Eleri jolted into action. But there was nothing they could do. Wade's legs shot out straight and tense, his entire body rigid in the grip of something. Then his head flipped back, knocking the oxygen mask off as he started into a full seizure.

67

As another bullet pinged off the bumper, Brian could feel his limbs shaking. *Was it anger that they were shooting at the car that he'd so lovingly pursued?* The one he spent his hard earned savings on. It was the first thing he'd bought once he had a decent salary and knew that his mother was covered. *Or was he just petrified?*

They would kill him, he knew. Even though he had no idea where this bullet had come from. He couldn't see the pursuit cars any longer. But that made this scarier ... bullets were coming from nowhere.

They had killed him once before by pushing him over the bluff, and they had killed the woman sitting in the passenger seat beside him too. It seemed their death would come by bullet this time.

"Get down!" he told her harshly, hunching his own shoulders as though that would help.

They'd left the top of the car down despite being followed. Then, when they'd been actively pursued and shot at it had been too late to pull over and go through the laborious process of putting it up. It hadn't occurred to them they would be shot at.

It was just a stupid mistake—one that might get them killed.

Mila had at one point jokingly told him it wouldn't have mattered if they had put the top up. "The top is fabric. All it does is obscure our view. It won't save us at all from bullets."

So here they were, looking like a horror movie joy ride gone wrong. Occasionally, bullets bounced off the trunk or doors, sending him into a deja vu tailspin.

He plowed along the gravel road, the tires sending the huge body of the car tilting and tipping, rocking until he was confident they would bounce right off the road. Though if he did, he would crash into the large trees that lined both sides of what was essentially a path that had once been graveled.

Behind them, they could make out the crunch of tires over the sounds of his classic boat of a car clomping its way through the woods where it didn't belong. He wondered if the noises were maybe just his own pulse whooshing through his eardrums.

The large SUV that had chased them had been joined by a second. When he got a good look at it, one side was scraped up and bashed in already. Not a good sign.

They'd passed the trail of three SUVs that seemed to have been chasing a smaller car at breakneck speed along the path in the other direction … but one had squealed the tires and turned around to follow him and Mila.

Later, the second had appeared.

Though their pursuers managed to close the gap on the main road, he'd taken a harsh right hand turn onto a nearly invisible gravel road. Brian had simply known it would be there … It seemed the SUVs hadn't. So he and Mila had gained the time it had taken for them to backtrack and find the point of entry.

When they came to a split, Brian had taken the lesser traveled path in front of them—another thing that he'd "just known" would be there. He also somehow knew that it would loop back out onto the main road … if they could make it. The SUVs not only had the advantage of speed on the paved road, but they would have the upper hand in here, too. Brian's only advantage was the thing that lurked just beneath memory that told him where to go.

The tire ruts in the other road had been deeper, and it was why he had chosen this one, but he heard the sounds of tires and gravel behind them. They weren't far enough ahead. They wouldn't make it back to the main road. He knew.

Not only did they hear the sounds of the other cars closing in, stray bullets started to find them.

Beside him, Mila turned around and suddenly began digging into the back seat. His fear spiked. She'd been trying to stay low, but the front of the car didn't have modern age bucket seats. The old style bench had no gap between the driver and passenger. So, she was hanging up and over the structure—an easy target if one of the other cars could get a sight on her.

Why? Why had he bought a big old boat? Why had he painted it cherry red? It was so visible through the trees.

"Leave the bag!" he commanded, though he could feel her refusal even as he said it. Then he got an idea. "In fact, toss it into the middle of the road. Maybe if they get it, they'll stop coming after us."

She had it in her hands now, cradling it like a large baby. "They won't. They know that we know."

"What do we know?" he demanded, turning to look at her, the anger feeling like it sharpened through his harsh stare. He didn't even glance at the path in front of him, his hands just turned the wheel one way then another from memory.

"I don't know what we know," she whispered, possibly the stupidest answer she could have given—if he hadn't been having the visions—if he hadn't *known* that he knew her from somewhere—if it hadn't been revealed to him that he loved the cherry red Ford Falcon because Ben Hartman had loved it three and a half decades earlier— Brian would have called her five shades of idiot.

With his eyes back on the gravel in front of him he paid closer attention. Calling it a road would be a dramatic overstatement as baby trees had taken root between the two ruts and now periodically scraped the bottom of his car. He'd stopped wincing at the damage long ago.

But he realized she was right.

"It's barely over three hundred thousand dollars!" he yelled at her over the rough sounds of the woods. His anger wasn't with her. "They have to have spent more than that pursuing us already!"

He watched Mila as the realization of his statement sunk in.

"Is it revenge?" she asked. "Are they mad because we stole it?"

"Maybe." He took another turn as he sighed again. Another ping, this time against Mila's door had them both cringing and remembering to stay low. "Maybe it's a mafia thing and they simply can't let anyone cross them for any amount."

She shuffled the bag in her grasp, slowly nodding, but then she shook her head. "That's not it. It's something else, Brian."

At least she hadn't called him Ben again.

"Do you remember the bag that we hid?" she asked quietly.

He nodded. It was stupid. He shouldn't remember something someone else had done a lifetime ago, but he did. He remembered Jennifer and Ben frantically cutting dollar shapes from old magazines. They'd had to pull out a bill and trace it because they didn't know the correct dimensions. They'd stacked the cut pages, rubber banding them together and piling them into the bag that they had purchased. It wasn't quite the same but looked close enough to the one Mila now held.

This one had been shiny and new the first time he'd seen it. Now it had dirt rubbed into it, bugs and soil pH had tried to eat holes into it over the years. It even had some grass seeds still embedded in the webbing straps from where he'd found it in the overgrown yard behind William's house. This bag had seen some shit.

But the one she referred to had been shiny and new like this one at the time. He remembered standing, holding one bag in each hand as Mila—actually Jennifer—had added stacks of magazine bills until he said they weighed the same. But the magazine paper was clearly much heavier than the linen of the bills. So, they pulled out all their fake bill stacks and stuffed some wadded paper underneath it to bulk it up enough to look better at first glance.

Then they buried it, knowing they were being watched. They'd thought it would work ... buy them enough time to get away, to start over, to have their baby. It hadn't.

Mila said she'd gone back to the spot and dug for the bag, but it was clear it had been gone a lifetime ago.

"So you know they found the fake. Do you think they're just angry that we duped them? Could they really hold a grudge for this many years?" That last part he wondered why he'd asked it out loud. But inside he didn't know ... *could* the original players still even be alive? Ben Hartman and Jennifer Barnes weren't.

"Did we ever even look through the bag?" Mila asked him. "I know we counted it ..."

As Brian searched his and Ben's memories, he slowly shook his head. They'd stuck their hands inside, stirred the stacks around. They'd pulled enough out to count down to the bottom layer and they'd counted one of the stacks specifically. Then they'd multiplied up, grabbed a piece of scrap paper and carried the one ...

But no, they'd never taken everything out of the bag.

"I think there's more here than we're seeing," Mila said.

Something cold and hard settled in the middle of his chest. Brian knew she must be right.

68

Eleri's phone clattered to the floor. Her hand had jerked as Wade's body began to shake and shiver uncontrollably. Aside from noting the sound it made, she didn't care. All her focus was on Wade.

Her hands reached out and held onto his shoulders as if she could press him down and hold him still, even though she knew she couldn't. Donovan was on his feet fast enough that his chair crashed behind him.

She watched as he turned his head to call out for staff, but even that proved unnecessary. They were already coming through the curtains, several nurses skidding to a halt as they realized their patient was not human.

Another younger nurse, her brown hair swinging in a ponytail pushed her way past the others and began taking vitals as if her patient didn't look like a massive dog. More kept coming at the sound of the machines alerting them.

Eleri hadn't noticed that either; everything was beeping and buzzing around her until it seemed the air was, too.

One nurse, a large blonde man who looked like somebody had stuffed a Viking into scrubs, was reaching out but then turned to look to Donovan. "What do you want us to do?"

"Push Lorazepam," Donovan rattled off a dose and Eleri watched as the staff reluctantly set to work.

Even though they were clearly not convinced of what they were or should be doing, they were fast. Only moments later, the liquid was sliding into Wade's IV line. Eleri watched his body calm as the medicine hit.

"That was a very low dose," the viking said.

Donovan nodded. "He's about a hundred eighty."

"That is a massive dog!"

It wasn't a dog at all, Eleri thought, and she was glad Donovan knew the dosing or at least thought he did. Wade's body might have stopped shaking uncontrollably but hers was only starting.

With one last touch to his shoulder, to be sure Wade was still breathing, she sat down and wove her fingers together to keep them still.

"They work with us a lot," Donovan said, "so we try to know the dosing to treat them if they need it." The "they" being ambiguous so the staff could interpret this as "large trained FBI dogs." Eleri tried to ignore the irony that Donovan was one of the "they."

With Wade calmed again, and her thoughts scrambling for something to focus on, she reached for the familiar. She was patting herself down for her phone, when she heard the crunch as the large Viking of a nurse stepped backward. His eyes flew wide. He had to have felt it beneath his foot.

"Oh, no." He looked between them.

Then Eleri tipped her head and offered a small shrug. "It was my fault. I dropped it, I left it on the floor." Of course, she had, her friend was having a seizure.

But as the Viking moved his foot, it was clear this was more than just a cracked screen. Reaching down, he picked it up. It stayed in one piece, though bits of it moved.

"Just toss it," Eleri told him and listened to the bizarre sound of multiple thuds as it broke apart mid air and each piece hit the trash can separately.

Donovan's phone had been packed away since Florida when she'd handed him over to Leonidas. It had been in the car at the time, and she'd carried it with her—but it was in the hotel room in the bottom of her luggage, still at the crime scene of the slaughtered housekeeper, not on her.

Wade's phone was at the bottom of Lake Superior, probably still in his pants pocket. Her phone was now in the trash at the hospital.

Christina, who was still in surgery, probably had the only functioning piece of equipment, but it would be stashed with her clothing somewhere in the hospital. Somewhere Eleri didn't know about.

It felt bizarre to be so cut off, but Wade and Donovan were in the room with her. Christina was in the operating room. Even if everyone wasn't completely stable, she could walk to where they were. The air around her felt so odd.

After a few moments of watching Wade and determining that the medication had worked, the staff talked amongst themselves and decided there wasn't anything else to do because their patient wasn't human. Slowly, they filtered out of the room.

"Is he better?" Eleri asked.

"Hopefully." Donovan sighed heavily. "It's not an uncommon side effect of hypothermia. I'm hoping that's all that it was."

Deciding she could live with that she didn't press further. She didn't want to know what else could go wrong. Reaching over, she placed one hand on Wade's shoulder and closed her eyes, working whatever small spell she could here and now so that this didn't happen again. It might be a side effect, but seizures were still serious.

Someone must have walked in behind her because she heard Donovan whisper, "Let her pray."

It wasn't wrong.

In a moment, when she'd finished, she looked up at him and said, "I was reaching to call Walter for you when Wade started seizing. I'm surprised you hadn't called her already or either Christina or me. You just showed up."

This was a conversation that needed to happen. Something important was at play here. Eleri just didn't know what yet.

Righting his chair, Donovan sat back down and the two of them stayed that way, on opposite sides of Wade's bed, their friend breathing steadily now between them.

"Once I was healthy enough to do something—once I got my brains to function for long enough—I managed to put a stop to the drugs they were feeding me to keep me docile." He almost grinned. "Planning and executing that plan while you're drugged is hard! Anyway, I stayed in the bed, flexing my muscles and exercising in a way that didn't look like it."

She must have frowned.

"I knew it was going to be difficult to get up. I'd had several surgeries, been in bed for a while, and was consistently drugged. I was in no shape to run away—"

"Which was the point," Eleri added.

"Once they took me from the vets at the clinic, they transported me halfway across the country and that made it a lot easier for me to take control of what was going into my system. I managed to get up and walk around. Later, they transported me again ... about three days ago. For twenty-plus hours as I rode north, they made several stops. I was kept in a tiny container which I later found out was packed into a shipping truck. But for the first time, I don't think they had a camera on me. So, I did everything I could. I got up, I exercised, I ate everything they gave me, I bumped up the dosing on the IV they'd left me with. I was ready."

But ready for what? She wondered.

"Then, once I felt it was the best it was going to get, I waited for the truck to stop, and I bolted right out the back."

Her mouth fell open.

"Were you naked?" she asked, almost laughing.

"No. I was in sweats by that point, but they didn't really fit. I looked ... not safe. I looked a lot like a fugitive on the run."

He wasn't wearing sweats now.

"An old lady was at the diner where I tried to panhandle some money. I couldn't access any accounts—that would alert MI. She took pity on me and said she was on the way with a donation of her deceased husband's clothes to the resale shop." He motioned to himself, and for the first time, Eleri realized that she'd been so excited to see him that she hadn't realized what he was wearing.

He was in chambray colored pants that were just a bit short. His button up plaid shirt had colors that had gone out of style around the time she'd been born. He didn't look like Donovan at all, except for the fact that he was clearly Donovan.

Again, she grinned at him, her hand coming out to rest on Wade's shoulder, reassuring herself that her grin was okay, that there weren't horrible things going down on the gurney between the two of them while they had this conversation.

"Then, I hitched a ride. From Indiana, where I was."

"And you knew we were in Minnesota?" She was incredulous.

He nodded. "I'd been paying attention. There's a lot of chatter. So, I hitched a ride up here to where you were."

"But why did you *hitch*? Why didn't you just call me? We would have come to get you."

"It's a good thing you didn't call Walter just now." Something about the way his expression changed told her there was more to this … certainly something she wouldn't like.

He added, "I couldn't call you."

"You could have used a pay phone. Or asked someone to borrow one!"

"It would have told them exactly where I was."

"What?" Eleri asked. "Not if you weren't using your phone or your money … Unless … Do you think they're tracking our phones?"

"No," Donovan replied. "I know it."

69

Donovan sat in an orange plastic molded chair that was attached to the hospital wall, one in a row that traced the long hallway.

He said he had needed to come to the vending machine for snacks, and even begged change off Eleri to do so. But in all honesty, he just needed a moment alone.

He'd been alone but not alone for so much of the last month and a half. In the veterinary office where he'd been kept initially, he'd either been hovered over or left in the room by himself. At least he imagined that was the case from the few memories he had. The times he'd been conscious enough to pay attention, he'd tried to hang onto what he saw and heard. He knew the two vets had done the surgeries on him in his alternate form. It had taken a while to heal to the point where he thought he might shift back. They clearly knew what he was.

Before that could happen—he'd been stupid enough to think he'd shift back, thank them, and be on his way—Miranda operatives had whisked him off. They'd monitored him even more, drugged him to complacency, and used the excuse that once Donovan shifted, he would be recognizable as an FBI agent. Surely the two veterinarians would not want an FBI agent found *fresh from surgery at their veterinary clinic, did they?*

At whatever MI compound he'd been taken to—he still didn't know—he'd been left in a small box of a room, occasionally treated and mostly ignored. He'd listened where he could. Sometimes they spoke when they were around him. If he did a stupid trick, and just pretended to be asleep, they spoke more freely, like idiots. Other times he heard things from beyond the walls. That was stupid on their part, too.

He told Eleri all of this.

Miranda was full of wolves. Wolves had excellent hearing. Or maybe it wasn't stupid, and they'd simply gotten so used to everyone hearing everything and they'd realized there was no way to stop it.

Somewhere along the line he'd overheard enough information to let him know they'd tapped multiple FBI agents' phones. He'd learned about a case that had everyone in action at MI. There was a car and two dead bodies.

Donovan heard that they thought they could finally get "the bag" back—whatever that meant. Even though he had no idea what any of those things were, he cataloged it all. Then he'd heard there were two agents in Minnesota, and they'd doled out just enough information for him to figure out that it was Eleri and Christina.

He'd escaped shortly after that—though he still didn't know if he'd actually escaped or if MI had just let him think he had.

From the moment he left the back of the transport truck, he hadn't been alone at all. Kind people had taken him under their wing, fed him or handed him a ten-dollar bill or both. Several had given him a leg of the ride to Minnesota. The last had dropped him near the Great Lake, and he'd walked four miles to the bluff where he believed they would eventually show back up, before walking into that stupid-ass, claw-and-gun-fight.

He was convinced that he'd arrived just in time to see his friends die.

He could have called ahead of time and let them know he was coming. Except he hadn't for exactly the reason he had told Eleri. He hadn't called Walter to let her know that he was okay, not until he'd managed to convince the viking of a nurse to lend Donovan his phone for a few moments.

The poor man felt guilty for destroying the one phone they had. Though Donovan didn't feel good about it, he played on the man's sympathies. Doing the only thing he could, he'd sent a coded text to GJ. GJ would figure it out—that he was alive and safe and healthy. That he was with Eleri and Christina and Wade. He didn't add anything else about Wade and Christina's current states, though at least they were doing better. Eleri or Westerfield could do that. Later.

Then, as he realized this was crazy and GJ would likely crack his code immediately, as it was one she'd designed, she would chat right back. He quickly composed and sent a second message, explaining that the first message was coded because Miranda was tracking their phones, and that she couldn't write back. Then he'd deleted both messages from the viking's phone and thanked him, next requesting access to Christina's belongings.

All of this was highly unusual. Eleri's badge gave him a number of perks, at least. She assured him she still had his and it was concerningly reassuring. The odd clothing, the lack of phone, badge, and gun, had all felt too surreal. Luckily, no one had demanded his own badge yet, or questioned the fact that he looked like he'd been dressed out of a bag of an elderly woman's donation clothing.

They'd stayed like that, alternating sitting beside Wade and Christina—after she'd come out of surgery—all night. This morning, another nurse had taken pity on him and given him and Eleri scrubs.

They'd now been in the hospital for over twenty-four hours, Christina had gone through recovery and been moved to another floor. They'd demanded Wade be put in the bed beside her and Eleri played every FBI card she had to make it happen, though she still hadn't called Westerfield.

He now had Christina's gun in his pocket. The two upright agents were concerned that Miranda operatives might follow them right into the emergency department. Dr. Anderson had insisted that their guns be set aside. When Donovan had explained his concerns, she had made it clear in no uncertain terms that he needed to "get that dog out of my ED!"

"It's not him they're coming after, it's *us*. And I can't get Christina Pines out of your hospital."

Anderson had relented under his determined assault, but she'd moved them all "out of her ED." Donovan and Eleri still held their guns.

No one was in the hall. He'd nearly lived in hospitals like this one during his rotations and later his residency. So much came flooding back. He'd been so alone—a wolf in medical school, not even knowing that anyone outside his own direct family could do what he did.

Now, he knew his lines went as far back as ancient Egypt. He had a brother he couldn't find and maybe didn't want to. He had friends—here in this very hospital, and in the Ozarks, and in other states. Hell, he had a *girlfriend*.

Pushing his long legs out in front of him, he leaned his head back against the wall. All the changes to his life didn't change his basic nature. He needed to go for a long run so bad. He needed something to die down or let up for just a little while.

Christina was out of surgery and doing fine. He'd grinned when she got mad that he hadn't given her the gnarliest scars possible.

Wade was awake but couldn't do anything until they took him out of the hospital, and he changed form so he could speak. The gash on the back of his head was finally healing nicely.

He tried to calculate the number of hours until they could leave.

There was already a new car waiting for them outside, courtesy of the Duluth BCA office. If Miranda Industries was smart, they'd already gotten someone out here to place trackers on it. Lord knew renting a car would be a bad idea, because MI could hack a rental company's tracking system far too easily.

It was entirely possible that MI had people embedded in this very hospital. He looked up and down the long hallway, as though one would just walk by and it would be obvious. But no one came.

They would be here—this area was an MI stronghold. If they didn't have employees in the hospital, they had access to the records. He was expecting that MI knew their captive had escaped. They likely knew exactly what damage they'd inflicted on the other agents. They knew there was a dog in one of the ER bays and now in a shared hospital room, courtesy of the FBI. And they knew the dog wasn't a dog at all.

Though Eleri had tried to bring him up to speed on the case, there were too many moving parts to keep track of. She'd told him he didn't want to dive back in and work for the FBI from the moment he showed up, but wasn't he already doing that?

He'd been shot at and clawed. There was no denying he had damage. Hadn't Miranda Industries already tried to shred him and left him with wounds that required butterfly bandages. There was no denying he was already in it.

Standing up, he declared his little down time over. Heading to the vending machine at the end of the long hall, he bought Eleri a pack of peanut butter crackers. They seemed to contain barely any actual peanut butter and the crackers were an unearthly shade of orange. He grabbed himself a bag of candy—which was somehow the only thing that appealed to him.

Then he headed back toward the room where his friends were. They needed to figure out why Miranda Industries was so hell bent on getting back three-hundred-thousand dollars they'd lost thirty-five years ago.

70

Mila slammed forward, her hands coming out to the dash to brace herself even as the seatbelt caught her. It stole her breath and her movement, the air choking in her lungs as the bag flew out of her grip.

It wasn't buckled in, and it bounced off the dash and back at her, adding insult to injury. It only took a moment to see why Brian had stopped so suddenly. A tree had grown up in the center of the path. This would be as far as the car could go. The old boat of a vehicle had barely made it to here. Branches had scraped the sides and they'd had to slow down and weave their way through obstacles in their attempt to flee.

This was the end of the line for the car. But not for her.

Mila was reaching for the door, but she looked at Brian as if to ask *what do we do now?*

He didn't even reach for his own door handle, just bolted up and over the side, motioning for her to toss him the bag and do the same. She threw the bag as best she could, but it was heavier than she estimated, and it didn't make it beyond the borders of the car.

Brian reached in, grabbing for it, but he watched her, too. As she was reaching for the door handle, he shook his head at her, quietly whispering, "No. No noise."

Ah, yes. That was smart. This wasn't a newer, quieter car model. She noticed now that he'd left the engine running. They were abandoning his baby, but they weren't going to give their pursuers any help.

Mila went up and over the door just as he had, her feet landing with a crunch among the leaves and twigs of the forest floor. In the distance, she heard bark exploding from another bullet.

They may very well just be firing into the trees in the hopes of getting lucky, or maybe with the purpose of sending the message that they were still back there and were determined to catch up with their quarry.

With one arm wrapped around the bag, holding it close to his torso, Brian reached back and grabbed her hand. Before she could process anything, they were on the move, running through the woods.

She remembered doing this before. Last time, Brian had been shot. The sharp streak of fear ripped through her that it would all repeat and he was about to be shot again. That she'd screwed up and she wasn't fixing anything.

But if they weren't in the car now, then they weren't repeating Jennifer and Ben's last day. And they weren't going over the side of the bluff to their deaths. If they *were* repeating history, and even if he were shot, he would survive this.

It still wasn't a comforting thought.

Mila stopped, tugging at his hand, begging him to just talk to her for a moment. "If they want the money, let's give it to them."

He frowned at her and it was fair, she'd been insistent that they couldn't just hand it over and walk away. Reaching for the bag, she unzipped it even as it stayed in his arms. She opened just enough to reach in and grab one of the stacks of bills, then she chucked it onto the path behind her.

"No!" He almost yelled it, but she could tell he was trying to keep his voice down. Offering the money had made him mad, really mad.

Brian was already heading back down the trail, grabbing the still banded stack of bills from where it lay on the ground. "You can't do that! You can't just give them the money!"

"You're the one who said we don't need it!" Her immediate reaction to fight back had her tension cranked even higher. Her voice was getting too loud, but in her panic she was unable to keep it down. Unable to remember why they'd decided they couldn't do this.

"It's not that we can't give them the money." He hefted the bills he'd picked up, then lobbed the stack into the car with near perfect precision. Then he reached into the bag, grabbed another stack and did it again. "It's not about that. It's about you leaving a trail of bread-crumbs right behind us."

He was right. She hadn't been thinking. She'd thought she'd just toss the money behind them, making them pick up the individual stacks, but that would let their pursuers know exactly which way they'd gone.

"Hell." He hefted the bag with two hands, then pausing to zip it shut realizing the mistake he had made. "Let's give them the whole thing."

He was heading back toward the car, when Mila protested. "No!"

This time she moved herself in front of him, jumping up and blocking Brian from making his shot. She pulled the bag from his hand. "It's not the money. They don't even really want the money. It's something else."

"Exactly! So, let's give them everything!" He moved to grab the bag back from her, but she deftly twirled away, evading him. Or maybe he just wasn't willing to yank it away from her.

"I think they're going to come after us anyway," she told him as another tree exploded nearby.

This one was much closer than the last and they both cringed and ran as though that would save them.

Grabbing her hand again, Brian dragged her farther down the trail. The two of them fit into places that cars didn't. Were they still leaving a trail? she wondered. Was anyone behind them going to be able to track it and see exactly where they had gone? She might as well have left the money leading right to them.

But they were running, crashing through the underbrush, until they decided they were out of harm's way. But what did they know?

At least the bullets seemed to have stopped. Brian didn't think it was enough, though. He offered to take the bag and she let him. Another bullet pinged nearby, and Mila felt another adrenaline rush of energy. Once again, they took off running until they were both out of breath.

She felt like they'd been running through the woods forever, though it had probably barely been ten minutes. She figured her fight or flight reaction was working overtime and she wasn't a runner so she was sorely overestimating.

Her breath was huffing in and out. If these guys had semi-decent hearing, that alone would probably lead them right to her. Glancing at Brian, between her own body-wracking breaths, she tried to find words. "They're horrible people."

"Duh," he replied, the stupid word making her smile even though he was bent over with his own rough breathing.

He held the bag tucked up under one arm, other hand braced on his knee as he, too, sucked in air. Mila was grateful that she only had to carry herself and not the heavy bag of bills as well this time. She told him, "They've been horrible for thirty years."

"I don't understand ... what you're ... getting at."

"Look at them. They chased us through the woods in dark SUVs. They killed us the last time they had us. Why? They *have to be* running trafficking rings or drugs, or ..." she didn't know.

But Brian understood now. Still huffing in not-quite-as-deep breaths, he nodded along. But she kept going.

"The only people who would mount that kind of a chase over this kind of money have to be into something deep. They are coming after two people who weren't fugitives. They have to be well connected. And they didn't get that way unless they've made that money and those connections in some improper way. We aren't being chased by a hospital or a legit oil drilling company. We just aren't!"

He was nodding along fully, starting to understand where she was going.

But she still said it out loud. They had to be on the same page. "They are the mob. Some kind of crazy drug-running mafia! We cannot let them have what they want."

This time she reached out to take the bag from him, hugging it as though it were precious. It might not be precious to her, but it was precious to them. And she and Brian needed to figure out why. "I can't be part of what they are doing. I can throw them the dollar bills, but I can't give them what they want. Because if they want it that badly, it's got to be something that's going to make their business that much easier to do."

He was on her side now, maybe not playing the hero but willing to agree to some minor heroism. "Then what do we do?"

"We hide. We hide until they leave."

He took the bag back from her, hefting it up and looping the too-short straps over his shoulders. He wore it now like a very awkward backpack.

"And after we hide," she added, "once we know we are safe, we call those FBI agents, and we turn ourselves in. We tell them what we have."

"What *do* we have?" Brian asked.

"We have three hundred and something thousand dollars in cash that we quasi-stole thirty-plus years ago. Beyond that, I don't know." As she turned to look over her shoulder, another tree exploded.

This one was too close.

In the distance she heard noises of an engine stopping.

"They found the car," Brian said, and she nodded as another tree beside her exploded.

She flinched and ducked. But this tree was too soon, too close. Not random firing into the woods. Whoever was behind them had found them.

Brian grabbed her hand and tugged her along, the bag bouncing against his back as they ran in fear for their lives. Whatever else they had, it was very, very valuable.

71

Wade rolled one shoulder, feeling the hair on his arms recede as he did it. Twisting his neck, he then flexed and unflexed his toes. It was almost painful—the stretch in the pull of muscles changing places and moving from one spot to another. But it felt good—sometimes necessary.

Beside him, Donovan sat on the ground already back to looking fully human. He was butt naked, his heels in the grass, knees up and elbows resting across the tops. If Wade hadn't known where to look for him he would have blended right into the shadows of the dusk.

"That felt good?" he asked Wade.

"Felt necessary."

It had been two days since Wade had been released from the hospital, since he'd been let out of the makeshift oxygen mask Donovan had devised. His friend had saved his life, but even though he'd padded the edge of the cut soda bottle he'd used to fit Wade's snout, it was still uncomfortable. Then again, nearly dying had been damned uncomfortable, too.

His headache had finally receded, the medication no longer necessary, and for all of those things Wade was grateful. Even for the run.

"We have to get back to Eleri," he told Donovan.

Nodding quickly in agreement, Donovan stood up and the two men reached for the bags that they left behind when they first headed out. Inside, folded clothing, shoes and FBI issue and burner phones waited for them and they quickly got dressed. It wouldn't do to be found naked out in the woods.

It had been three hours and the run had done him good. Wade was truly hungry for the first time in a while. The four of them were finally back together. Though Christina's injuries had not been quite as life-threatening as his, they were going to take longer to heal. The three of them had been trying to keep her off her bad leg but keeping her still wasn't going well.

The surgery had done wonders but as talented as the doctors had been they hadn't simply put her to rights like she wanted. It would take time—time Christina didn't have the patience for.

Though Eleri had at first insisted on coming out with the guys, she realized relatively quickly what was likely to happen if she left Christina alone. So, Donovan and Wade had taken the keys and come out themselves. It wasn't as if either of them needed a babysitter, as if either of them hadn't been doing this entirely on their own without getting caught for all of their adult lives.

Carrying the empty bag over his shoulder and his fingers hooked into shoes, Wade enjoyed the feeling of leaves, twigs, and all the little fuzzy flowers that fell off the pines squishing and crunching beneath his feet. It had been too long since he was out in nature.

"We were all looking for you," he told Donovan.

"I know and when I finally got free, I couldn't even call anyone and let you know I was safe."

"It's that serious? Miranda Industries is tracing every call we make?"

"Absolutely. Every single one of you. Had I called, they would have known exactly which pay phone I was calling from or traced back the number to whomever's cell phone I had borrowed. They've tried to embed someone everywhere that could be useful," Donovan explained.

"What do you mean?" Wade wanted to ask if they were just tracing the numbers called or if they had the means to listen in, but Donovan was full of other information.

"They have someone at the cell phone companies. Someone with enough access to pull up the records on any number they want and embed tracking programming. They have someone at the power company …"

Wade felt his eyebrows rising.

"Someone in the department of transportation, in each police unit, and so on."

Wade had believed that Miranda was balls deep in everything, but maybe he hadn't given them quite the kind of credit they deserved. It sounded like they'd strategized their way into every possible way to cut someone off or track them. Then again, they'd come to his family home in the middle of nowhere, showing up with an army that seemed to simply materialize at the property lines, ready to invade and fully outfitted.

As he and Donovan made their way back to the car that the Duluth BCA had loaned them, Wade tugged the handle on the passenger side and tried to find out what Donovan might know from his time on the inside. "Eleri and Christina have been following a pair of bodies pulled up from the lake. The case traces back to the late eighties and a missing stash of money from a grocery store robbery."

Donovan nodded along, starting the car and turning it around in the parking lot. Then he headed to the main road and away from the national park. Wolves, Wade thought, would always be able to find the nearest space full of trees and free of cameras available for a run. They had about a thirty minute drive to get back to the new hotel, though.

"There's definitely chatter in Miranda about the case. Mostly about the bag," Donovan said. "There's a little about the money, but mostly they just said they wanted the bag. Whatever that is."

"It was a bag with just over three-hundred-K in cash. Eleri seems to think someone has it now. That it was taken out of play back in the eighties and has remained missing all this time. But now something has put it back into play."

"Why now?" Donovan asked, pulling the car out onto a wider state road. "Identifying the bodies doesn't identify the bag if it's not with them."

"Maybe it triggered some information that Miranda was able to use to find it. We haven't figured that part out yet."

About halfway back Wade's official phone rang. He was a little startled to see the name but of course once he thought about it for a moment, he realized Donovan still didn't have an official phone. They were trying to keep him under the radar as much as possible. "Hey, Walter."

Next to him, Donovan's expression perked even though if they were tracking the calls as clearly as Donovan said they were, maybe he shouldn't speak.

"Hold on a sec," Wade told Walter and turned to Donovan. Covering the microphone, he very softly asked his earlier question, "Do they know what we're saying or just who we called and when?"

"I don't know. I know they're tracking the calls. I don't know if they can listen in. These should be secure FBI lines, making that impossible, but ..." He shrugged at the thought and took the next turn.

Exactly, Wade thought. It should be impossible for them to trace even the numbers as they came in and out. But MI could clearly already do that.

Turning his attention back to Walter, he asked, "What have you got?"

"You won't believe who just called me."

72

Eleri stood abruptly as the doorknob began to move. Her heart rate jumped but calmed quickly as she saw Donovan and Wade come through.

They looked a little disheveled and probably needed showers, but she needed help. Sitting on Christina was not an easy job. And it was impossible to outvote the other agent as only herself. She was grateful that they would now once again be three on one.

"Oh, you're back! Was it good?" she asked and smiled as they simply nodded.

It had likely been too long since Wade went running. And she knew it had almost definitely been too long for Donovan. She'd learned that running as a wolf was a good way to release stress. Lord knew, they'd both had plenty of it recently.

She was waiting for them to comment about the weather or the fact that they had two suites—this time with a connecting door in the middle—so they could both shower upon return. She particularly enjoyed the need for all the extra rooms. Despite all that had happened and the way that they'd been attacked, she was grateful they were all together.

But the guys just looked at her and Christina oddly. Finally, Wade spoke.

"Walter called while we were on our way back."

"Interesting, what did she say?"

"Only that we wouldn't believe who called her."

When she raised her eyebrows to ask *who?* He only shrugged.

That was stupid, she thought. But then Wade spoke up.

"We put her off. Get your burner phone."

It wasn't stupid. These guys, they weren't stupid.

Picking up the phone, she flipped open the old school clamshell. The older technology was often harder to hack. They'd even picked up a specific model that Wade recommended for just that reason.

Eleri dialed the number from heart and wasn't surprised when GJ answered. The two west coast agents were sharing the burner hoping that it would draw less attention than two.

"Hey, El," GJ said happily.

"The gang's all here." It was a phrase Eleri was incredibly pleased to be able to say.

"Wonderful. I've got Walter." In a moment, all six voices were on the line— a cheerful reunion that, for a long time, Eleri had feared would never happen.

Then she'd spent the last several days being afraid again. Luckily, Wade had recovered nicely. Even after the run, she could see that his color had still improved. Donovan had seemed healthy from the start —just missing for so many weeks. Now, if Christina could get back to her usual hundred-percent ...

"I got a call from one Mila Panas."

"The young woman who saw Olena Barnes, who claimed to be her long dead daughter reincarnated?" *The one Eleri had seen digging in the forests just outside Duluth?*

"Exactly that one. She and Brian Abadi are still together." There was a grin in GJ's tone. "Would you like to guess where they are?"

Eleri didn't need to guess. "Minnesota."

"Got it in one!" Even across the continent she could hear that GJ was proud.

Around the small coffee table in the suite, eyebrows shifted up, wondering what the hell was coming next. Still, Eleri explained her reasoning. "I think she came here because at some point, they buried that bag in the woods."

"They must have dug it up because it was here, wasn't it? At the Barnes' home." Walter asked. "Olena said they went down to the shed. When we checked it out, we found where they obviously pulled some things aside and didn't quite manage to put them back together. The place was clearly very recently disturbed and looked like what they removed could have taken up the space of a bag holding about three-hundred-grand in cash."

GJ picked up the story. "So, we think they went to Olena Barnes and made friends with the woman. That they convinced her that Mila was Jennifer, and they used that trust to get the bag of cash."

"Have you been tracking credit cards and phones?" Wade asked, but of course, they had.

"And we have absolutely jack shit," GJ replied. "They've been smart. Must be cash only."

"Are we able to follow the car?" Eleri asked.

"You would think, but the thing about Falcons is that there's actually a decent number of them still on the road." Walter explained. "So, we can't quite place any sighting as theirs."

"Even though it's red?" Eleri pushed.

"That's the most popular color," GJ informed her.

Of course it was.

Wade jumped in. "Did Mila or Brian say anything about the bag?"

"That," Walter said, "is exactly the beautiful part—"

"Well, not *beautiful*," GJ added.

"Apparently they were chased through the back roads in the woods, a few days ago by several black SUVs."

Not beautiful, but far too familiar.

"When exactly?" Wade pushed.

"Five days ago. Mid-afternoon."

Eleri felt her eyes fly wide. "On the way to the hospital, we passed a red convertible! Going the other way, toward the bluff ... And I didn't put it together."

"I suspect you probably had several other things you were thinking about." Christina's tone was wry.

But she was right, Eleri was likely the only one who'd seen it. Christina had her head tipped back and her eyes closed as she'd simply tried to manage her pain. Wade wasn't even conscious. And Donovan's attention had been entirely on him.

"I know where they were." *Well, five days ago she did*, she thought. "But where are they now?"

GJ answered again. "They say they were chased and shot at. They tried to leave some of the money behind, but it was apparently not enough to make it stop."

"So, how did they get in touch with you?" Donovan asked.

"Called on their cell phone," Walter replied, with a touch of disdain. "So, we sent them to get a burner and move to a new location. And when they called back, they told us about the bag."

"Where are they?" Eleri repeated looking frantically around the room, as if she could find her car keys and run right out the door. But she couldn't.

Christina needed to stay behind and probably Wade too. Which only left Donovan.

Hell, but for the fact that she'd had a bullet go straight through her arm and she hadn't even noticed, she was the healthiest of the bunch. *Son of a bitch.*

"They said they're hunkered down in a barn off of Route 3."

Donovan looked up at her. "I guess I'm not going to get that shower."

73

Donovan lifted his hands to his mouth and felt like an utter idiot. He called out, "Hoo hoo. Hoo hooooo."

Eleri rolled her eyes and stared at him. Her expression made it clear that the attempt at sounding like an owl was as horrifically bad as he thought it was.

"You do it." He told her. "I don't think my mouth makes that shape."

This time her expression said *bullshit*, but she lifted her hands to cup her own mouth and did a fairly reasonable impression of an owl.

Still nothing happened.

GJ had given them the directions she'd gotten from Brian, which mostly sucked monkey ass. Brian Abadi was an investment banker who'd apparently never done anything resembling going anywhere. He didn't seem to understand north and south or even quite how they'd gotten here.

Apparently, the couple had run for several days, trying to stay under the cover of the woods. They'd eventually found a safe barn per Walter's instructions and climbed into the loft. The whole story, though, meant they hadn't come on any roads and the directions Eleri and Donovan had were pretty pointless—as evidenced by the fact that this was the third white farmhouse they'd stopped at.

It seemed they all had a large, old, dull red painted barn in the back. Apparently, this was just how one painted everything around here. So, Brian and Mila's "identifying marks" on the farm they'd decided to squat at weren't even helpful.

Donovan thought there was a reasonable chance they'd only called the FBI because they were hungry. And he was also beginning to believe that he and Eleri weren't going to find the couple tonight.

How long should they search? How many more properties could they trespass? How many more barns should they hoot at?

The first three they'd checked had yielded nothing. And Donovan wouldn't have been surprised if he found out later that Mila and Brian had actually been in one of them and had simply let the agents walk on by.

They had to be terrified. Though they were close to his age, they certainly didn't have his training or Eleri's. As a medical examiner, he had been exposed—even before his time in the FBI—to the horrors that people could inflict on each other. As a profiler, Eleri got into their minds when they did it. But Mila and Brian? It sounded like they weren't prepared for anything like this at all.

Brian was an investment banker who'd clawed his way out of a poor neighborhood. Mila an artistic middle child of a middle class family. She was doing well enough for herself as a graphic designer, but neither had been prepared to have someone else's memories, let alone to be shot at and chased by a shadow organization that was funded to kingdom come and back.

"Mila? Brian?" Eleri called out softly. There was always the issue that the two agents weren't the only ones looking for the missing couple.

Miranda had to be searching high and low as well. GJ relayed that she had given the pair instructions to find a safe place to hide and reject it. To find another place to hide and reject it, too. They were to only stay at the third suitable location they found. If Miranda Industries was onto them at all, they might very well have been able to make an excellent guess about where Mila and Brian would choose to hunker down.

Turning to Eleri he asked, "Can you get anything?"

He couldn't even pick up a scent and follow a trail here. He had no idea what Mila or Brian smelled like, and there wasn't time to find where they'd abandoned the car and track them outward from there.

Eleri shook her head. There wasn't much either of them could do about it, but they needed to find Mila and Brian before Miranda Industries did.

Calling their names again, this time Eleri added, "This is FBI Special Agent Eleri Eames."

"Badge number?" The voice came back softly, but Donovan's ears perked.

That was an interesting request for a password. Would they even know if Eleri got it right? He was willing to bet that GJ had fed it to them.

Sure enough, as Eleri rattled hers off, the door on the barn slowly slid open. Two bedraggled adults, clutching a black bag for all that they were worth, began to step out cautiously.

Mila moved forward grabbing the bag from Brian and holding it outward toward him and Eleri. "Take this! Just take it! I don't want it anymore." She sucked in a breath and before he could say or do anything she shook it again. "Take it and we'll leave. You'll never see us again."

Eleri grabbed at it but only because Mila motioned as though she would throw it and Eleri would have to catch it if she didn't take it voluntarily.

Before they could comment or even say hello, Mila turned away. In a moment she was running across the field, startling Donovan.

Brian began to follow, but Donovan reached out. He only managed to barely snag Brian by the arm, though he noted that he didn't have to tug hard. Brian seemed torn between following Mila and staying and answering the agents' questions.

"You can't go," Donovan told him. "It's not safe."

"We don't even know what's in the bag," he pleaded as though that were enough. "I mean, we know about the money and we left some of it behind. But we don't know why it is that they're after this or us."

"It doesn't matter." But Donovan wasn't looking at Brian. He was focused in the distance, were Mila had stopped, realizing that Brian wasn't with her.

Brian still looked confused, as if there was an easy way out of this. Donovan could feel his pulse racing where he still held onto the man's forearm. The agents couldn't afford to let these two go. Not anymore than Miranda could.

"They already chased you and they shot at you," he reminded Brian.

In the distance he could catch Mila's expression. She wasn't so far away that she couldn't hear. "All they had to do was steal the bag back from you and leave you alone. They could have done that, but they didn't. They either aren't convinced that you don't know, or they are afraid that you might know enough to put it together in the future. Either way, you're not safe."

The two stared hopelessly at each other. Donovan tried to wait patiently while they made a decision. Though there was only one decent decision to come to, it would be better if they made it themselves.

Beside him, Eleri rifled through the bag as if she might find something the other two had missed.

His attention was torn. He didn't want to hang on to Brian and force him to stay, but he didn't feel he could let the man go either. He knew the result of a bad choice already.

He was turning to ask Eleri what she thought but the sharp pop of a bullet exploding into the wood of the barn ignited screams from the horses inside.

The sound had all four humans face down in the grass in a heartbeat. Even Brian and Mila had recognized what the sound was and reacted immediately. They might not know what was in the bag that was so valuable, but they clearly knew their only chance of surviving this was to stay as small as possible.

74

Eleri shifted her weight to get lower down. She'd landed on top of the bag, and it was making her too big of a target.

With it up beside her, it would be harder for them to hit her. They might hit the bag with one of their stray bullets, but something told her they would work to be sure the bag stayed safe.

There wasn't enough time now to think about what she'd seen when she grabbed it. Lifting her head cautiously, she noted that Donovan did the same. The two of them made eye contact. But, as if by some unspoken agreement, they both turned their heads at the same time to see Mila trying to crawl her way back to the group.

Next to Donovan, Brian was aiming himself toward Mila, starting to crawl out to get her. Eleri watched as Donovan's hand shot out, lightning quick, and grabbed onto Brian's leg.

"Don't. We've got her covered!" Donovan demanded of the man.

Brian's head snapped back, his eyes staring at them. It was clear to Eleri that Brian didn't believe it.

With a slow breath sucked in through her nose, she focused all of her feelings in one intense laser beam. Then she reached up and snapped her fingers.

The air shifted around them. She knew what she'd done even though she still couldn't identify exactly what it was. It caught Brian and Mila unaware and, for a moment, it surprised Eleri that they could see it, or feel it or …

"What the hell is that?" Brian demanded. He glared at her as if knowing she was responsible for it. He shifted his gaze to Donovan, as if to demand that her partner let go of him. Neither of them flinched.

Brian's expression cooled and Eleri knew he considered her and Donovan now as much of a threat as whoever was shooting at them.

"Eleri has Mila covered," Donovan said not quite saying out loud what the small dome of shimmered air was around them.

It moved, just enough to see an outline of where it ended, but filmy enough that no one would quite be able to clarify that they'd actually seen it. Mila stayed down—frightened and still—in her own much smaller bubble further away.

"You can crawl back toward us," Donovan called out.

With tentative motions, the woman started to move. It was all scary but being with Brian and the federal agents had to be the better of the two options. She stayed low in the grass which made her difficult to see. But the way the grass moved, then didn't, it was clear she was hesitating.

Brian had watched Mila for a moment before turning and glaring at the agents as though all of this were their fault.

It was interesting, Eleri thought, his fear of the bubble around them made it clear that he had not seen anything of the Miranda Industries operatives other than their human faces and their human guns.

She knew there were wolves all throughout the company. But what about other creatures? They'd encountered Neveah Johnson a few cases ago, though she hadn't quite worked directly for Miranda, at least not as far as Eleri could tell. So maybe she was an oddity, a creature of the sea, and not one of thousands like the wolves.

There was far more in the world besides wolves and witches, Eleri knew. But Brian Abadi and Mila Panas seemed not to have encountered any of it before now.

How had they gotten this far and stayed this naive? Whatever they were carrying in the bag, it was important.

Miranda Industries had probably never wanted the money. Or if they had, they hadn't cared in the end. The startup stash had been enough to get them going even without it. She'd felt something powerful when she wrapped her arms around it, though not when she'd held it by the straps, or pawed her way through, looking for whatever the others had missed. Only when she'd turned it upright, held the zipper close, and hugged it with her hands touching the reinforced flat bottom, had it zinged through her.

She might not know what it was, but she was beginning to get an idea of how powerful it was.

In the middle of the open field, Mila inched forward, finally crawling along slowly and surely. But as another shot ricocheted through the air, she froze for a second before squeaking and flattening back down.

Brian pushed up as if to bolt, but Donovan—with fast wolf reflexes—shot his hand out and snagged the man's leg. Brian's leap was cut short and he wound up sprawling face down in the grass.

"The bullets won't hit her. I promise you." Donovan's voice was low and comforting, and Eleri hoped Brian wouldn't think too hard about the *why* behind the words. "Tell her to keep crawling toward us."

Donovan knew that Mila would take the instruction better coming from Brian, but Brian didn't know if they were saving her or leading her into something worse than where she already was. He hesitated and Eleri tried this time.

"We can't get out of here until we are all together." But Brian still didn't call out and get Mila moving again.

Another knowing look passed between herself and Donovan. She turned to Brian. "Put your head down and close your eyes. Donovan is going to go get Mila."

Why he had to close his eyes Brian didn't know—and hopefully never would. He seemed about to refuse for a moment until her glare closed both his mouth and his eyelids.

With his face squished enough for her to be sure he wasn't looking, Eleri nodded to Donovan and turned away.

She kept watch around the borders, looking for movement at the edges. Her gun was already in her hand. Again, she'd pulled it on reflex, ready to take all comers or just provide cover.

But there was nothing to shoot at—nothing she could see anyway. An odd feeling crept over her that her partner was staying stuck in the tiny bubble with her as she felt first his shirt then his pants hitting the ground between them.

A moment later, a low growl alerted her that he was ready.

She snapped her fingers again, giving him his own space of

protection. Brian's eyes popped open for a moment and he saw Donovan's changed form but he quickly squeezed them back shut, as if to deny anything he might have witnessed.

With a look to let her know he was going, Donovan slunk off into the distance though what he was going to do, Eleri didn't quite know. Would he herd Mila, as if he were a sheepdog? Growl at her and scare her into running toward Eleri? Or use his teeth on the back of her shirt and drag her all the way over?

She had no idea, and it didn't matter because another heavy pop cut through the air and Donovan let out a sharp noise and dropped out of sight.

75

Reacting quickly and staying low, Donovan turned and checked his flank.

No blood. He would have tasted it if it was there. *Interesting.*

He'd felt as it hit his side, but now the reaction seemed more like the bruise he felt if a bullet had hit a Kevlar vest and not his skin. *Go Eleri,* He thought.

It was difficult to stay crouched down in this form and make progress forward. He considered it for a moment before standing up on his feet, no longer scooting along.

Timing was of the essence—it was why he'd shifted in the first place. He was faster this way. It might make him a slightly larger target, but the speed would give him an advantage and he had to get to Mila. He could only see the edge of her shirt through the tall grass, but he could hear her whimpering. Though whether that was because gunshots were pinging off things around her or because a large black wolf was now headed her way, he didn't know.

Mila was about to get an education in the things she'd never dreamed could happen. It probably wasn't going to make her very happy, but it would save her life.

With a low growl, he sprung forward, the pads of his feet crunching through the dry grass of late summer. Areas around this farm were lush, but this particular plot of land just beyond the barn was a prairie fire waiting to happen.

It didn't matter right now, he thought, not until and unless one of these bullets lit it up. With his ears in this alternate form, he pointed them in different directions to hear what was going on.

There were people hidden in the cover of trees, hunkered down in the grass at the edge of the fence. That's where the shots were coming from. He flicked his ears back even as he moved forward. *Not the safest gesture.* But again, he didn't have the time to stop and wait.

Behind him, he heard the neighs and whinnies of the horses in the barn. One screamed. It had probably been shot. And he could only hope that the owners would find it soon. He also had to hope that they weren't home now.

Was the farm really abandoned right now? Was that why Mila and Brian had chosen it? Had they been forward thinking enough to choose a place with few humans about?

Mila looked up at him just then and screamed bloody murder. She clearly hadn't noticed the wolf coming toward her until just then, and she began furiously backing up, her hands and legs scrambling to get away. Donovan tried to issue whatever noise would make her follow him. But it didn't work. Luckily, he was faster than she was.

Within half of a hair's breath, he was behind her, compelling her forward. She screamed and clawed, jumping forward as if to stand and run. The wolf behind her was suddenly far more threatening than the bullets.

She was wrong about that, so he snapped with his jaws, grabbing at her pant leg. It was a good catch—no skin, just fabric. He could only watch as she planted, face down, in the thick dry grass. It crunched as she landed, and he wondered if the wolves at the fence could hear her.

Bullets broke the sound barrier above her. *Yes, they heard her.*

Mila screamed again and this time he used his nose to nudge her forward. She'd looked back at him, only this time the terror in her eyes wasn't about him. She seemed to understand—if nothing else— the direction she needed to go in and that he wasn't going to be the cause of her demise.

Still crouching down, he stayed close behind her. She was so much slower than a wolf. He could have covered the distance in half the time if left to himself. But she was the whole reason he was here, the whole reason he had changed. If he didn't save her, Miranda Industries would kill her or take her. If they took her ... Donovan had no idea what they would do.

No. He continued to push her forward, because he did know what they would do to her. He used his nose again to nudge at the back of her feet as she crawled quickly, whimpering and crying the whole way.

Miranda Industries might torture her for information. They would definitely attempt to trade her for the bag. Whatever was in the bag, Eleri had felt something from it. Now he was more than curious.

But none of that mattered if they couldn't get safely out of here. He could hear Brian yelling, "Mila, come on! Come here!"

He held his hand out to her, as if he could will her to grasp his fingers.

Donovan wasn't quite certain what kind of couple the two of them were, but they were very close now. Terror could do that to people.

He watched as Brian crawled forward, the air around him shimmering just the slightest, letting him know that Eleri's protection moved with Brian.

Another bullet cut the air too close, sending them all once again flat.

Then, slowly, they picked up and began to move again

Whatever spells Eleri had put into place, they now melded together, the four of them at last in one spot. Eleri elbow crawled over to Mila, grasping wrists with Mila as Mila did the same with Brian on the other side. The two of them hauled Mila in closer, Eleri offering her own body as a shield. His partner, at least, still wore the protective vest they'd arrived in.

With the three human forms lying down in the grass together, Eleri still clutched the bag, even as she held tightly onto the woman.

"Close your eyes," she instructed them.

Donovan believed he had shifted in many strange places. It was one thing to do as he'd seen the Miranda soldiers do up on the bluff—through the trees he'd watched awkwardly as they'd simply shed their clothing, leaving it on the ground behind them, shifting right there before they leapt into action. He'd only done that once or twice himself: Times when the need for a run had itched so badly beneath his skin, that he hadn't had time to place his clothing somewhere safe, when he hadn't cared if he made it back at all.

But now, under the cover of whatever protection Eleri offered, with three people nearby, their eyes closed, trying to stay low so he wouldn't get hit … well, this was a new one even for him.

He rolled his shoulders, cracked his ankles, and pushed his feet out until the toes were human again. His skin tingled as the hair once again moved back, changing him on the surface from a wolf's fur to the skin of a man who was simply a little naturally hairy.

Bless her, Eleri had pushed his clothing into a small, neat pile, making sure it was all ready to easily climb into. Doing it while staying low was another challenge. When he was done, with even his shoes jammed back on from where he'd never unlaced them in the first place, he rolled over. "Okay."

Mila and Brian both stared at him. Mila was obviously uncertain how the wolf had shoved her back to the fold, but the man now sat beside her. Donovan figured she could push it to the furthest recesses of her subconscious, let her think she hadn't seen what she had, and she would remember it but never quite believe her own memory.

Looking at Eleri, they'd checked the first thing off their very dangerous list: get the four together and get Mila and Brian protected. Next: get out.

They were positioned near the door of the barn. Mila was the only one who'd moved away from the structure before the shooting started. The building offered shelter on one of four sides, the door still slightly ajar, so Eleri motioned them all inside as a volley of shots split the air.

76

Wade looked up at the sound of Christina's voice, though he wasn't quite sure what she'd said.

Her foot remained elevated on the coffee table, the sock and sneaker looked relatively normal despite all the damage. It was her thigh he was worried about. The claws had raked all the way through her flesh, even chipping her femur, the surgeons had said.

The muscle had been shredded and had to be carefully pieced back together. The force required to do that was far beyond what Wade would have expected. He wondered if wolves could generate the kind of force a bullet did.

When a bullet ripped through flesh, it opened a hole ten times bigger than the diameter of the metal. The energy rippled and widened behind it, the way a sonic boom looked behind a plane in a photo. As the bullet left the body, the skin and muscle and all the tissue closed back in, filling the space, so all that was left was the gap the bullet itself had torn.

From the surgical photos Donovan had showed him later, he imagined the physics for Christina's gashes to be much the same. What was seen on the surface had not conveyed the extent of the damage her leg had taken. What they had initially thought of as deep cuts had been more like having her flesh flayed from her body.

But she looked well put back together now. Enough to be deceptive. She wore a brace on her leg that kept her from bending her knee. Her one arm was in a sling, protecting the area where they had pieced together muscle there as well.

"Something's wrong," Christina told him.

He shook his head. He didn't know of anything. Maybe she meant something about her injuries, something he couldn't see. Maybe her pain meds were just wearing off.

"I called Eleri three times and she's not answering."

Not something with her meds. Christina had his attention now. He asked, "Times?"

As simple and stupid as the question was, she fully understood. "Every ten minutes. Three times. It's been just over twenty minutes now that I've been trying her with no answer." She paused, then added, "No reply. Not even a single letter in text."

"Burner?" he asked.

"The only thing she's got with her tonight." Christina glanced across the room and Wade's vision followed her direction, as if they both needed to assure themselves that the FBI issued—supposedly secure—phone was still where she'd left it. She hadn't wanted MI to be able to track where they went.

She and Donovan had both taken their burner phones. Wade asked, "Donovan?"

"Nothing from him, either. And look." This time she held up the phone.

Though the burners were all clamshells, they had rudimentary screens on the top half. They were small, nowhere near the size that Wade was used to these days, but Christina showed the map on her tiny screen and the red dot showed that Eleri's phone was just off of State Route three.

Again, he didn't see anything wrong, but he trusted Christina's worry now—medication or no—that something was up. She enlarged the map with a few clicks of buttons, no touch screen here.

"It hasn't moved. The whole time I've been calling her the dot hasn't budged at all."

With those words, he felt it almost as though her worry transferred into him.

"Do you think she dropped the phone?"

"Does it matter?" Christina volleyed back quickly. She was right. Unless the phone was casually dropped, and Eleri hadn't noticed—

which would be a problem itself—then the dropped phone was just as concerning as the lack of answers.

"We have to go find them," Christina said even as she began the cumbersome task of pushing herself up off the couch.

"What do you mean *we?*" He looked her up and down trying to find a way to make it work.

"I'll drive! I can use my left foot."

"You can't bend your right leg at all. How are you even going to fit?" he countered.

"I'll make it work." Though Christina continued to protest, he couldn't figure out the physics of that one. If her right leg was out straight, how would she ...?

"I'm better and faster if I go by myself," he told her, though he knew she would hate being out of the action. "You have to stay here for *you*. And you have to stay here for *me*. So that I can move faster and get to them."

He could see the look on Christina's face telling him that she didn't like it, but she understood. As he was gathering his things—shoving his badge into his pocket, checking for his own burner phone—he grabbed his FBI issued phone and slapped it down on the sofa next to Christina. "You could monitor from here. Stay in touch with Walter and GJ. Use my phone so MI thinks I'm here."

"I'll find out if they know anything."

But even as she spoke, he was already headed to the door.

His hand clasped around the knob, and he heard the noises outside in the hallway that made him pull up short.

Footsteps. Not uncommon for a hotel hallway, but not what should be happening in a hallway they'd entirely commandeered.

His pause alone must have alerted Christina. With large clunky movement, she turned and looked out the window behind the sofa. She twisted in a way that he knew she shouldn't, but he let her check the parking lot below them. Because he was hearing multiple sets of feet in the hall, and there was no good reason he could think of for that.

Luckily, his hearing was stellar and they were still at the far end. But Christina ducked down too quickly for her health, and too quickly for it to be anything good.

As she turned back to look at him, her eyes darted to the side, as though she could see down the long hallway. When they returned to him there was a question in her gaze.

His hand still on the knob, Wade nodded a slow *yes*.

Christina kept her voice low, not a whisper as whispers carried further than people expected. "Coming down the hallway?"

He nodded. Wade saw her resignation set in.

Christina softly announced, "Then we're surrounded."

77

F uck. She hated this.

Her fists pulled in tight near her chest, Eleri worked to maintain whatever safety she could for herself, Donovan, Mila and Brian. They might be in the barn and behind the wood walls, but the horse that was still screaming in his stall was evidence that the guns on the other side were powerful enough to send bullets through.

Though she and Donovan wore protective gear—mostly just their Kevlar vests to protect their heart and their lungs, but not their heads —Mila and Brian had nothing. It was the agents' job to keep the civilians safe, even if the civilians were the root cause of all of this going wrong. She tried not to think how this might have been better if Mila and Brian had just listened when she and Donovan wanted to immediately leave.

But she pulled her fists in close and worked what spells she could with just her voice. Eleri hated doing this in front of the newbies. It was weird enough operating spells in front of Christina and Donovan. The thing she'd easily grown up doing with Grandmére and her sister felt awkward and strange with others around.

Sure enough, Mila turned and looked at her. "What are you doing?"

It was Donovan who answered, "Keeping you safe," as he put his hand on Mila's arm and turned her away.

Eleri was grateful. They'd both revealed far too much but had felt that it was the lesser of the two evils. The other option would have been leaving Mila and Brian to the Miranda operatives.

Eleri still clutched the bag tightly to her. Her arm looped through the short straps, holding it close, as her fists stayed clenched for her spells. When she finished, she reached one hand up underneath it to relieve the pressure the straps had put on her arm. With her palm flat against the bottom, she could still feel the zing that came from whatever was in there.

"Christina will be getting worried about us," she told Donovan, knowing that she'd failed her check ins. Pulling out her phone, she clicked out a short message.

If Christina and Wade were en route, hopefully, that would stop them from walking into the middle of this shit show. Also, hopefully, Christina hadn't moved from the couch. Though Eleri doubted that would be the case.

"What do we do?" Donovan asked.

They were likely surrounded. But they couldn't tell for sure; they had no way to see where the shooters might be, so they couldn't even plan the best escape route.

She shrugged. "It's entirely possible we walked right past several operatives on the way toward the barn."

"No." Donovan shook his head. "I would have smelled them."

Mila frowned and Eleri ignored her. "At least that's good to know. So that tells us how to get out of here."

"It makes sense that they're over on that side of the property," Brian said. He was better than his partner at ignoring the strange things going on right in front of their faces. "If they tracked us here that's the direction they would have followed us from."

Taking a risk, Eleri walked closer to the wood, putting her eye up to a crack at one of the doors and looking out. She almost jerked her head back. *"Oh, hell no."*

"What?" Donovan asked. He knew better than to shove her aside and put his own eyes at the place where she was peeking, but his impatience was clear.

She voluntarily stepped aside, almost hoping he wouldn't see what she'd seen.

The jerk of his head said he did.

The young, dark-skinned woman in the long green gown

appeared to walk directly through the fencing at the edge of the property.

"Alesse?" he asked.

Eleri shook her head. "Gisele."

The youngest of the Dauphine sisters. The surviving members of the family who had stolen Eleri's own younger sister, Emmaline, when she was just a girl. Eleri was almost more afraid of Gisele than Alesse. Alesse was better trained and more ruthless. But Gisele was a wild card. Chaos walking barefoot in a green dress.

"Whatever's in this bag," she told Donovan, "It involves the Dauphines now."

Brian looked first to Mila then to Eleri and Donovan as if they might fill him in.

They weren't going to.

Eleri watched as Donovan's expression changed to say, *You're in way way over your head.*

"Who are the Dauphines?" Brian asked anyway.

"Forget you ever heard that name," Eleri told him in no uncertain terms.

Gisele's appearance would make it much harder to escape. But they would have to do what they could. Turning back to Mila and Brian, Eleri told them, "Stay out of the way. Don't let them know that you're still in here."

Though MI had to know that anyway. Maybe Gisele was just following the lure of the bag, it gave off that much of a feeling. If Gisele Dauphine had ever held it, she would know.

Donovan patted himself down. "We have flashbangs and smoke bombs. Guns and ..."

"Pepper spray," Eleri added wryly, as if that would do any good.

"Ku-batons," he added with a slight grin, but those were only good in close contact which Eleri hoped they never had to deal with.

"Elereeeee ..."

Her head turned with the words, and Donovan's head tipped too, his human ears perking. She wasn't imagining it. Whether Gisele had said her name out loud or not didn't matter. She had called to them.

But Donovan wasn't going to be distracted. "If I use the physical weapons, and you use what you've got, can we cover ourselves enough to get everyone out?"

"Maybe."

She turned back to Mila and Brian but didn't hand them back the bag. It could mean death for them. Miranda operatives would mow them down, take the bag from their corpses, and leave happily. "You're going to hear an explosion." Then she gave them directions for what to do.

With her hand at the edge of the door, ready to slide it to the side just enough for the two of them to step out, Eleri took a deep breath and tried to cover herself more than she already had.

"Elereeee ..." Gisele's voice came again. This time from closer.

Donovan nodded. Even as she pushed the door, her foot crossed the threshold and stepped on to the grass, Eleri called out. "Gisele! We're here."

78

W ade looked to Christina. *Could he get her out of here?*
He knew she was wondering the same thing. Then she
confirmed it. "I could make it seem as though I'm fully healed."

"Yes, but you can't *make* yourself fully healed," he countered. "And
if you walk on your leg like you *are* healed, you'll just damage it
further."

She threw a look over her shoulder, even though she couldn't see
down into the parking lot from the couch, and said, "It beats the
alternative."

"You can't go out into the hallway. And we can't go out the
window." He followed her assessment as she pushed herself up
awkwardly to stand on her one good leg.

It was almost the only functional limb she had left. Though she
had one arm she could use, Wade knew it wasn't working at capacity.

"They know we have both suites." So even though the two of them
stood in one of the main areas, the idea that they could walk out of
the other door was just as ridiculous as walking out this one. But the
idea stuck with him.

"How long do we have?" she asked.

"I don't know." He was scrambling to find a way out.

"In the closet," she said, "there's a vent. Can we go up?"

The thought of Christina climbing anything was ridiculous. The other option, though, was cutting through the floor and going down, and he thought that might be just as bad.

But maybe they could go *sideways*. "What about the next room?"

Aside from some soundproofing, they should be able to get through the wall. It made sense and Wade was already moving. The two bedrooms flanked the main space like stacked wings on either side of the conjoined living rooms.

Bolting into the one furthest back from the hallway he looked for safety. The operatives in the parking lot could maybe shoot up into the third floor. But it was risky, and they likely wouldn't hit him or Christina.

He closed the door, counting on the several walls and a couple of doors between them and the people in the hall. Behind him, he heard Christina hobbling, but there wasn't time to go back and help.

He shoved the bed to one side and saw the headboard stayed attached to the wall. "The tools!" he called out.

They carried a small kit with them. But Christina was smart, and she called out "Heads up!"

She'd already thought of it and managed to pick them up from the front bedroom.

Jesus, she was moving way too fast. Wade wanted to tell her to slow down and rest, but with the footsteps rapidly approaching the door out front, he knew there was no time.

He didn't have a sledgehammer, but he used the slightly smaller than normal claw on the back of the hammer and had the headboard off in just a few seconds. It should have been a longer job, but desperation made him fast.

He swung the head next, small taps finding the studs. Once he had the space—the studs were eighteen inches on center, just big enough —he smashed through the middle. He only had to get through one space, there wasn't time to take out any studs. It wasn't an old building, no lathe and plaster, just thin drywall and a foamy stuffing between.

He was through in minutes. But as he stopped his own noises, he heard scratching at the door to the other suite. They didn't have a key that could get them through the deadbolt and flip the lock he'd thrown. They'd have to break their way in, and that might just buy him enough time.

As expected, the room was empty, no one was on the other side.

The wall had given way easily enough that the work wasn't even that noisy. At least he didn't think it was. Then again, the operatives on the other side of the door were likely wolves.

The front door of their suite now rattled and shook as the operatives upped their efforts. Wade was surprised it had held this long.

Had they not copied the key? Wade wondered. The Agents had demanded physical key access so that phones and even card keys couldn't be hacked. But somewhere in the building was someone with a master key. Surely, Miranda had gotten that. But from the sound of the door still rattling back and forth, they hadn't. Maybe the flip lock was better than it looked. They were going with brute strength.

Well, so could he. He turned, nearly running into Christina, who was already waiting right behind him. She had a bag in her hand and kevlar vests strung over her arm. "Grab the tools," she told him before she started to climb through the just-big-enough hole he'd made.

It was awkward, and she shouldn't have stood on her bad leg to lift her good leg up and through, but it was the only option. Neither of them complained, though he could tell from the expression on her face that something had caught fire in her leg.

They were quickly into the next suite, opening doors and dashing through. It wouldn't be enough. Miranda Industries likely knew exactly which two suites they occupied. Coming out the next one would dump them into the hall too close.

There would likely still be operatives in the hallway as he and Christina exited into it.

"One more," he told her, dashing through the empty suite.

Once again, he used the hammer as a crowbar, this time to get through the lock at the conjoining door. Then he pushed his way into the matching bedroom. They would come out two suites over. The next door should get them almost at the end of the hallway.

He hoped it was enough.

79

Gisele floated forward, her feet stepping softly, rolling heel then toe, moving silently through the grass. But she moved with an unearthly speed.

Behind the witch, the operatives flooded the field—an army Eleri had not expected. They wore gear from head to toe and held rifles to their shoulders, aimed and ready to fire. With a twitch of a single finger, Eleri or Donovan could be dead ... if her spell didn't hold.

Gisele floated to an odd stop ten feet away from Eleri and Donovan.

Too close, Eleri thought. She almost held her hand up to warn the woman to stay back. *As if that would do anything.* Telling Gisele to stay back was just an invitation to move in closer.

Eleri worried that Gisele would notice everything they did, but Donovan had been smart. He had flashbangs and smoke bombs already in his hands, the pins looped over his fingers. He was ready to activate and toss them in a single motion.

He didn't have to reach for them and let Gisele know what he was doing. Unless, of course, she already knew. There was every possibility the other witch could read their minds and knew everything going on.

None of this was the kind of thing Eleri would put past any of the Dauphine sisters. She had to act as if Gisele was as well or better informed than she was.

Should she announce that they were leaving with the bag? It didn't seem wise.

"Let's negotiate," Gisele said, smiling too serenely for the situation.

"Of course," Eleri replied with a forced smile.

Donovan understood that as the signal that it was.

With two hands flinging forward, he splayed his fingers wide, pulling the pins from flashbangs and smoke bombs as he moved. The small cylinders landed between them, closer to Gisele than to them.

With lightning speed, they ducked toward each other, covering their ears and squeezing their eyes shut. The warning of their movement had not been enough for the operatives around them to move fast enough to protect themselves.

Though her eyes were closed and her hands were cuffed over her ears, Eleri could still see the wolves falling back from the blast of sound and light. They didn't sprawl onto their backs but it had definitely caused pain, likely to their sensitive ears.

The flashbangs had definitely bought them a moment—but *only* a moment.

Eleri's body reacted almost before her mind did, running to keep up with Donovan who was already gone. She could barely match his long strides and only hope that Mila and Brian understood the signal and followed the instructions.

Luckily, in a moment, she felt them sprinting beside her.

Donovan had done his part, now it was her turn. Even as her feet kept the rhythm, she held her hand up in a fist, close to her chest, repeating the incantation.

"I hear you, Eleri Eames!" Gisele's voice came from over the distance, but Eleri didn't let it stop her.

Gisele was trying to break into her spell. "Eleri Eames!" she yelled at the top of her voice the second time.

Her anger was delicious, because it meant Eleri's success.

Even Gisele Dauphine could not see them.

Keeping one hand wrapped around the bag, Eleri hoped the spell would hold as she unclenched her fist and reached back and found herself in contact with Brian Abadi. Grabbing on to his nearest limb, she held on tight and pulled him along with her, knowing Donovan would do the same with Mila.

The two agents raced forward, dragging the others behind them. Now if they could just get to the car ...

80

"Three ... Two ..." Wade counted silently. He didn't say any of the words he just mouthed them. If he did speak, the wolves in the hallway might pick up the sound. Hell, they might have already heard it.

He could only hope that the noises he detected behind him—of wolves crashing through the suite door and pouring into the space they'd occupied minutes ago—was enough cover for him and Christina.

The two of them would hopefully burst into an empty hallway.

If they were lucky, the wolves would have all piled into the suite, searching for them in both directions.

On *one*, he threw open the door of the suite they now stood in and shoved Christina through. Neither of them were protected enough, nor had time to get into their protective vests. Christina still held them looped over her arm.

She hobbled the short distance down the hallway. Wade ducked out behind her, using his body as cover for hers. If someone got shot, it should be him. Despite his near death experience, he was miraculously the healthier of the two. He would survive a wound better.

He'd barely looked back but breathed one easy breath that the hallway was clear.

The distance was so short, and yet so long between them and the stairwell. Once they got to the stairs, they had the additional problem of how Christina would even make her way down.

But they didn't even make it.

Behind him he heard the sub-audible creak of a hinge.

The operatives had found the place empty, they'd likely discovered the hole in the wall. They were coming back out into the hall.

Reaching forward, Wade pushed at Christina's back. He didn't want to shove her, but he needed to make them go faster. As much as it was preferable that he were the one of the two that took the bullet, it would be better if neither of them did.

She had her hand on the silver, utilitarian knob to the stairwell, throwing the door open as he heard the voices behind them, shouting that they'd been seen.

Luckily, the stairwell opened easily, letting them slide right in. Unluckily, it didn't provide a metal barrier. Wade both felt and heard the slice of a bullet through the air nearby and he could only pray that his body wasn't protecting him from the shock of already having pierced his skin.

He slid in, pushing the door shut and looking for something to brace it with.

Of course, there was nothing. The job of a hotel stairwell was to give people a safety exit. The ability to block it would ruin all of that.

In front of him, Christina kept moving forward, placing her hands on the stairwell rails. They were perfectly round, painted but unsmooth. Still, she lifted her bad leg and mostly slid down like a fireman. *It had to hurt.*

Following quickly, he did the same, feeling the skin at his palms peeling even as he heard the door behind him jiggling.

They made it around the first corner before the footsteps echoed above them. The Miranda Industries ops were in much better shape than Christina and himself. *Did they even stand a chance?*

The men and women in dark clothing ran down the first steps and jumped the remaining distance. Their feet clumped on to the metal and cement landing.

He and Christina were almost around the next corner. *But not close enough.*

He could see them coming over his shoulder. Their guns were raised. They had far too long of a barrel for the distance they were shooting—a ridiculous piece of weaponry for a stairwell.

But it didn't matter. If they got the guns aimed, the bullets would still kill him just as quickly.

Though they kept moving, Christina slowed. She flattened herself against the wall but Wade tried to grab her and drag her along as he moved past.

But she fought him, saying only, "Let me."

He paused just long enough to see a wall of flames rush up the stairs.

The operators began to fall back, but he wondered how long this would hold them. They'd been exposed to Christina's fake fire before. So, this time she allowed him to grab her and drag her with him as he practically flew down the remaining stairs and prayed they made it out alive.

81

Bullets pinged off the car doors. Eleri heard Mila's screams piercing the air.

Though Brian managed to keep himself together better, and they'd all made it into the car, they weren't safe yet. With the bullets flying, they wouldn't be safe until they were clear of this place.

Eleri pushed her foot and mashed the gas pedal, even as more bullets pinged off the back, even before all of the doors slammed closed.

They were all adults. It was their own job to stay inside the fucking car. She was getting them and the bag the hell out of here.

She squealed the tires, leaving rubber on the road as Donovan slowly and carefully pulled the bag off of her lap, putting it onto his own. He yelled into the back, "Duck! Get low!" even as he tried to make his own large form as small as possible. They each needed to be the tiniest possible target. Getting killed by a stray bullet now would simply not be acceptable.

Eleri had only just gotten him back; she couldn't lose him again now.

She and Donovan also had Mila and Brian under their care. They possessed the bag. All should be good but, behind them, Gisele Dauphine was still standing. She'd chased them to the car, following far too closely.

With her scream of rage, the wolves had stood up, recovering quickly from the flashbang. Luckily—as Eleri had just discovered—flashbangs and smoke bombs had greater effects on wolves than even on humans. Their greater sensitivity to smell and hearing had knocked them even harder than regular people. For that she was grateful.

She sped down the road, fishtailing as she went, waiting to see the SUVs pull into line behind her. But they didn't.

She looked sideways to Donovan. "There weren't MI cars here when we pulled up. Are they going to be able to follow us?"

"I told you we didn't pass any operatives nearby on the way in. I would have scented them. I think Brian was right that they had been tracked here so the operatives were clustered on the other side of the field."

Eleri glanced into the rearview mirror, seeing Mila and Brian still hunched down low in the back seat, working at keeping their heads out of sight. *Good.*

Mila at least had the decency to look contrite, Brian was harder to read.

"They might find us soon," Eleri said, then added, "message Christina."

Though she was breathing a little easier, she wasn't breathing easy enough. Even if Miranda operatives had to run back and get to their SUVs, it didn't mean they couldn't pull in behind them at any point or —God forbid—get in front and intercept them.

"We have to get to the hotel." Donovan replied even as he tapped out a message on the ancient keyboard. "We need to pick up Wade and Christina. Then keep going."

Eleri nodded along. She took every turn in the road, watchful and fearful of what might pop up behind them or in front of them.

When they finally made it into town, she worried that Mila and Brian might go off their rockers. The pair had been through a lot, and she hadn't had a chance to see if they had anything trackable on them … aside from the bag itself.

Eleri still feared that Miranda Industry SUVs would cross the road in front of them at any time. Anything could happen. Hell, the bag might even blow up.

Though MI hadn't had it in their possession for over thirty five years, it was possible they'd rigged it long ago and still knew how to trigger it. Anything was possible. And that was the problem.

She skidded through another turn. Close to the hotel now, she issued more directives into the back seat. "You two need to get into the center of the seat ... in fact, Mila, you sit on his lap."

When they were a little slow to comply, Donovan added, "We've got two more coming in, and one is severely injured."

Seatbelts weren't even a consideration in a situation like this. As far as surviving a crash? That would be about prayer and maybe Eleri's skills.

She was taking the turns harshly, flicking glances into the rearview mirror to watch as Brian held one arm around Mila's waist. The other reached out to brace them against the door each time she turned.

Then it happened. They'd arrived, and Eleri squealed her way through the hotel parking lot.

She saw them then: large black SUVs, with dark tinted windows. Three of them.

Had the MI team beaten them here? The cars looked empty. No one moved inside. Unless of course the tinting was dark enough that she couldn't see.

Her head snapped to Donovan even as the car moved forward, her expression asking *how had this happened?*

"Any word from Christina?" Eleri asked.

When Donovan double checked his phone then shook his head, she added, "Wade?"

He shook his head again.

Fuck!

Had the operatives somehow looped around and arrived before them? Had they raided the rooms? Was this another team? Were Christina and Wade going to be held hostage and used as negotiating tools for the bag?

Eleri didn't know.

She did know that Christina would make an excellent hostage. They couldn't afford any more damage to her.

Smashing the gas pedal yet again, Eleri spun her way through the parking lot. Trying to avoid the front door, Eleri once again took the turns too sharply as she made her way around to the side of the building. She watched as Donovan reached for his door handle, even before the car came to a stop. He would run up the stairwell to see what was going on. She noticed that he checked his pockets, his burner cell phone in one hand, and he now held another flashbang in the other. He was ready to grab his gun at any moment.

But as he stepped out of the car, the side door of the hotel flew open wide.

Christina stumbled out, running awkwardly on one straight leg. Wade was behind her, but he moved quickly around in front and grabbed her by the hand. Both of their gazes searched the lot for somewhere to go.

Only then did Eleri remember that Wade and Christina had no car at all. Eleri and Donovan were in the one on loan from the BCA in Duluth. It had been stupid to leave the other two here with no exit strategy.

"Here!" Donovan yelled.

It all happened so fast that Wade and Christina had only made it five feet past the door when they looked up and saw him.

Donovan reached back, opening the back passenger door. Eleri put her hand up, fingers moving in a swirl before clenching into a closed fist. She tried to give Christina an extra lift and help the woman fight the gravity that was hurting her so much.

"Go!" Donovan shoved at Wade, taking Christina and helping her awkwardly into the back seat. But, true to form, she shoved him away. "I've got it!"

Wade was racing around the car, trying to climb in on the other side. He was the last one still exposed. Eleri was waiting for him. Christina's door slammed and so did Donovan's as the stairwell door erupted with Miranda Industry operatives streaming out.

Eleri couldn't even count the guns that were raised at them.

In the rearview mirror, she could see as Mila and Brian tried to become the smallest possible ball they could be. She had to move. *Wade could get his own door shut.*

But, as she moved to hit the gas, a dark skinned hand came through her window and her head snapped to the left.

Just outside the car window, Gisele Dauphine stared down at her.

82

There was no way Gisele had made it here in this timeframe, Eleri thought.

She and the other operatives could not have made it back to their cars and then arrived here before Eleri and Donovan did. Could they? Was there another route between here and the barn they'd found Mila and Brian in?

This had to be a different set of operatives. They'd been flanked, Eleri now knew.

But Gisele Dauphine ... How was she here?

For a moment too long, Eleri froze. The hand stroked at her hair, somehow passing through the glass of the window. It was a creepy feeling, Gisele's magic attempted to reach into her soul and twist in a way that made Eleri want to hand over the bag. But she herself wanted to fight.

She needed more than just this moment to figure out how, though.

Beside her, as she tried and failed to twist away, she could feel Donovan's anger rising out of his body. In the back, Mila and Brian radiated a fear that seemed to take over the whole car.

In a flash of insight, Eleri saw the truth. Though they all saw her and though she touched Eleri, *Gisele Dauphine wasn't here.*

In fact, she hadn't even been in the field. She'd moved too fast. Wherever she was, it wasn't Minnesota. She was projecting.

Slamming her hand down frantically, Eleri jammed the buttons on the car door and mistakenly hit all of them. All the windows moved down far too slowly for the speed her brain was going at.

"Shit!" she said. Gisele just smiled at her, hopefully not realizing what Eleri's right hand was doing as she fumbled through her pockets and along her belt.

"Eleri," the voice said, the accent soft and lilting. It was the kind of tone one expected before the tarot reader told you that you were about to receive a great fortune.

The window passed down but Gisele's arm stayed exactly where it was. She wasn't really here.

The witch's other hand now reached over the edge, curling around the car door. Still smiling oddly, she leaned in. "Give me the bag, Eleri."

When Eleri didn't move, she spoke again.

"Do you not know what you hold?"

"I know what I hold!" Eleri almost yelled it.

She lifted the pepper spray, hoping it would work. So she smashed her finger down on the plunger and sprayed Gisele's face.

83

Donovan heard the scream ricochet through his skull. Gisele Dauphine was wilder than a banshee and far angrier.

But as he watched, she jerked back and faded from existence.

"What?" He must have said it out loud, and he heard the same from at least one of the people crammed into the backseat.

But there was no time to answer. Wade had leaned forward, beating at the back of Eleri's seat. *"Go, Go, Go!"*

His frantic command was punctuated by a bullet. The operatives that had followed him and Christina out the side door were now shooting at them.

Donovan tried to duck as he heard glass shatter, though he couldn't see the damage on the car. "Go!"

He reiterated Wade's words, but it didn't matter. Eleri had already lurched the car forward and cranked the wheel.

Behind them, he heard a door slam. Someone getting into the dark SUVs? Would they have more gas, fresher cars than what they had?

Cars weren't like horses, they didn't tire, but the Duluth BCA sedan wouldn't likely outrun a small army of the SUVs. Eleri clipped the curb, sending the car rocking as they pulled out of the hotel lot to the sounds of horns and swearing. She'd cut at least two people off, but no one in the car could bring themselves to care.

They ducked in and out of traffic, weaving between cars and

angering the other drivers. But Donovan knew they'd be angrier if the SUVs barreled down the road shooting at everyone.

He held his breath, trying not to issue commands to Eleri who clearly knew what she was doing. But it was hard to sit quietly and let others work, despite the fact that he loved it, too. He'd made it out of MI's hands.

He wasn't going back.

"One," Wade called up from the backseat.

Donovan's eyes darted to the side mirror. It wasn't aimed for him, but he could see the SUV exiting the parking lot behind them. They had a good lead but would need to make use of it. So he finally spoke up. "Here."

He pointed to the right, and Eleri, almost presciently made the turn. Then she blurted out, *"Where next?"*

Three quick turns later, she looked up and asked Wade, "How many?"

"None right now."

Reaching out, Donovan put his hand over hers. "Park. Then we wait."

84

E leri nodded along as the two US Marshals gave instructions to their new detainees. The men had shown up with hats and accents and a firm embrace of their jobs.

Eleri had touched each of the officers, in turn reading them and making sure that they were actually marshals with the US service and not someone that Miranda Industries sent in.

But once they cleared, Donovan filled in the information they would need to know. "The mafia that's after them is deep. They have infiltrations everywhere ... even into the FBI."

The marshals gave a sad grin back to him as if to say, *well, they might have infiltrated you, but they won't infiltrate us.*

Eleri turned and glared at them, but it was unnecessary. Christina —from her position on the couch with her leg elevated and pain meds talking—said, "You will take this seriously or you won't take our people."

The pointed glare that followed the words and the shift in the Marshals' stance let Eleri know Christina had pushed them into belief.

How many times had Christina had to do that on this case?

Eleri didn't know, but she knew it was more than Christina would have wanted. Still, she couldn't help but be grateful.

Within a few moments, Mila and Brian were whisked off into

WitSec despite their protests. Brian had wanted to write a letter to his mother explaining why her payments wouldn't be coming.

It had been all she could do to glare down the marshal who obviously wanted to say, "They won't be coming because you're dead."

Eleri would make sure the woman won enough money to take over for what Brian had been sending her.

Mila had demanded a call and was still very upset it had been denied. The prospect of not seeing their families ever again was more than either of the two were prepared for. But there was no way to send Mila Panas and Brian Abadi back into the world under those names. Miranda would hunt them down just to stop what they might know.

Eleri tried again. "If you don't do this, one day, Miranda Industries will show up and kill you. And that's if you're lucky."

Mila's eyes had flown wide, but Eleri couldn't let her be naïve. "If you're not lucky, you fly under their radar long enough for them to get their hands on someone you love. So you have to go. It's the safest for everyone."

Though Brian and Mila were only reluctantly agreeing to the process, the marshals had handled this before. It wasn't their first rodeo and Eleri thought snarkily that they looked like they were dressed for their fifteenth or thirtieth rodeo.

Once Mila and Brian were safely whisked away, Eleri only managed a moment's breath before the four remaining agents picked up and moved again.

It had taken two hours after she pepper sprayed Gisele to know they'd escaped Miranda.

Eleri had assumed correctly that if she could feel Gisele's touch, then Gisele could feel hers. But the damage broke the hold. Maybe the operatives couldn't track them as well with their witch out of the loop.

But each time Eleri had seen a black SUV on their way here, she'd made another evasive maneuver. Honestly, she'd probably evaded more than one partier returning home from a night of drinking, or a family, just getting back into town after a trip. Large black SUVs were a dime a dozen. But she couldn't be too safe.

The car still felt like a target as they climbed back in. At least there were only four of them now. The trunk still held all of Eleri's necessary things that she'd taken to carrying with her: The copper bowl, the Book of Shadows, the herbs and the little hand-stitched bags that came from Grandmére. Beyond the tool bag and the gear that Christina and Wade had brought with them, most everything else had been left behind. Eleri understood a little of what Mila and Brian were going through.

She remembered too late that they'd left their FBI-issued phones. Though Eleri and Donovan had purposefully left theirs in the room when they left to keep Miranda Industries from tracking them out to meet Mila and Brian, Christina's had been a necessary sacrifice as they fled.

They'd carefully followed Christina's earlier advice, finding first one, then a second, then a third place where they might buy an additional burner phone. They rejected the first two and only bought a phone at the third before tossing the other three out the window.

Donovan contacted Walter with another coded message for GJ to decipher.

They told each other about their escapes. Wade and Christina talked about their plans to go up or down, and finally sideways. Eleri and Donovan said how they'd encountered Gisele out in the field.

"How did you know you could pepper spray her?" Christina had asked it before, and Eleri had answered. But the medication she was on was strong and Eleri didn't mind explaining again.

"She was projecting, she wasn't real. But I could feel her. I banked on the fact that if I could feel her, she could probably feel me. So, I tried it."

Christina asked two more times on the trip. They drove for hours and hours and hours. They stopped for restroom breaks and changing out drivers. They took meals from drive-throughs open all night so they wouldn't have to leave the car.

In Indiana, they passed near one of the FBI branch offices. With only a few minutes warning to the local officers, they stopped by, trading out the car for another with little explanation. They let the local agents know the abandoned car should be returned to the Duluth BCA. In Missouri, they did it again. And they kept going with only a few short stops.

They arrived at the de Gottardi/Little compound, once again giving only five minutes warning. Wade called and checked with his cousin.

"Tell no one any details. I've got three agents and a valuable piece of intel."

"What is it?"

"We don't know yet. That's why we're coming here. We think we're going to need your help."

It was midday as Wade's cousin came to greet them and ushered them into the center of the compound with little fanfare. Aside from the strange new car, no one should even know that they had arrived.

They were quickly handed off to Jen Crunk.

"Wade!" she said, reaching out and clearly happy to see him again as she made a motion to offer a hug.

He leaned in, sparing her the awkward moment. "It's good to see you. I'm glad you're still here."

Though Eleri hadn't been here for the incident with the Dauphines, she'd met Jen afterwards.

"Agent Eleri Eames." She held her hand out to remind the new compound researcher they'd met before. Then she watched as Donovan and Christina did the same.

But Jen clearly remembered Christina. "It's good to see you again. Are you okay?"

"Not yet," Christina admitted—a bold move for her—but she followed it with, "But I'll get there. Soon."

"Follow me." Jen turned, issuing her command over her shoulder. But as she led them down through the winding underground tunnels, she occasionally looked back to be sure Christina kept up.

Wade had put one shoulder under Christina's arm and helped her walk along. Eleri realized they should have stopped for crutches. Surely there were some here at the compound. Unfortunately, Christina would have to wait until later. For right now, it was important that they get into the bag and figure out what they had.

Her burner phone buzzed in her hands, surprising her that it had signal down here. She stopped. She recognized the number.

"GJ?" she asked, hanging back from the group.

But the group stopped. GJ's voice came across the line, grabbing everyone's attention. "We got the fingerprints back from the gun in the trunk of the car and you're not going to believe who they belong to."

85

E leri pressed the burner phone to her ear. GJ's information meant the prints were recognizable. "Whose?"

"Anton Leonidas."

Eleri felt her own surprise and watched as Donovan's eyes went wide. His hearing was superb, but it was Wade who leaned over and asked, "Anton Leonidas?"

He'd held the gun in the robberies over thirty years ago?

But GJ said it before she even had a chance to put it together. "He's Victor Leonidas' father."

Getting herself together, Eleri managed to ask, "Where is he now?"

"He died four and a half years ago."

Donovan frowned at the news, then Eleri and Christina looked to each other.

Christina shook her head, her medication was excuse enough for not putting the numbers together. But Eleri couldn't quite compute it.

GJ filled them in. "It was two months after Victor Leonidas went undercover with Miranda."

Holy shit! She was struggling to put it all together. "Was Anton with Miranda the whole time?"

"Looks that way," GJ said. "I'll let you know when I get more."

It sounded like the other agent was about to hang up. Eleri cut in before she could. "Did you tell Westerfield any of this?"

She could hear GJ hesitating on the other end of the line. "A lot of it's in the official documents. It matched through AFIS, so it's in the digital records. But no, I didn't tell him anything else. And there's no official report on it yet."

"Keep it that way," Donovan leaned in and said, "We'll update you once we know about the bag."

The phone clicked and the line went dead. Eleri, still reeling from the news, managed to click her phone to turn it off. Best not to be trackable down here at all.

Christina's gaze caught hers again and they had to be thinking the same thing.

Whose side was Victor Leonidas really on?

With a look at the four of them, and not really following this part of the conversation, Jen motioned them to move further down the long tunnel. She didn't know what the connection to Victor or Anton Leonidas was, but she'd been given a task.

Opening the doorway into a chamber, Jen walked in easily, but Eleri felt this was a moment. She watched as Wade and Christina passed through the door in front of her. Just coming in here changed something in them. *This had been where it happened.*

"We fortified it," Jen told them. "We've had several wolves getting into some of the old spell books. It was made clear before that we don't necessarily need a witch to run them."

Once they were all in the room and Jen closed and bolted the door behind them, Donovan put the bag onto the table and Jen went to work.

She pulled on latex gloves, unzipped it, and carefully pulled the remaining stacks of money out. She set them aside on a clean sheet of paper to be inspected later.

As they all peered in, they saw the bag was empty.

"It can't be empty," Donovan said. "Or is there something about the money?"

Eleri looked from the pile of cash back to the bag. "No, it's the bag. The bottom of the bag."

Eleri nodded at Jen. The woman reached for a small, hooked knife and began cutting at the bottom of the bag. She tugged at the stitching, ruining it in an irreparable way.

As she lifted the front corner of the lining, an old, yellowed piece of parchment was revealed.

They all looked silently on as Jen tugged and ripped at the seams, revealing more and more. The writing had faded. It covered the page as far as they could see. The edges were ripped, the writing trailing off or torn in half. As far as Eleri knew, none of them could read it.

When Jen had the pieces fully separated, she reached in, but Eleri stopped her.

"No. Don't touch it. I'm afraid it will activate something." She looked around the group. "It's part of something much, much bigger."

ABOUT THE AUTHOR

AJ holds an MS in Human Forensic Identification as well as another in Neuroscience/Human Physiology. AJ's works have garnered Audie nominations, options for tv and film, as well as over twenty Best Suspense/Best Fiction of the Year awards.

A.J.'s world is strange place where patterns jump out and catch the eye, little is missed, and most of it can be recalled with a deep breath. In this world, the smell of Florida takes three weeks to fully leave the senses and the air in Dallas is so thick that the planes "sink" to the runways rather than actually landing.

For A.J., reality is always a little bit off from the norm and something usually lurks right under the surface. As a storyteller, A.J. loves irony, the unexpected, and a puzzle where all the pieces fit and make sense. Originally a scientist and a teacher, the writer says research is always a key player in the stories. AJ's motto is "It could happen. It wouldn't. But it could."

A.J. has lived in Florida and Los Angeles among a handful of other places. Recent whims have brought the dark writer to Tennessee, where home is a deceptively normal-looking neighborhood just outside Nashville.

For more information:
www.ReadAJS.com
AJ@ReadAJS.com